Quicksands

of

Crime

by
Peter Winstanley-Brown

Quicksands of Crime

A catalogue record for this book is available from the British Library.

ISBN no. 978-1-4196-6453-3

Manuscript prepared by Campaign Trail Ltd.

DEDICATIONS

At her request, I am reluctantly not naming the lady who tracked down serious amounts of research information for me. She also patiently processed seemingly endless updates, all of which makes her deserving of my thanks.

Regrettably, spending years delving into the darker side of life, added to the sheer grinding volume of work, has left us with some scars, but fortunately, we are resilient characters. It is my hope that the eventual publication of "Quicksands" early in 2007 will be accepted by the public as a genuine opportunity for some countries to get really serious about crime – probably for the first time.

My 14 year old daughter Shoshi is a wonderful girl who typifies that sector of our younger generation which already has high personal standards but are nevertheless still at serious risk from growing criminality. Perhaps, in due course, she will find some way to lead her peers into a more civilised and peaceful world, but I would not wish to impose any expectations upon her which did not sit happily in her heart.

I have also had support in a variety of ways from my sons Cass, Cal and Sean and it is so sad that Cass will never see the finished version of "Quicksands".

Following a courageous five and a half year fight against cancer, Cass died in January 2007, having given enormous encouragement to other sufferers via his website and his book "Cancergiggles – Mountains are easy". His wit and cheerful irreverence, and his remarkable ability and willingness to solve even the most difficult computer problems suffered by relatives and friends, will be very sorely missed. It was Cass, many years ago, who first dubbed me "Pancho", a nickname which I have long preferred to my given name, its origin being from really fun times.

Quicksands of Crime ~ Warnings & Lifelines

Quicksands of Crime ~ Preface

My early experience of injustice took root in the business world where I quickly discovered that some major corporations would use almost any tactics – however dirty, devious, distasteful or even illegal – in order to suppress emerging competition and achieve their dubious objectives.

Taking on media cartels as a young nobody entrepreneur led me into a decade- long David and Goliath battle because unfortunately, there was no single stone around for me to sling, and the vested interests I was taking on had far better protective armour than had Goliath. Through sheer cussedness, I survived, amongst other things, death and injury threats, numerous nuisance and silent telephone calls and spurious law suits designed only to run me out of money and energy. Eventually, with limited resources, I chose to try to bring my corporate persecutors under the microscope of the UK's Monopolies & Mergers Commission and the Office of Fair Trading. Not an easy thing to achieve, particularly whilst simultaneously having to deal with the gutter tactics used by my adversaries who saw me as a troublesome upstart who had to be squashed. In the event, the UK M.M.C. on three separate occasions, ruled against the major companies I had chosen to challenge. My victories though, had not been without personal cost, but at least I had learned that even powerful establishments could be beaten if they were behaving badly, provided that one is determined and prepared to pay the associated price, which is not just financial.

My first serious brush with day-to-day criminality was getting myself beaten up in broad daylight by three thugs when, as a bystander, I asked them to stop giving a young lad a seriously dangerous kicking. One of them knocked me unconscious by hitting me between the eyes with a bracketed scaffolding pole because I was getting the better of the scrap with his two mates who had turned on me. Thereafter, with most of my business battles won, I decided to start researching crime seriously and eventually, in 1994, I founded The Society for Action Against Crime – a not-for-profit Non-Government Organisation – as a vehicle for identifying the causes of crime and searching for solutions. Lobbying Governments to take appropriate corrective action was the necessary follow-up to my findings and that has proved a real education and a serious disappointment.

I am grateful for the encouragement of those who have appreciated our Society's research and campaigning. This has come from a cross section of people from a number of countries, including criminals, but regrettably several groups whose interest we sought to arouse, have been conspicuous by their lack of concern about high crime levels. Lack of concern is, in fact, putting it mildly, because these particular cartels are major obstructions preventing us all from enjoying almost crime-free lives.

Hence the writing of this book, to engage more with the public and spell out the serious crime-related dangers and the many initiatives necessary to escape them.

Right now, more than half of my acquaintances have suffered serious crime and whilst many of these were burglaries and car theft, they also include frightening attack. My daughter-in-law Debbie, for example, had a young thug come into her beauty parlour in June 2005 and put a gun between her eyes just to get the modest amount of cash she had in her till. Despite the fact that this occurred less than 2 miles from where Marion Bates had earlier been shot dead in her jeweller's shop by an as yet unfound killer accompanied by a supposedly electronically tagged serial offender, the police were remarkably unconcerned about the armed raid on Debbie's salon, even though the villain who fired the fatal shots into Marion Bates is still at large, as of this writing.

The ramifications of such crimes go far beyond their obvious damage. They leave serious scars which may never heal. A fact which few of those involved with our judicial processes seem to understand. It seems that the police in Nottingham are too busy pointing radar guns at motorists who may be doing 40 miles an hour in a 30 limit, because by January 2007 (20 months later), Debbie has had only one police visit since suffering the frightening armed robbery.

My sister and brother-in-law had 3 armed men force open the door of their motorhome in France and rob them of their money, passports and vehicle keys in the middle of the night. Not being prepared to risk a repeat nightmare, they sold their motorhome, which of course diminished their chosen lifestyle.

You and we can change this dreadful culture and this book puts the means so to do into your hands. Unlike Government Inquiries, my book cannot be pigeon-holed, sexed up or down, edited or ignored. It has been commissioned by no-one and is therefore free of any censorship or influence from vested interests.

The required root and branch changes necessary to escape the quicksands of crime will inevitably tread on the toes of some lofty establishment figures as well as the criminal fraternity - so be it - because without the necessary fundamental changes, there will be no serious diminution in crime in those countries which suffer it unduly.

Bringing what needs to be done fully into the public domain by publishing this book is not, of course, without risk. Hopefully, the outcome will justify and outweigh the dangers. You, the reader, can play your part in the fight against crime by taking up with your political representatives, those of the solutions I propose herein with which you are in agreement. You will find help in this and other respects in the final pages, including, as you read along, some imaginative solutions to change the minds of those who may continue to refuse to listen to your genuine grievances.

Particularly, I am hopeful that young people in many countries will join me and The Society for Action Against Crime in our up-coming campaigns and whilst of necessity, much of the book's content is American and European based, the problems and their solutions are essentially global.

It is true that a disproportionate amount of crime is committed by young people, but it is equally true that most of the victims are also youngsters, many of whom are profoundly unhappy with the violent and deteriorating environment which surrounds them. They despair at their politicians, their police and their Courts who have so miserably failed to make serious inroads into crime and they deplore the hypocrisy of their statistics-spinning politicians and their stream of ineffective tinkering.

"Quicksands", which is essentially a **Crimedown Blueprint**, provides a rallying point for all of those, young and old, who see crime – particularly violent crime – as a serious blight on their lives and I will be happy to discuss licensing adapted and translated versions of my book covering any country suffering high crime. I am hopeful that the disclosures, ideas, information and guidance herein will give encouragement to those who despair about crime levels and persuade them instead, that together we can force our politicians to take the necessary serious anti-crime measures without which the world will be condemned to suffer the numerous associated problems in perpetuity. In effect, this book is about defining the nature and dangers of the crime quicksands, warning of their whereabouts and offering lifelines to those who have strayed or been pushed into them.

It may not be easy, at first reading, to recognise a direct connection between my observations and crime as most people see it. In such instances, I ask for your patience and hope that you will come to understand that the causes of crime are very complex and the way they interact not always obvious without a little reflection.

Two strong rivers of belief flow through the following pages – the confidence that criminality can be substantially overcome and the need to return more freedom to the law-abiding. It is absolutely not necessary for Governments to interfere with the liberty of the latter in order to achieve the former.

I hope "Quicksands" will help you understand that beating the bad guys and having less interference by Government into the lives of the good guys are not mutually exclusive. Listen to no-one who claims this to be impossible. They have neither your security nor best interests at heart.

Peter Winstanley-Brown – A.K.A. Pancho
Email: **quicksands@crimedown.org**

CHAPTER 1

LIFE CAN BE WONDERFUL
WITH MINIMUM CRIME

Imagine living in an environment where you can go out where you wish without thinking about the risk of being attacked – possibly even killed.

Imagine being able to leave your car, knowing that no-one is going to put a brick through its window, steal your possessions, drive off with it, or simply ruin your paintwork by running a screwdriver along your car's length.

Imagine being able to suggest to litter louts that they dispose of their rubbish responsibly, without the fear of being verbally abused and possibly thumped, seriously kicked or stabbed.

Imagine knowing that no-one in your area or of your acquaintance has suffered a burglary in recent times.

Imagine not having to lock/bolt/chain your doors and windows, boats, cars, cycles, motorbikes and caravans.

Imagine living in a country where you can let your kids go to play in the park or out to a disco, knowing they can walk home safely.

Imagine being able to go into any bar without someone getting a broken glass or bottle in their face, or being head-butted by some drunken thug.

Imagine that your elderly relatives live where no conman or woman is going to trick them out of their savings – or into some wholly-inappropriate purchase or building repair at a grossly over-inflated price.

Imagine living where your eyes are not constantly assailed by ugly graffiti sprayed on every available and even some very difficult-to-access surfaces.

Imagine the peace you would enjoy if the threat of bricks or bullets coming through your home's windows no longer existed.

Imagine there being no "happy slapping" in your country, and for those of you who have yet to come across this disgusting term, happy slapping is the depraved and sickening practice of beating someone up - without warning or justification – just so their "mates" can capture the attacks on their mobile phones to send on to other of their moronic gang members.

Imagine that your Government has stopped interfering with and invading the privacy and freedom of its law-abiding citizens – and concentrated instead on catching and punishing the criminal fraternity.

Imagine your children and grandchildren going to school without the fear of being bullied, kicked, stabbed or even shot.

Imagine schools where neither out-of-control pupils nor their ill-tempered parents verbally abuse or physically attack the teaching staff.

Imagine being able to drive anywhere without some lunatic road-rager attacking you because you didn't get out of his way, or because you had made some minor misjudgement. In his or her opinion, of course.

Imagine a country where almost no-one drives without insurance, often leaving injured or dead victims or their families with insurmountable financial problems in addition to their physical and emotional sufferings.

Imagine there being no town or village centres left stinking of urine and vomit by drunks and druggies.

Imagine living in a country which is not cowed by terrorism, but is determined to take it in its stride and not be panicked into allowing its traditional freedoms to be cynically stolen from the entire population by its power-hungry politicians.

Imagine having an honest and open Government which did not incarcerate people without charge, confine them in appalling places, fly them secretly around the globe and give lip-service against abuse and torture, whilst participating in it behind very closed doors, either themselves or via third parties.

Imagine living in a country where the criminals and their victims get the justice they deserve and where Judges and Magistrates do not give wildly fluctuating sentences for very similar sentences.

14

Imagine living in a country whose politicians thought more about protecting you from crime than about their own careers and financial benefits.

"Dream on" some may say. "If only"; "No chance"; "You wish" say others.

Well, I have news for you. Some communities already enjoy most of these happy circumstances and we can all do so if we demand it of our politicians. Quicksands of crime develop, not just because of the criminals, but because the politicians have failed to dissuade, control and punish them with sufficient wisdom and vigour. Many countries suffer high crime because their idea of education is limited to ever more exam passing, to the almost total exclusion of personal development and responsibility.

Imagining, dreaming and wishing alone will not give us all crime-free societies of course, because some countries have very nasty, very dangerous criminals whom their Governments have tolerated or even used. Such is the level of criminality and general lawlessness in even first-world countries such as America, Australia, France, Russia, China, Ireland and Britain though, that only a multi-headed approach can now successfully bring it down to tolerable levels.

This Blueprint for crime reduction offers you multi-directional solutions - somewhat like a jigsaw puzzle, wherein each piece makes its contribution to the final picture. Many of the individual pieces - which years of research have led to my chosen recommendations - are radical, controversial, even unique. Others are refinements of what has already been toyed with, but badly implemented due to their lack of understanding. Individually, each of my jigsaw pieces have merit, but on their own, some will only bring down crime a little. The maximum reduction in crime will only come when action is taken on most or all of the recommendations contained herein simultaneously – a significant multiplication benefit factor akin to compound interest. That said, as you read on, you will learn that there are three particular areas where, if my recommendations are put into effect, crime will drop substantially and quickly.

Those of you living in a high-crime country have a choice. Do nothing and crime will, at best, decrease marginally, but more likely will become worse, or you can grasp the lifelines identified in this book and pull yourself and others out of the quicksands.

I have neither time nor respect for the pessimists or the apologists because I know that no nation need suffer high crime. They do so only by default, by the inertia of those who control the levers of power, and because of those who so gullibly vote for them.

Having spent around 45,000 hours researching, discussing and writing about crime in the last 15 years, aided by countless investigation, processing and recording work by others, I have expertise in this area which no politician or Government Department could possibly match. I itemise this simply to demonstrate that my certainty that high crime can be beaten, is not merely wishful thinking, but is based upon years of hard work, brainstorming and deep, at times almost reclusive searching for solutions. Unlike most politicians, academics and others who think themselves important, I have discussed crime with thousands of people who would describe themselves as absolutely ordinary and I have huge respect for the commonsense wisdom I have learned from so many of them. Much of their down-to-earth thinking has helped my search for solutions to crime which have eluded so many for so long and I am indebted to countless strangers in bars and pavement cafes around the world who have shared their opinions so openly with me.

This book then, is the outcome of my years of research - a Blueprint for crime reduction, the merits of which will hopefully become clear to you as you progress through its pages.

However, neither I, this book, nor any Reports published by The Society for Action Against Crime can succeed in rescuing millions of potential victims from the quicksands of crime without your help.

Politicians, bureaucrats, lawyers etc. essentially prefer to stick with the cosy privileged lifestyles they have manipulated for themselves, but they *can* be stirred out of their complacency if sufficient of their citizens take action to bring them to account where they have failed to deal adequately with crime.

Read on to find out what needs to be done to bring crime hurtling down in high-crime countries and at the end of this Blueprint, I will show you what you, as an individual, can do to help achieve this. Life can be so much better, when you have what, right now, you are only allowed to imagine.

But first, you have to want it.

Then you have to do something about it.

At the end of the book, I show you what you should do and I will reveal some of the unusual tactics we can all employ to wake up or by-pass those politicians who have allowed their citizens to suffer high levels of crime and are content to continue so doing.

Should you, as an individual reader, feel that you may see the need for new initiatives on crime, may I ask that you consider reading this book twice. Once to get an overall impression of my work and thinking, and then a second reading to mark your agreement or disagreement with what I am saying.

By highlighting in green, those sentences which strike a favourable chord with you, and in red those with which you disagree – you will then be able to assess the extent to which we may be on the same wavelength.

There are, of course, almost no aspects of any subject which enjoy universal agreement and few people will concur with everything I have to say, some because of ignorance or misinformation, some due to personal vested interests and some down to genuinely different viewpoints which I will always respect and be happy to consider.

No matter. What counts is the number of people who agree with much or most of what I am proposing because if sufficient of my readers are in this category, then there really is a good prospect that the countries suffering high crime levels really can be made far safer and happier places to live and bring up our children.

CHAPTER 2

AN OVERVIEW

Unless we effect some serious changes of direction, we will all be at huge risk of adding to the millions who have already fallen victim to crime. That we have quagmires of crime, I have no doubt, with some countries already under the control of criminal gangs and corrupt politicians, whilst in others, daily life is impoverished for the law-abiding who are driven to confining their lives in ever-decreasing circles of (hoped) security in their attempts to either avoid suffering or witnessing violence, or being confronted by disgusting behaviour.

Crime has increased exponentially since the 1960s in many countries and the phenomenon is in no measure restricted to emerging nations. America, Australia, Britain, China, France, Ireland, Russia and others, all suffer unacceptably high crime levels. This book is part of my personal campaign to see crime reduced by 70% or more in the short to medium term, and by 90% in the foreseeable future. Many believe this to be impossible, but the following pages demonstrate that such negativity is unfounded. Given the will and the honesty to acknowledge past mistakes, the battle against criminality can certainly be substantially won.

Crime, of course, is unlikely to be completely eliminated any time soon, but it can be massively reduced where it is high and there is no reason why we should all not enjoy the more tranquil lifestyles of countries such as Andorra, Canada, Denmark, Finland, Singapore, Switzerland, Botswana and Uruguay. Nor need it take decades to bring crime down very significantly, with reductions achieving 50% or more perfectly possible within 3 years in most high-crime countries, continuing albeit at a slower rate thereafter.

There is no good reason for us to continue living at the daily risk of being stabbed; shot; kicked into unconsciousness or death; raped; spat at; verbally abused by disgusting foul-mouthed yobs; burgled; mugged; cheated; bullied or threatened. Nor should anyone have to suffer the stench or sight of urine and vomit in our streets, or our hospital and emergency staffs, family doctors and teachers disrespected and violated. Right now, instead of moving towards a more civilised society, many countries are speeding in precisely the opposite direction and, whilst I will do everything within my power to seriously loosen the grip which the criminal fraternity has on the windpipes of far too many nations, I do need your help if success is to be maximised.

This book makes no attempt to catalogue the horrific crimes which are commonplace in many countries because the dreadful statistics speak for themselves. They can also be seen in newspapers and our Courts with depressing regularity and one has to conclude that the media are far more interested in using the morbid interest in crime, in order to boost their circulations, than they are in supporting anti-crime measures.

Researchers at The Society for Action Against Crime believe that the sensational media coverage of crime outnumbers that of seeking or promoting solutions by a factor of more than 50 : 1 in most high-crime countries. If you are waiting for our Society's campaigning to be supported by the media, don't hold your breath. Some of them are part of the problem and truly investigative journalism into crime causes is about as likely as virgins in a brothel.

The causes of crime are of course numerous and consequently, the necessary corrective measures, as outlined in this book, need to be wide-ranging. Some of these will bring crime down quickly. Others will take longer but are just as important if crime is to be brought down significantly year-on-year until it reaches far more tolerable levels.

Neither I nor the Society which I formed are alone in being concerned about crime, but few others, if any, have devoted most of their waking hours for many years studying and campaigning on the subject.

Having researched crime and sought opinions and ideas from thousands of people over many years, I have not the slightest doubt that crime can be massively reduced and that this can be achieved without taking away the freedoms and liberties of law-abiding citizens and without denying the proper protections which any civilised country should afford to suspects, to accused persons, or even to convicted criminals. Working towards major reductions in crime means not only catching and punishing criminals, it means rolling back the stasi-like police states which are increasingly being developed in America, Britain, France and elsewhere. Regrettably, these are beginning to copy the early tactics of Stalin, Hitler, Mao Tse Tung and sad to say, Vladimir Putin, who has reverted to type by riding roughshod over Russia's citizens' freedoms.

20

Later you will read proposals on the subject of sentencing the guilty which, though unique, would certainly be a major improvement on the current hit or miss systems which pass for justice. People commit crimes for many reasons, included in which are:

- Human nature (including national characteristics)

- Ridiculous mass of counter-productive laws and regulations

- Wrongly focused education

- Poor parenting

- Greed

- Pathetic Politicians

- Anger and frustration

- Psychiatric problems and drugs involvement

- Religious or other extremism

- Political oppression and hypocrisy

- Flawed mythical democracies

- Resentment against injustice and unfairness

- Excess population/uncontrolled immigration

- Environmental rape

- The low risk of detection

- The absence of meaningful consequences for convicted criminals

- Inadequate prison capacity

- Drugs and alcohol abuse

- Misdirected resources

- Problems with debt repayment

Clearly, with such a wide variety of factors responsible for a considerable range of crimes, there can be no single solution – or even a handful of solutions – although changes in drugs regimes can produce major reductions in crime very quickly. Our years of research confirm this and we have seen many initiatives from Governments fail because they focused on only one, or at most, a few of the problems which should have been addressed. Most political proposals to deal with crime over the past 20 to 30 years can best be described as "tinkering". Not always wrong, just wholly inadequate and at times, completely counter-productive.

In order to bring about "major" reductions in crime, we must deal with its numerous causes *simultaneously* and with unremitting determination. Our primary aim of course should always be dissuasion, deterrence, call it what you will. Far more needs to be done to stop people even considering turning to crime and there are short and long-term steps which can be taken to achieve this, but only if politicians are willing to challenge current practices and look seriously, with open minds, at the solutions proposed throughout this book.

Included in the short-term measures are significantly increasing the chances of detection and compounding these with more certain and more serious consequences for those found guilty. We must also reduce the instances of criminals escaping justice via the misapplication of technicalities of law, so beloved by those lawyers wishing to demonstrate how clever they are. Better education is high on the list, where meaningful changes would prevent many youngsters from embarking on a life of crime, but the full benefits from this source – necessary though they are - will not come to fruition for some years. All the more reason not to delay the introduction of a new subject **"Concern & Consequences"** as an obligatory examination in all schools. Right now, many of our schoolchildren have no respect, no manners, no standards and are completely out-of-control and I have no doubt that much of this is due to mothers handing their young kids over to nurseries and crèches instead of giving them the emotional support and guidance which they can only get from a happy home environment. Some kids calculate, quite rightly unfortunately, that taking knives and even guns into schools is worth the gamble because the odds of being caught and subsequently punished are very low indeed. No deterrent there then.

22

I have been campaigning for a ***Concern & Consequences examination*** for many years and The Society for Action Against Crime has a 57-page Report on the link between Education & Crime which is available via its website **www.crimedown.org**. Not a single Government or individual politician has offered to even discuss the contents of this Report, preferring instead to ignore it, in the hope that it will disappear. It will not. An adapted version of the C & C examination curriculum should also be used in prisons as part of the rehabilitation and parole application process.

Suffice it to say for now, that Governments' continuing failures to properly position crime and associated social issues in their schools and prisons is a significant contributory factor to the levels of crime in some countries rising exponentially over a 40 to 50 year period. The following pages will cover all of the most important causes of crime and show how high crime countries can become low crime ones and how low crime nations can avoid the very real and ever present danger of becoming high crime countries.

I must warn though, that whilst crime ***can*** be massively reduced, we are running out of time to bring such happier times to fruition.

The longer our politicians delay taking the many corrective measures which are necessary, the stronger become the criminal gangs and those establishments which, for often conflicting and dubious reasons, do not see it in their interests to see crime disappear. You will likely be surprised to learn that some highly-respected groups are amongst those resisting meaningful anti-crime measures – some due to their naivety, others having darker motives.

As of now (early 2007), the law-abiding citizens in countries such as America, Britain, France and Ireland who wish to see crime seriously reduced, outnumber those who do not. However, there is a hidden danger looming. The number of criminals is being allowed to grow and – here lies the danger - their power is being added to by other misguided groups who, for a variety of reasons, are burying their heads in the sand and refusing to support the changes which are necessary to deal with the criminals.

This unholy alliance may well now be approaching a majority which could, in future, prevent the law-abiding and concerned sector from using the ballot box to elect a more enlightened breed of politicians prepared to get serious about crime.

Since George Bush came to power 6 years ago, crime has risen continually in the USA whilst the freedoms of its citizens have been progressively trampled upon. Increasingly, political judges in America have been leaned on to drive a coach and horses through the thoughtful protections which the Founding Fathers so wisely wrote into the Constitution in order to protect all free citizens from Federal and State interference, control and abuse.

Should you wish to try to deny or justify your Government's trashing of its own Constitution Mr. President, I will happily debate this with you on live television. Not in America though, where my outspokenness about its dirty political system would likely see me arrested or seriously harassed.

Since Jacques Chirac became President of France, crime in that country has leapt ahead, whilst he himself is only free from criminal investigation and possible prosecution by virtue of the nonsensical law which affords protection for any French President from being subject to the same laws as the rest of that country's citizens.

Correct me if I am mistaken Citizen Chirac, but wasn't the French Revolution about removing laws which favoured only the privileged? Little wonder that France is now such a dysfunctional hypocritical country, setting itself alight despite the ratcheting up of its Police State.

Tony Blair – he of the sound bite New Labour Party – promised, prior to his election as the UK's Prime Minister, to be *"tough on crime, tough on the causes of crime"*. *If only!* Since he came to power, there are now 50 million unsolved crimes in Britain. That is such an outrageous number I had best spell it out to avoid any assumption that it could be a typo. *Tony Blair is now the custodian of fifty million unsolved recorded crimes with a further nine to ten million crimes being added year-on-year.*

Any country with 20 or more recorded crimes per thousand head of population I assess as suffering high crime and I base this on having visited more than 30 countries and researching crime and corruption data on many others. Below this 2% level most people feel unthreatened, without any need to adjust their lives and feeling free to walk around without fear of harassment and able to speak their minds anywhere in their countries.

Where recorded crimes rise above 2% of population, this comfort level progressively decreases. People become more careful about where they go and fearful of admonishing youngsters dropping litter, doing criminal damage or even bullying. They barricade themselves in at home and understandably, some feel it unwise to go out and challenge gangs of yobs vandalising their cars or other property.

My 2% crime level is an arbitrary figure and is not necessarily applicable to all populations but, it is based on years of study and experience. It is though, a benchmark; a starting point; a target which all countries should aim to get below. Others may believe 1.5% or 2.5% would be a better comfort level, but really, any figure is substantially subjective and not necessarily worse for that. The important thing is to stop just drifting around, but to have a focus point – a figure beyond which any society must realise that crime is getting beyond what is tolerable and needs corrective measures as a matter of urgency.

Many are the people in Britain and elsewhere who tell me that their country is unrecognisable from the one in which they grew up and that nowhere is either safe, free or civilised. Henley-on-Thames, for example, was once one of England's quietest and safest towns but in recent years it too has suffered from Britain's now ubiquitous high crime level. It had not, though, suffered a murder since U.S. Army Sergeant Johnny Waters, in 1943, killed Doris Staples, his lover, because she tried to end their relationship. For this crime of passion, Waters was hanged. Britain had capital punishment in those days.

Flash forward to December 2006. Active Round Table member and local businessman Steven Langford was viciously punched and kicked to death by a gang of thugs *only 20 metres from a manned police station.* This is how safe you are in Britain (and elsewhere) in 2007. Steven Langford's murder was no crime of passion, it was just a brutal attack by a group of feral yobs whose only motive was to indulge their own sadistic inclinations and the buzz they get from assaulting innocents.

This book is my attempt to not only learn more about the causes of crime but more importantly, dissuade or punish those who see crime as an easy or exciting way of life.

What the UK Prime Minister's 9-year reign has produced is not the promised "tough on crime, tough on the causes of crime" but *soft on the criminals, tough on the victims and oppressive on the freedoms of every law-abiding citizen*. Predictably though, Tinkering Tony tinkers on, with mountains of rhetoric and molehills of action and using the ill-conceived British Crime Survey to try to pretend that crime is less serious than the reality. Even the Government's own Audit Commission, in June 2002, reported massive waste of funds which still resulted in a failing criminal justice system, with only 6% of crimes leading to convictions. The Audit Commission, by stating that the criminal justice system was too complex, too slow and in need of total overhaul, was at last reflecting what The Society for Action Against Crime had been saying for more than a decade.

On Christmas Eve 2006, a leaked Report from 10 Downing Street revealed that crime from 2007 is expected to rise by 25% and that not 80,000 but 100,000 prison places will soon be needed.

Well, I have been writing to Tony Blair at Downing Street and to a string of British Home Secretaries and Shadow Home Secretaries for more than a decade, warning them that absent some seriously new thinking and initiatives, crime would reach runaway proportions. Now, apparently, it is official.

After ten years of tinkering Tony's tinkering, not only Britain but other countries now suffer high levels of crime because they believed that the words of a great snake oil salesman were a substitute for real anti-crime measures. Blair's legacy will be that even a hundred thousand prison places will not now be nearly enough and if justice is done, he, Chirac and Bush will go down in history as doing major damage to the very concepts of democracy and freedom.

This book is, in effect, an International Blueprint for massive crime reduction on the basis that if the cap fits, wear it. It is for you to decide whether or not you are happy with the level of crime in the country or area where you live. Certainly the U.K. Audit Commission's Report did not result in the necessary overhaul of the crime scene in Britain, which is an indicator of the obstacles which vested interests bring to bear in order to maintain the status quo.

As at January 2007, the UK's already sky-high level of crime was still rising. Despite Tony Blair's ten-year old promise to solve it, crime and street robbery is up a further 5% and theft is up 12%.

Hopefully, by better understanding what needs to be done, you will feel sufficiently concerned to take whatever measures you feel to be appropriate. I realise, of course, that not everyone will agree with all of my conclusions and recommendations, if only because there is almost nothing in life about which there is universal approval. One thing which we should all do though, is pay far more attention to what our political representatives are up to.

In my final chapter, you will find a summary of measures which every high-crime country should be taking if it seriously wishes to achieve minimum crime and I would like to think that you will demand these of your Government.

If no-one bothers, we will all continue to live in a callous world of declining standards and high crime, but hopefully, when you have finished reading this book, you will feel sufficiently strongly to follow at least some of its recommendations and encourage others to do likewise.

CHAPTER 3

CRIME REDUCTION
WILL BRING HUGE FINANCIAL BENEFITS

At first sight, the costs involved in the implementation of the proposals I recommend in this book may seem high. Absolutely they are not. In fact, the good news is that monies spent wisely on major crime reduction are not only affordable, they will be incredibly profitable. Anti-crime investments can soon be handsomely repaid many times over, both to Governments – which is you indirectly, as a taxpayer – and to you on a personal level.

Some of the proposals contained herein, such as the introduction of a Concerns & Consequences examination subject in all schools, will incur only modest set-up costs and will very quickly become self-liquidating, then profitable as more of our youngsters are persuaded away from crime. With a *C & C Exam* in place, you could look forward to a sharp reduction in the number of anti-social yobs currently being churned out in their thousands by the education systems of so many countries in recent decades.

Other measures needed to catch, convict and confine increasing numbers of criminals, necessitate more police, more prison places and more community service controllers, but not all of these require new money, because a re-assessment of priorities can and should switch funds from wasteful bureaucracy to front-line services. In any event, all additional early costs will quickly be more than wiped out as the costly devastation caused by crime is eliminated. In high-crime countries, the costs of keeping a criminal in prison ranges between 15% and 28% of having that criminal loose in society. A very big monetary gain to the taxpayer.

This, of course, needs handling with some finesse – an attribute which is missing from most politicians' expertise. It will need vision to develop those of my proposals which, by their very nature, must encompass some volatility. Some countries, for example, urgently but only temporarily need a significant increase in police and prison places but these, combined with other of my proposals will, by their very improved effectiveness, make such increases necessary for only a few years. We must therefore build prisons with dual purpose use and prepare those working in them for subsequent alternative careers – environmental protection perhaps.

In other words, each nation should match its resources to its needs, on the understanding that beating crime will initially require more expenditure which will drop significantly in subsequent years due to its own successes.

Reducing crime will undoubtedly result in numerous advantages, some of which will bring huge financial benefits, others which can best be valued for their lifestyle improvements. Burglary, for instance, causes millions of people worldwide to move home within months, because they feel insecure living in a property which has been violated. Around 9% of marriages also break up within a few months of suffering burglary. Although not quantifiable, the costs of these must be enormous.

Right now, the high crime nations are spending mega sums dealing with crime on a whole range of related matters. Governments spend hugely on police, prison and probation services and although such spending should increase in the short-term, it will subsequently reduce to around 50% of current expenditure as they succeed in bringing crime down to the levels possible. We are talking here of many billions of £s, $s, €s of savings *every year*, as in future years, far fewer security services will be required, because if my recommendations are put into effect, there will be far fewer criminals in total and many of the incorrigible ones will spend longer behind bars.

Right now, companies and individuals spend fortunes on security, installing locks, burglar alarms, electronically-coded gates and doors, hiring security personnel, paying elevated insurance premiums etc. CCTV cameras have become ubiquitous and you and I pay for these and for people to monitor and review them. Low crime countries do not have to bear the costs of tens of thousands of such cameras. Most unfortunately do, seeing them as a substitute for preventing crime, which they absolutely are not. Priorities the wrong way round yet again. Britain, for example, has gone camera-crazy and its citizens are now the most spied upon on earth. Since Tony Blair came to power, Britain has rocketed to the top of the Big Brother surveillance league. With only one percent of the world's population, Britain has an amazing twenty-five percent of the CCTV cameras on the entire globe. Low crime countries such as Andorra and Uruguay on the other hand, seem to have almost none, because their politicians have not made the mistakes which lead to high crime. Canadians and Germans are the least spied-upon people and although vested interests are trying to destroy this happy level of privacy, they are, at the time of writing, meeting determined resistance from populations who have better priorities than their counterparts in Britain and America. Ironic, isn't it, that Britain and America defeated Germany in World War II, supposedly in the protection of freedom, yet Germany now has far the greater measure of freedom than have the victors.

When one looks, as I have done over many years, it is easy to see how the costs of crime escalate so easily and go largely unnoticed and without comment.

Sports clubs could save significant sums if the necessity for paying huge fees for policing their events was removed or substantially reduced.

Protecting our politicians costs taxpayers a fortune. Money badly spent, in any event, you may say. Quite why our politicians feel deserving of such massive expenditure on their personal protection is never satisfactorily explained. Surely it cannot be because they perceive themselves as being of greater value than you and I.

Crime of course results in mountains of direct losses ranging from bank robberies, muggings, break-ins, criminal damage, burglaries and stolen cars, bikes, boats, caravans, works of art and animals etc.

Graffiti has to be removed, usually by Local Authorities having Departments and workers employed full-time to deal with the problem. Again – you pay if you live in a high crime environment.

Ditto for litter. It is easy to drop but it is costly to pick up and it is you who pays the clean-up bill.

All medical services in high crime areas bear additional costs, again paid by taxpayers, which should not even arise. They have to devote their time, skills and our resources to caring not only for the victims of crime, but often also the perpetrators. When the drugs peddlers have a shoot-out or a stabbing frenzy, those who survive are still restored to health, usually at our cost. Allowing criminals to add unnecessarily to the burdens of already over-stretched emergency services has proved to be enormously expensive.

In Ireland, Dr. Nicola Ryall, a leading consultant in brain damage, despairs that so many often educated and affluent young men think nothing of kicking a victim's head in. The results can and sometimes are fatal, she says, but even when not, the results are often tragic in the extreme. Victims are left with lifetime disability from diffuse brain injury with society left to pick up the tab for their permanent medical care. Dr. Ryall, who has often given evidence in trials where brain damage features, is quite sure that all too often, those found guilty of inflicting the appalling injuries all too frequently receive sentences which, for the ruining of a life, are disgracefully too lenient.

Even fire-fighters and ambulance personnel are now routinely attacked in some countries, which is not only unacceptable, mindless violence, it imposes costs on their taxpayers which can be eliminated by overcoming the problem.

The aforementioned are just some of the monetary losses which most countries suffer as a direct result of crime.

Neither I nor anyone else can put a figure on these costs for individual countries, but what I can say with confidence is that the real cost is so enormous that when it becomes significantly reduced, it will equate to several percentages off company and personal taxes and substantial savings across the board, from which all can benefit.

Perhaps some universities would care to try to quantify the national costs of crime in their own countries. I would willingly participate in such studies if this was felt to be helpful.

Over and above the obvious monetary losses are the more personal lifestyle ones which truly are incalculable. How does one value the loss of peace of mind and well-being? No-one can put a price on the introduction of long-term fear into the lives of those who have been burgled, beaten, mugged, threatened or raped.

Nor is it only the direct victims who suffer as a result of criminal activity. When a child is abused or murdered, or a rape committed, there is a circle of relatives and friends who cannot avoid the dreadful scenarios constantly intruding into their thoughts.

No amount of surveys or counselling can ever determine the effects suffered by both direct and indirect victims as they replay over and over again, the often horrific crime scenes in their minds. Nor can we measure how such crimes subsequently cause all concerned to adjust their lives into a more defensive and fearful mode.

Sadly, many a relationship has also foundered as a direct result of a loved one being murdered, mugged or raped because guilt, self or mutual recrimination and if-only's eat remorselessly away at those left behind. All too often, these secondary victims find the aftermath too difficult to bear.

Every single crime we prevent is of huge value, so it is stating the obvious that eliminating millions of crimes every year is of profound, almost infinite benefit, both in straight financial savings and the prevention of shattered personal lives.

This Blueprint shows how these benefits of huge crime reduction can be achieved.

CHAPTER 4

TERRORISM

I cover this subject early on, not because it merits priority in the overall debate on crime, but because Governments have recklessly allowed themselves to be skilfully manipulated by a tiny number of crazy fanatics into a series of disastrous knee-jerk blunders. Either that, or they may simply be doing what authoritarian Governments have traditionally done, which is to take every opportunity to instil fear into their citizens in order to get an even greater stranglehold on every aspect of their lives.

It was Paul Craig Roberts, a former official in President Reagan's Government, who rightly observed that the Bush Administration's hype about terrorism serves no purpose other than to build a Police State that is far more dangerous to Americans than are the terrorists. He wonders if anyone in Washington reads and understands the U.S. Constitution and the Bill of Rights. I can answer that question. Those gas and oil barons currently controlling America know the Constitution only too well, which is why they fear it and seek to sabotage it at every possible opportunity.

There can, of course, be no agreed definition of terrorism because it means different things to different people. To some, it is the use of murder and fear via clandestine tactics against an overwhelmingly superior conventional force. To others, it is the reverse – America, Israel and British lashing out with massive arms and air power without care for innocent civilians. There can be no global conclusion as to the state of mind of terrorists – if that is the prevailing term – because they cannot be assessed in the period prior to their murderous acts. Some may have simply been brainwashed and their anger and frustration fed and fuelled by fanatics. Others have undoubtedly become mentally unstable, seeking revenge for either actual or perceived injustices suffered by themselves, their family, their religion or their country.

Bush, Rumsfeld, Cheyney, Rice, Blair, Blunkett, Clarke, Reid, Putin & co. have already handed a string of victories to a range of terrorists around the world and they have done so at enormous expense to their taxpayers. They have also done this on money borrowed from foreigners, which puts every American citizen at huge risk.

Compared with China, for example, the American debt burden leaves them incredibly vulnerable.

China already has more than the equivalent of US$ 1 trillion in foreign currency reserves, much of it actually in U.S. dollars.

The U.S.A. on the other hand, has debts of 8 trillion dollars, much of it owed to China.

China is adding 720 million dollars to its piggy bank every day.

The U.S.A. is *falling further into the red* by adding 1.92 billion dollars of debt every day, much of it from China and much of it wasted in Iraq and on George bush's manic spending on stripping Americans of their freedoms, all under the pretext of defeating terrorism.

One might well ask how clever Bush and his college boy colleagues have been when they have put the destiny of their nation into the hands of the Chinese. China could now legitimately buy a controlling interest in almost every publicly traded corporation in America, including those in the vital energy and agriculture sector.

China now has sufficient funds to buy most of the really productive agricultural land in every State in America. So – just how bright is George W.'s supposedly "bright" team?

My view – and I doubt anyone has claimed this before – is that those claiming to be capable of governing us should have *three sights*, namely *insight*, *foresight* and *hindsight*.

Insight is needed in order to keep tabs on what is happening and analyse what is going right, what may be going wrong and what adjustments can beneficially be made. America and Britain have failed miserably.

Foresight is the ability to accurately judge the consequences of policies and actions pending and see problems ahead which necessitate changes of direction now, if they are to be avoided. Excess population, ridiculous constant pushing for growth, rape of the environment, abuse of energy sources and unnecessary wars are all demonstrations of the lack of foresight.

Hindsight seems easy. We all have it at times, but it can be a positive "sight" if we really do use it to examine what has passed, with a genuine wish and determination to avoid making the same mistakes again. Readers everywhere should ask themselves if their Leaders have demonstrated the positive or the negative sides of hindsight. Many, I know, learn absolutely nothing, even from their most catastrophic blunders.

These macho masters of rhetoric are spending – or, more accurately, forcing their citizens and businesses to spend – hundreds of billions of dollars under the pretence of protecting:- their nations; democracy; and their citizens' freedoms. These claims are false. As false, in fact, as some of these same politicians' lying assertions that Iraq had weapons of mass destruction which were an imminent threat to the west.

I am not talking hindsight here because I am on record writing to Tony Blair and George Bush telling them long before their invasion of Iraq that Saddam Hussein, after the Gulf war, was no threat to any other country and I gave them chapter and verse why he was not. Neither Britain's Prime Minister nor America's President wanted to hear this of course, I presume because they were already determined to invade Iraq the following year for reasons very different from those given to the public. Four years later, it is crystal clear that Bush and Blair's seeking of a United Nations resolution to invade Iraq was nothing more than shoddy window dressing. Do not be surprised if Tony and Cherie end up accepting lucrative offers to relocate to the U.S. shortly after the U.K. Prime Minister's handing over his poisoned chalice to Chancellor Gordon Brown or some other power-seeking ego-tripper.

Tony Blair's successor would be wise to consider the Canadian story about a visiting fisherman who hired the lake Warden to row him around for the day. After hours without a bite, the fisherman took out a small stick of dynamite, lit its fuse, then threw it into the lake – and bang – up came some stunned fish. The Warden was furious and started rowing back to the boathouse, yelling "that is not how we fish in this State. I'm going to report you to the Authorities." Unfazed, the fisherman lit another stick of dynamite and tossed it to the Warden with the words "I suggest you quit bitching and start fishing."

Are terrorists a threat?

Absolutely they are.

Can - as Bush claims – the war against terrorism be won?

No, it cannot be won, if by "winning" one means the elimination of all terrorists and hence, the prevention of any future attacks. Bush and Blair can thump their chests and make all the rousing patriotic speeches they like, but the day will never come when the war against terrorism will be won, when the terrorist threat is gone forever. Just like aeroplanes, terrorism, cannot be uninvented. I forecast long ago that invading Afghanistan and Iraq would not eliminate terrorism but would result in one year's occupation becoming two, then three, then five and quite possibly more than ten years. So it is proving.

Having invaded Afghanistan and Iraq, one might expect Americans to know where it is and what kind of people live there, but the National Geographic Roper Affairs 2006 Study of the Middle East discovered that 87% of college-aged students couldn't find Iraq, even on a map of the Middle East. Nor could 83% find Afghanistan.

Not everyone knows much about the Shiite/Sunni balance in Iraq, but one man particularly demonstrated his ignorance on this important matter. When asked by Jeff Stein, Congressional Quarterly's Editor, if Al Quaeda is Shiite or Sunni, Silvestre Reyes said – "They have both". He then stumbled on to say – "predominantly Shiite". But for his job, this would have been funny, but what can one say about a nation which invaded Iraq, supposedly on the basis of "credible intelligence" confirming weapons of mass destruction, when Silvestre Reyes, it's House Intelligence Committee Chief, **whose job it is to oversee Middle East intelligence**, is blissfully unaware that Al Quaeda is staunchly Sunni, to the point of considering Shiites as heretics. Oops – so much for intelligence.

What America should have done following 9/11 was to issue Letters of Marque which its Constitution allows it to do. These fully legal "Letters" allow the Government to offer substantial rewards to bounty hunters to track down and bring in any criminals and that is exactly what the 9/11 perpetrators were. It was never an act of war by Afghanistan and no Afghans were involved. Fifteen of the criminals and Osama Bin Laden were Saudis, so why did Bush choose to invade Afghanistan and not Saudi Arabia? Why did they rush into what became two unbelievably expensive wars and subject its entire population to the disgusting Patriot Act instead of issuing Letters of Marque which would have produced better results at a fraction of the cost? Control, dear reader. The bully's drug – control.

Terrorism is not a phenomenon just of the 20th/21st century and history shows that America, Britain, France, Belgium, Ireland and Spain are just some of the countries who have encouraged, financed and armed terrorists when they saw it in their own interests to try to overthrow even democratically elected Governments which morally should have been none of their concern. So, why the hypocrisy?

There are, of course, many reasons why some people resort to terrorism, including:-

Injustice, which can be real, perceived or falsely aroused.

Religious Hatred is almost an inevitability, because within some religions there will always be the zealots who will search their scriptures to find justification for their wish to consider all who do not share their beliefs as the enemy. Regrettably, religious writings and teachings all too often allow for contradictory interpretations, particularly by those with dysfunctional personalities.

Outside Interference i.e. one or more nation(s) exerting unacceptable pressure upon another country. This is a sure-fire way of ensuring the creation of patriotic terrorists, and politicians who fail to recognise the dangers in this are in the wrong job. There have been warmongers since time immemorial – people whose bank balances and prestige can only increase by encouraging conflict. It is time we stopped listening to them because they all have their own disreputable reasons for promoting wars, invariably from behind-the-scenes positions of cosseted safety.

The damage which warmongers such as Donald Rumsfeld have done – and I suspect continues to do behind the scenes – is incalculable but certainly enormous. Devious Donald, whom a previous U.S. President described as a "ruthless little bastard" was typical of the breed. Cosying up to ruthless, disgusting regimes around the world one minute, by supplying them with arms, intelligence (sic), money and media support, then turning on them when they were no longer flavour of the month.

39

Rumsfeld was a friend of Saddam Hussein for years, despite knowing his record as a murderous, torturing, brutal Dictator, then enemy when Iraq's Ruler was no longer any use to them against Iran. Rumsfeld, Bush, Cheyney, Rice & Co. were only ever interested in creating conflict. Where no reasons for conflict exist, these devious people are quite happy to manufacture them, even to the extent of conspiring in attacks on their own citizens and serving military. When it comes to making enemies whom they can then justify attacking, "whatever-it-takes" is the motto of the warmonger establishment with huge financial interests in arms and surveillance equipment manufacturing corporations. Add in the Generals and the supposed intelligence-gathering organisations and you have the world's greatest cartel of elite criminals.

Invariably, crime starts at the top then filters down to the petty chancers at the bottom of the money-grabbing chain.

No-one should forget that it was Donald Rumsfeld who pleaded with the President to send Iraq weapons of mass destruction and supply Iran with nuclear technology. On my! What short memories some folk have.

In October 2006, a group of top security experts – whatever that means – claimed that Britain was now the number one target for a revitalised Al Quaeda and would remain so for at least a generation. Well, they would say that wouldn't they, because if we swallow it, the way some swallowed their 'weapons of mass destruction' claims, that is their jobs secure for at least another 10 to 30 years.

Truth to tell, neither the security experts nor anyone else knows either the Muslim Fundamentalists' aims or their capabilities. One does not, of course, need more than a handful of brain cells to realise that when you invade foreign countries and kill hundreds of thousands of their innocent civilians, you create a pool of anger and hatred which may well result in retaliation by some of the victims' compatriots. That though, is no reason to be other than quietly vigilant and apart from this, we should ignore the regular *P.R.* campaigns of politicians and security experts trying to keep us in constant fear, just so they can take away ever more of our freedom and privacy.

Elite groups always make millions/billions out of selling war and anti-terrorist equipment and are only too keen to join with power-hungry politicians in keeping their citizens in an on-going state of fear.

40

Revenge can be such a vicious circle and nothing demonstrates its corrosive effects more than the terrible Beslan school tragedy where Chechen terrorists took terrible revenge, not on those Russian soldiers responsible for torturing, raping and killing their own families in Chechnya, but on innocent Russian children and their relatives.

Compounding the 1st September 2004 tragedy, children aged 7 to 12, who took part in a documentary film a year later, swore revenge on the Chechens saying they would never forgive them and wished only to cut their throats. These children, of course, were told nothing of the atrocities committed in Chechnya by Russian soldiers over generations and so were unaware of their own country's role in the vicious circle of terrorist atrocities. In any event, who amongst us can know what our own reaction would have been had we seen our friends and relatives butchered in such an appalling manner.

Quite understandably, some of the Russian adults hold President Putin responsible for many of the Beslan deaths because of the way the Russian military were allowed or encouraged to storm the number one school. Again, it was the macho knee-jerk reaction of a buttoned-down political mind, hell bent on sending a tough-guy message to Chechnya, with a total disregard for the lives of even their own Russian citizens, including so many innocent and frightened children.

Vladimir Putin, of course, is still a leopard. He has not changed his spots. He just hid some of them for a while. At heart, he is still a ruthless, devious manipulator, still leaning heavily on his KGB methods of old. Those expecting either freedom or democracy should put no trust in Comrade Putin. Boris Berezovsky and Mikhail Khodorkovsky are just two of many who found to their cost that trying to work with Russia's arch bureaucrat can result in catastrophe. One has been driven into exile, one railroaded into gaol for 9 years. Others have not been so lucky, Alexander Litvinenko for one, poisoned in London by Polonium-210, a highly radioactive substance which only States with limitless funds could possibly have afforded.

The lesson to be learned, is that all nations can and should avoid inviting revenge attacks by refraining from unnecessary or unjustified interference in the affairs of others and in oppressing their own people.

I am in no way advocating submission to blackmail, nor am I suggesting walking away from disputes, but neither nations nor terrorists can win over hearts and minds by blowing people up. In October 2005 the U.S. military launched yet another sweep against insurgents in Fallujah, a small Iraqi town and as before, innocent civilians suffered the highest fatalities. Fifteen thousand, in fact, were murdered by Americans and more than 50% of those slaughtered were women and children. With typical American arrogance and insensitivity, they code-named their own assault "Operation Iron Fist". Gee Mr. Rumsfeld, you really do understand how to persuade Iraqis to love your soldiers don't you. Early in 2003 it was threats of shock and awe and by the end of 2005, it was Iron Fist. Some people just do not learn.

In October 2006, NATO bombers managed to bomb 52 innocent Afghans to death, again mainly women and children.

Anyone believing that none of the families of the hundreds of thousands of victims of the American/British invasion of Afghanistan and Iraq will not seek revenge, is living in Fantasy Land.

The terrorists have won!

It grieves me to have witnessed how our politicians have already handed a succession of victories to a tiny number of warped terrorists. One must question either the sanity or the motives – or both – of those of our control-freak politicians who have so eagerly given the terrorists so much of what they want.

"It's people's lives at stake here!" pontificated U.S. Marshall George Walsh. "We're not playing a game of craps", he thundered – attempting to justify the evacuation of a Washington D.C. federal courthouse and the closure of several streets, including a section of Constitution Avenue – all because an unpleasant smell had caused some hyped-up goon to suspect nitrogen-based explosives. Turned out it was nothing more than the malodorous whiff from a homeless guy's unwashed clothing. A tad paranoia bureaucratica I believe and just one of many thousands of costly mini-panics resulting from petty officials being unjustifiably wound up by politicians with dubious agendas of their own.

I don't pretend to know the extent to which terrorism is centrally directed by the likes of Osama Bin Laden or by small independent

42

groups of misguided fanatics, not all of whom, by the way, are Muslims. Nor do I believe that our Governments' much-vaunted "intelligence" services know either. This, remember, is the same bunch of no-hopers who claimed to "know" that Iraq had weapons of mass destruction, so let's get real here.

Like almost all bureaucrats, those in "intelligence" seriously exaggerate their own importance and they are supported in a scam created and run by senior politicians and business interests for their own disreputable reasons. So-called intelligence services do not protect their countries, they only pretend so to do because this gives politicians the opportunity to do what the public would not tolerate if they were made aware of the truth. Secrecy is the enemy of truth and we will always have terrorism and crime whilst ever our politicians connive to mislead their own citizens by avoiding bringing "alleged" lawbreakers to public trial.

The Bushes, Blairs, Cheyneys, Rumsfelds, Rices, Clarkes and Reids should realise that the world is weary of their mantra of last resort – "we obviously cannot reveal what we know because this would put our intelligence sources at risk". Such deceitful garbage comes only from those wishing to maintain power for their own reasons, which has nothing whatsoever to do with the national interest.

Former U.S. Congressman Bob Barr, a Conservative from Georgia, was absolutely right when he said – "The American people are going to have to say, enough of this ridiculous business of justifying everything as necessary for the war on terror". "Either" he said, "the Constitution and the laws of our country mean something or they do not" and it is truly frightening what is happening in America. Little wonder that lifelong lovers of America, such as Irish political commentator Eamon Dunphy, now conclude that the America of yesteryear no longer exists, other than in some people's imaginations. Thanks to President Bush, the country is now simply ugly, he wrote in November 2006.

- It is **not** in any nation's interest to spend billions of dollars/pounds spying on and interfering in the lives of law-abiding citizens. This is just what the terrorists want, because it moves their target countries deeper into debt and creates divisions between politicians and their own people. George Bush fell straight into the terrorists' trap by recklessly committing America to the most outrageously misguided expenditure any taxpayers anywhere in the world have ever had imposed upon them. We, our children and our grandchildren will be paying for his expensive macho tantrums for decades to come via higher taxes, inflation, shrinking pensions, postponed retirements and decaying infrastructure.

- Worse still, Bush, Blair and co. have bent the knee to the terrorists by hammering the final nails into the coffin of freedom. Not the freedoms of the bad guys but those of their own law-abiding citizens. These citizens never wanted to live in a society where their bankers, accountants, lawyers, motor distributors, travel agents, insurers etc. were all obliged to be spies for power-crazed Governments. Nor do they want, or see the need for these professionals to have mountains of bureaucratic forms, restrictions and other demands imposed upon them – the huge costs of which can, in the final analysis, only be borne by the consumer. Governments of course, have no money, so everything spent unwisely – whether directly as a taxpayer, or indirectly because thousands of businesses and service providers are forced into unnecessary costs imposed by the bureaucrats – is paid by you and by me.

Another victory to the terrorists - handed to them on a plate by our own politicians who, once they achieve power, quickly become strangers to the whole concept of freedom.

For years, America hid the fact that it operated secret prisons around the world but in September 2006, President Bush admitted – or was it boasted? – that his C.I.A. had in fact being doing exactly that and had no intention of giving them up. He claimed that operating secret prisons gave them information unavailable elsewhere and saved lives. Easy to say, especially when everyone involved is kept incommunicado and denied public trials.

The Associated Press reported that British Member of Parliament Andrew Tyrie accused George Bush of just playing with words and he called upon him to make clear, exactly what techniques have been used in the C.I.A.'s secret prisons.

German Member of the European Parliament, Elmar Brok, called upon the European Commission to ask Washington about the location of America's secret detention centres. I would like to see such an approach and its outcome given maximum public exposure. The E.U.'s Dick Harty said that Poland and Romania are unlikely to have *large* (our italics) detention centres for C.I.A. use, but may have put cells at their disposal for a short time.

In November 2006 though, Poland was accused by Members of the European Parliament of obstruction and non-co-operation with its enquiries into illegal rendition flights. Polish Airport Manager Jerry Kos told Italian M.E.P. Claudio Fava that an alleged rendition flight no.313 on 22nd September 2003 never landed at Szymanow Airport but Polish official Marek Pasionek said it had landed there but could not be inspected – *because it was dark.*

Now I don't know about you, but I sure as hell would not like to be in any secret detention facility, large or small. Europe should have got tough with the U.S. on this long ago.

My next chapter deals with the whole subject of treatment whilst in detention. Suffice it for now to say that it has been and still is deeply shameful.

Bush also conveniently forgot to mention the hundreds of thousands of deaths and the immeasurable amount of structural damage, homes wrecked and lives ruined as a direct result of his indiscriminate macho lashing out.

By far the greatest number of the dead, injured and dispossessed were innocent of any crime and were never any threat to America and only a fool would not realise that causing such death and destruction inevitably breeds more hatred, more enemies, not less.

• I believe I speak for the overwhelming majority of the ordinary people around the world when I say that we never wanted to see people held incommunicado for weeks, months or years without a public trial in open court, before a jury.

Even less do civilised people condone torture or abuse; or kidnapping and sending suspects to third party countries to suffer such evil treatments in greater secrecy.

Our politicians have sunk to these depths and have jumped on the tragic activities of terrorism as an opportunity to throw out hundreds of years of established law. More victories to the terrorists, who now understand very well that just the occasional murderous operation brings knee-jerk reactions from our politicians which result in ever more impositions on every one of us.

The terrorists must rejoice in America's Patriot Act and Britain's escalating anti-terrorist laws *because they have achieved precisely what the terrorists wanted :-*

- Serious disruption of daily life in many western countries.

- Massive expenditure adding to each country's already high debt. America cynically portrays itself as the richest country in the world, but that is pure spin and propaganda. Already, it has not billions but trillions of dollars of debt. More debt, in fact, than every other country in the world put together and their gross triggering and mishandling of the terrorist threat is adding to this debt every day, with no end in sight.

- I am grateful to Congressman Jim Cooper for revealing information from the U.S. Treasury's Financial Report showing the disgraceful level of debt in America. In addition to their own personal mortgage, overdraft and credit card debt, every American now owes – via national debt – an amazing 156,000 dollars and this equates to 375,000 dollars for each working American. These are debts which cannot even begin to be re-paid, unless of course the Fed prints up trillions more dollars causing hyper-inflation. This is the cost of pretending to be an empire.

Financial columnist Robert Kiyosaki got it about right when he wrote "Most Americans live in La-La land. They're clueless about what's going on in the world. They still think we're the richest country in the world when in truth we are the world's biggest debtor nation". Now I have no objections to the delusional thinking themselves rich, but I do have a serious problem with them when they start acting the part and throwing their weight about.

Even the U.S. Government Accountability Office's Comptroller General, David Walker, blandly admits that America has "*a broken business model*". That, dear reader, is an understatement. It can only end in tears.

We could all, of course, "appear" to be the richest person in our area if we repeatedly borrowed money from our neighbours in order to live a lavish lifestyle, but our status would be illusory because the day would inevitably come when our neighbours tire of paying for our extravagances.

Just like individuals, the bombast of highly leveraged nations can very quickly melt away as one slides into bankruptcy, with creditors dividing up any assets.

You know, one way to knock out a business competitor has traditionally been to lend them so much money which they would not be able to pay back, then bingo, its takeover time. Many of America's enemies now own mountains of dollars of US debt and many of the country's assets. Not surprisingly, some of this is already being converted to gold, to alternative currencies and to other physical commodities, leaving America increasingly vulnerable to the growing threat of wholesale dollar desertion.

Communist China, for example, can overwhelm America at any time of its choosing and without firing a single shot. That is because a succession of Republican and Democrat Governments have hidden from their electorate the staggering level of China's ownership of America. By 2005, China alone holds hundreds of billions of dollars in U.S. Treasuries. Selling these would immediately collapse the U.S. bond market and send the fictitious mighty dollar crashing towards its true value, i.e. close to zero. Rest assured, China is not keeping America afloat due to altruism and at some point it will call in these loans and quite probably spend some of that released liquidity buying even more American land, businesses and other tangible assets at knock-down prices because the Chinese can seriously depress the values of these U.S. assets at any time of their choosing.

I make this point simply to confirm that America is not the professed richest country on the globe and that fundamentally, they are broke and should not be charging around the world 'kicking ass' when the facts show that they cannot even pay for their own boots. Ever the ones for papering over the cracks, the Federal Reserve's fraudulent tactic has been to repeatedly print more dollars, thereby reducing the value of every other dollar already in circulation.

It should have been payback time for Gobbledegook Greenspan but by the skin of his teeth, he ducked and dived just long enough to let his successor Ben Bernanke take the rap. This book is about crime of all kinds and it was certainly criminal that Mr. G. built a gigantic housing bubble by encouraging massive debt at federal, state, corporate and personal levels. Another two million Americans became bankrupt in 2005 alone and I have not the slightest doubt that a substantial number of these will resort to crime in an attempt to maintain their former standard of living, which in any event was only supported by irresponsible borrowing. That, of course, was precisely what the pathetic Alan Greenspan was doing with his nation's economy.

• **Note.** Since writing the above, in September 2005, I note that in Bill Bonner's Daily Reckoning of 24th November 2005 Dr. Kurt Richebacher was quoted as saying "The whole thing (the American economy) is a monumental fraud and Mr. Alan Greenspan is merely an extraordinary criminal." Dr. Richebacher is arguably the world's leading economist and Bill Bonner – jointly with Addison Wiggin – published their take on the U.S. economy in their November 2005 book "*Empire of Debt*". This underscores what I have been saying for years, but my beat is mainly that which impacts upon crime whilst their speciality is finance and *Empire of Debt* puts the American economy under the microscope far better than my limited analysis. Everyone in America, everyone owning U.S.-denominated debt and everyone who does not believe in the Fed's supposedly magical debt-fairy, should read *Empire of Debt*.

USA fiscal policy has long been fraudulent, starting with a string of Presidents removing the traditional necessity for the paper dollars held by banks to be backed by gold. It was President Franklin D. Roosevelt in April 1933 who made it compulsory for US citizens to hand over all of their gold and silver coin, bullion and certificates to the Government at the Government's own paltry gold valuation of 23 dollars an ounce. By 1934, that same Government cynically "re-valued" gold to 35 dollars an ounce. By any measure, that was blatant fraud and the fact that it was committed by politicians, on their own people, in no way makes it any less of a crime. Subsequently, cutting a long tragedy short, Richard Nixon – when he took America off the Gold Standard - ensured that the US dollar, like all fiat (paper) money, would eventually become worthless.

By failing to understand the motives of terrorism and by borrowing billions of dollars every day to support a profligate Homeland Security Department, Bush, Rumsfeld, Greenspan & co. have simply brought forward the day when the rest of the world will be able to force America into bankruptcy. American author, Gore Vidal, understands this better than most and like millions of his countrymen whose warning voices went unheeded, he has chosen to live abroad. He, like me, came to the conclusion long ago that no American now has freedom because their neo-cons have, for years, been trashing what America was built upon - a mainly commonsense Constitution and Bill of Rights.

Terrorism is a disturbing, disgusting tactic and must be dealt with, but if we are ever to reduce it to a minimum, we must face these and other unpleasant realities which our Governments have so far failed to address. Few people are aware that America has its military stationed in more than 100 countries. Why is this? and how would Americans feel if these countries had their troops on U.S.A. soil?

• The foreign policies of America and Britain have contributed hugely to terrorism instead of diminishing it. Instead of holding up true freedom as a shining example to the whole world, America has joined the Taliban, Al Quaeda, Russia, Zimbabwe etc. into the gutter by ruthlessly stealing the freedoms of their own law-abiding citizens. Other cowardly countries have allowed themselves to be bullied by Bush, Rumsfeld and shop window-dummy Condaleeza into the mire of oppression.

Along with millions of others, even ex-UK Labour Party Minister Roy Hattersley is railing against his own Party's attacks on freedom. Under the headline *As Bad As The Taliban*, he wrote for the Daily Mail (a Conservative-leaning tabloid) about his opposition to Tony Blair's anti-terrorist law which resulted in Peace Campaigner Maya Evans being arrested for nothing more than reading out the names of British servicemen killed in Iraq. She was arrested by 14 police officers for doing this at the Cenotaph where Britain has traditionally honoured those fallen in conflict. Why? - because it was within one kilometre of Parliament, the "supposed" seat of democracy. This new restriction was just one of many slipped into Tony Blair's latest anti-terrorist laws.

Ex-Minister Hattersley reflects my own concerns in saying "the culprits are those who offended every tradition of British liberty", i.e. those Members of Parliament who passed this indefensible Act. Freedom-lovers the world over deplore terrorism but are absolutely certain that limiting free speech and preventing the reading out of a list of those killed in Iraq, is both a denial of fundamental liberties and a propaganda gift to the terrorists seeking to undermine our society.

I have further questions of both Tony Blair and Metropolitan Police Commissioner Sir Ian Blair :-

"Disregarding for the moment your foolish law, why did it take 14 police officers to arrest Maya Evans – a demure, known peace advocate who was simply reading out a list of dead soldiers' names?"

"If terrorism is the apocalyptic threat which you pretend it to be, surely these 14 officers would have been better deployed trying to track down information about the plans and whereabouts of terrorists with a view to finding evidence sufficient to arrest and charge <u>them</u>?"

Maya Evans should not have been arrested. Two minibuses of police officers should not have been sent to remove her. Nor should she have been charged and subsequently criminalised. If some moron in the Met. foolishly decided it was necessary to arrest a lady peacefully reading out a list of names, one old-style British bobby would have had no problem carrying out his superior's orders, however unwise they were. Perhaps the lady can think herself lucky she did not end up having 8 or 9 bullets fired into her head.

- Consequently, having poured petrol onto the Islamic fires for years, terrorism cannot now be quenched. It can, only at best, be contained and politicians' macho rhetoric about waging war and ranting on about victory has already proved counter-productive and is likely so to continue.

- *Identity cards* will not stop terrorists, but they will reduce the effectiveness of the police by further alienating them from the public and by soaking up numerous billions of pounds, some of which could have gone, and could still go into better policing and more savvy community relations. Should they ever be introduced, ID Cards will cause huge anger amongst many otherwise law-friendly citizens and would be another victory for the evil but clever terrorists.

- Politicians beware! Supporting intrusive Identity Cards and other invasions of privacy will have precisely the opposite effect to that which you are trying to sell. There will be more crime, not less, and this could well have serious consequences which you seem to be incapable of imagining.

- Paying billions to surly, aggressive, security personnel will not stop terrorism and the multi-million pound expenditure which British MPs have voted to erect a House of Commons security screen for themselves would have been far better spent elsewhere. Clearly, the arrogance of the 646 British Members of Parliament shows that they feel themselves to be more important than the remaining sixty million of their citizens. I will come later to how much more could have been done to reduce terrorism but with considerably lower expenditure.

- Spending vast sums trying to keep tabs on who is flying where; taking toenail clippers from grannies; stopping families from flying because their 3 year old child bears the same name as someone on a list of supposedly questionable people, will not stop terrorists, but it has made flying an extremely unpleasant experience, particularly in America.

- The farcical security scare started in Britain in summer 2006 over carry-on liquids cost British Airways alone a hundred million dollars and because it spread faster than bird flu, its knock-on financial losses were incalculable. It was just blind panic which could and should have been managed far more efficiently. The entire nonsense was, of course, centred initially on flights to America.

I recommend all of those with a choice not to visit the U.S.A. until that country learns to be less dictatorial, more civilised and more respectful of privacy and freedoms and unless you want to lose your shirts, sell any property you have in America before the bubble bursts big-time.

Our security services should, of course, be on the ball, but being offensive, surly or predictable is not the way to catch terrorists. Nor does it make any sense confiscating manicure sets whilst allowing potentially dangerous glass bottles to be sold on aeroplanes, available to every passenger thereon. Our own military are trained in unarmed combat and it would be remiss in the extreme, to assume that there are no terrorists with similar skills which would enable them to overcome the crew of any passenger airliner even without anything remotely resembling a weapon. Aunties with knitting needles and granddads with pipe cleaners pale into insignificance by comparison and I make this point only to demonstrate that there should be limits to how much we spend on anti-terrorist measures because no amount of money can guarantee to protect us, so it should be far more cleverly prioritised.

I have personal experience of abuse and completely unjustified threats from airport security officials and I have lost count of similar instances brought to my attention by others. Many people, of course, just tolerate such disgraceful treatment rather than risk the wrath of the bullies by either complaining at the time – highly risky – or writing about their experiences, which I recommend all to do.

Sister Glenn Ann McPhee is the U.S. Conference of Catholic Bishops' Secretary for Education, a high-profile job which obviously afforded her better-than-average access to some pretty influential people. Not that this led quickly to the correction of bureaucratic errors, as Senator Edward Kennedy and others also discovered, to their chagrin.

Without warning, 62-year old Sister McPhee – a very busy traveller – was suddenly prevented from boarding her booked flight. She eventually discovered she was on a no-fly list - for absolutely no valid reason - and over a 9-month period, this meant numerous missed speaking engagements due to her being denied access to a succession of flights and highly-aggressive and intrusive searches. The U.S. Transportation Security Administration treated her queries and eventual complaints abysmally. Only when Karl Rove, who was George Bush's Chief Political Adviser, was persuaded by Church Hierarchy to intervene, did things begin to improve. He contacted Tom Ridge, who was the Chief of Homeland Security, who in turn passed the matter to that Department's top lawyer.

Sister Glenn Anne McPhee eventually discovered that her many months of trauma was caused, for no better reason, than the T.S.A. claiming than an Afghan had used the name McPhee as an alias. No forename – just McPhee – so perhaps everyone with this name is on their no-fly list. Certainly 62-year old Dominican nun Sister McPhee was on it and she feels sure that many ordinary people would not have got off the dreaded list because they would not have her access to high-level contacts.

Typical of failed bureaucracies, the Transportation Security Administration has bolted on yet another layer of parasites, this time known as Secure Flight. Already it is earning serious criticism and doubtless will continue to attract the negative attention it deserves. Like every hugely-expensive Government computer-driven programme, that of the *T.S.A.* is full of holes and errors. Seems that not only do they never learn, they spend huge resources trying to bully other nations into adopting similarly invasive and counter-productive tactics.

Cravenly, the EU is caving in to America and throwing years of costly individual data protection into the bin, giving any Government direct computer access to private information about you which is none of their business.

More about how to take back our freedom later in the book.

Sister McPhee describes her months of trauma as the closest thing to hell she ever expects to experience and whilst she and I endorse the need to prevent terrorists from boarding planes, we expect a far higher level of competence and civility in the systems necessary to achieve this. One can question and even search passengers just as efficiently with a smile and kind words as one can with a sour and threatening attitude. Try joking with airport security, or even complaining about unacceptable behaviour – in America particularly – and you will quickly find yourself in a back room, handcuffed and even imprisoned by a series of scowling, staring, scary officials who make it quite clear to you that you are completely within their power. How civilised.

Right now, we are paying taxes to employ these tyrannical, Gestapo-style "security" morons to bully us. Is there no end to what we must suffer under the veil of supposed protection from terrorism which even our Governments admit cannot be guaranteed?

The costs involved in "mistakenly" persecuting a nun are incalculable, but all told, they certainly amounted to tens of thousands of dollars. Multiply this by the endless number of similar "mistakes" and you will begin to understand how much of *your* money your political appointees and their obnoxious Little-Hitler officials are wasting.

My advice is to fly as little as possible until such time as airport immigration and security officials learn to treat all travellers with respect, tolerance and good humour. Tourism and airlines are of great value to most countries and our refusal to support those employing abusive officials may eventually produce some better behaviour.

Nowhere amongst the billions of words written about ID Cards and passports have I come upon any comment on a matter which to me typifies the hypocrisy of Government.

Viz

The inside cover of the European Union, United Kingdom of Great Britain and Northern Ireland passport says :-

"Her Britannic Majesty's Secretary of State requests and requires in the name of Her Majesty all those whom it may concern to allow the bearer to pass freely and without let or hindrance, *and to afford the bearer such assistance and protection as may be necessary.*"

Fat chance.

Perhaps Tony Blair would explain why he colludes with his Secretaries of State to introduce regulations authorising officials to ignore and override "Her Britannic Majesty's" specific requests and requirements.

Perhaps George Bush would explain why he puts up two fingers to those visitors travelling to America under the protection of a British Passport. Or could it be, Mr. President, that as with other embarrassing issues, you pretend to be ignorant of your officials' abuses? Like torture, perhaps.

Terrorism in perspective

I simply do not believe that there are hundreds of suicide bombers or thousands of terrorists living in each of the western countries. If there were, we would be suffering atrocities every week, possibly every day, because that is allegedly what the extremists would like to inflict upon us, if what our scaremongering politicians tell us is true.

Ask yourself – If there are so many terrorists living in Europe, America, Canada and Australia who hate our guts, why aren't they attacking us continuously? It isn't lack of money, because massive death and destruction could be inflicted at almost no cost. No. The answer is that we do not have thousands of terrorists living in or visiting western countries. That does not, of course, make the modest number we probably do have, any less of a concern.

All countries can and should keep their borders as tight as possible and those Governments who have kept out individuals known to preach hatred and violence are quite right having done so. Those nations coming late to such a policy have much to explain to their electorates, having let in dangerous troublemakers in the first place. Anyone, of course, should be free to criticise any Government, but no-one is entitled to accept the hospitality of a foreign country then abuse its generosity by preaching or in any way participating in violence against innocent citizens. Any immigrant with such a record should be refused entry and returned to their departure country. Any immigrant allowed entry should be advised that such concession is granted strictly on condition that they do not involve themselves in any terrorist activity or encouragement. Failure to comply must result in deportation or prosecution in a normal public Court.

Iraq was not responsible for the attacks on the twin towers and Bush and Blair lied about their reason for invading that country and killing hundreds of thousands of innocent people.

Even the U.S. Senate, having studied the subject for 3 years, produced a Report in September 2006 which admitted that American Intelligence (sic) had been seriously faulty; that there had been no weapons of mass destruction and that Iraq had never colluded with Al Quaeda to mount any terrorist attack on the U.S. Saddam Hussein had, in fact – the Senate concluded – distrusted Bin Laden and refused his suggestions to join forces against the U.S.

Bush's response was that Saddam Hussein had been shooting at American planes. Wow. A country defending its own airspace. Would President George W. Bush not have had Iraqi planes shot at if they were flying over American territory?

The hypocrisy of so many so-called World Leaders I find staggering. I have not the slightest doubt that their attitude of "don't do as I do, do as I say" contributes to both terrorism and everyday crime.

Whilst two wrongs do not make a right, no-one should be surprised that some Moslems were subsequently fired-up by the fundamentalists to seek revenge. Bush and Blair seem to have invented two new concepts of international dispute. The first is that of a one-sided war in which they can attack a country which is no threat to them, but the invaded nation is not expected to retaliate. The second is the creation of enemy combatants stripped of any of the legal standings which every civilised country should honour. Such sly abuses of power have achieved precisely nothing in fighting terrorism but they have brought disgrace on America, Britain and others, of which many of their own citizens tell me they are deeply ashamed.

I absolutely and unreservedly deplore every form of torture or brainwashing, including its disgusting proxy participation by some so-called civilised countries. Indeed, I am working with others to take a major and unprecedented anti-abuse initiative following upon the publication of this Anti-Crime Blueprint.

On the torture and extraordinary rendition issues, I am at one with Amnesty International and other Freedom Bodies, but where I do take a contrary view to them is on the question of returning some illegal immigrants to the countries from which they came.

I see no just alternative to returning any immigrant to his/her country of origin if such an immigrant incites, promotes or participates in terrorism or serious criminal activity in any host nation which affords them refugee status or where they may be applying for entry. Under those circumstances only, I believe that such immigrants forfeit their right to refugee consideration, having left their own country intending subsequently to cause trouble in another.

It is proper that a country returning troublemakers to any regime with a reputation for torture should seek assurances that those returned will not be subject to abuse. However, such assurances are of very dubious worth, so no-one should pretend that they constitute any kind of guarantee. Perhaps one value of such assurances of non-abuse though, would be to monitor their effectiveness, hopefully to improve the climate of human rights in the countries concerned. It should also be borne in mind of course, that people in glass houses should not throw stones. Anyone for Belmarsh Prison; Guantanamo Detention Centre; Abu Ghraib; secret torture venues used by America throughout the world? What, I wonder, would America's response be if another country asked for assurances from the U.S. that any returned person would not suffer any kind of torture.

Those seeking to live in another country other than their homeland are aware of the risks involved and if they choose to abuse any host country, they do so in this knowledge and should not whine when they are sent back home, however unsavoury their own Government's practices may be.

Terrorists, and particularly those inspiring them, are not fools. They are well aware that they must constantly vary their tactics, which is why they have developed home-grown terrorists in their target countries in order to avoid the risks of having hit-men from the Middle East being apprehended at border entry points.

Instead of installing tens of thousands of extra cameras and spending tens of billions on ID and recording the movements of innocent people, we should spend around 25% of those largely ineffective, wasted billions on more police officers and more prisons. Many more of these police officers should be deployed under cover, infiltrating everywhere terrorists may be incubating and making friends with those who may be able to provide valuable information. Rewards should also be available to those volunteering information about terrorist activity as appropriate. The number of uniformed, *on foot* police officers, should also be hugely increased for both anti-terrorist and anti-conventional crime purposes.

We should get our police out of their cars; away from their desks, and out onto the streets – not with a "your papers please" attitude, which would be counter-productive, but to chat and expand their personal contacts with local communities whose eyes and ears could be invaluable in identifying the bad guys (and girls). Being on first-name terms with as many people as possible on their patch is one of the surest ways our police officers have available in the fight against crime.

Governments should stop trying to frighten their populations about terrorism,

a. because the threat – though real - is miniscule and

b. because no Government, ***however much it blusters***, can guarantee to protect us from terrorist attack.

c. Those who think terrorism is a 21st century phenomenon should ask themselves what Guy Fawkes and his co-conspirators were doing putting barrels of gunpowder under the British Houses of Parliament.

Tony Blair, David Blunkett, Charles Clarke, John Reid and the rest of the terrorist scaremongers should stop their lying about a whole new ballgame and cut out the garbage about the rules having changed. They have not.

• Robert Gatesby, Thomas Wintour, Francis Tresham, Christopher Wright and other conspirators – including Guy Fawkes – succeeded in getting 36 barrels of gunpowder under the British Houses of Parliament, sufficient – had there not been a betrayal – to blow up the King, the Prince of Wales, the entire House of Lords and numerous bystanders on a particularly busy day.

In my modest opinion, Mr. Blair & co., that was just as much a terrorist plot as 7/7 or 9/11 and, contrary to your "new situation" spin, the year was 1605. That's right – ***terrorism was alive and dangerous in the seventeenth century***.

The cause of the Gunpowder Plot was the anger and frustration of those on the receiving end of anti-Catholic laws. Religion and abuse of political power yet again. Nothing new there then. You guys just never learn, do you? Wind people up and frustrate them for long enough and some of them will use whatever means they can devise to bite you back. It was ever thus. It will ever be thus and pretending that it is some new scary phenomenon is simply spin to trample on even more of our freedoms.

Since time immemorial, Governments have exaggerated threats to their nations' security in order to grasp the opportunity to introduce anti-freedom legislation. The 21st century is no different. There are, of course, numerous areas where we will always be vulnerable to murderous attack, but bringing in Draconian laws and oppressive control systems can never protect us from these, so we should not be impoverishing or bankrupting ourselves pretending otherwise. Those politicians making fatuous claims such as "we are living in a different world" – or – "the rules of the game have changed", are either fools, knaves or both. The world has always been a dangerous place and imposing ever more distasteful and intrusive regulations on the law-abiding sectors of society will not stop terrorism. It will though increase the public's antipathy to all authority, which never seems to run out of excuses to further enslave every one of us.

Ex-U.S. Congressman Bob Bauman saw the dangers immediately after the attack on the twin towers and true enough, the neo-cons seized their chance to force through their disgraceful Patriot Act, which smashed holes through their Constitution. Five years on, Congressman Bauman now fears for freedom, not only in America but in much of the world where complacency rules.

The Society for Action Against Crime is aware of many new ways in which terrorists could inflict damage on any nation and although some of these will doubtless already be known to the terrorists, I have no intention of listing them here, for obvious reasons.

My point, is that one does not need to be very bright to think of cheap and easy damaging, murderous activities which no amount of money, scrutiny, new laws or oppressive controls could possibly prevent. This being so, we should quit the pretence, cut out the wasted expenditure and stop the macho rhetoric and knee-jerk closing of stable doors after the horses have bolted.

So, what _do_ we do about terrorism ?

We should put terrorism into perspective by relegating it to its rightful place in the scheme of things in a far from perfect world. We are far more likely to die in an air crash caused by pilot error, poor aircraft maintenance, computer/instrument failure or deep vein thrombosis, than we are from being aboard a hi-jacked plane and we would save far more lives if we spent more money on these safety and health issues instead of wasting it on ID Cards and spying on the private affairs of millions of law-abiding individuals.

Your chances of suffering from terrorist activity are tiny compared with being murdered or seriously injured in a regular criminal attack.

In India, about 3,500 die each year on the railways, but draconian measures to try to save most of these lives would be counter-productive. Philosophically, the Indian Government is doing what it reasonably can afford to do, which is to bring down the number of tragic deaths year-on-year, but without crippling the railways, either operationally or financially. Sure, it would be wonderful if all countries had train services as efficient as those of Switzerland but, as with terrorism, we live in the real world and the Swiss are smart enough to know that if you don't go around threatening other countries, you can afford far more of the good things of life in your own.

Unfortunately, politicians do not portray the reality of terrorism. Tony Blair for example, pretends the threat to be far greater than the reality, in order to make what he thinks are rousing speeches about not allowing terrorists to change our lives in any way. We should carry on as usual, he lied, whilst hypocritically trying to force through mountains of repressive regulations, including Identity Cards and measures to imprison people without charge or public trial for 3 months instead of the traditional 7 days. What is usual about that? It is Tony Blair, David Blunkett, Charles Clarke, Hazel Blears and John Reid who gave the lie to the claim that the terrorists will not make us change our way of life. It is *they* who have introduced laws and regulations which absolutely have changed the British way of life dreadfully, so why the hypocrisy? Why the lies? Control, dear reader, it is all about control.

Unless you live in Iraq, Afghanistan or Israel, you are vastly more likely to be killed on the roads than you are by terrorist activity, so why have our politicians overreacted to terrorism but done almost nothing about the dangerous or uninsured criminal drivers who kill people with far greater regularity?

Worldwide, your chances of choking to death, being struck by lightning, dying from a bee or wasp sting or from food poisoning are infinitely higher than dying from terrorist attack, but we quite rightly do not get into a funk about such things, we simply take sensible precautions without giving up any of our freedoms.

And how about this for hypocrisy. Bush and Blair have sworn to take out terrorists wherever they may be in the world, supposedly to save a few hundred or a few thousand lives, *but* around 100,000 people (*yes, that is one hundred thousand*) are attacked and *killed every year by snakes* – with another million victims suffering non-fatal bites. Bizarrely, not only is there no war declared on snakes, it is actually illegal in some countries to kill or harm them. At first sight, drawing attention to this inconsistency may seem flippant, but I promise you it is not. It is a serious attempt to persuade everyone to stop and think; to question what our politicians are up to; to calmly establish priorities and not to be panicked into knee-jerk headless-chicken reactions, because whittling away our freedoms is just what the terrorists want.

The Two Blairs – and we don't mean Cherie

82-year old Labour supporter Walter Wolfgang was manhandled out of the September 2005 Labour Party Conference in Brighton, England by obese "stewards" and held by police under the Prevention of Terrorism Act. His offence? He had shouted a few words of disagreement during Foreign Secretary Jack Straw's speech. Oh dear! Disagreement with a Labour politician – now there is a serious crime which cannot possibly be tolerated. The episode also introduced to us yet another Labour Party definition of terrorism.

Recognise the similarity between this conduct and that of the American airport security goons or of those who had Maya Evans arrested for reading out the names of British soldiers killed in Iraq?

27-year old Jean Charles de Menezes was manhandled by Labour Government employees under the control of Police Commissioner Sir Ian Blair and whilst incapacitated, was shot numerous times in the head from close range in a public underground station in London, England. His offence? None. He was an innocent young man who had been secretly pursued for miles by a variety of armed Government agents then callously shot dead.

"I wasn't even there" said Blair No.1 when apologising for the "mistake" at the Labour Party Conference.

"I wasn't there" said Blair No.2 when apologising for the "mistake" of Jean Charles being murdered in cold blood – F.B.I. fashion - by Government personnel. That, of course, was after Commissioner Blair had publicly announced a false and incomplete account of the tragedy which attempted to portray Jean Charles as a terrorist. Almost copycat tragedies of many which the American security services have inflicted on numerous innocent victims since long before the 9th September 2001.

61

What neither of the two Blairs is honest enough to admit, is that these were not accidental "mistakes" at all. They were the inevitable results of unacceptable control freakery. They were typical of what happens in States which do not put freedom of speech, privacy and liberty right at the top of their unassailable priorities.

Tony Blair's Labour Party Conferences are scripted, totally controlled, stage-managed and carefully spun farces which tolerate no outside or spontaneous opinions from unauthorised sources.

Following the July 2005 London bombings, Police Commissioner Sir Ian Blair, in conjunction with the then Home Secretary Charles Clarke, wound up the police force in such a macho shoot-to-kill campaign that tragedies and unnecessary interference with daily life were certain to result.

Having been told to be seen to be doing something, the police either lost their heads or put on a "show" of manic activity, orchestrated between the two Blairs and Charles Clarke. Whole areas were cordoned off at the drop of a hat and police cars and motorcycles were charging around, sirens blaring, just because someone was seen opening a backpack for access to his sandwiches or doing highly-suspicious things like raising a walking stick to hail a taxi.

Murdered Jean Charles did none of these things and cynical official apologies are wholly inadequate when the real cause of his death was a crazily wound up police force made even more dangerous by the promotion of a secretive shoot-to-kill policy which never results in those responsible for the supposed "mistakes" being punished.

The completely innocent Jean Charles lost his life.

I doubt very much that those guilty of his murder will lose either their liberty or their pensions.

At the time of writing this Crimedown Blueprint, his killer(s) name(s) are still being kept secret, more than a year after the event.

I know why the U.K. Government persists in trying to hide Jean Charles' killer(s) – it is because they fear what would emerge if those responsible had to face a public trial.

The American-approved Iraqi General in charge of his country's serious crimes division (post Saddam) was shot through the head by an American soldier who – here we go again – "mistook him for a suicide bomber".

An Iraqi heart specialist was on his way to his hospital in Baghdad in 2005 but he never arrived there to do his life-saving work because the U.S. military shot him dead because they thought he "might" be a suicide bomber.

With allies and security forces like this – who needs enemies?

I am in no way trying to deny the dangers of terrorism nor to ignore the sword of Damocles scenario of dirty bombs, biological attack etc. which Governments employ to keep us afraid. Were politicians able to **guarantee** to prevent any such dreadful event, then some of the current massive expenditure on anti-terrorism would be worthy of consideration, but on their own admission, they cannot do this. That being so, they should tell the terrorists on our behalf that whatever they do, we really will not let them blackmail us into wasting billions of pounds, nor will we give them the satisfaction of knowing that they have succeeded in forcing us to give up our traditional freedoms.

Quietly, but without giving the terrorists the oxygen of publicity which they so dearly love, we should do everything possible to track down potential terrorists and use every available surveillance technique **to secure evidence against them which will stand up in open court**. Our efforts though, should **not** be wasted trawling billions of emails, phone calls, bank accounts or spying on the library records of **innocent** people because these are amongst the private freedoms which every Government should be protecting, not trying to destroy.

Above all, we should be calm and laid-back about terrorism and not give it the importance which the murderous, misguided perpetrators seek. Terrorists are criminals and by panicking and giving them any special status other than that, serves only to encourage their deplorable activities. In no way are they as dangerous as either snakes, mosquitoes, global warming, flu pandemics or many other difficulties and those pretending otherwise show either naivety or serious lack of judgement.   There are, of course, other disturbing explanations which our politicians are not willing to reveal.

You know, life is full of risks, of which terrorism is just one, and to each individual, it is way way down the danger list. There are no valid reasons therefore, to throw hugely disproportionate amounts of money tying ourselves up in knots, stripping us of our long-established freedoms and privacy and turning us into a society where half the populations are Maoist-style spies, reporting innocuous trivialities to Big Brother.

What we need are more and better police behaving as Peace Officers, but in far better touch with both the law-abiding and criminal sectors of society.

We have always had laws against everything which terrorists do, so there was never any need for new ones which served only to sneak in further freedom-trashing elements designed to give the Executive greater control over even the law-abiding sector of society.

We have Courts which need changing and prisons requiring expansion and restructuring. I explain in later chapters how best to do this in order to achieve maximum crime reduction without sacrificing *any* of our freedoms, of which we should have more, not fewer.

And what we absolutely need, is to stop panicking and stop continually bending the knee to terrorists by spending billions and billions of $s/£s/€s whatever, for absolutely no valid reason. Unless we stop this profligate expenditure, we will never afford decent pensions, good infrastructure, or the money initially needed to reduce basic domestic crime. We will also be pushing off into Never Never Land, the prospect of ending both local and global poverty, but on this issue, the evidence is that world Leaders are not serious anyway.

Later chapters include a revolutionary approach to sentencing, explaining how I believe those found guilty of terrorism or general crime should be dealt with. Still to come are suggestions for deterring all crime and more effective ways of using our prisons. Plus much more to hopefully enlighten sufficient readers to make a difference.

The Police case for 3 months' detention without evidence or charge

Having seen the 06 October 2005 letter from Metropolitan Police Assistant Commissioner Andy Hayman (specialist operations) to UK Home Secretary Charles Clarke, it is clear that this diatribe was *invited* in order to support the Labour Party's wish to hold people without charge for 3 months instead of 7 days.

The Metropolitan Police letter begins, and I quote – "Thank you (Home Secretary) for giving me the opportunity to comment on the issue of extending the maximum period of detention".

P.W.B comment – This means that the initiative came from Charles Clarke to a senior policeman who, being concerned with his career, was only too willing to comply with the Home Secretary's known wishes of detention-without-charge for 90 days. Presumably the letter was asked of Andy Hayman, the Assistant Police Commissioner, because the Commissioner himself, Sir Ian Blair, was, at the time, under a cloud due to the Met. (or intelligence agents) shooting dead Jean Charles de Menezes, an innocent Brazilian living in London.

Met. Police letter says they (the Police) can no longer wait until the point of attack before intervening.

P.W.B. – I agree, but that is not sufficient argument to justify detention beyond 7 (now 28) days without charge. Suspicion and tittle tattle without evidence are not enough and in any event, improved continuing surveillance of terrorist suspects may well give them sufficient rope to hang themselves. Britain does not have thousands of suicide bombers willing to blow-up themselves and us. If it did, we would be suffering terrorist atrocities every few days, as they are in Iraq.

Met. Police letter parroted the mantra of Tony Blair and Charles Clarke precisely, i.e. "public safety always comes first", inviting us to believe that if we allow our police and politicians to force ever more draconian laws onto us, we will suffer no harm.

P.W.B. – That, of course, is arrant nonsense. No matter how many of our freedoms they extract from us, neither our politicians nor our police or armed services can *guarantee* that we will not suffer further terrorist attack. What they have succeeded in doing is spending billions of pounds of our money, not on infiltrating terrorist cells, not on better surveillance or genuine terrorist suspects, not on befriending those communities likely to spawn terrorists – but on wasting money and manpower resources attacking the rights, the privacy and the freedoms of every law-abiding person in the country. That is not what we pay our politicians to do. Whilst they play around with all this control-freak garbage, they have all allowed everyday violent crime to increase from its already unacceptably high levels. So much for their rhetoric about public safety always coming first. It is, in any event, a quite meaningless phrase of pompous rhetoric.

Terrorists and public protectors of course are often a reversible garment but, however described, both are wrong when they kill innocent people. Assistant Commissioner Hayman should be reminded that the British Police have killed many innocent people without any of the perpetrators suffering any consequences, so he should not be surprised that there is no universal gullible acceptance of the control-freak arguments of some politicians and some senior police and intelligence personnel who seem hell bent on playing politics instead of devoting all of their supposed cleverness to catching criminals.

The Met. Police letter – Lists copious information about the considerable volume of work which the police have to process in their enquiries - forensic examinations, computer analysis, forgery assessments, obtaining mobile phone records, allowing time for detainees to pray, shortage of interpreters, shortage of police officers etc. etc. etc. supported by actual and (inexplicably) theoretical cases. Everything, in fact, which an authoritarian Government could possibly try to use as an excuse for forcing through more draconian anti-freedom laws. Uncle Tom Cobley and all.

P.W.B. I accept that the police have a huge amount of work in trying to pre-empt terrorist attacks and find those responsible who have not been prevented from carrying out the occasional cowardly and murderous activity. Not for a moment do I underestimate either the volume, the danger or the complexity of what we expect of our police, but I do take issue with this being used by politicians and by those senior police and intelligence officials prepared to use police difficulties as an excuse for trampling on freedoms which Britons have had and refined for centuries. Certainly, there are those in the ranks of Britain's police forces who do **not** want to see longer detention without trial, fearing quite rightly that the constant erosion of individual liberties will make their job far more difficult.

The Difference between myself and the control-freaks is that I believe that we should **never** trade-in our freedoms for any reason. They have been too hard won and hundreds of thousands of our servicemen and women gave up their lives to protect them. Giving them away is simply spitting on the graves of those who fought for them.

In any event, stealing our liberties and nose-poking into what should be our private and lawful matters will not guarantee that we will never again suffer terrorist attacks.

Assistant Commissioner Hayman tells us that processing and enquiring into suspects cannot be done within 14 days and he cites a "theoretical" case of 15 terrorist suspects being arrested. He tells us that manpower and other restraints would make it impossible to bring charges within 7 to 14 days, so he makes the huge leap to 3 months' detention without charge. With such logic, if the number of people arrested was 150, the Assistant Commissioner would "need" 2½ years for his officers to complete their investigations. He conveniently does not mention this, but what is the betting that what was 7 days, then 14 days and if Blair & co. get their way, 90 days, becomes 150 days, becomes open-ended, as it is now in America, to its shame. In civilised countries the State is not allowed to confine anyone - without charging them with a specific crime – for more than two or three days.

Assistant Commissioner Hayman claims, in his support for 3 months' detention without charge, that the use by terrorists of mobile phones as a secure means of communication is "a relatively new phenomenon" – his words.

P.W.B. What planet is this guy on? Does he really not know how long mobile phones have been around? Or is he just clutching at straws, trying to find endless reasons for increasing police powers? I don't know about Andy Hayman, but certainly my company was using mobile phones more than 20 years ago, when undertaking survey work for the Central Office of Information, so they surely cannot be considered relatively new to terrorist organisations as Hayman claims.

In his "theoretical case study" sent to the Home Secretary Charles Clarke, Asst. Commissioner Hayman paints the prospect of the security services being told by "an Agent" of a group of men in various parts of the country planning terrorist attacks on the Houses of Parliament and the British Embassies in Pakistan, Istanbul and Morocco in 3 months' time. The (hypothetical) Agent is "reliable" says Andy Hayman, so the information must be acted upon for public safety reasons.

Yes, the police should act on such information. Yes, they should arrest those where there is evidence and yes, they could also arrest some, perhaps, on suspicion only. But no – those arrested on suspicion only should not be detained for more than 14 days unless some firm evidence of their danger can be put before a judge. If not, they should be released and put under 24-hour surveillance – which may well lead police to other villains who may be involved or to the hard evidence they need to both detain and charge those concerned.

I do not accept detention beyond 14 days without charge and when the Assistant Police Commissioner glibly talks about their Agent being reliable, I must remind him that it was supposedly "reliable intelligence Agents" who provided Tony Blair, Jack Straw and David Blunkett with supposed evidence that Iraq had weapons of mass destruction. This misinformation has already led to the deaths of hundreds of thousands of completely innocent people, in addition to those in the military fighting a war which was certainly not justified by the reasons given.

So much for reliable Agents.

Whenever the general public is denied information for security reasons, they should smell a very large rat because invariably the politicians involved have hidden motives of their own which they know would be unacceptable if leaked out.

Asst. Commissioner Hayman's letter claimed that there were too few explosives specialists to examine and make safe suspect premises. He even reckons there is *only enough of these specialists to attend one property at a time*.

P.W.B. If this is true - which I find difficult to believe – why, instead of cosying up to the Home Secretary by giving him the arguments he knew Blair and Clarke wanted, to sell their 3 months' detention-without-charge proposals, did he not instead, campaign for a lot more forensic and explosives specialists who could attend simultaneous crime scenes? Why?

I realise that foresight is a stranger to most politicians, but surely even Blair, Blunkett and Clarke should have seen the rising need for such specialists years ago. So why do we have too few now? It cannot be lack of funds, because the UK Labour Party is throwing money every which way on their ever-increasing army of snoop bureaucrats and crazy Identity Card ideas.

Asst. Commissioner Hayman also painted an outrageous picture for the Home Secretary which theoretically depicted mountains of evidence, often in foreign languages. His letter said – of videos seized – that a cursory viewing showed them to be of an extremist nature but because they had Arabic voiceovers, there is *little point in (police) officers viewing them* because they cannot understand them. His words.

P.W.B. Little point in viewing them! Having, quite rightly, spent millions on surveillance and identification, seizing hundreds of computers and boxes of videos, I would have expected every single video to be scrutinised over and over again, regardless of whether the lingo voiceover was in Arabic, Pottywicky or Bureaubabble. I would want to know who and what was on those videos. They could show already-suspected terrorists who will never be caught by ID Cards; they could show recruits undergoing training; they could contain clues about the venues of the videos; they could show weapons or chemical warfare preparations. And Yet Assistant Commissioner of Police Andy Hayman tells the Home Secretary that there would be *little point in his officers viewing them* because they would not understand their language content.

This beggars belief and one must question the judgement of Charles Clarke who uses such crap to support his own agenda for stealing more of your and my freedoms. These I will always resist and if they are forced upon us, I and many others will do our utmost to see such draconian measures reversed and hopefully, those responsible for them, removed from Office.

Supporters of Tony Blair's attempts to allow the police to detain people for 90 days without charge or trial, were promoted using some incredibly stupid arguments, amongst which were those of:-

Keith Vaz, Labour Member of Parliament who, when interviewed on 9th November 2005 incredibly came out with the following craven and cowardly statement – "I was elected 6 months ago to give my 100% support to my Party and to Tony Blair". Well, I have news for Mr. Vaz. That is **not** why you or anyone else is elected to Parliament. Were it to be so, there would be no need for anyone but the Prime Minister to be in the House of Commons at all, because all the rest would simply be android lobby fodder. Fortunately, some of Keith Vaz's Labour Party were not so spineless and were prepared to vote their consciences and slow down at least some of the Blair/Blunkett/Clarke assaults on traditional liberties.

Gordon Brown, Britain's Chancellor of the Exchequer, who is manoeuvring to succeed Tony Blair, claimed on the 8th November 2005 that one must go along with the police wanting to hold people for 90 days without charge in order to be able to "interview" suspects.

"**Interview**" Mr. Brown? For 90 days Mr. Brown? How many "interviews" have you attended?

When one is in custody for more than a few hours Mr. Brown, you are not being interviewed –

- You are being denied your freedom which, without evidence suggesting guilt, should not happen

- You are likely to be subjected to "good cop/bad cop" interrogation

- You may well be denied adequate sleep

- Independent legal association may be denied to you, as may suitable medical attention

- Your family may well not be informed of your arrest and if they know of it, they will not be allowed to visit you

- No-one knows what physical and psychological abuse may be metered out because everything is kept very secret

• You can be kept totally isolated

• You are being browbeaten - hour after hour after hour after hour.

And most important of all, you may suffer any or all of the above and be completely innocent and may never even be told what it is you are supposed to have done.

In one day's "interview" there would be sufficient time for a suspect to be asked – and answer – more than a thousand questions. Multiply that by 7 days and there simply cannot be any more questions to ask. Can you think of even a thousand questions to ask anybody about anything? Does Gordon Brown – a supposed man of figures – know of any "interview" (his word) that lasted 90 days with the potential to ask 90,000 questions? I would like to know.

Britain should hope that such a confused man, sheltered from anything approaching reality, is not the one to appoint future Cabinet Ministers.

In the course of my research I of course come across many a fanciful conspiracy theory and the occasional one which merits further examination. Shannara Johnson, writing in "What We Now Know" (a Casey Research publication) highlights the flaws in the claims of the British and U.S. Governments that terrorists were to use TATP – Triacetone Triperoxide – to simultaneously bomb U.K. to U.S.A. planes into oblivion by carrying on a range of liquids in ordinary containers, then mixing them in the planes' lavatories to create lethal explosives. The science shows that such an operation was never a starter and that no terrorist organisation would ever have contemplated such an impossible project. Chemists also reveal that the fumes created by even the early stages of the various mixing processes would have killed anyone trying to carry out the required procedures, particularly in the confines of an aeroplane toilet compartment.

Add this to the fact that none of those arrested in Britain had either plane tickets or reservations and the reluctance of the U.K. Home Office to bring the supposed villains to trail and one must ask what the huge panics and disruptions at British and American airports in August 2006 were all about. Was it for real? Or was it a diversion? A further attempt by Tony Blair and George Bush to keep ratcheting up the fear of terrorism in order to force their publics to give up ever more of their freedoms and provide ever more information to Governments who will add it to their all-encompassing data bases.

What may happen to this information is not known. It may end up in the wrong hands. It may result in a "mistake" causing you, a relative or a named contact to suffer serious harm. It may end up with Government tracking your every movement. It will certainly further convince every petty security official that they are entitled to subject you to any indignity their mood chooses.

Me? I will suspend judgement on the liquids-on-planes episode until those arrested in its connection are put on public trial. The longer this is delayed beyond November 2006, the more concerned I will become.

Clare Short, who resigned from Tony Blair's Cabinet over Iraq went on, in September 2006, to identify Gordon Brown as a champion of 90-day detention and a serious danger to the people's freedom and liberty. She was absolutely spot on, of course.

I have spoken to many people who have wrongly been detained by the police for just a few days. They all found it a dreadful experience and some switched from being pro-police to anti-police as a result of the trauma they suffered. The dangers of damage to the relationship between police and the public from Detention-Without-Charge for more than a few days are far greater than the supposed theoretical benefits suggested by the control freaks.

My Proposition is that everyone arrested should have access to a lawyer and a doctor upon request; that no-one can be detained for more than 60 or 72 hours without appearing before a judge who could extend the detention up to 7 days, subject to the police persuading the judge of such necessity.

A further 7 days' detention should be available via a second (different) judge. End of confinement.

Bear in mind that the police can charge any suspect any time they wish and could also charge them for a lesser offence for which they believe they have evidence, giving them yet more time to perhaps compile a good case to warrant adding a charge of a more serious crime.

I recommend that instead of detaining anyone – and remember, it could be you – beyond 7, possibly 14 days without charge, the police should release any arrestee unconditionally unless a judge attaches a G.P.S. tracking and surveillance order as a condition of release in cases where the judge can be persuaded of the need for the imposition of such a restrictive condition. This would necessitate a state-of-the-art tracking device affixed to the suspect for the same 3-month period for which Assistant Commissioner Hayman wants to be able to lock people up without charge.

I am not talking about the crude devices used on everyday probationers, but state-of-the-art technology tied into a permanent supervision-of-movement tracking system. More expensive, yes, but we are not talking about tracking thousands of burglars or football hooligans – but supposedly just a small number of people who may or may not be involved in terrorism.

I for one do not believe that draconian laws are necessary to protect us all from terrorism. Detaining people for 90 days without charge may not be limited to terrorist suspects, and those Police States which suffer such anti-freedom laws soon discover that their police and judiciary use them to confine and question those suspected of far more mundane offences. Be warned. Your liberty has been hard won. Never put it at risk.

I come now to the practice driven by America known as *Extraordinary Rendition*, which is the moving around of arrested people from one country to another for a "different" kind of "interrogation". Allegedly these prisoners are terrorists, but America seems never to have sufficient evidence of this to charge them of any offence and bring them to trial in open Court. In its attempt to spread Gestapo-style fear throughout the world, George Bush, Donald Rumsfeld, Dick Cheyney and Condoleezza Rice have pulled every dirty trick imaginable. They have created, authorised, condoned or failed to prevent deplorable practices resulting in:-

- The arrest of people without evidence, often during what can only be described as "hoovering" operations

- Hooding and Manacling

- Flying suspects from one country to another, to another, in secret,

73

without the knowledge of their families, the International Red Cross or Amnesty International

- Asking cowardly third party countries, known for their abuse and torture of suspects, to interrogate prisoners on behalf of America's Secret Services

- Misleading the world's media and Human Rights groups about the processing and treatment of arrested persons who may or may not be terrorists

- The kidnapping by U.S.A. agents of people in foreign lands without either the knowledge or consent of those sovereign countries' Governments.

My questions of President Bush are:-

- What possible justification do you claim entitles you to fly suspects around the world if the purpose is not to have them tortured in the foulest manners?

- Do you, or do you not have or use any kind of detention centres in foreign countries? **Stop Press**. Since first writing this, G.W.B. has finally fessed-up to his C.I.A. running such secret prisons.

- Why do you not either deal with suspects in the countries where they are arrested or – if sufficiently confident of their guilt - why do you not fly them to America, without all the cloak and dagger nonsense?

- Why is America afraid to put suspects on public trial? Do this and your Courts will deserve every support in handing out very serious sentences to anyone found guilty of terrorism or the support of terrorism?

- By what right, under its Constitution, does the U.S.A. have military bases in more than a hundred countries around the world?

- Would you support the proposal that anyone accused of torture should be subject to a trial in an International Court?

My questions of Prime Minister (or ex-Prime Minister) Blair are:-

• Why was your strongest condemnation of America's Guantanamo Bay Detention Centre never more than describing it as *an anomaly*? And why did you use such a meaningless word which in no way addressed the serious nature of the subject?

• Why did neither you, your Foreign Secretary Jack Straw, nor your Attorney General Lord Goldsmith speak out fully and publicly against Detention Centres if, as you eventually claimed, you sincerely believed it wrong to keep people locked up and without recourse to due process of law?

• It was always clear to me that just "talking" to the Americans diplomatically behind closed doors would not persuade them to give up illegal imprisonment and torture. Why then, did you not take a tougher line and tell President Bush that unless he closed down his Star Chambers, Britain would withdraw from Iraq and Afghanistan?

• What do you think your neo-con President friend could have done had you faced him with such a legitimate choice?

• How would you like to see those involved in any way with torture, dealt with?

I doubt that any act of terrorism has ever been prevented by information emanating from torture, nor would it validate such disgusting practices if it had.

Torturers are sick brutes. Who else could tear out fingernails; pierce eyes with red hot needles; slash penises or female genitalia; beat people senseless; deprive human beings of sleep; assault their hearing with hours of 200-decibel sound; force a fellow man or woman to live for weeks in their own excrement; subject religious believers to practices known to be offensive to their beliefs; bring victims close to drowning by "waterboarding" or continually spraying them with ice cold water whilst being forced to stand naked for many hours; use electric currents applied to sensitive body parts.

These and other foul practices are still, in the 21st century, commonly carried out in many countries throughout our wonderful world. Sometimes the victims die. Sometimes they survive. Sometimes they are not believed, despite the medical confirmation of the abuse suffered.

Proof, of course, is not easy to come by, because the vile perpetrators carry out their cowardly torture in great secrecy.

As evil – and arguably even worse – are those who commission, tolerate or turn a blind eye to torture or use double-speak on the subject, which is tantamount to authorising it.

I find it very difficult to believe that some world leaders – including George Bush, Donald Rumsfeld, Dick Cheyney, Condoleezza Rice, Tony Blair, David Blunkett, Charles Clarke, Jack Straw etc. – believe that no-one is being tortured. If they persist in pedalling their sham innocence, I would like them to join me on television to talk face-to-face with a number of people who claim to have been tortured by the Americans or their nominees. Let the viewers hear what the victims have to say about their maltreatment and let the viewers make up their own minds about whether they believe their stories and whether or not they accept the hand-washing claims of the politicians.

My original research was intended to find the causes of general domestic crime and to find solutions to bring crime levels down significantly. However, as time passed, it became clear that Government crime was at least equally important and until such Governments improve their own standards, they have no moral authority to preach to anyone. Many of the public are gullible of course, but a growing number now disbelieves almost everything their politicians spout. Abuse, threats and torture are not the way to persuade people as to the merits of democracy and unless democracy means freedom, openness and honesty, it is a sham which is not worth fighting for.

As a separate issue, I and others will shortly be cutting through all the nonsense denials about torture and terrorism and identifying some of those involved.

Meantime, no more weasel words on the subject. Believe me, we will better defeat the terrorists by having higher moral standards than theirs. Right now, too many of our politicians are allowing their countries to be dragged by the terrorists to join them in the gutter of indiscriminate killing, torture, inhumanity and cowardice. That gutter – just to bluster about being tough – is not where I want my country to be. Hopefully it is not where you want your country to be either, so together we must act to bring about change.

Barging around the world trying to force a few people's warped view of democracy down everyone's throats is not only arrogance in the extreme, it will prove to be counter-productive unless and until our Governments begin to conduct their own affairs more honourably.

Many of the world's leading politicians claim to have no knowledge or involvement in either torture or extraordinary rendition. They could, of course, be pro-active against such disgraceful practice and their failure so to be speaks volumes about their real motives.

I have a question which should be asked of all of these politicians :-

"If it is proven that such practices have been carried out whilst you were or are in Government – will you resign from public office and forego all of the pension rights which you have accrued during your time working as a public employee?"

A simple "Yes – or – No" will suffice.

Finally on the subject of terrorism, it is interesting to note that in 1997, the highly thought of war correspondent Robert Fisk, interviewed Osama Bin Laden by invitation in the mountains of Afghanistan. The Muslim fundamentalist claimed to have forced the Russians out of Afghanistan and been a significant player in the demise of the Soviet Union as was. The degree to which this claim was valid is difficult to establish, but what is not in doubt is Osama Bin Laden's involvement. Osama B. L. went on – in 1997 remember – to tell Robert Fisk that he intended to reduce America to a shadow of its former self .

To the extent that the U.S. has been hurtled into bankruptcy, with the world's greatest ever level of debt, and by tempting Bush & co. to trample on the freedoms and privacy of its own citizens – to say nothing about the same freedoms of millions of others around the world – it is crystal clear that Osama Bin Laden has prevailed. The tragedy is, that even capturing or killing this guy will make no difference, because whenever politicians take away people's freedoms, they hang on to them tooth and nail.

I must also draw your attention to the joint fear-rousing speeches in Britain in the run-up to the Queen's speech by Tony Blair on 15th November 2006. The timing of the Head of MI5's and the UK Home Secretary's speeches were clearly orchestrated. John Reid, in fact, hours before the Queen's speech, admitted that the words of MI5's Dame Elizabeth Manningham-Buller a few days earlier were likely to receive less suspicion that the same words coming from him.

Dame Elizabeth claimed that 1,600 individuals were under surveillance; that 30 active plots existed and that Britain had 200 terrorist cells. Quite how she knows this but allows them to continue, she doesn't say. Home Secretary John Reid let slip that what they had on the people may only be "information" and not evidence. Now, I immediately recalled that John Reid and his colleague Ministers in league with Tony Blair had intelligence "information" that Iraq had weapons of mass destruction. Yeah, right.

Dame Lizzie M-B also called for greater help from the public, without actually spelling out what she wanted the public to do which it is not doing already. Her exhortations are, in fact, no more use than the ridiculous rising levels of terrorist alerts which give no helpful advice whatsoever. Don't shake hands with a suicide bomber perhaps. No. All these warnings are about two things – being able to get through legislation to detain people without charge for ever longer periods and forcing Identity Cards on the entire population.

My take on this is that if one takes the figures of MI5 and the Home Office at face value, what they confirm is that 60 million Britons (out of 60 million one thousand six hundred) are not terrorist suspects. This being so, why punish these 60 million citizens, most of whom are completely law-abiding?

If either the Good Dame or the Home Office genuinely want our help, why do they not publish the names, addresses and photographs of some of their suspects, inviting the public to keep them under surveillance and also report anything of interest about them to the police. There must, of course, be some real reason to choose particular terrorist suspects and some must obviously be left undisturbed for a while, in the hope that they lead to other terrorists or become involved in acquiring the tools of the terrorist trade. Once any terrorist suspect is publicly "outed" they will, of course, be rendered useless to their cause because the Authorities would quickly be told by the public about who they meet and where.

In her announcement on 10th November 2006, the Grand Dame Director General of Britain's Security Service was long on accusations about terrorism but unbelievably short on facts or evidence. She claimed grandiosely that 99 defendants were awaiting trial in 34 terrorist cases. I would like MI5, the Lord Chancellor or the Home Secretary to first publish the names of these alleged 99 terrorists then provide information about their fate. It will be interesting to track how many are found guilty or innocent and if guilty, what sentences are given to them by the Courts.

Dame Eliza M-B is typical of all vested interests insofar as she exaggerates the threat in order to hype-up the importance of her Department. She asks us to imagine (in November 2006) a plot to bring down several passenger aircraft succeeding, claiming there would be thousands dead and major economic damage across the globe. Well, I have news for the lady and her political scaremongering friends – there was such an event on the 11th September 2001 and tragic though it was, by far the most economic global damage was not that caused directly by the terrorist attack, it was, in fact, the hugely disproportionate response of George W. Bush and Anthony Blair who have recklessly trashed their own citizens' freedoms and turned the entire world into a mania of security, paranoid surveillance and military expenditure. This forces unbelievable costs on taxpayers globally and almost all of both the public and private sectors. Almost all of this is both unnecessary and unaffordable. It is on borrowed money, leaving America particularly in deep financial trouble. Just as the terrorists planned.

What was it I said about foresight, insight and hindsight?

Post Script. In January 2007, it seems that the UK's Director of Public Prosecutions is beginning to catch on about terrorism. Contrary to the bangings-on by his Home Secretary John Reid, Sir Ken MacDonald, the D.P.P., is reported to have come out against fear-driven responses to attacks, describing terrorists as deluded inadequates who never merited a war on terror, notwithstanding their atrocities.

CHAPTER 5

TORTURE

Now I come in more detail to the most heinous, sickening, disgusting crime of all – **TORTURE**. That darkest and destructive perversion of human nature.

It was Madame Roland, minutes before being guillotined, who bowed to the Statue of Liberty in Paris's Place de la Resolution and spoke the immortal words "*Oh liberty. **What crimes are committed in thy name?***"

I can also announce here that, in association with other interested parties, I am, shortly after the publication of this book, to initiate a major step forward in combating this most despicable, cowardly practice. I am doing this because all of those august bodies, including the United Nations and its eventual 1984 Convention Against Torture, and the crocodile tears of many Governments, have failed to prevent torture from rolling on into the 21st century. Contact **torture@campaigntrail.org.uk** if you wish to help or participate.

It took the U.N. decades even to come up with their 1984 anti-torture measure. It was and still is, long on bleeding-heart rhetoric and convoluted legal verbage, but woefully short on practical solutions. Kofi Annan should bear much of the responsibility for the U.N.'s tardiness on torture. His office, as Secretary General, gave him enormous clout but he chose not to use this to instigate and bring into effect, practical protections against torture. This is borne out by the fact that torture is still rife and used either directly or indirectly by many countries, including, I am ashamed to say, America, Britain and France, in addition to the more obvious perpetrators – Russia, Turkey, Iraq, Egypt, Zimbabwe, Saudi Arabia, Haiti, China, Nigeria etc.

These are "only allegations" some so glibly say. There is no **proof**, they claim, cynically ignoring the pain, trauma, psychological damage and terrified deaths suffered by so many. Well, I have news for these creeps who dismiss torture so lightly. When someone is water-boarding you, dropping acid into your eyes, slicing your penis, shoving over-large objects into other of your natural orifices, hanging you by the neck whilst you are standing (just), and increasing the height of the noose by a centimetre every half hour, stamping on your already broken bones, forcing hot needles up your finger and toe nails; denying you sleep, quiet, food or drink – the perpetrators do not allow witnesses with camcorders in to watch and record their evil foul deeds. Even worse is the depraved practice of carrying out such torture in front of the victims' friends, colleagues or loved ones before eventually killing them all in attempts to prevent the evidence of their actions from ever seeing the light of day.

Torture, by its very nature, is difficult to prove, being highly-secretive operations where its practitioners are in total command – usually the inevitable outcome of unrestrained political power. I have nothing but contempt for those who are so casually dismissive of torture simply because (they say) there is no proof. Fortunately, some do escape their captors and occasionally, those on the periphery, have an attack of conscience and reveal all.

I am not naive enough to believe that all allegations of torture are true, but there is overwhelming evidence of its continuing use. Those doubting this should start by looking at some of the case files of Amnesty International; they should look at the mountain of medical evidence, most of which could not possibly have been self-inflicted or caused accidentally; they should sit face to face with some of the victims, like Martin Mugamba who was kidnapped in Zambia by British and American agents then flown to Guantanamo Bay to be tortured and they should listen to the harrowing accounts of their sufferings. They should talk to people like Canadian Doctor William Sampson and Briton, Sandy Mitchell, both mercilessly tortured in Al-Hajr, Saudi Arabia's high security jail for more than two years. Statewatch (**http://database.Statewatch.org/search.asp**) also has an excellent record of raising specific issues related to torture as has Clive Stafford Smith, who is the Legal Director of Reprieve, a charity which helps victims of Human Rights abuse. They have masses of evidence of torture. Visiting **www.reprieve.org.uk** is a good starting point for anyone concerned.

Those trying to downplay torture should explain why they think the International Red Cross is denied 24/7 unannounced access to places such as the U.S.A.'s Guantanamo Bay Detention Centre in Cuba and why so many countries are so uncooperative to the point of blatant obstruction of those investigating allegations of abuse. By late 2006, there has reportedly been a major up-grading of Guantanamo with some access to certain Bodies, but if George Bush thinks that those mistreated in America's star chambers will forget or forgive their years of abuse he is very mistaken.

They should ask why America wants such dirty facilities and why, in any event, they hide many of them off-shore instead of having them openly on their own soil, available to be inspected by and reported upon by reputable independent persons or Bodies. As at 21st September 2006, even the U.N.'s Special Rapporteur, Manfred Novak, confirmed that torture was by then worse in Iraq than when Saddam Hussein was in charge.

A few people, like U.S.A. Army Captain Ian Fishback, have been brave enough to report upon horrendous atrocities committed by American troops during his service in Iraq and Afghanistan. These included serious beatings, pouring burn-causing chemicals on prisoners' faces, shackling in positions so unnatural as to guarantee physical collapse into unconsciousness. When he reported to his superiors what he had witnessed, he was warned to stop or suffer serious consequences. Only Senator John McCain, who himself had suffered years of torture by the Vietcong, chose to support Captain Fishback's efforts to stop Americans from ignoring the Geneva Convention. Subsequently, John McCain, along with his Republican colleagues Susan Collins, Lindsey Graham and John Warner, Chairman of the Senate's Armed Services Committee, took a stand in September 2006 against George Bush's abuses of his position as President. They and others thwarted, at least temporarily, Bush's attempts to allow the C.I.A. to employ coercive interrogation methods, by-pass the Geneva Convention, and establish forms of kangaroo courts where accused can be sentenced to death without seeing the supposed evidence used to convict them.

Every so often, someone within the torture-friendly Governments breaks ranks and gives us just a peek into the cauldron of cruelty. Ex-C.I.A. spy Robert Baer stated that Jordan is the place to send people for serious interrogation; Syria is the place for torture and if you want your suspects to "disappear", then render them to Egypt – a Middle East country to which America gives millions of dollars' worth of aid every year. Why would they be so benevolent, one wonders?

According to Robert Baer, his Government and Tony Blair's are complicit in extraordinary rendition with the British S.A.S. having lifted people in Afghanistan on behalf of the Americans, and the

C.I.A. doing the same in Gambia, getting their hands on British Citizens helped by Tony Blair's MI5.

Whether countries such as Egypt, Morocco, Syria, Jordan, Uzbekistan, Britain's Diego Garcia, Afghanistan, Albania etc. voluntarily offered disgusting gulag facilities to America is not known for certain, but I think the likelihood is that they caved in to serious pressure applied by the U.S.A. Regrettably, naked bullying has been a significant feature of America's foreign relations for many decades. One need look no further than their neighbours in South America for proof of this.

When energy sources reach critical shortage levels in a few years' time, America will find some pretext to invade those countries which still have oil, gas, valuable minerals and even fish. Countries such as Brazil, Iran, Saudi Arabia and Venezuela are amongst the obvious candidates but – and remember you read it here first – do not be surprised if America's solution to its own insolvency and energy problems is to lay claim to Canada, its much wealthier and far more civilised neighbour to the North. A rigged spoof attack by "supposed" Canadian troops on U.S. territory would be par for the course. A typical C.I.A. sting giving America the excuse it needs to invade yet another country. Fanciful? Don't be too sure. But forewarned is forearmed. Canada and Mexico should be very wary of their neighbour in its last days of empire. It will first try to suck you into its web via trading treaties and a common (de-valued) currency and when these fail, look out Canada, look out Central America and look out you independent Caribbean nations. If the U.S.A. continues under neo-con and mega corporation direction, it will stop at nothing to solve its energy deficits and its inability to pay its mountainous debts by conventional means. This is foresight. Don't say you weren't warned.

Colin Powell added his voice to that of the President's opponents and having been Chairman of the Chiefs of Staff during the first Gulf war and Bush's Secretary of State in the second (current) conflict, he cannot be accused of being an unpatriotic dove. Colin Powell pulled no punches and warned Americans that trying to circumvent Article 3 of the Geneva Convention could result in the C.I.A. and its political masters being at risk of being charged with war crimes.

George Bush is well known for the difficulty he has with language and nowhere is this more evident than the problem he has – or purports to have – with the word **_torture_**. "Alternative interrogation" he prefers to call it or "harsh or cohesive interrogation" is another of Bush's euphemisms for torture and in September 2006 he opined that "waterboarding" was only "a policy to question suspects". This contradicts his own C.I.A. who admit that few suspects can endure more than 30 seconds of waterboarding without being sure they are about to drown. Because no marks are left, this technique, claim the C.I.A. creeps, is not torture. **_YUK!_**

America's native Indians learned long ago, that some U.S. Presidents speak with forked tongues and George W. Bush is certainly a successor in the same mould. He pretends to be against torture but persists in wriggling about what it is. He also claims that the Geneva Convention does not apply in the war against terrorists and whilst this view of Bush, Rumsfeld, Rice, Rove and co. pertains, there is little chance of instilling standards of decency and honour into soldiers who have been thrown into impossible situations which cannot be overcome simply by superior force of arms. There can only be one outcome when senior politicians tell the military that "the gloves must come off".

Presidents of many nations seem to have an affinity with torture. Doubtless it has helped some of them become President (or Leader with another title) in the first place.

Ramzan Kadyrov, for example, Chechnya's hard man, is well-documented to have led a 7,000-strong militia – the Kadyrovtsy - who regularly abducted and tortured to death, anyone suspected of opposing his Russian-backed regime. In 2005, Russia's Vladimir Putin, ex-K.G.B., who knows a thing or two about torture, gave Kadyrov the Hero of Russia medal, its highest honour. As they say – it takes one to know one.

Ismail Mutayev claims to have numerous burn marks on his body, caused personally by Kadyrov and the well thought of Human Rights Society of Endangered People produced a Report in which they too had information that Kadyrov had personally tortured civilians.

Let no-one ever forget that courageous journalist Anna Politkovskaya was shot dead in Moscow on the 7th October 2006, just before publishing research into torture by the Kadyrovtsy and that since Vladimir Putin came to power, 19 journalists have either been killed or have disappeared in Russia without a single person being brought to trial. Anna herself had already been kidnapped by Russian Security Services and held in a dark pit without food or water for several days, during which she was subjected to a mock execution. This brave lady, who openly accused Putin of being a K.G.B. snoop comparable to Stalin, simply could not ignore the disgusting crimes being committed by Russia in Chechnya. Her book "Putin's Russia" was refused publication in that country, but her principle reason for writing it was simply that she did not want her kids to grow up in a country responsible for such appalling atrocities. Others, including Russian Central Bank official Andrei Kozlov, an anti-corruption campaigner, have also been killed in suspicious circumstances.

Blair and Bush claim to want to spread their values (heaven forbid) around the globe, so why then do they do nothing meaningful about that slimeball thug and torturer Robert Mugabe of Zimbabwe? All Thabitha Khumalo, General Secretary of the Women's Advisory Council of the Zimbabwe Congress of Trade Unions did was start a campaign for feminine sanitary products to be made available and affordable in her country. For this humanitarian stand, Mugabe's torturers beat her so severely that her front teeth were knocked into her nose and a rifle barrel forced into her vagina.

Others, including actors Anna Chancellor, Jeremy Irons and Stephen Fry are making efforts to support Thabitha and her campaign, but what I want to know is why those claiming to have higher standards and values – Bush, Rumsfeld, Rice, Blair, Blunkett, Straw, Clarke, Blears, Reid etc. – have done bugger all to either protect this brave lady or ensure that the women of Zimbabwe get the sanitary products they so desperately need? They drop bombs on civilians at the drop of a hat – why do they not drop supplies of these lightweight female necessities with equal enthusiasm? Nothing could stop such a humanitarian operation if the will exists to carry it out. Let's do it and show the women of Zimbabwe that they have not been abandoned to the total control of their disgusting Dictator.

Another despicable practice is that of sending prisoners, enemy combatants, mere suspects – call them what you will – to other countries with reputations as torture specialists. Just how barbaric have the political and military elite of supposedly civilised nations sunk in order to achieve their own slimy purposes?

Maher Arar, a Canadian citizen, suffered torture in Syria after being arrested on "mistaken" information in the U.S.A. then flown by the Americans to Jordan. Quite why or how Jordan sent Mr. Arar to Syria is not yet established. What is known is that the Royal Canadian Mounted Police had mistakenly provided the Americans with inaccurate information about this man, but of course, that was no reason for him to be flown to the Middle East, where he was tortured.

To their credit, the Canadian Government acquiesced to public concerns and authorised a Commission of Inquiry into the actions of Canadian Officials in relation to Maher Arar. This was a brave decision, particularly when Canadian investigators had spent considerable time and money trying to implicate Maher Arar in terrorist activities.

On 18th September 2006, Commissioner Dennis O'Connor published his Report in which he stated, quite categorically, that there was no evidence to indicate that Mr. Arar had committed any offence or that his activities constituted a threat to the security of Canada. See **www.ararcommission.ca**.

Commissioner O'Connor is to be applauded for revealing misconduct of the R.C.M.P. and Canadian Officials who leaked confidential and inaccurate information to the media designed to damage Maher Arar's reputation in order to protect the self-interest or interests of the Government. No evidence was found to suggest that either the Royal Canadian Mounted Police or the Canadian Security Intelligence Service had any involvement with the American Security Department's rendition of Mr. Arar to Syria. How refreshing though, that Canada put itself under the microscope, admitted its own mistakes, exonerated an innocent victim and recommended that the Government consider Mr. Arar's claim for compensation. Would that America and Britain were so enlightened.

Having trawled through mountains of material about the secret rendition of untried terrorist suspects, I have not the slightest doubt that this pernicious practice has been commonplace and has been driven by America. Bush's disgraceful regime has bullied craven nations into turning a blind eye to secret flights moving people on to torture destinations and in some instances, into active participation.

On other occasions, America has ignored all international law and convention and simply sent its own secret service agents into other countries in order to kidnap suspects, some of whom were innocent of any crime. Now, a 10-month investigation by European Members of Parliament has confirmed 170 illegal rendition flights in Britain. More than 140 such flights were allowed via Portugal.

Hundreds more dirty renditions were found to have taken place in at least eleven European States, including Britain, Ireland, Portugal, Spain, Cyprus, Poland, Greece, Germany and Romania. Germany seems to have been the major co-operator with the Americans, allowing 336 rendition flights and Italy, Britain, Germany, Austria and Sweden had people snatched from streets and whisked away to be tortured and/or incarcerated in other countries without charge. Exterior numbers and other aeroplane markings were often changed and on occasions, excessive and secret "landing charges" were paid in cash in order to keep the flights off the record books.

The evidence against America is now damning and extensive and at the close of 2006, Italy looks about to prosecute 26 American agents for the abduction of Hassan Mustafa Osama Nasr from the streets of Milan. With European Arrest Warrants likely to be issued, it will be interesting to see if the U.S. is prepared to hand over those charged to their Italian accusers. Highly unlikely.

Did we fight two world wars, the cold war and numerous minor ones only to copy the basest methods of the Gestapo, the fiendish Japanese war machine and the darkest deeds of the Soviet K.G.B? Our forebears, who believed they were fighting for true freedom and human dignity, must be turning in their graves.

I have witnessed decades of **talk** about stopping torture. I have read the conclusions of hundreds of meetings supposedly designed to result in treaties to outlaw torture. I have studied mountains of legal opinions and international conferences on the subject. I have listened ad nauseum to politicians, civil servants, lawyers and security functionaries even disagreeing about what can or cannot, should or should not, be described as torture. I have known these legal and political luminaries argue for days, weeks, months and years over a form of words which pay lip-service to opposing torture whilst leaving loopholes to allow their Governments to continue its use by applying different interpretations of the craftily-agreed words.

88

These pathetic people have no real interest in ending torture. *Their* interest is in attending more conferences; in more discussion groups comprised mainly of their own kind; in writing Academic Papers and Reports to impress their political masters – or to get their Governments off the hook of public anger. These conference organisers incidentally, choose some of the world's most beautiful and expensive venues in which to play their word games.

Millions of man hours have been paid for by the taxpayers of many countries to produce documents and even laws related to torture, but what have they achieved? *Precisely nothing.*

Anyone doubting this need look at just one example of hundreds of documents – CAT/C/USA/CO/2 18 May 2006, the Advance Unedited Version of the Committee Against Torture, 36th session 1 – 19 May 2006. It is ten pages of waffle, legal legerdemain and opposing opinions dressed up in excessively "diplomatic" language with neither the Committee nor the Party representing the United States of America willing to call a spade a spade.

Reading this one document will give you just a flavour of what is going on. Note the number of meetings to which it refers – 702nd, 705th, 720th, 721st – and that is only the United Nations. Thousands of meetings on torture have been held by others elsewhere – all nothing more than talking shops with no worthwhile positive outcome.

Another Human Rights Committee Report dated 10-28 July 2006 referred to the *two thousand, three hundred and ninety-fifth meeting held on 27th July 2006*.

It did not say where the meeting was held, nor who attended, nor what was said by anyone. What it did say, without any implication of consequences, was that:-

The Committee notes the submission of the State Party's second and third periodic combined report, was "seven years overdue". *Seven freaking years overdue!* What are these cushy-life overpaid creeps up to?

I have been commissioned, over the years, by major corporations and Governments to investigate and report on well over a hundred media campaigns. Not once did I miss a Report date by even a single day, so I can conceive of no circumstances, other than political and bureaucratic stalling, which would result in any report being 7 years overdue.

The following eleven pages are a straight, word-for-word reproduction of just one of hundreds of official Reports on torture and one must ask why, in May 2006, it was still necessary for scores of delegates to waste their time and our money churning out such garbage.

You can be forgiven if your eyes glaze over as you read the following pages, or your brain has difficulty accepting how our supposed highly-educated Government servants can talk around such a serious subject as torture for the umpteenth time with neither the hope nor the serious intention of stopping it.

Distr.
GENERAL

CAT/C/USA/CO/2
18 May 2006

Original: ENGLISH

ADVANCE UNEDITED VERSION

COMMITTEE AGAINST TORTURE
36th session
1 – 19 May 2006

CONSIDERATION OF REPORTS SUBMITTED BY STATES PARTIES
UNDER ARTICLE 19 OF THE CONVENTION

Conclusions and recommendations of the Committee against Torture

UNITED STATES OF AMERICA

1.   The Committee against Torture ("the Committee") considered the second report of the United States of America (CAT/C/48/Add.3/Rev.1) at its 702nd and 705th meetings (CAT/C/SR.702 and 705), held on 5 and 8 May 2006, and adopted, at its 720th and 721st meetings, on 17 and 18 May 2006 (CAT/C/SR.720 and 721) the following conclusions and recommendations.

A. Introduction

2.   The second periodic report of the United States of America was due on 19 November 2001, as requested by the Committee at its twenty-fourth session in May 2000 (A/55/44, para. 180 (f)) and was received on 6 May 2005. The Committee notes that the report includes a point-by-point reply to the Committee's previous recommendations.

3.   The Committee commends the State party for its exhaustive written responses to the Committee's list of issues, as well as the detailed responses provided both in writing and orally to

the questions posed by the members during the examination of the report. The Committee expresses its appreciation for the large and high-level delegation, comprising representatives from relevant Departments of the State party, which facilitated a constructive oral exchange during the consideration of the report.

4.   The Committee notes that the State party has a federal structure, but recalls that the United States of America is a single State under international law and has the obligation to implement the Convention against Torture ("the Convention") in full at the domestic level.

5.   Recalling its statement adopted on 22 November 2001 condemning utterly the terrorist attacks of 11 September 2001, the terrible threat to international peace and security posed by acts of international terrorism and the need to combat by all means, in accordance with the Charter of the United Nations, the threats caused by terrorist acts, the Committee recognizes that these attacks caused profound suffering to many residents of the State party. The Committee acknowledges that the State party is engaged in protecting its security and the security and freedom of its citizens in a complex legal and political context.

B. Positive aspects

6.   The Committee welcomes the State party's statement that all United States' officials, from all Government agencies, including its contractors, are prohibited from engaging in torture at all times and in all places, and that all United States' officials from all Government agencies, including its contractors, wherever they may be, are prohibited from engaging in cruel, inhuman or degrading treatment or punishment, in accordance with the obligations in the Convention.

7.   The Committee notes with satisfaction the State party's statement that the United States does not transfer persons to countries where it believes it is "more likely than not" that they will be tortured, and that this also applies, as a matter of policy, to the transfer of any individual, in the State party's custody, or control, regardless of where they are detained.

8.   The Committee welcomes the State party's clarification that the statement of the U.S. President on signing the Detainee Treatment Act on 30 December 2005 is not to be interpreted as a derogation by the President from the absolute prohibition of torture.

9.   The Committee also notes with satisfaction the enactment of:

    a)   The Prison Rape Elimination Act of 2003, which addresses sexual assault of persons in the custody of correctional agencies, with the purpose, *inter alia*, of establishing a "zero-tolerance standard" for rape in detention facilities in the State party; and

    b)   That part of the Detainee Treatment Act of 2005 which prohibits cruel, inhuman, or degrading treatment and punishment of any person, regardless of nationality or physical location, in the custody or under the physical control of the State party.

10.   The Committee welcomes the adoption of National Detention Standards in 2000, which set minimum standards for detention facilities holding Department of Homeland Security detainees, including asylum-seekers.

11.   The Committee also notes with satisfaction the sustained and substantial contributions of the State party to the United Nations Voluntary Fund for the Victims of Torture.

12.   The Committee notes the State party's intention to adopt a new Army Field Manual for intelligence interrogation, applicable to all its personnel, which, according to the State party, will ensure that interrogation techniques fully comply with the Convention.

C. Principal subjects of concern and recommendations

13.   Notwithstanding the statement by the State party that "every act of torture within the meaning of the Convention is illegal under existing federal and/or state law", the Committee reiterates the concern expressed in its previous Conclusions and Recommendations with regard to the absence of a federal crime of torture, consistent with article 1 of the Convention, given that sections 2340 and 2340 A of the United States Code limit federal criminal jurisdiction over acts of torture to extraterritorial cases. The Committee also regrets that, despite the occurrence of cases of extraterritorial torture of detainees, no prosecutions have been initiated under the extraterritorial criminal torture statute. (articles 1, 2, 4 and 5)

> **The Committee reiterates its previous recommendation that the State party should enact a federal crime of torture consistent with article 1 of the Convention, which should include appropriate penalties, in order to fulfill its obligations under the Convention to prevent and eliminate acts of torture causing severe pain or suffering, whether physical or mental, in all its forms.**

> **The State party should ensure that acts of psychological torture, prohibited by the Convention, are not limited to "prolonged mental harm" as set out in the State party's understandings lodged at the time of ratification of the Convention, but constitute a wider category of acts, which cause severe mental suffering, irrespective of their prolongation or its duration.**

> **The State party should investigate, prosecute and punish perpetrators under the federal extraterritorial criminal torture statute.**

14.   The Committee regrets the State party's opinion that the Convention is not applicable in times and in the context of armed conflict, on the basis of the argument that the "law of armed conflict" is the exclusive *lex specialis* applicable, and that the Convention's application "would result in an overlap of the different treaties which would undermine the objective of eradicating torture". (articles 1 and 16)

The State party should recognize and ensure that the Convention applies at all times, whether in peace, war or armed conflict, in any territory under its jurisdiction and that the application of the Convention's provisions are without prejudice to the provisions of any other international instrument, pursuant to paragraph 2 of its articles 1 and 16.

15.   The Committee notes that a number of the Convention's provisions are expressed as applying to "territory under [the State party's] jurisdiction" (articles 2, 5, 13, 16). The Committee reiterates its previously expressed view that this includes all areas under the *de facto* effective control of the State party, by whichever military or civil authorities such control is exercized. The Committee considers that the State party's view that those provisions are geographically limited to its own *de jure* territory to be regrettable.

The State party should recognize and ensure that the provisions of the Convention expressed as applicable to "territory under the State party's jurisdiction" apply to, and are fully enjoyed, by all persons under the effective control of its authorities, of whichever type, wherever located in the world.

16.   The Committee notes with concern that the State party does not always register persons detained in territories under its jurisdiction outside the United States, depriving them of an effective safeguard against acts of torture (article 2)

The State party should register all persons it detains in any territory under its jurisdiction, as one measure to prevent acts of torture. Registration should contain the identity of the detainee, the date, time and place of the detention, the identity of the authority that detained the person, the ground for the detention, the date and time of admission to the detention facility and the state of health of the detainee upon admission and any changes thereto, the time and place of interrogations, with the names of all interrogators present, as well as the date and time of release or transfer to another detention facility.

17.   The Committee is concerned by allegations that the State party has established secret detention facilities, which are not accessible to the International Committee of the Red Cross. Detainees are deprived of fundamental legal safeguards, including an oversight mechanism in regard to their treatment and review procedures with respect to their detention. The Committee is also concerned by allegations that those detained in such facilities could be held for prolonged periods and face torture or cruel, inhuman or degrading treatment. The Committee considers the "no comment" policy of the State party regarding the existence of such secret detention facilities, as well as on its intelligence activities, to be regrettable. (articles 2 and 16)

The State party should ensure that no one is detained in any secret detention facility under its de facto effective control. Detaining persons in such conditions constitutes, *per se*, a violation of the Convention. The State party should investigate and disclose the existence of any such facilities and the authority under which they have been

established and the manner in which detainees are treated. The State party should publicly condemn any policy of secret detention.

The Committee recalls that intelligence activities, notwithstanding their author, nature or location, are acts of the State party, fully engaging its international responsibility.

18.   The Committee is concerned by reports of the involvement of the State party in enforced disappearances. The Committee considers the State party's view that such acts do not constitute a form of torture to be regrettable. (articles 2 and 16)

The State party should adopt all necessary measures to prohibit and prevent enforced disappearance in any territory under its jurisdiction, and prosecute and punish perpetrators, as this practice constitutes, *per se*, a violation of the Convention.

19.   Notwithstanding the State party's statement that "[u]nder U.S. law, there is no derogation from the express statutory prohibition of torture" and that "[n]o circumstances whatsoever (...) may be invoked as a justification or defense to committing torture", the Committee remains concerned at the absence of clear legal provisions ensuring that the Convention's prohibition against torture is not derogated from under any circumstances, in particular since 11 September 2001. (articles 2, 11 and 12)

The State party should adopt clear legal provisions to implement the principle of absolute prohibition of torture in its domestic law without any possible derogation. Derogation from this principle is incompatible with paragraph 2, of article 2, of the Convention and cannot limit criminal responsibility. The State party should also ensure that perpetrators of acts of torture are prosecuted and punished appropriately.

The State party should also ensure that any interrogation rules, instructions or methods do not derogate from the principle of absolute prohibition of torture and that no doctrine under domestic law impedes the full criminal responsibility of perpetrators of acts of torture.

The State party should promptly, thoroughly, and impartially investigate any responsibility of senior military and civilian officials authorizing, acquiescing   or consenting, in any way, to acts of torture committed by their subordinates.

20.   The Committee is concerned that the State party considers that the *non-refoulement* obligation, under article 3 of the Convention, does not extend to a person detained outside its territory. The Committee is also concerned by the State party's rendition of suspects, without any judicial procedure, to States where they face a real risk of torture. (article 3)

The State party should apply the *non-refoulement* guarantee to all detainees in its custody, cease the rendition of suspects, in particular by its intelligence agencies, to States where they face a real risk of torture, in order to comply with its obligations

under article 3 of the Convention. The State party should always ensure that suspects have the possibility to challenge decisions of *refoulement*.

21.   The Committee is concerned by the State party's use of "diplomatic assurances", or other kinds of guarantees, assuring that a person will not be tortured if expelled, returned, transferred or extradited to another State. The Committee is also concerned by the secrecy of such procedures including the absence of judicial scrutiny and the lack of monitoring mechanisms put in place to assess if the assurances have been honoured. (article 3)

When determining the applicability of its *non-refoulement* obligations under article 3 of the Convention, the State party should only rely on "diplomatic assurances" in regard to States which do not systematically violate the Convention's provisions, and after a thorough examination of the merits of each individual case. The State party should establish and implement clear procedures for obtaining such assurances, with adequate judicial mechanisms for review, and effective post-return monitoring arrangements. The State party should also provide detailed information to the Committee on all cases since 11 September 2001 where assurances have been provided.

22.   The Committee, noting that detaining persons indefinitely without charge, constitutes per se a violation of the Convention, is concerned that detainees are held for protracted periods at Guantánamo Bay, without sufficient legal safeguards and without judicial assessment of the justification for their detention. (articles 2, 3 and 16)

The State party should cease to detain any person at Guantánamo Bay and close this detention facility, permit access by the detainees to judicial process or release them as soon as possible, ensuring that they are not returned to any State where they could face a real risk of being tortured, in order to comply with its obligations under the Convention.

23.   The Committee is concerned that information, education and training provided to the State party's law enforcement or military personnel are not adequate and do not focus on all provisions of the Convention, in particular on the non-derogable nature of the prohibition of torture and the prevention of cruel, inhuman and degrading treatment or punishment. (articles 10 and 11)

The State party should ensure that education and training of all law enforcement or military personnel, are conducted on a regular basis, in particular for personnel involved in the interrogation of suspects. This should include training on interrogation rules, instructions and methods, and specific training on how to identify signs of torture and cruel, inhuman or degrading treatment. Such personnel should also be instructed to report such incidents.

The State party should also regularly evaluate the training and education provided to its law enforcement and military personnel as well as ensure regular and independent monitoring of their conduct.

24.   The Committee is concerned that in 2002 the State party authorized the use of certain interrogation techniques, which have resulted in the death of some detainees during interrogation. The Committee also regrets that "confusing interrogation rules" and techniques defined in vague and general terms, such as "stress positions", have led to serious abuses of detainees. (articles 11, 1, 2 and 16)

The State party should rescind any interrogation technique, including methods involving sexual humiliation, "water boarding", "short shackling" and using dogs to induce fear, that constitute torture or cruel, inhuman or degrading treatment or punishment, in all places of detention under its _de facto_ effective control, in order to comply with its obligations under the Convention.

25.   The Committee is concerned with allegations of impunity of some of the State party's law enforcement personnel in respect of acts of torture or cruel, inhuman or degrading treatment or punishment. The Committee notes the limited investigation and lack of prosecution in respect of the allegations of torture perpetrated in areas 2 and 3 of the Chicago Police Department. (article 12)

The State party should promptly, thoroughly and impartially investigate all allegations of acts of torture or cruel, inhuman or degrading treatment or punishment by law enforcement personnel and bring perpetrators to justice, in order to fulfill its obligations under article 12 of the Convention. The State party should also provide the Committee with information on the ongoing investigations and prosecution relating to the above mentioned case.

26.   The Committee is concerned by reliable reports of acts of torture or cruel, inhuman and degrading treatment or punishment committed by certain members of the State party's military or civilian personnel in Afghanistan and Iraq. It is also concerned that the investigation and prosecution of many of these cases, including some resulting in the death of detainees, have led to lenient sentences, including of an administrative nature or less than one year's imprisonment. (article 12)

The State party should take immediate measures to eradicate all forms of torture and ill-treatment of detainees by its military or civilian personnel, in any territory under its jurisdiction, and should promptly and thoroughly investigate such acts and prosecute all those responsible for such acts, and ensure they are appropriately punished, in accordance with the seriousness of the crime.

27.   The Committee is concerned that the Detainee Treatment Act of 2005 aims to withdraw the jurisdiction of the State party's federal courts with respect to _habeas corpus_ petitions, or other claims by or on behalf of Guantánamo Bay detainees, except under limited circumstances. The Committee is also concerned that detainees in Afghanistan and Iraq, under the control of the Department of Defence, have their status determined and reviewed by an administrative process of that Department. (article 13)

The State party should ensure that independent, prompt and thorough procedures to review the circumstances of detention and the status of detainees are available to all detainees as required by article 13 of the Convention.

28.   The Committee is concerned by the difficulties certain victims of abuses have faced in obtaining redress and adequate compensation, and that only a limited number of detainees have filed claims for compensation for alleged abuse and maltreatment, in particular under the Foreign Claims Act. (article 14)

The State party should ensure, in accordance with the Convention, that mechanisms to obtain full redress, compensation and rehabilitation are accessible to all victims of acts of torture or abuse, including sexual violence, perpetrated by its officials.

29.   The Committee is concerned by section 1997 e (e) of the 1995 Prison Litigation Reform Act which provides "that no federal civil action may be brought by a prisoner for mental or emotional injury suffered while in custody without a prior showing of physical injury." (article 14)

The State party should not limit the right of victims to bring civil actions and amend the Prison Litigation Reform Act accordingly.

30.   The Committee, while taking note of the State party's instruction number 10 of 24 March 2006 which provides that military commissions shall not admit statements established to be made as a result of torture in evidence, is concerned about the implementation of the instruction in the context of such commissions and the limitations on detainees' effective right to complain. The Committee is also concerned about the Combatant Status Review Tribunals and the Administrative Review Boards. (articles 13 and 15)

The State party should ensure that its obligations under articles 13 and 15 are fulfilled in all circumstances, including in the context of military commissions and should consider establishing an independent mechanism to guarantee the rights of all detainees in its custody.

31.   The Committee is concerned by the fact that substantiated information indicates that executions in the State party can be accompanied by severe pain and suffering. (articles 16, 1 and 2)

The State party should carefully review its execution methods, in particular lethal injection in order to prevent severe pain and suffering.

32.   The Committee is concerned by reliable reports of sexual assault of sentenced detainees, as well as persons in pre-trial or immigration detention, in places of detention in the State party. The Committee is concerned that there are numerous reports of sexual violence perpetrated by detainees on each other, and that persons of differing sexual orientation are particularly vulnerable. The Committee is also concerned by the lack of prompt and independent investigation of such acts and

that appropriate measures to combat these abuses have not been implemented by the State party. (articles 16, 12, 13 and 14)

The State party should design and implement appropriate measures to prevent all sexual violence, in all its detention centres. The State party should ensure that all allegations of violence in detention centres are investigated promptly and independently, perpetrators are prosecuted and appropriately sentenced and victims can seek redress, including appropriate compensation.

33. The Committee is concerned by the treatment of detained women in the State party, including gender-based humiliation and incidents of shackling of women detainees during child-birth. (article 16)

The State party should adopt all appropriate measures to ensure that women in detention are treated in conformity with international standards.

34. The Committee reiterates the concern expressed in its previous recommendations about the conditions of the detention of children, in particular the fact that they may not be completely segregated from adults during pre-trail detention and after sentencing. The Committee is also concerned by the large number of children sentenced to life imprisonment in the State party. (article 16)

The State party should ensure that detained children are kept in facilities separate from those for adults in conformity with international standards. The State party should address sentences of life imprisonment of children as these could constitute cruel, inhuman or degrading treatment or punishment.

35. The Committee remains concerned about the extensive use by the State party's law enforcement personnel of electro-shock devices which have caused in several deaths. The Committee is concerned that this practice raises serious issues of compatibility with article 16 of the Convention. (article 16)

The State party should carefully review the use of electro-shock devices, strictly regulate their use, restricting it to substitution for lethal weapons and eliminate the use of these devices to restrain persons in custody, as this leads to breaches of article 16 of the Convention.

36. The Committee remains concerned about the extremely harsh regime imposed on detainees in "supermaximum prisons." The Committee is concerned about the prolonged isolation periods detainees are subjected to, the effect such treatment has on their mental health, and that its purpose may be retribution, in which case it would constitute cruel, inhuman or degrading treatment or punishment. (article 16)

The State party should review the regime imposed on detainees in "supermaximum prisons," in particular the practice of prolonged isolation.

37.   The Committee is concerned about reports of brutality and use of excessive force by the State party's law enforcement personnel, and the numerous allegations of their ill-treatment of vulnerable groups, in particular racial minorities, migrants and persons of different sexual orientation which have not been adequately investigated. (article 16 and 12)

> **The State party should ensure that reports of brutality and ill-treatment of members of vulnerable groups by its law enforcement personnel are independently, promptly and thoroughly investigated and that perpetrators are prosecuted and appropriately punished.**

38.   The Committee strongly encourages the State party to invite the Special Rapporteur on torture and other cruel, inhuman or degrading treatment or punishment, in full conformity with the terms of reference for fact-finding missions by Special Procedures of the United Nations, to visit Guantánamo Bay and any other detention facility under its effective *de facto* control.

39.   The Committee invites the State party to reconsider its express intention not to become party to the Rome Statute of the International Criminal Court.

40.   The Committee reiterates its recommendation that the State party should consider withdrawing its reservations, declarations and understandings lodged at the time of ratification of the Convention.

41.   The Committee encourages the State party to consider making the declaration under article 22, thereby recognizing the competence of the Committee to receive and consider individual communications, as well as ratifying the Optional Protocol to the Convention.

42.   The Committee requests the State party to provide detailed statistical data, disaggregated by sex, ethnicity and conduct, on complaints related to torture and ill-treatment allegedly committed by law enforcement officials, investigations, prosecutions, penalties and disciplinary action relating to such complaints. It requests the State party to provide similar statistical data and information on the enforcement of the Civil Rights of Institutionalized Persons Act by the Department of Justice, in particular in respect to the prevention, investigation and prosecution of acts of torture, or cruel, inhuman or degrading treatment or punishment in detention facilities and the measures taken to implement the Prison Rape Elimination Act and their impact. The Committee requests the State party to provide information on any compensation and rehabilitation provided to victims. The Committee encourages the State party to create a federal database to facilitate the collection of such statistics and information which assist in the assessment of the implementation of the provisions of the Convention and the practical enjoyment of the rights it provides. The Committee also requests the State party to provide information on investigations into the alleged ill-treatment perpetrated by law enforcement personnel in the aftermath of Hurricane Katrina.

43.   The Committee requests the State party to provide, within one year, information on its response to its recommendations in paragraphs 16, 20, 21, 22, 24, 33, 34 and 42 above.

44.   The Committee requests the State party to disseminate its report, with its addenda and the written answers to the Committee's list of issues and oral questions and the conclusions and recommendations of the Committee widely, in all appropriate languages through official websites, the media and non-governmental organizations.

45.   The State party is invited to submit its next periodic report, which will be considered as its fifth periodic report, by 19 November 2011, the due date of the fifth periodic report.

What, of practical value, did this document achieve?

Was the Report given wide public exposure? No.

Did it stop the U.S.A. torturing suspects? No.

Has it changed America's opinion that it can use its lawyers to wriggle out of its international obligations to prohibit torture? No.

Did it bring about an end to extraordinary rendition? No.

Will it prevent anyone from being tortured in the future, either by or at the behest of President Bush's war machine? No.

Like the years and years of committee meetings, Treaties, Reports which preceded it, CAT/C/USA/CO/2 18 May 2006 has not reduced torture one jot.

Some nations have paid lip-service to minimal anti-torture measures, but even the United Nations' Convention Against Torture is pathetic, despite taking a decade to be brought into being and now having been in existence for more than twenty years. The truth is, that the U.N. has always given torture a very low priority and never created a sufficiently-aggressive action plan to eliminate it.

Another talking shop, the European Commission, had numerous meetings and communications culminating in banning the trade in instruments of torture – electric chairs, leg irons, guillotines etc. What a pathetic waste of time and money! I very much doubt that such trade existed, but in any event, these and many other items can be locally sourced in any country and torture can and is often carried out by a variety of items in everyday innocent use. Someone should tell these bureaucratic boobies that it is *people* who abuse and torture and it is these *people* and not their equipment who need controlling.

Torture *can* be almost eradicated but first, all countries should be required to make an unequivocal declaration against it and commit themselves to positive measures to replace the interminable roundabout of talking shops. What are needed are clear, serious and simple actions.

Like what? I hope I hear you ask.

Well, as an early step, any country refusing to outlaw torture absolutely should be highlighted, warned and if necessary, subjected to sanctions, including, in the final analysis, losing its vote in the United Nations.

As this is unlikely to happen quickly, I and a number of interested parties will begin a very focused Anti-Torture Campaign shortly after the release of this book.

It is time to stop just talking about torture. It is time for action and we will be naming names, raising questions and calling people to account.

Nothing will be achieved if we leave things as they are because our politicians and their secretive security arms are skilled at obstructing even worthwhile organisations such as Amnesty International and the International Red Cross. All, of course (they say), in the name of a mythical national security interest – that global cover-up which gets rolled out whenever the public is getting uncomfortably close to discovering Governments' dirty deeds and dealings.

We are supposed to accept this all-encompassing "national security" cop-out and keep our noses out of matters which Governments treat as their own exclusive domain. Problem is, the "secret intelligence" is all too often either trivial; unreliable; planted by cleverer opposing "intelligence" agents; wholly inaccurate; or spun by the receiving civil servants, politicians or generals to support their own pre-conceived plans. Unfortunately, these secretive security blankets, which are portrayed as being for the public good, very rarely protect anyone other than the miscreants using them. Invariably though, they end up costing thousands of *innocent* lives. I and many others want to see far greater transparency and accountability in these so-called national security areas because increased openness would improve the public's understanding of what we are facing. The more the public knows, the more they will be willing and able to assist the security services with information about all categories of criminal activity, including terrorism. The converse is also true.

Can one person's solutions to torture succeed where all others have failed?

Well, I believe it can and will, given the support of ordinary people throughout the world. People just like you perhaps.

My belief is that sometimes problems are best solved by *not* trying to build onto previous bodies of work, but by stepping back and searching for more simple answers. My Anti-Torture Campaign will bring completely new approaches to bear on the issue. You can register your early interest in this by emailing **torture@crimedown.org** or you can keep watching **www.crimedown.org** which will announce its availability. Anyone with a serious interest in this or other of my work to bring about major crime reduction is welcome to contact me in the run-up to what I believe will be exciting times ahead.

Our approaches to politicians will put many of them on the spot in such a way as to raise very serious questions about the fitness of some of them for public office.

The Intelligence and Security Committee of the U.K. House of Lords on 10 March 2005 stated very clearly that intelligence personnel were not sufficiently trained, some not even knowing the Geneva Convention – a particular necessity when going abroad to "question" detainees, the Committee said. The House of Lords usually brings far more common sense and wisdom to bear on its deliberations than does the Lower House and the yah-booing of its ideologs but regrettably, its Law Lords failed to strike a blow against torture on one important issue.

No-one and no State should have immunity from prosecution for torture and I want an end put to the nonsensical legal shenanigans used by some to try to evade justice.

A typical example of this is the case of Les Walker and his British colleagues who claim to have been arrested in Saudi Arabia on false charges, then imprisoned and tortured over many months. They sought eventually, justice via the British Courts. This was refused on the spurious grounds that the State concerned – Saudi Arabia – had immunity from prosecution. A disgusting piece of sham law if ever there was one. The UK Court of Appeal though, agreed with the plaintiffs, but regrettably the UK Law Lords overturned the Court of Appeal decision on 14th June 2006 ruling that on a matter of law, the State of Saudi Arabia did have immunity from prosecution. The matter may now go to the European Court of Human Rights, at huge cost of course, in terms of time, money and the enormous additional stress and mental anguish suffered by the victims and their families.

It is high time that our Judges stopped treating the law as academic ping pong and put principle before practice. One presumes that the Law Lords concerned have never been tortured. Had they been, I suspect that their decision to accept Saudi Arabia's claim to immunity from prosecution would have been quite different.

Not dissimilarly, it has taken Chile more than fifteen years to strip Augusto Pinochet of the immunity from prosecution which he himself had brought into law in 1990 whilst Head of State. Only now, in late 2006, can Chile's former Ruler be charged with ordering the torture or "disappearance" of those who spoke out against his dictatorial Police State regime.

The General is now 90 years old, but whatever his state of health, I believe he should face trial, if only to demonstrate to the world that no-one suspected of association with torture can expect to evade justice.

December 2006 Update – The crafty General beat the system in the end by dying before Chile's impossibly slow lawyers could get their criminal justice system into gear.

Rulers who authorise, condone or turn a blind eye to torture should know that they will be tracked down, arrested, put on trial and suffer the most serious consequences, whatever their age or state of health.

Society should long ago have addressed the questions – "What kind of person becomes a torturer?" and "How do these twisted personalities progress to positions where Governments employ or commission them to carry out their evil practices?"

Regrettably I know of no politician who has attached sufficient importance to the many questions surrounding torture to mount a campaign against it as part of their own personal manifesto. Do please let me know if you are such a person who has not shown up on my radar screen.

UK Foreign Minister Ian Pearson was a perfect example of politicians' duplicitous attitudes to torture when, despite being one of Tony Blair's spokesmen on Human Rights, he appeared to suggest that the practice of "water-boarding" may be legal in certain circumstances. Looks to me like Mr. Pearson and his American counterparts have been on the same torture-spinning courses.

Water-boarding, for those unaware of the term, is blind-folding and strapping a helpless victim to a board overhanging a bath or water tank. The torturers then force those being interrogated under the water for ever longer periods, sufficient to convince them that they are about to die from drowning. Not surprisingly, many of the abused make whatever confessions they hope their torturers want to hear, whether true or not.

Sometimes of course, the victims do drown and on other occasions – as with many forms of torture – their hearts simply fail. Any who do survive suffer serious psychological problems for indefinite periods.

How can anyone believe that this may be legal in some circumstances? What circumstances can there possibly be to justify such dirty, cowardly torture? Perhaps Ian Pearson was misreported and if so, he may care to make his position on any kind of torture absolutely clear, leaving no room for doubt. He will have to be very careful of course, knowing what happens to those honest enough to speak out. Robert Grenier, for example, one-time top counter-terrorist official at the C.I.A. in America, was sacked in February 2006 for opposing water-boarding and other forms of torture and because he was unhappy about the Bush/Rumsfeld programme of kidnapping, extraordinary rendition and flying people around the world in secret to a variety of scary prison venues.

Similarly, Britain's Ambassador to Uzbekistan, Craig Murray, was smeared and withdrawn from his post for speaking out against the use, by Britain and America, of information gained by the Uzbek Government's use of torture. He later openly accused Bush and Blair of selling their countries' souls for intelligence, which was never more than dross, having been obtained by torture – a traditional practice of President Karimov's security services.

I will be inviting Robert Grenier, Ian Pearson and many political Leaders, to participate in my Anti-Torture Campaign from 2007.

Their reactions will be interesting to compare.

Torture is not, of course, limited to that effected by Governments and their security nominees. Sadly, there are individuals who, without any encouragement or justification, take pleasure in causing pain and distress to fellow human beings. Their methods vary from the sudden kidnapping of total strangers to enticement via initial friendliness and to the taking advantage of domestic situations and the necessary degree of privacy which this gives them. All too often, even children are tortured and depressingly, not always by strangers.

Again, all too often, there have been warning signs of abuse which the police, education and social services personnel overlooked or ignored, sometimes with tragic results.

Instead of getting away with the standard condolences and the glib parroting of "we must learn lessons from this" – yet again! – should not the Government employees who are paid to protect the vulnerable sectors of our societies, pay a serious price when they fail so to do?

Until every Government official understands that they too will suffer meaningful consequences if they fall below acceptable levels of competence and responsibility, the abuse/torture will continue, albeit at a lower frequency if my new sentencing principles (later chapter) are brought into effect.

- It is, unfortunately, too late to prevent Marc Dutroux's years of kidnapping, raping and torturing a string of females, at least four of whom died as a result, the youngest being only 8 years old.

  Dutroux had been on the Belgian judicial system's radar screen for years and in 1986 he and his wife were accused of drugging, kidnapping and raping five other young females. As the driving force, he was sentenced to thirteen years in gaol, but disgracefully, the parole authority released him after only three years, supposedly to care for his grandmother. As a direct result, Dutroux was able to continue his masochistic practices, including using the date-rape drug Rohypnol to procure his victims, some of whom he buried, still alive, in his garden. So much for parole "experts".

- Paedophile Thomas Titley actually asked, in 1996, to be locked up for life because of his inability to control his urges for indecently assaulting young boys.

The judiciary thought they knew better. He was sentenced to only four and a half years, but in the event, was released after only three. Immediately his social workers and probation officers ended their contact with him, Titley reverted to his previous practices, including imprisoning a 7 year old boy in a dark two-metre hole underneath his floor boards. This did not come to light until late in 2003, despite a sex offenders order being made against him in April 2002.

No-one will ever know how many children had been terrified and abused by Titley but what we do know is that the number would have been much smaller had the victims not been let down by those who should have been more alert to the very obvious danger signals.

One has to wonder how many of these evil private abusers and torturers stay below official radar screens only to become paid torturers for security services at a later date. Not a happy thought, but less disturbing than the alternative, which is that Governments themselves actually train people to do the torturing.

Just getting people involved in my Anti-Torture Campaign will not, of itself, stop all torture but it will increase the profile of this disgraceful crime and will be one of the building blocks leading to major reductions in the practice.

Other measures must be to call upon every Government to outlaw torture absolutely. They must do this unequivocally. No weasel words about what is or what is not torture, or what category of person may be tortured, and no turning of blind eyes where the practice occurs.

Too many politicians, such as White House Legal Counsel Alberto Gonzales, deliberately muddy the water on crime. This gun-slinging lawyer told the Republic Judiciary Hearing that he "absolutely did not" approve of torture, but official U.S. Government documents show that this same Gonzales had argued that Al Quaeda prisoners (if that is what they really were) did not qualify for Geneva Convention protection, but even if they did, George Bush had the authority – he did not say whose – to ignore the Geneva Convention and/or American law which forbids torture. So, just like Abraham Lincoln, President Bush perceives himself as being bound by neither the law nor the Constitution which both he and Lawyer Alberto Gonzales swore a solemn oath to uphold.

I am not the only one to have rumbled U.S. Attorney General Alberto Gonzales. Robert Parry, writing for the Baltimore Chronicle, considered his interpretation of the U.S. Constitution's granting of habeas corpus rights of a fair trial, to be one of the most chilling public statements ever made.

Word-mangler Gonzales told a Senate Judiciary Committee on January 18, 2007 that the Constitution contains no explicit bestowing of habeas corpus rights – only a prohibition against taking it away. Republican Senator Arlen Specter was aghast at the squirming lawyer's claim, wondering how even a Government lawyer could posit that anything could be taken away if it never existed in the first place.

Looks to me like U.S. Attorney General Alberto Gonzales, the U.K.'s Attorney General Lord Goldsmith and his bosom pal, Prime Minister Tony Blair, have all been taking the same lessons in how to portray black as white.

Clearly the American Administration has not listened to Theo Van Boven, the U.N.'s Special Rapporteur on Torture, Cruel, Inhuman or Degrading Treatment. He has repeatedly criticised attempts by Governments constantly trying to get around international laws against these malpractices. In his Report to the U.N., he stressed that *there are no circumstances whatsoever* which can possibly justify such abuses and that anyone violating these international laws, even by order of a superior or Head of State, should be held to account. He made it very clear, as do I and many others, that no argument for necessity, including terrorism or suspected terrorism, internal security or state of emergency can ever be valid and cannot be used in any way to justify torture. Problem is though, Theo Van Boven's excellent Reports to the U.N. General Assembly were – just like so many others – just Reports. They have failed to stop torture because as of now, there are no meaningful consequences for those nations choosing to ignore them.

Regrettably, Europe has shown itself to be extremely weak-kneed on the matter of extraordinary rendition, relegating the matter, on 14th September 2006, to a simple "press line" which is its lowest form of comment. A robust official statement on the whole issue of torture is still long overdue.

We must change this.

For starters, I would like every country to create an ***Independent Torture Protection Panel*** which should be well-publicised and available for anyone to contact and report suffered, witnessed or suspected torture. This service should, of course, be in absolute confidence when requested and be funded sufficiently to both investigate complaints and trigger prosecutions as appropriate. I will be happy to consult on this once my Anti-Torture Initiative is announced.

Underscoring these changes should be changes in law where needed, to reflect the seriousness of either carrying out, authorising or failing to report torture. The level of punishment afforded to these crimes should be mandatory and my recommendations on the subject can be found in a later chapter on sentencing.

If you wish to live in a country which claims to be civilised, I hope you will join me in my pro-active campaign against all forms of torture. This innovative campaign is scheduled to begin sometime in 2007.

Another Crime/Torture Link

Try just having a nightcap and slipping peacefully into sleep when:-

• A loved one has gone missing, presumed abducted

• Your young son or husband has been kicked to death and his body dumped in a rubbish skip

• Your ten year old daughter or granddaughter has been gang raped

• Your live-alone grandparent has been severely beaten and robbed of his/her survival-level pension cash

• Three of your family did not survive a head-on car crash caused by a young tearaway unconcerned about the consequences of overtaking on a blind bend, perhaps even driving whilst disqualified or drunk

• Your father was tortured to death by State interrogators

I could go on, because there are millions of people suffering the mental torture which involuntarily invades their minds, re-running what is either known about their loved ones' suffering, or what their imaginations perceive as being the likely appalling scenarios.

110

Each victim may have a wide circle of relatives and friends who suffer this anguish and for them, there is no slipping peacefully into sleep each night. For some, the dreadful mental images which, unbeckoned, take over their minds, never fade and some say that this torture by proxy has essentially destroyed their wish to carry on. This, of course, is exacerbated if the perpetrators are neither found nor adequately punished.

Inevitably, these secondary victims get sucked into the quicksands of crime along, of course, with the primary victims.

Only serious affirmative action can significantly reduce the number falling victim to all kinds of torture, whether by security personnel, individuals on their own accounts or everyday violent criminals causing secondary torture. Hopefully, by the time you reach the end of this book, you will be persuaded that such action is a very real prospect which really can bring crime tumbling down.

Late in the day, by 15th September 2006, there is a ray of hope in America concerning the detention of suspected terrorists and their treatment whilst in custody which, we should not forget, is already more than 5 years in some instances. For the first time, George Bush faced some serious and outspoken criticism from some of his senior colleagues who joined forces with opposition members to throw out the President's attempts to have suspects tried by a very dangerous form of military tribunal. Even the Government's own lawyers appointed to defend Guantanamo Bay prisoners criticised the tribunal system and both Lt. Commander Philip Sundel and Army Major Mark Bridges openly admitted that those whom they had been instructed to defend would not get a fair trial. Both condemned the Appeals process which ludicrously, amongst other things, allowed the Pentagon-appointed official, who had approved the charges against their clients originally, to also be the final adjudicator.

Perhaps, just perhaps, the message of ourselves and very many others is just beginning to convince even some of the U.S.'s thick-skinned neo-cons that America's prevarication on torture and matters judicial has turned America into a pariah. This is not only in other countries. Many Americans are also deeply ashamed of their Government's behaviour both in Iraq and in its treatment of arrested individuals. Bush & co. will not be forgiven their crimes and may well someday face trial for their actions.

Meantime, the suspects – and that is all they are right now – are still languishing in scary, secretive detention centres, despite America's Supreme Court having declared President Bush's attempts to by-pass the judicial system as being unconstitutional. Of course he knew this perfectly well. It remains to be seen how long the American people will tolerate the salami-slicing of their original Constitution by a bunch of business-driven warmongers.

I wish to make it quite clear to all of those involved in this dirty business, that every suspect should be brought to trial without delay. By trail, I mean public trial, not some other deviant form of tribunal or whatever, where the accused are not permitted to see or hear all of the supposed evidence against them.

Any accused found guilty should, quite properly be given harsh sentences appropriate to their crimes.

Any found innocent should receive both an apology and substantial compensation for their wrongful imprisonment and any harm or trauma suffered by themselves and their families. Just think for a while, how you would feel if your son, husband, father or brother suddenly "disappeared" for some months or years and the effect this would have on your family.

Having spent a substantial part of my life researching crime, I am in no mood to see justice denied by those in America and Britain whose politicians are too closely connected to mega businesses whose Directors are getting fat on contracts to supply goods and services, the only use for which is destructive to people. When it becomes difficult to do this, Bush's and Blair's military are authorised to blow up everything and everyone in the hope that a few of the enemy will be amongst the dead.

So much for the values which the dictatorial duo profess to want to spread around the world. Values? Neither Bush nor Blair know the meaning of the word.

I have more to say about politicians in a later chapter but for now I will simply re-state my determination to campaign against all crime, whether individual, terrorist, organised by gangs or State inspired.

Come to think of it, the last two categories could be condensed into just one. What, after all, are the upper echelons of most Governments

112

than organised gangs hell-bent on increasing their power and stifling all opinions but their own?

We of course expect to be kept as safe as is reasonable. We want terrorists discouraged and where they are not, our military and security services should catch, confine and put on public trial anyone planning or committing acts of terrorism. I absolutely do not want though, to see our world sink further into the quicksands of crime by torturers claiming to be adding to my security. Rather than have anyone tortured on my behalf, I prefer to run whatever increased risk this may entail.

No-one has the authority to torture or murder in my name and that no-one includes power-crazed Presidents and Prime Ministers.

CHAPTER 6

SENDING OUT ALL THE WRONG SIGNALS

Politicians in many countries have, for decades, been sending signals to all and sundry which have inevitably led to high levels of crime.

Regrettably I have to conclude, after many years of research into crime, that our political leaders are not only short of the three previously discussed assets – foresight, insight and positive hindsight - they are mainly missing an equally-important quality – commonsense.

- School kids have, for decades, picked up on the fact that they can misbehave, be abusive, get drunk, take drugs, kick heads in, shoplift, damage property etc. etc. with little or no chance of suffering anything approaching consequences which would cause them undue concern.

Organisations such as the Centre for Crime and Justice Studies should bear much of the responsibility for this, campaigning as they do for the age of criminality to be increased to 14, claiming that we should not be criminalising the little darlings so early in life.

These academic airheads try and make it seem that it is we, the law-abiding people, who are doing something terrible to these young offenders, but that is arrant rubbish. It is the young criminals who criminalise themselves, so why do those playing around with the subject at the Centre for Crime and Justice Studies try to switch things around and make it seem that society and not those committing offences – and very often their parents – who are to blame?

Right at the heart of high crime is the realisation, by those with neither standards, morals or respect, that there are a variety of factors which they can exploit in order to be able to commit crimes but not pay the penalty, even if caught. True, there are some juveniles who may break the law without being fully aware of the consequences, but that is a failure of parents, inadequate education on social issues, crazy judicial systems and misguided Bodies such as the Centre for Crime and Justice Studies. It is listening to such Bodies which has resulted in some countries suffering high levels of crime and I wonder how much those working in them are paid, and by whom, for pedalling their dangerous opinions which, by any measurement, have failed to persuade the criminally-inclined to mend their anti-social ways.

- Politicians in Britain, for example, are running around like headless chickens, despairing about the high level of gun and knife crime. Had they listened to me over the years, they would not now have the problem. Nor would Judges have been sending only 16% of knife carriers to gaol.

- Compounding this, even on the rare occasions when they are taken to Court and are found to be guilty, offenders are confident that few will know of their crimes because – happy for them, but disastrous for their victims and potential victims – young villains are protected at law by complete anonymity and secrecy.

I am sick and tired of hearing - "*The offender cannot be named for legal reasons!*" Why the hell not? If we want fewer crimes, we must stop shielding those found guilty of committing them.

Are politicians barking mad or what? telling their youngsters that no matter what they do, neither they nor their parents will suffer any public shame or accountability. Nor will their neighbours be aware that they are rubbing shoulders with criminals.

Preventing the names of criminals being released because of their youth is arrant nonsense and sends out a dangerous signal which inevitably results in even more crimes being committed. Youngsters should be taught, from the earliest age, at home and in school, that if they break the law, they will be held responsible and be punished and shamed and that this shame will inevitably attach to their parents.

Some judicial systems are full of serious defects, and protecting criminals - instead of actual or potential victims - is certainly one of them. We should be telling every parent that if their children - for whom they are responsible – commit a crime, their kids, and by association, the parents, will not be given the comfort of anonymity. If a child is found guilty of any crime, whatever his or her age, it is important that this should not be hidden from the community in which they live.

Because of the current law in some countries, whereby the names of juvenile criminals cannot be revealed, there are many parents who care little about what their kids get up to, because it is never going to reflect on them. With such a ridiculous law, there simply is no imperative for parents to instil good standards, if those who fail, suffer no public exposure for their misdeeds. What a crazy signal to be sending out to the criminally-inclined.

My belief is that a shopkeeper is entitled to know if any child in the community has been found guilty of stealing, regardless of their age. No reason to ban the kid from the shop of course, but good cause for a little more quiet vigilance when a convicted criminal is known to be on the premises. Protecting the identities of the guilty, whatever their age, is one reason why some countries have so many repeat offenders. These countries are quite simply giving their youngsters a perfectly protected incubation environment in which they can develop their criminal inclinations and skills in complete anonymity. This is a crazy and quite illogical message to be sending out to both kids and parents.

More and more serious crimes are being committed daily by ever-younger juveniles and it is both illogical and counter-productive to protect them and their parents by sticking to the failed practice of saying that their names cannot be revealed for legal reasons because they happen to be on the convenient side of an arbitrary age.

Two young London boys were caught with their pants down, filmed by a friend – mobile phone again – raping an 11-year old girl. They were charged with the offence but by some mystery, the case was never processed and because of their ages, their names were protected. Quite how such lenience is supposed to deter crime and protect the public, those responsible for this judicial lunacy did not care to explain.

The filming of even young teenagers having full sex and being whizzed around the internet is already commonplace in some countries.

In Perth, Scotland, 16-year old Callum McKinley circulated video evidence of his friend having sex with a 14-year old girl. How would you feel had that been your daughter, granddaughter or sister? The Sheriff's Court let him off so that he could pursue his football career. Well that's okay then. Perhaps it also gives us clues about why professional soccer players, who should be setting good examples to our youngsters, are all too often involved in scandals where their behaviour has been appalling.

As a parent myself, I should not be put in a position of unknowingly allowing my young daughter to go and play in the park with a young boy who may already have been found guilty of taking part in a gang rape – a crime which even pre-teenagers are increasingly committing, protected by the nonsensical law of anonymity for which there never was any justification. Every parent should be allowed to protect their own children by knowing the risks to which they may unwittingly be exposing them and they cannot do this if juvenile criminals are allowed to wander around incognito.

This totally illogical law does nothing to reduce crime and until it is scrapped, it will continue to be responsible for many crimes which otherwise would not have been committed, had it been made clear to all that the protection of anonymity was no longer available.

I know of no politician campaigning for the removal of this law, which sends precisely the wrong signal to both children, who may be on the edge of criminality, and to those parents who don't care what their kids get up to, provided that it does not become public knowledge and hence, a source of embarrassment to the whole family. Change this crazy do-gooder law which over-protects the guilty and we will find that the brains of many irresponsible parents will pretty quickly click into gear.

Most criminals weigh up the risks of being caught; the likelihood of then being taken to Court; the chance of then being convicted; and, if found guilty, the minor prospect of suffering any serious sentence for their crimes. Each of these elements, combined with ridiculous rules of evidence, represents a series of possible escape routes for the criminals and by loading the dice against the police, prosecution and prison services, politicians in some countries have been sending out clear messages to the criminal fraternity, that committing crime involves a very low risk of suffering any nasty consequences. The statistics clearly confirm that many criminals feel this low risk to be well worth taking.

Another wrong signal sent out by some judicial systems is that any guilty person can escape justice if some smart-ass lawyer can find that some aspect of "procedure" by either the police or prosecution has not been followed.

That the perpetrators of even serious crimes can avoid trial on any misjudged technicality of procedure is not only profoundly unjust for the victims, it gives the criminal fraternity yet another potential route to get off the hook. It makes a nonsense of the law and no country should allow any accused person to avoid a full trial and its verdict, just because somewhere along the line, correct procedure may not have been followed to the letter.

Procedural regulations are important of course, but in order to ensure that they are not ignored by those concerned, my proposal is that those failing to adhere to them should face sanctions. In serious cases, these could include personal fines and/or demotion. This, though, should be a separate issue to that of the innocence or guilt of any defendant.

I profoundly disagree with lawyers such as Nick Freeman (dubbed Mr. Loophole) who claim to deplore drink drivers and other criminals but see it as their "job" to defend them. Defend? Fine, if by defending, one puts forward plaintiffs' cases and challenges or disproves the prosecution's evidence. Regrettably though, it has become common practice for some lawyers not to do this, but to seek to help even their dubious clients evade justice and avoid a full and fair trial on nothing more than ferreting out mistakes in procedure. Any lawyers doing this, particularly those specialising in trying to get cases dropped on technicalities are, in my view, a disgrace and to do this whilst claiming to deplore the offences in question is the height of hypocrisy. I wonder if their reasons for doing this have something to do with the high fees they earn from helping criminals evade justice.

Unless we want to continue throwing justice into the trash can, it is imperative that we stop letting criminals walk free - or accused allowed to escape from even facing a full trial – just because a police officer has allegedly not read a suspect his rights about remaining silent; or a prosecution person had not properly submitted documents by a given time; or any other of a number of things had not quite been done by the book.

There are good reasons for many of these required procedural practices but they should be no more than good practice rules. Mistakes get made because even police officers, lawyers and court officials, including Judges, are human, but they should never be jumped onto to prevent any trial going ahead and the Court's verdict fully implemented. The victims of any crime deserve nothing less.

Having suffered the crimes, victims then agonise in uncertainty for the period of the police investigations, hoping their perpetrator will be caught before perhaps returning to do them more harm. If and when a suspect is apprehended, the victims then have the trauma of identity parades and assisting prosecutors in their preparation of the cases. Very often, they know with certainty that the accused is guilty but quite properly, the final verdict must be that of the Court.

Just imagine how those victims feel when, after their own suffering and stress and all of the time, money and other resources spent, the accused is got off the hook because some smart lawyer has outwitted the prosecutors on a point of procedure.

The people who should suffer the consequences of the breaches of rules should be those who breach them, either by fine, demotion or, if sufficiently serious, imprisonment for contempt of Court. The people who should not gain are those accused of crimes. They should face trial, regardless of any technical breach of procedure. Otherwise, the public suffers the dangers of criminals walking free and returning to commit further offences when a trial may well have seen them behind bars, perhaps for a very long time.

It is time to stop this nonsense, stop this huge waste of money preparing for trials which never come to fruition. Stop sending signals to criminals that they may be able to "buy" a breach of procedure.

Further decreasing the risk of suffering meaningful consequences, particularly for young criminals, is another highly-dangerous signal sent out by our judicial system. This is the practice, now well-established, of pleading for – and often getting – *leniency for first offences*.

Having spent many years researching then reflecting upon solutions to crime, scrapping first-offence leniency is high on my recommendations to politicians everywhere the practice has taken root. Here's why :-

• An undeniable truism is that if we could stop all first offences, there would be no crime at all – end of story, problem solved. Depressingly, few people recognise the fundamental importance of this. We all, therefore, have a responsibility to prevent as many first offences as possible and by being lenient towards them, we send out messages which, instead of deterring crime, actually encourages and increases it.

• In reality, *only very rarely are so-called first offences the first offence committed by the accused in question*. Invariably, those for whom defence lawyers plead "first offence" in Court, have already committed crimes for which they have either never been caught; been caught but only received one or more cautions from the police; been let off by the prosecution service; or been found not guilty of a crime which they had actually committed.

I long ago wrote to David Blunkett when he was Tony Blair's Home Secretary, taking issue with him about first offences, reminding him that technically, Ian Huntley, the murderer of two young Soham schoolgirls was a first offender, but only because his earlier offences had not been properly processed. Had they been, Jessica Chapman and Holly Wells would have been spared their terrible ordeals and would still be alive today.

Being lenient with those claiming to be first offenders therefore, is both illogical and counter-productive. I believe it is nonsense to broadcast to all and sundry that everyone is allowed to commit a "first" crime and probably not suffer the full rigours of the law appropriate to the offence. Many criminals are as smart as insurance assessors at weighing up risk. They consider most of the factors involved in the possibility/probability of getting caught and suffering serious consequences and wherever they calculate that, even if apprehended, they stand a good chance of getting away with a crime, this significantly increases the likelihood of them chancing their arm.

This is just one of the numerous causes of crime, but it is one of those which can quickly and easily be remedied – simply instruct all of those involved in the judicial process that they must ignore each and every plea for leniency based upon "first offence" excuses.

Taking this simple measure will also save many thousands of police investigation hours being thrown onto the scrap heap. It is hugely damaging to police morale when, having worked hard to discover the perpetrators of crime, often over long periods of time, they see the criminals walk away unpunished or given derisory sentences. If we are serious about crime reduction, our police services need supporting, not sabotaging and it is hugely counter-productive to throw their hard-won successes into the bin instead of giving them every possible help.

I long ago realised that sentencing the guilty amounted to little more than a lottery which sends out all the wrong messages to the criminal fraternity. Researching many aspects of judicial procedures, I found none which provided both protection for the public and fair consequences for those who committed the crimes. Any independent person or group seriously considering sentencing could not but conclude that in most countries, it is in a mess. Unfortunately, few politicians, bureaucrats or senior police officers set aside time to allow for serious contemplation, which is one reason why they fail to get to grips with the fundamentals of crime. Why, for example, do some countries allow the previous criminal records of accused persons to be hidden during any subsequent trial until after the Juries' verdicts.

In a 2006 UK survey, 77% of those questioned, disagreed with this nonsensical hiding of past criminal records and I have no doubt that this has resulted in many guilty parties escaping justice because the Courts did not perceive them as being capable of the crimes of which they were accused.

Past records should be made available during trials and prior to verdicts. Juries are not stupid. They are not going to convict anyone on their past record, but all too often, jurors feel cheated when they give an accused the benefit of the doubt only to find out later that they had had the wool pulled over their eyes.

Giving criminals the knowledge that their previous convictions could not be made available at an appropriate time in Court, is yet another wrong signal to be sending out to anyone contemplating crime.

My own system is to do masses of research, separate the facts from the myths, then spend hours, weeks or months searching for practical solutions – something which politicians and superficially successful people simply do not do.

My chapter "Chaotic Sentencing" is a good example of what results can emerge when individuals do not set aside ample time in which to think. Unfortunately, those climbing the career ladder, seeking to secure power, or chasing big bucks, do not appreciate the necessity for quiet contemplation, which is why they constantly tinker with crime instead of analysing the facts and thinking seriously about finding solutions to the problems.

The more thoughtful the country, the fewer the counter-productive signals, the lower the crime.

Very very few crimes would be committed if those contemplating them:-

- Knew that 75% or more offenders and not the 3% to 10% (according to country) were caught and punished.

- Knew that the Courts had no power to treat them with undue leniency.

- Knew that unprovoked violent offenders are certain to go to gaol, as may some who had suffered some provocation but responded with unnecessary violence.

- Knew that a lifetime sentence meant exactly that and those serving lesser sentences would get no more than a 5 to 10% reduction in time confined, which could only be earned by achieving "co-operative prisoner" status.

- Knew that Courts could not allow age, first-offence, being under the influence of alcohol or other drugs, as mitigating factors in crimes committed.

It is years of uncertainty about these and other crime-related causes which persuades many a criminal that the risks of getting caught and put away for a meaningful period of time are so small as to be well worth taking.

I have not the slightest doubt that sending out such signals of encouragement to the criminal fraternity is absolutely the wrong thing to do and those countries persisting with such practices have no hope whatsoever of escaping the dreadful and often deadly quicksands of crime.

Britain is one such country, having listened for far too long to the likes of Lord Chief Justice (as was) Lord Woolf, who insisted that **murderers**, no less, should have their sentences reduced by a third, simply for admitting their crimes. Whilst Lord Woolf was contributing to crime in Britain, Mayor Giuliani was doing exactly the opposite in New York. He energised his police force to rid his scary city of even low-level crime – graffiti, tramps, beggars and rough-sleepers. Harlem is now transformed, as are other previously no-go areas and one can walk Central Park without constant harassment. Armed muggings, robberies, rapes and murders have all dropped significantly. All because Mayor Giuliani scrapped many of the wrong signals which had been sent out for years and started sending out the right ones to the criminal fraternity. It did not take long for them to get the message.

Regrettably, Britain's current Senior Judge, Lord Chief Justice Phillips, is following his predecessor's failed practices. He is quite rightly proposing better use of Community Service Orders but still he does not campaign for a large increase in prison places for the really dangerous criminals. Telling these scores of thousands of still-to-be-caught guys that there are no prison places for them is dangerous in the extreme.

Had the judicial changes I am recommending in this book been in effect 6 to 10 years ago, Damilola Taylor and many many others would still be alive. His killers, both with criminal records, would not have been free to wander around and commit manslaughter. His killers, Danny and Rickie Preddie, who gave the police and prosecuting authorities more than a 5-year multi-million pound runaround, got away with manslaughter and 8-year sentences to Secure Youth Detention Centres and if the past is any guide, they are likely to be released early if they feign remorse, which they certainly did not show at their trial.

Damilola's father, Richard Taylor, quite rightly considers the sentences to be too lenient and too little of a deterrent. They were sentenced on 9th October 2006. Don't be surprised if they are let our before 2010.

You will read more about my proposals as you progress through my book, but to summarise their benefits, the Preddie brothers would have been taught from primary school age, via my proposed new examination subject (next chapter), that a whole range of seriously unwelcome consequences befall all law-breakers. They would also have learned that Courts could not give seriously discounted sentences for juveniles, nor could they have been treated lightly for any first offence – which their killing of Damilola Taylor of course was not. This pair of creeps were just cowardly thugs whom society had failed to dissuade from becoming gang member criminals. With my proposals, there would have been far more obstacles for the Preddie family to overcome if they wanted to continue along an anti-social path and in the event of them ignoring the rules, their killing of Damilola would have landed them in gaol, not for 8 reduced years but for 10 to 20 years – more if they had committed previous crimes.

Knowing all of this, it is unlikely that the paths of the Preddie brothers and their victims would ever have crossed and certainly not with the tragic results which caused Mr. Taylor to tell the world that his family felt so badly let down by all of the sectors of British society which had failed to deter his lovely son's killers.

What a pity that a lovely, talented young doctor and Oxford graduate died because those operating Britain's judicial system had sent all the wrong signals to 19 year old Nolan Haworth.

It has long been my contention that the term "serial offender" is a disgraceful admission of failure by any civilisation which permits such a phenomenon to develop.

No-one will ever know the true number of crimes Nolan Haworth committed, but within a few days of being released from a young offenders' institution (guilty of twelve crimes of violence and theft), he was involved in an affray with a knife, which resulted in two students being violently beaten.

Behind the wheel of a vehicle, he was a dangerous maniac. He frequently drove unsafe cars whilst banned from driving and he simply ignored such matters as road tax, M.O.T. certificates and vehicle insurance. By now, society should have either dissuaded this guy from his life or crime or put him in prison for a very long time. They did neither. The signal they sent out to Nolan Haworth instead, was that he could break whichever laws he chose without suffering any serious consequences and so it was, that on his way to Court in Banbury to face charges for the aforementioned violent affray, he borrowed a clapped-out old car and ended the promising career of recently-graduated Dr. Margaret Davidson. Margaret, despite her working-class up-bringing, was just about Nolan Haworth's opposite – responsible, hard-working and delightful.

Witnesses testified as to Haworth's driving like a lunatic, overtaking at high speed on a narrow road, overtaking suicidally on a blind bend and finally on the brow of a hill without visibility. Margaret Davidson was the unlucky one driving quite properly on her side of the road, coming the other way. She was killed instantly.

It could have been you; it could have been one or more of your loved ones, but on that day, it was Elizabeth and Joe Davidson's beautiful daughter. Their little girl.

The maximum penalty in England for causing death by dangerous driving is 14 years in prison – too little, in my view, for the most serious offences. In September 2006, Nolan Haworth was astonishingly gaoled by Oxford Crown Court for only 4 years, of which he will likely serve much less. Go figure.

Just another tragedy resulting from a dysfunctional judicial system.

Sensitively interviewed by John Humphrys on BBC Radio 4's Today programme, Margaret Davidson's mother Elizabeth read out her statement written for the Court. Added to the facts of the case, I find it wholly unacceptable that Mr. Haworth will be out on Britain's streets again in less than 4 years. Taking away his driving licence of course, only theoretically "bans" this creep from driving, because the Courts tried this unsuccessfully before. Like many others, Mr. Haworth simply puts up two fingers to the judiciary, to society – and to you.

Every day there are tragedies similar to those suffered by the Davidson family and friends. Our politicians, our Judges, our educationalists, our Social Services and our legal professions have known this for many years and have done nothing to seriously reduce it. I do not believe that you and I should tolerate such a disgraceful state of affairs and this book is all about identifying unacceptable crime and the solutions thereto.

Sadly, I cannot bring back Margaret Davidson or other victims, but I can provide those interested with solutions which will save many lives and injuries in the future.

Read on – and let 2007 be the start of sunnier times ahead.

Let us also stop the practice which in Ireland virtually tells potential criminals that they can escape a prison sentence, or at worst, get a seriously reduced punishment, by bribing the victim. Barry Duggan, for example, suffered a vicious beating from Dermot Cooper and Stephen Nugent. They gave him a fractured eye socket, a broken jaw and a fractured skull. A librarian, Barry Duggan was unconscious for hours, spent twelve days in intensive care and subsequently suffered anxiety attacks, loss of memory and the inability to read. For this disgracefully violent attack, Cooper and Nugent were give a 3-year prison sentence, but, because they paid an undisclosed sum in cash to the victim, their prison term was reduced to 22 months "suspended" and 3 months in a cushy training unit, which is better than many people's homes. This pair should have spent at least 5 years in gaol for such a violent attack. Mr. Dugan's G.P., Dr. Michael O'Tighearnaigh quite rightly was appalled that anyone inflicting serious head injuries should avoid a substantial prison sentence. Clearly, cases like this do absolutely nothing to deter others from committing violent attacks as their mood takes them. Nor was this an isolated instance, as my research attests.

The Republic of Ireland suffers huge violent crime, despite having such a small population and the lenience afforded even those found guilty of the vilest offences causes both the Gardai and the law-abiding to despair.

What signal does it send out to youngsters when David Naughton, 15 years old at the time and therefore driving illegally, was given a custodial sentence of only 3 years for his admitted dangerous driving. Tearaway Naughton absconded from Ireland where, despite having killed 2 friends and neighbours, he had been given bail.

Due to a whole series of blunders by Justice Minister Michael McDowell's department, it took three years to bring this irresponsible lout to Court. Mistakes in documentation resulted in Dangerous David avoiding completely being charged with driving without car tax, without insurance and without a driving licence. Despite being guilty of all of these serious offences, he escaped being tried for them – *on a technicality of bungled procedure*.

What kind of signal are you sending your youngsters, Minister McDowell? Could this be why tiny Ireland suffers one road death every day instead of the less than two hundred a year which would be more appropriate to its size?

I wonder, Minister McDowell, if you visited the relatives of the dead girls, Stacey Haugh aged 16 and Lorna Mahoney aged 13, the teenagers killed by David Naughton and explained to them why he is not spending at least ten years behind bars. I would also like to know if David Naughton will ever, legally, be allowed behind the wheel of a car again.

Until Ireland addresses these serious issues, many of its youngsters will continue tearing around like lunatics in cars which they mistakenly believe they can control.

People of Ireland – you have a vote. Chapter 19 shows you how to use it to express your dissatisfactions.

Another example of Ireland's wrongly-educated youth was the sickening attack by Sean Hayden who, simply to have his mates record the attack on their mobile phones for display on the internet, double drop-kicked Hazel O'Neill in the face. Taken completely by surprise by this cowardly flying kick in her face, Hazel was hurtled back fifteen feet before crashing over a bollard, adding a smashed arm to her facial injuries. Welcome to happy-slapping – the trendy game which our educated kids think is "fun".

Because of a legal technicality connected with the perpetrator already being under caution associated with a Garda Diversion Programme, coward Sean Hayden is unlikely to have to face trial. What king of signal is that, Mr. McDowell, to be sending out to your young people?

Until Hazel O'Neill's outraged father went onto a national radio programme in Ireland, the Gardai were disinclined to do anything significant about one of the most appalling crimes to come into my orbit. All the Gardai did was give this nasty low-life, who incidentally was already known to them, a "talking to" when in fact they and the D.P.P. should have thrown the book at him, starting on day one, when Hazel was hospitalised due to Sean Hayden's brutal attack.

I have news for Ireland's politicians, security services and judiciary – start catching and putting away far more criminals for longer terms or force your citizens to continue suffering high levels of crime. Carry on as you are doing and at some point, perhaps sooner than you think, you will deservedly suffer the wrath of the law-abiding people upon whose support you rely. Ireland's judicial system is in meltdown right now, typified by the pre-Christmas 2006 spat between the Chief Justice and Minister McDowell over revealing the names of 23 gangland suspects allegedly associates of murdered top drugs criminal Martin Hyland. The whole episode is a disgraceful can of worms, showing the entire Irish judicial system to be in total disarray.

Not that Ireland is alone. In Tony Blair's Britain, a hundred people in the last two years have been murdered by villains let out early from gaol on probation by the "Authorities" and what can one say about a nation where a young father dies in his 10 year old son's arms having been beaten to death after confronting trouble-making yobs outside their home? The thugs responsible were given two and a half year gaol sentences but of course, they will be released much earlier, simply because prison capacity is grossly inadequate. Could these ludicrous signals be the reason why UK citizens are so dissatisfied with their Government?

Britain also has its martial art, drop-kicking thugs, two of whom – unnamed by the Court for legal reasons (yuk) – knocked down 17-year old Willem Haymaker with a flying kick then beat him unconscious. Not content with that, these disgusting louts put their cowardly attack into a rap song, telling how they stamped and stamped and stamped and stamped until his whole ████ face was diminished. The song got worse, but one of the brutes was ordered to work with youth offender experts for 9 months and the other is being supervised for 2 years by the Probation Service. Yeah, right. Both had to pay £50 to their victim. How is that for sending out all the wrong signals, Messrs. Blair, Reid, Brown and co?

In December 2006 YouGov poll people reportedly claimed to be thoroughly fed-up with foul language, loutish behaviour, vandalism, graffiti and most of all, immigration. 62% said Britain has become a worse place in the last 5 years and more than 50% believe politics to be hugely corrupt. Having tracked all of these falling standards for more than a decade, I propose solutions in later chapters which hopefully will take root and reverse these terrible trends.

STOP PRESS 18 February 2007

Today is my last day for writing Quicksands of Crime – there has to be a deadline somewhere.

On this last day, Tinkering Tony is at it again, this time panicking about a recent spate of youth gun murders in South London. Yet again, T.T. sends out all the wrong messages to the country's criminal classes. He was confused about the current state of the law because he announced that the five-year mandatory sentence for gun possession is to be applied to 17-year olds – down from 21. In fact, his Government had already passed a 2004 law bringing it down to 18.

These arbitrary age limits make no sense whatsoever because parents and the drug traffickers get the message that, below a certain arbitrary age, these often dysfunctional youngsters will suffer no serious consequences even for carrying or using a gun. I very much doubt that Blair's announced summit on the subject (yes, I know – another summit) will send out the message which all of Britain's parents should receive, which is "If your child, or whatever age, commits a serious crime, they are going to be confined for at least 5 years." Send out this important and unequivocal signal and even the most dilatory of parents will begin to take a greater interest in what their kids get up to. They may even begin to search their rooms for guns and other weapons.

CHAPTER 7

WRONGLY-FOCUSED EDUCATION

The abandonment of discipline and the dilution of punishment for misbehaviour which began in the 1960s and which has continued progressively ever since, has been paralleled by falling respect, rising surliness and increased crime. Not all countries suffered serious juvenile crime at the same rate, but America led the way, with Britain, Ireland, Australia and others following, one to two years behind.

My research leads me to conclude that most countries have now lost sight of what we should expect of education. No longer does our Education Establishment strive to turn out well-rounded individuals with a thirst for genuine knowledge covering a wide range of interests. Instead, we have a sausage machine system designed only to force more of our kids through a straight-jacket examination regime. Very cleverly, the combined efforts of Government and some of the larger teachers' unions have dumbed down examinations, scrapped true learning, reasoning and creativity and substituted them with exam-passing tricks and shortcuts. Little more really, than a bunch of clever-clog nerds publishing and trading in a range of "How to Second Guess the Examination Boards" dodges.

This dumbing down is not, of course, the fault of our youngsters who have been taught that passing exams is not only life's primary purpose, but that any means of so doing is fair game. Little wonder therefore, that the seeds of discontent and destruction, sown year upon year in the fertile grounds of our Education Establishments, have now produced a plethora of dysfunctional weeds, hell-bent on sabotaging as much of the healthy harvest of students as possible

Serious damage has been done in our schools and universities, but all may not be lost. We still have plenty of fine young people, many of whom are concerned at the rise of disruptives in their midst. Unfortunately most countries are failing them.

Much of what needs to be done to reduce the criminality in schools and the number of anti-social yobs they are turning out, features in The Society for Action Against Crime's *"Education & Crime Report"*. This can be accessed via **www.crimedown.org**. It shows that I have been pressing Governments over many years to introduce a comprehensive *Concerns & Consequences* examination into all schools. Finally, Britain introduced a very inferior version of citizenship in 2002, but only in a very diluted and unimaginative form, devoid of any enthusiasm or understanding. On the very day that Tony Blair was delivering his final fantasy euphoria speech to the Labour Party Conference (26th September 2006) extolling the successes of his education reforms, it was reported that the teaching of Citizenship in Britain's schools was a dismal failure.

I have no doubt that failing education systems will continue churning out substantial numbers of criminals unless and until some radical new corrective measures are brought into effect.

At the same Conference, Prime Minister Blair waxed lyrical that all children have equal access to a quality education. Pity he had not read the Report roundly condemning the disgraceful education of 60,000 children in the State's care (via Social Services). Listening to Tony Blair one would expect the disadvantaged kids under the total control of the State would be better educated than the rest, but in fact, they were and still are so disgracefully treated as to give the lie to Blair's claims that his schools offer equal opportunities to all.

My recommendations are :-

• The introduction of a *Concern & Consequences* subject into the curriculum of every primary and secondary school in those nations which suffer high crime.

   It should be made a compulsory examination subject with running, term-time marks for behaviour featuring as a substantial percentage of the final certificate. This will eliminate the prospect of academically-gifted children being able to gain a good exam result even though their attendance and conduct records may have been below acceptable levels.

   Part of the *C & C* curriculum should continually show the benefits to students of the subject in later life and the importance which employers will undoubtedly attach to it. After my years of promoting the introduction of a *C & C* examination, the 'Power to The People' Report (February 2006) has caught up and recommends a "Citizenship" curriculum which they say should be shorter, more practical and lead to a qualification. I agree absolutely with the latter two conclusions but not the "shorter" aspect, because the prospect of any pupil straying into criminality is constant from primary school right through to leaving secondary education. To make the **Concern & Consequences** curriculum short would be a serious mistake.

The curriculum for my proposed **C & C** examination should, of course, be available to all home-schoolers and its importance to employers and higher education should be emphasised to all. This should not be a problem because home-schoolers turn out far fewer anti-social misfits than do conventional education systems.

It is hugely regrettable that some countries such as Germany ban home- schooling. Such suppression of their citizens' freedom to choose is a dangerous move in the direction of totalitarianism and I recommend every country to stop asserting that children belong to the State. In fact, they "belong" to no-one, but one thing for sure is that those mothers and fathers who take their responsibilities seriously have far more right to decide how their offspring are educated than does any Government.

German Authorities have constructed a database of suspect parents in order to raid those believed to be educating their children at home. Hmm. Remind you of anything?

From an early age, and continuing throughout, all pupils should be taught that there are **no** excuses for committing crimes. It should be made absolutely clear to them that whilst they may be deserving of our sympathy and support, neither poverty, having drunken parents, being abused or deprived of the electronic goodies which get thrown at their peers, can ever justify crime. That so many sociologists and smart lawyers plead leniency for young criminals on such grounds has served only to perpetuate the nonsensical myth that disadvantages entitle those who have suffered them to turn to crime.

Whilst it behoves parents to instil this message into their offspring, we all know that some of them fail in this duty, so it is doubly important that schools ensure that none of those they claim to be educating are left in any doubt that consequences inevitably follow criminality. It is not society's role to search around looking for reasons why young Jimmy is a sadistic little bully, or why Sally steals from shops and her classmates. It is society's role to protect the innocent by making it clear to all, that those ignoring its laws cannot escape the consequences of their actions, whatever their prior disadvantages.

I usually have little respect for the mumbo jumbo of social scientists, but one of their number, American Charles Murray, has obviously studied crime sufficiently to conclude that only retribution-based judicial systems can work and he recognised that in Britain, Tony Blair's promise to be tough on crime was always a non-starter. On one essential matter at least, Charles Murray and I are in absolute agreement. Britain will not substantially reduce its high levels of crime unless and until the culture of no – or minimum – punishment of the guilty is binned.

On the practical side, I would like to see included in the curriculum, visits to hospitals, police stations, Courts and prisons and victims of crime brought into the classroom to talk with pupils about the effects of crime. The *C & C* examination itself, should be compulsory and its passing, a requirement for entry into higher education or landing a worthwhile job.

• A tight anti-bullying programme is advised, with every pupil having to fill in a Bullying Report Form every week. This would give not only the direct victims an opportunity to name their bullies, it would allow any pupil to report, in confidence, the suffering of others, thereby enabling teaching staffs to identify both bullies and victims early and take appropriate action before events become tragedies. If politicians continue to resist the introduction of an on-going Bullying Report Form regime, concerned parents should run the system themselves at the school gate. Contact **pancho@crimedown.org** if you wish to discuss.

• Head Teachers to have the absolute right to expel any pupil for either serious violence, bullying, threatening behaviour or criminal damage. Neither Governors nor any Government Education Authority should be permitted to overturn any Head Teacher's disciplinary decisions, but they should, of course, always have the opportunity to ask for a reconsideration of any specific case.

• All serious crimes must be reported to the police for possible prosecution. All too frequently, schools prefer to sweep even serious bullying and criminal damage under the carpet, simply to present themselves in a good light, which is often contrary to the reality. This can and has led to vulnerable kids being murdered by bullies or being so desperate that they end their own lives. I am sure I don't need to ask how you would feel if it was your son or daughter stolen so cruelly from your life.

- Sufficient special needs schools should be available to rehabilitate disruptive or seriously disturbed pupils. It is crazy to allow the criminally inclined, or those constantly challenging the authority of their tutors, to prevent their conscientious peers from enjoying a trouble-free environment for their studies.

Changes to current education practices can contribute significantly to lower crime, but of course, they will take time to come fully on stream. All the more reason to take the necessary decisions without further delay.

To make this happen though, requires much greater public awareness of how badly most children are currently being educated. I have tried all of the conventional routes to encourage debate on these matters, but our politicians show neither understanding of the problems nor interest in seeking solutions. This is a major reason for writing this book, which I hope will stir many of you to action and open up wider debate in the high-crime countries where Governments and Educators are failing their communities.

Not that the problems are confined to schools. One only has to see the naked bullying which Political Parties use as a common tactic in forcing even members of their own Parties to abandon their consciences and judgement and vote for measures with which they fundamentally disagree.

Where Governments forsake reason and resort, instead, to blatant bullying in order to force elected representatives to toe the Party Line, they are showing our young people that if they cannot persuade, then blackmail, arm-twisting, threats and even violence are acceptable practice. That is what Parliamentary whips are all about. If the slaves don't obey, get the whips out.

Discipline alone, of course, will only solve some of the problems of schools turning out social misfits. To many pupils, of all capability levels, schools are little more than bastions of boredom, teaching far too little of either interest or value to adult life.

Many of the recommendations elsewhere in this book will, if implemented, have a far more immediate effect on driving down crime than those dealing with education, which inevitably needs years to feed through to maximum benefit. Nonetheless, continuing to neglect juvenile crime in schools would be a serious dereliction of duty and would, to some extent, sabotage what can be achieved by other initiatives. I not only want to see mature criminals deterred from crime or put out of circulation for longer periods, I want this done without our schools replacing them by feeding-in an endless supply of anti-social yobs at the bottom end of the chain.

Nor should we accept that the problems are confined to the bottom end of the social scale. It was four "supposedly" well-educated, upper middle class students of Dublin's Blackrock College who were involved in the beating and kicking to death of Brian Murphy (aged 18) on the 31st August 2000.

French "happy-slapper" Thomas Wehrung is not exactly a deprived person either. This "respectable looking" 22 year old and his friend decided it would be a great wheeze to attack an innocent bystander just to record it on their mobiles. What were the consequences? A £1,000 fine reduced by Judge James Scarry to £600. This privileged lout was in Dublin from France on a gap year before doing a Master's Degree. Educated? I think not.

Nor have some societies taken on board the fact that whilst at school and university, many young people are already on the road to drinking themselves to death. Indeed, for many students, binge drinking is their main pleasure in life and sadly, many continue drinking to falling over, vomiting or anger point into later life. Educated? Not by my understanding of the word.

When parents like Anne and Michael Plunkett, a Head Teacher and Probation Officer guided their son David through university, little did they think that he would succumb to the pervasive uni-drinking culture leading to his death. David was found 13 days after speaking gibberish on the phone to his parents. An excess of alcohol seemed to have caused him to fall into and drown in a canal after being thrown out of an "organised" student drinks event. Sadly I have many other tragic stories of drinks-related tragedies on file about students at a wide range of universities. You may well ask what on earth is going on at these seats of high learning and why those running them have allowed it to become the accepted norm for thousands of their students to have getting-out-of-their-heads-on-booze as their principle passion. Drinking at our universities has now reached epidemic proportions which contradicts the very words "higher education".

Constantly getting high on drink or drugs is not clever. Nothing wrong with a few drinks of course, and even occasionally going accidentally over the top may not be too disastrous. The problem lies in the university culture of going out with the single intention of getting smashed out of one's skull and being sniffy about others not wishing to do the same. That is downright dangerous.

Some serious re-education is needed and many groups are already aware of this, but seem devoid of solutions. ***Addicted Britain***, a Social Justice Policy Report reckons that in Britain, 3,000 to 4,000 kids as young as 11 years old end up in hospital with alcohol-related problems. Something is going seriously wrong when half of young teenagers admit to having at least one binge-drinking session every month, involving 5 or more alcoholic drinks.

Iain Duncan-Smith has quite rightly pointed the finger at family breakdown as a significant contributory factor. His Party's Social Policy Group commissioned YouGov to poll 40,000 people who had suffered social problems. It discovered that those from broken homes were far more likely to fail at school; become addicted to drugs and alcohol; get into debt; and claim social security benefit.

Going on to university seems not to beneficially improve these depressing trends.

Highly-educated Irishman Nialle Clarke in October 2006 was caught red-handed after having carried out an armed robbery at the Bank of America in Maine, U,.S.A. Clarke was acclaimed as one of Trinity College's (Dublin) highest-flying students and not only had he mastered all of the usual academic qualifications, he was sufficiently inventive to win accolades such as the Technology Innovation and the Enterprise Ireland student awards. Considered as an I.T. genius, he had earned substantial fees and yet this man's education – like that of so many others – was lacking in some fundamentally vital areas.

Nialle Clarke had been interviewed by the BBC expressing anger at the police response to the London underground bombings and their brutal extermination of innocent Charles de Menezes and he claimed to feel safer in third world countries than in London. These disturbances do not, though, explain how such an academically gifted man should turn bank robber and one's thoughts must go to his parents, who obviously thought that his educational qualifications had set Nialle up for a happy and successful life.

Harvard, the world's self-proclaimed best university, is also guilty of playing Power Politics and attempting to bully even its own teaching staff, to the dismay of most of its students. Facing a second faculty vote of 'No confidence', which he seemed sure to lose, President Lawrence Summers resigned, having challenged this august university to examine its teaching practices. Specifically, he wished to see more professors teaching a wider knowledge of their subjects instead of ever more narrowly-focused specialisation, which was their particular addiction. The tenured professors saw this as a threat to their wonderful cosy lifestyles, in which they can choose to teach the most ephemeral microscopic subjects of their own choice - the magnetic orientation of racing pigeon droppings perhaps. Even better for these permanently-embedded academics, if they teach nothing at all, they still get paid.

This, dear reader, is where making a God of education leads. Not to wisdom, not to common sense, just to playing the academic equivalent of a political power game designed to protect cosy and rewarding lifestyles which were never justified in the first place.

The problems causing high crime are many and they must all be tackled more or less simultaneously if we are to overcome them.

Better focused education is, though, one of the major elements in the Crimedown jig-saw puzzle. Right now unfortunately, it is little more than a scam, pretending that everyone, by passing a few exams, is "clever" and will be rewarded with a top job and a happy life. No-one will need to empty the bins, clean the streets and toilets, stack the shelves, make new roads, man the toll booths or checkouts, clean the buses, trains, ferries and planes, do millions of boring office jobs, staff the bars, hotels and restaurants etc. because they will all have passed some exams or other and so expect something much better.

Again, at his Farewell Party Conference, Tony Blair was puffing up his educational achievements - 50% of youngsters going to university, with ever more to follow. Necessary, he said, because China and India were churning out many more graduates. What he conveniently did not tell his audience was that China's and India's graduates are a tiny proportion of their populations and that no country needs 50% or more of its people to have university degrees. Why would they? Working for and getting a degree implies getting one of the better jobs as a result, but within a very few years, the folly of this "education, education, education" obsession will be there for all to see.

Having 50% or more of school leavers gaining degrees is frankly a crazy overkill because in no workplace is there – or will there be – sufficient numbers of higher paid jobs to employ all of these over-qualified graduates. Tony Blair of course is an excellent communicator, a class act – "**act**" being the operative word. He has honed his skills at persuading the gullible very deliberately but his image will, in my view, tarnish very quickly as the reality of his premiership becomes exposed. Very soon, Britain and some other countries will have some very angry graduates on their hands when they find themselves without the kinds of jobs to which they were misled into believing they would be entitled. When they discover, instead, that having studied for a further number of years and taken on tens of thousands of dollars/pounds/euros of debt and cannot get a job commensurate with their qualifications, Mr. Blair's promises of a wonderful world will be seen for what they were – smoke and mirrors.

Parents are conned into believing that if they do not get their children into the "good" schools or if they do not pass exam after exam, they are doomed. Parents are also falsely told that they have a choice of school. What utter garbage. I am constantly amused that parents swallow such lies. Clearly, however clever these parents consider themselves to be, they are devoid of basic common sense. Nor do they show much faith in their own kids if they believe they could not survive and progress in whatever school is closest to home.

Those parents who move house for no other reason than to be close enough to a "preferred" school are, in my view, contemptible because they are stealing a place at that school from someone more entitled to it. They are also aiding and abetting those who massively oversell the type of limited education peddled in most countries.

When we are turning out pupils who *all* understand that happy-slapping, kicking, thieving, bullying, spitting, stabbing and threatening are not what they wish to do – then, and only then, can we claim to be educating our youngsters.

It matters not if 80/90/100% get a Y+, an A-, a PPP with Honours in this, that or the other exam if a substantial percentage are still quite happy to indulge their criminal preferences. We should not be turning out young people, whatever their exam grades, if they do not fully understand the workings of the police, the Courts, Jury Service, the dangers of drugs and the effects of crime upon the victims.

Most anti-drugs education has frankly been either a pathetic failure or even counter-productive, largely because however skilfully the factual information has been presented, it simply does not strike the right chord with kids. What is needed is far more practical exposure to those *suffering from drugs and crime*, including face-to-face chats with people already in – or having been in – serious health and financial difficulties as a direct result of using drugs, including tobacco and alcohol. Yes, this will require radical re-structuring of most countries' education systems, talking time away from exam cramming and transferring it to matters of far greater practical worth. So be it.

The time is long overdue for us to stop wasting so much of the valuable time spent in schools. Time to concentrate a much higher percentage of this on teaching standards, behaviour, honesty, friendship, financial and health responsibility. We used to turn out youngsters far better prepared to deal with the practicalities of everyday life. This book is not the place to comprehensively deal with this, but I will give you just one example to show what is going wrong.

We have produced millions of students with excellent exam results in maths. How come then, that these youngsters go on to put their entire lives in hock by falling for the disgraceful entrapment by the financial services industry selling them highly-irresponsible mortgages on the most outrageous terms? Why were these students not educated to avoid such dangers? Why were they not warned that falling for such mortgage garbage would turn them into slaves for life? Or bankrupts.

Educationalists, really at the behest of Governments who in turn have pandered to big business and Trades Unions, have been criminal in their neglect of the environment in their curricula. I will discuss the hundred-year rape of our planet in a later chapter, but it is important to understand the connection between environmental damage and education.

There are eminent scientists such as James Lovelock who have known about the dangers and been warning Governments about them for decades, but politicians did not want the truth about environmental damage to be taught to our up-coming generations. Had they listened, our schools would, by now, have turned out millions of citizens far better able to care for planet earth. Their failure so to do has been short-termism of the highest order of irresponsibility which has damaged our world, very possibly beyond the point of its salvation.

Even now, in 2006, the seriousness of the situation is still being kept under wraps and I know of no country which is providing students in our schools and universities with the information they will need if they are to escape the appalling legacy we are dumping on them. It is no exaggeration to say that unless we immediately start giving today's and tomorrow's youngsters the information and tools they need to understand how to handle a century's abuse of our environment, there will be no hope of even beginning to correct what is already close to being irreversible.

Too many of our over 30s are already difficult to energise on this vital subject, often because they have become entrenched establishment figures who simply do not wish to acknowledge that we all have many lifestyle changes to make. With the help of a few scientists and thinkers, it will be down to today's kids to save the planet for themselves and for future generations. This will necessitate urgent changes to every country's education system. Failing this, things worldwide will get very ugly. The question is – "Are our Political Leaders serious about the environment? – or are they just making speeches about it and tinkering with matters which in fact require fundamental changes *starting today*?"

I tell you plainly – there is not a moment to lose.

For more than 15 years I have advocated votes for 16-year olds and the prospect of more countries introducing votes at age 16 does now seem to be improving. Perhaps my campaigning has made a contribution. Again, the Isle of Man leads the way with its recent enfranchisement of its 16-year olds.

That said, it would seem sensible to restrict voting rights for all ages to those who have demonstrated a knowledge of their social responsibilities by passing the *Concern & Consequences Examination* which should be certificated as a stand-alone subject.

Passing the C & C examination should also be a condition for getting a driving licence and driving should feature significantly in the curriculum throughout each child's life.

See later how driving licences also feature in my new Court sentencing solutions.

A significant factor in wrongly-focused education in many countries is that from a very early age, *kids know almost everything about their rights but almost nothing about their responsibilities*.

It is for you to decide whether or not you are living in such a dysfunctional environment.

CHAPTER 8

THE POLICE AND SECURITY SERVICES

It is appropriate here to differentiate between a Police State and a State where there are plenty of street cops in evidence. Police States are those countries where politicians impose ever more rules, regulations and restrictions on its *law-abiding* citizens. Police States spy on innocent people and insist upon businesses spying on their customers and reporting to the Authorities (secretly) the most trivial transactions. Police States pass laws requiring everyone to carry Identity Cards and seek to keep suspects – that elastic word – in detention for long periods without charging them with any crime. Police States conduct surveillance of even law-abiding citizens' phones and computers without the authority of a Judge and they similarly invade people's homes, often secretly.

In June 2002, Dr. Ron Paul, Republican Member of Congress, was asked "Is America a Police State?" His response – "Not yet, but it is fast approaching" and he went on to give chapter and verse why. Whilst I believed the U.S. to already have been a Police State in 2002, events since have proved us both right. Long before 9/11 (2001) – in January 2000 in fact – Congressman Paul, on the floor of the House, prophetically warned "We are placed in greater danger because of our arrogant policy of bombing nations that do not submit to our wishes. This generates hatred towards America and exposes us to a greater threat of terrorism." What a pity his warning was ignored. Had it not been, the attack on the twin towers 19 months later may never have taken place.

Randy Weaver failed to turn up in Court to answer a minor gun charge, of which there are many thousands in America due to a myriad of highly-technical regulations which are clearly only there to trip up those who cannot keep abreast of them. I have tried to study these regulations but they vary State to State and contain thousands of items which can only be described as trivial, often nonsensical, affecting neither the safety nor the danger of the weapons in Question.

America's F.B.I. agents stormed Randy Weaver's Ruby Ridge home and without cause or warning, shot dead his wife and son.

No-one was held to account for those State-inspired murders, yet George Bush bangs on about spreading American values around the world. Those not wanting to live in a Police State should hope that President Bush fails in his attempts to spread his warped values around the world.

Democracy is the drum which Bush and Blair bang, but I for one cannot reconcile the destruction of privacy, liberty and freedom with their warped kind of democracy.

To the serious detriment of their citizens, many Governments, in their never-ending drive for greater control, have opened up a huge gap between the Security Services and the people. Those Governments mistakenly choosing this route fail to understand (or care) that Police Forces operate most effectively when locally focused and when accountable to the local communities which they are there to serve and protect.

Listen to what Gordon Brown, Britain's Chancellor of the Exchequer and wanabee Prime Minister said at two highly-public events within two weeks.

On the 25th September 2006, at the Labour Party Conference in Manchester, England he said :- "Governments must be the servants of the people" and "people should take power from the State".

Unfortunately, he must have suffered a serious loss of memory because on the 10th October 2006 he made a public address which, in essence, was exactly the opposite of his previous utterings. It was, in fact, a diatribe of ever more invasions by the State of personal and business freedoms, all of course excused on the grounds of protecting us from terrorism.

Longer detentions without charge – already upped from 7 days to 28 days, yet Gordon Brown wants more, as I always forecast he would.

More freezing of suspects' bank accounts, leaving "intelligence" to decide who is a suspect – like they knew that Iraq had weapons of mass destruction – and many other control-freak measures which gave the lie to his Party Conference speech about the State giving power back to the people.

It is easy, of course, and a time-honoured tactic for politicians to scare some of their people about ever more threats to their security and yes, we do face dangers, but not of sufficient magnitude to merit our traditional freedoms being stripped away step by step.

I do not want your kind of world Mr. Brown - your world of finger-printing, iris recognition, recording private health, banking, travel and library information of every law-abiding citizen about whom you already have too much data on file. I and many others do not want a "your papers please" society. We do not want to take time off work to turn up to your designated locations to be interviewed, measured and photographed just to provide you with a document to which you and your ilk will add ever more information about us, accurate or not we may never know.

We far prefer, Mr. Brown, for you to use the brains which are supposedly available to Governments to dissuade and apprehend terrorists without impinging in any way on the rights and freedoms of law-abiding individuals.

We prefer to accept whatever risk there is from terrorists because terrorism is just another of life's risks and for each individual, it is far from being the most dangerous. I do not need you Mr. Brown to protect my identity. I do not need you to save me the bother of carrying other cards because I am free to choose whether or not I carry these other cards, nor are they on some mega database available to a whole range of petty bureaucrats. In short Mr. Brown, do what David Cameron claims to want (yet to be proven) – get your Government out of our lives.

Only those countries aiming to create Stasi/K.G.B. type Police State regimes seek to have centrally-controlled Security Services to whom they inevitably give excessive powers of surveillance, secret search, asset seizure, arbitrary arrest, detention without charge, etc. – not just of seriously suspected villains but potentially of every law-abiding person. This does massive damage to the relationship between police and public which in turn results in more crimes being committed and fewer crimes being solved.

No Police Force can operate in a vacuum, although some seem to believe they can. Senior police officers, often those who see policing as a career more than a service, are too often out of touch, not only with the public but with their own officers. They too readily suck up to politicians without regard to the damaging consequences. Too many Sheriffs and Chief Constables spend far more time courting their political nabobs than they do preventing or solving crime. One way to correct this in Britain, which has an appalling level of crime, is to disbar police personnel from ever receiving knighthoods or, on retirement, being handed a cosy quango job for having cosied up to their elected representatives. They should be full-time occupied with crime. They should at all times be personally responsible for at least one crime investigation and they should spend a minimum two days a week on the beat, either alone or with a constable colleague. In other words, they should never be allowed to lose touch with the coal face.

Police officers, of every rank, are there primarily to keep the peace; to do this as peacefully and as courteously as the circumstances permit; to find evidence sufficient to bring law-breakers to Court; and to be as visible and available as possible to those who need their help. They are not there to be punch-bags for the drunks, the malcontents or the short-tempered and it is to their credit that in many countries, most of them handle such abuse with considerable restraint.

Nor should police officers be forced by politicians and civil servants to spend ever-increasing amounts of their time filling in forms and recording for recording's sake. This is hugely wasteful, morale-sapping, counter-productive and it is a major factor behind the appalling statistic that between 90 and 97% of crimes are never punished. These are truly dreadful facts and these depressing levels of unpunished crimes are the direct result of gross mismanagement and interference by inept administrators. This is why so few police are seen walking the streets, chatting to people from every walk of life, getting to know as many individuals by name (and vice versa) and generally keeping their eyes and ears open. Until we get away from career, behind-the-desk ladder-climbers, and return to community policing, those crazy levels of 90%+ of crimes going unpunished will not be lowered.

One of the complaints I constantly hear from sheriffs, Deputies, police constables, sergeants and inspectors is the mountain of forms they are expected to process and I have no doubt that if all of the senior officers were regularly required to do the same work, there would be a marked reduction in the number of new forms continually being dreamed up. Whenever bureaucrats set "targets",

146

whether in policing, health or education, down, not up goes the actual service because those faced with operating the system do not wish to be seen as missing the targets, however crazy they may be. Inevitably this leads to prioritising the soft options instead of the more important ones.

Police officers are simply citizens authorised to keep the peace. It is a job which has unpleasant and sometimes dangerous aspects and those who choose to do this honestly and to the best of their ability deserve our respect, our thanks and our support. Officers such as P.C. Henry Garrod have risked much, including death threats, in their determination to bring peace via zero tolerance to their previously unruly areas. Quite rightly, they get the approval of their law-abiding citizens. Britain needs more officers like Henry Garrod just as America needs more like Bill Bratton who halved the murder rate using zero tolerance in New York, then went on to seriously diminish the power of Los Angeles' vicious gangs – resulting again in a drop of more than 40% in the murder rate. It can be done.

All too often though, in recent years, the standard of leadership, from the Home Office down to Assistant Chief Constable level, has been so misguided as to seriously damage morale and consequently failed to reduce crime to the far lower levels which I know to be possible.

High crime levels are not, of course, only due to misguided police forces. They are simply one of many factors which I include elsewhere in this book - just another piece, albeit a very important one, in the jigsaw puzzle of crime. Over-riding forces such as America's Federal Bureau of Investigation and the Bureau of Alcohol, Tobacco and Firearms and numerous Drugs Enforcement and Anti-Terrorist organisations have simply made basic policing much more difficult and far less effective. Many readers will know nothing about these centralised Agencies' appalling and disgusting records of abusing, bullying, threatening and even deliberately murdering their own citizens. America's Central Intelligence Agency, for example, has developed into an out-of-control, restrained by no-one organisation which has respect for neither the Constitution, the law, justice or human rights.

Every country, of course, should have a completely independent Body or Bodies available at all times to consider complaints against every arm of the police, revenue, intelligence, military or other such service. These independent Complaints Authorities should have full investigative powers and the freedom to report to the public, not just to Governments who invariably suppress or tinker with any findings likely to cause them embarrassment.

I have been lobbying for all serious complaints against the police to be heard in public by some kind of revolving, independent Complaints Body. At long last, the UK Government announced on 3rd January 2006 that it was to make the first tentative step in this direction by authorising an initial case heard in public (in England and Wales). This is welcome, but it should not be allowed to be no more than gesture politics.

Any nation wanting to reduce crime must have security personnel whose standards are seen by the general populace as being high. The natural reaction amongst any organisation to complaints is to close ranks, obstruct, obfuscate and be secretive about any evidence which may put them in a bad light. That is not acceptable because, quite apart from the injustice of the truth never emerging, enormous damage is done to the trust which the people should have in its security services. My preferences would be for all **Complaints Bodies** to be comprised of seven independent persons chosen from an available panel of say one hundred people, at least two thirds of whom should be ordinary citizens, not unlike jurors in fact. The selection of the seven to consider each case should be random. A small standby fee would be appropriate with a daily payment made to those chosen to adjudicate in individual cases.

Centralised policing is bad policing. It is local coppers, sheriffs, gendarmes or Garda on the ground, operating locally, who can best deal with every type of crime, be it domestic violence, burglary, organised crime, terrorism, fraud, mugging or kidnapping. Countries such as Andorra, Switzerland, Finland, Uruguay, Canada and Botswana have very low levels of crime because they understand that successful policing is almost entirely down to good quality local units and not supposedly cleverer centralised special bodies.

After the Iraq war debacle, the world now knows what I have long warned about – that **Intelligence** in the military/surveillance/information gathering context is little short of a joke. Little more, in fact, than a plaything of politicians and senior civil servants, used as an excuse to enable them to do things which they know the

148

myriad of signs, signals, camera warnings, cameras etc. instead of doing what I should be doing, - which is examining the road and my mirrors – not looking down at my speedo every few seconds. This constant checking of speedometers and excessive signage and cameras is downright dangerous and the cause of numerous accidents, including deaths.

Glib comments from the Chief Constable Richard Brunstroms of this world, that speed kills, are as pathetic as they are dangerous. As a straight fact, of course, speed can kill, but it is usually not the only factor. The combination of speed with other factors are highly relevant and Mr. Brunstrom should know that the first recorded road death occurred at 4 (yes, that's four) miles an hour. Had Brunstrom been around at the time, he would probably have been sounding off to the press, calling for a 2 miles per hour limit.

Britain is the speed camera capital of the world and North Wales is the speed camera capital of Britain.

Unfortunately for the publicity-seeking Chief Constable Brunstrom, the obsessive promoter of these cameras, their increase has had three unfortunate side effects, namely huge costs to the public, loss of licences for various periods and surprise, surprise, an 18% increase in road deaths in his area - this compared with significantly falling deaths in areas with far fewer cameras.

So, let's get real here. Be as honest as I am. Just about everyone exceeds some speed limit or another almost every time they drive and some have had their licences suspended in what is nothing more than a reverse lottery. Make no mistake, it could as easily have been you, your political representative, any off-duty police officer, lawyer, priest, entrepreneur or grannie. Don't get me wrong. We need speed limits and their enforcement should not be abandoned. However, some countries – America and Britain being prime examples – spend far too many resources persecuting and prosecuting minor speeding offences where there is absolutely no suggestion of careless or dangerous driving.

A perfect example of this in Britain was the driving ban imposed on the Queen's cousin, the Duke of Gloucester, caught speeding for the fourth time in three years. He was doing 70 m.p.h. on a 60 m.p.h. road – and which of us has not, I ask? Because of this, he faced dismissal from the position he had held for more than thirty years – that of the President of the Institute of Advanced Motorists. Now – I am absolutely not suggesting that his rank and position should have resulted in a different outcome. No – he was quite rightly treated like everyone else. What I am saying is that the entire system of fines, points on licences and driving bans for non-dangerous offences are a farcical, illogical lottery. It took the Duke of Gloucester almost three years to rack up his four "offences" but many do this within weeks or months. Such is the nature of this nonsensical attitude to technical transgressions of arbitrary speed limits which are all too often pulled willy-nilly out of the air.

It is not always the police who are responsible for injustice, of course. All too often the Courts act in a manner which can best be described as bizarre.

Compare the disqualification of the Duke of Gloucester for doing 70 on a 60 m.p.h. road with that of professional soccer player Diomansy Kamara. The police, quite rightly, pulled over Kamara for doing **110 m.p.h.** on a 70 m.p.h. road but, inexplicably, the Court did not disqualify the Senegalese footballer. Instead, they fined him £1,000, which was no more than a naughty-boy slap on the wrist to a player reportedly earning £60,000 a month. I propose practical solutions to such ridiculous inconsistencies in later chapters.

How about this for crazy justice?

An off-duty policeman claimed to be honing his skills as a traffic cop when caught driving above Britain's maximum 70 m.p.h. speed limit. Not just above it. Not just 10 m.p.h. above it, as did the Duke of Gloucester. Oh no. Police Constable Mark Milton was recorded on a police patrol car's video camera doing 159 m.p.h. Yes, you read me correctly – *one hundred and fifty nine miles an hour*, which is 89 miles an hour *above* the top speed limit.

Only after a lot of legal shenanigans was PC Milton eventually charged, quite rightly, with dangerous driving. He was originally cleared but the High Court overturned the acquittal and ordered a retrial. He was then found *guilty*. His sentence? Zilch, didley squat, zero, nowt.

He wasn't fined.

He suffered no points on his licence.

He was not given a prison sentence.

He didn't lose his job.

He wasn't even demoted.

We will never know, of course, what if any pressures had been brought to bear on District Judge Peter Wallis to cause him to treat a dangerous driving police officer with such incredible leniency, declaring that he had "suffered enough" with two and a half years of Court proceedings. What we do know though, is that had it been you or I travelling at such high speeds, we would have had the book thrown at us.

Such perversion of justice is highly damaging to relationships between the police and the public and as far as I can tell – speed kills, camera-happy Chief Constable Brunstrom did not rush into print, as is his wont, to register his disgust at the leniency shown to this officer. Nor, to my knowledge, is he campaigning to have PC Milton removed from either the force or from traffic duty. Doubtless he will correct me if I am wrong.

Will PC Milton still feel justified in handing out tickets for minor speeding offences and possibly losing safe drivers their licences? Very likely.

If so, how would you feel if you were the recipient of such a ticket which may be the one which results in your driving licence being suspended? I can't speak for the Duke of Gloucester of course, but having discussed the case with many others, I know how they and I would feel. Outraged.

The serious question which should be asked of every Home Security Department is "Why are you allowing your Police Authorities to devote manpower and money chasing millions of minor speeding offenders instead of focusing on the really serious criminal fraternity?"

Are we talking stealth tax revenue here? Or are our police forces so mismanaged that they are allowed or encouraged to waste their time on benign drivers because this is easier than going after the really bad guys. Almost everyone involved in Homeland Security constantly complains that they have far too few resources, too little money, too few personnel. This being so, there is something very seriously wrong with their priorities when both the police and the Courts waste so much of their limited time and resources on motorists driving in a perfectly safe manner.

I warn those countries who are criminalising their law-abiding citizens for minor speeding infractions – where there is no evidence of dangerous driving – that they are planting very dangerous seeds which will grow to haunt them. Ditto for the myriad proposed schemes for road-use tracking and pricing, charging to park outside one's own home and selected vehicle discrimination.

Some bureaucrats and politicians believe that motorists are nothing more than individuals of little consequence who will do nothing more than send the occasional letter to a newspaper editor (little chance of publication) or perhaps even their political representative (a complete waste of time and postage). They believe road users, because of necessity, will tolerate any amount of financial milking and suffer any amount of attacks on their freedoms and livelihoods. My research tells me that they are very mistaken and that a very dangerous head of steam is building up against the Governments of those countries prosecuting millions of otherwise upright citizens. Some are beginning to organise themselves into a range of protection and protest groups and I have no doubt that the politicians in the countries abusing their motorists have succeeded in breeding yet another family of potentially home-grown terrorists.

My advice is to stop persecuting those responsible for the minor infringements of speed limits; to immediately abandon all road tracking and pricing schemes and charging for parking in non-congested areas; to be more pro-active in finding and persecuting those without valid insurance or, where required, road fund licence; those driving unroadworthy vehicles; those driving dangerously; and those driving under the influence or alcohol or other drugs.

People of different nations have already demonstrated their – albeit reluctant – tolerance of high fuel taxes which vary between very low to around 80% of paid pump prices. This level of tolerance is really a question of how much tax the Executive can persuade its electorate

156

to accept, but I believe tax on fuel to be the fairest system of road pricing which acknowledges environmental concerns whilst keeping bureaucracy costs and injustices to a minimum. It is the burden and unfairness of the multiple impositions on everyday motorists which is rousing them to anger and action and my earnest advice to those responsible is that if they continue to disregard their concerns, they do so at their peril and I do not issue such an advice lightly.

Unless and until our police services significantly reduce the growing number of violent deaths and injuries suffered at the hands of hardened merciless criminals, they have no moral right to be wasting time on people driving at 50 m.p.h. in a 40 m.p.h. area. Every day I am on the road, I witness appallingly dangerous driving – lunatics overtaking several vehicles on blind bends; tail-gating; undertaking then forcing a way back into original lanes; shooting out at junctions; ignoring red lights etc. etc. Not once, in the numerous countries I drive in, have I ever witnessed any perpetrator of these truly dangerous driving practices pulled up by the police.

I also had a serious run-in with the UK Home Office when I was taking them to task about the damage, personal injuries and deaths caused by uninsured drivers. David Blunkett showed no interest whatsoever in my concerns and his civil service flunkies attempted to fob me off with tales of maximum fines for driving whilst uninsured. It took months of determined research to discover that no-one had ever been fined the maximum, but still, no-one at the Home Office gave a damn. Likely because of public campaigning, the police in Britain can now instantly check any vehicle's road tax and insurance standing – a system which I have long fought for and which other high car crime countries such as Ireland and France should adopt a.s.a.p.

What we next need is better support from the Courts to ensure that, when apprehended, those guilty of either dangerous or uninsured driving, suffer suitable consequences. Too many families have been decimated by their loved ones being maimed or killed by irresponsible drivers and the seriousness of this is reflected in my later chapter on New Sentencing Solutions. In short, all police forces and the Courts should tread more lightly on the non-threatening drivers and much more heavily on those who drive dangerously and every country should permit its traffic police to stop any driver without reason and require them to take an alcohol or drugs test with serious consequences for those exceeding permitted limits.

We should cut out the knee-jerk conditioning that all excesses of arbitrary speed limits are either dangerous or criminal because, as the song says – it aint necessarily so. Furthermore, if everyone stayed within all speed limits at all times, instead of safely exercising their own judgement, the countries concerned would often come to complete gridlock at significant cost to their economies. Not only that, the cost in lost fines and additional labour hours would be huge. The fines, of course, are primarily a stealth tax and, as with the billions of dollars/euros or pounds of taxes levied on tobacco, politicians welcome the contributions made to our Exchequers by those who marginally exceed speed limits without danger and those who smoke or partake of the hard stuff.

The environment would also suffer hugely if everyone stayed scrupulously within speed limits because many transport jobs which can now be done in one day, with the drivers playing catch-up when running late, would not be possible. Inevitably this would impose huge additional costs on every commercial vehicle operator for having to fund extra journeys and in the final analysis, both the additional financial and environmental costs are paid by you and me. Driver productivity would also fall because in each of their legally permitted periods of driving time, they would travel short distances if staying strictly within speed limits. This would result in one day's work being unfinished and causing an expensive chain reaction throughout work schedules.

I would also like you to think about another piece of road traffic hypocrisy wherein the police and some Courts are shooting themselves in the foot. If you warn other motorists of their approach to any kind of speed detection system, the police are likely to charge you with a criminal offence and regrettably, Courts seem not to recognise the illogicality of this nonsense.

The police and road traffic authorities cannot have it both ways. They claim that speeding is dangerous, but then promptly try to thwart the efforts of the responsible motorists who try to warn other road users to slow down (if they are speeding).

Yet another example of absurd priorities, where it has become more important to "catch" someone than it is to stop hundreds of motorists from travelling at speeds which the police themselves purport to cause accidents. This is bizarre and it is doubly damaging because it quite unnecessarily widens the gap between the police and the public. Nor is it sensible to further burden overstretched Courts with such nonsensical cases when there are huge backlogs of really serious offences queuing up to be determined.

Many countries cannot, or will not afford the funds required to properly deal with every breach of the law, so it behoves them to concentrate on serious crime and not waste their limited resources on offences which can, at best, be described as technical transgressions.

Around the world there are millions of murders, rapes, child and animal abuses, muggings, con-tricks, burglaries and corruption which remain unsolved and these and other serious crimes are the ones which every police authority should be focusing upon, if necessary at the expense of more trivial offences. To do otherwise simply confirms that the authorities are more concerned with grabbing easy fines than they are with catching the real villains.

As you will see in later chapters, I am not advocating a free-for-all for minor offenders, just a serious re-adjustment of priorities which will improve co-operation between the public and the police, instead of further sabotaging them.

Good local policing is the answer, with each Police Authority covering an area as small as is geographically sensible. Those advocating ever larger Police Authorities will inevitably cause more crime, not less. Success will only come from both uniformed and non-uniformed officers having close ties with as many people on the ground as possible.

In Britain, Tony Blair has a record of picking hopeless Home Secretaries with all four, in nine years, failing to reduce violent crime. Jack Straw was simply a nonentity. David Blunkett, Charles Clarke and John Reid were chosen as tough-talking bully-boy types, but as with most bullies, they never took on the tough opposition. They chose, instead, to attack the freedoms of the mainly passive law-abiding sector of society and, to rub salt into their citizens' wounds, they used billions of pounds of their taxpayers' own money to do it. Had Blunkett and Clarke not wasted so much of their time and taxpayers' funds trying to force Identity Cards onto an electorate which neither asked for nor wanted them, many more serious criminals would have been caught, more prison places could have been created and violent crime would be around half of today's level.

I make no secret of my behind-the-scenes campaigning to have David Blunkett and Charles Clarke removed from their roles as Home Secretaries because both were dangerous to the freedoms of law-abiding Britons and deficient in tackling violent crime and providing prison places sufficient to deter the UK's huge criminal element.

Unfortunately, previous Home Secretaries and Tony Blair have left John Reid between a rock and a hard place with expanding violent crime and nowhere to put the perpetrators. He has yet to show a real understanding of the seriousness of crime in Britain and one should only make limited allowances for his being Home Secretary for less than a year at the time of writing because in my view, every politician should at all times have ideas in mind for tackling crime.

Tony Blair, of course, has left any Home Secretary and his successor with the millstone of ID Cards around their necks. His successor will feel very disinclined to call an early General Election to confirm his/her public acceptance because as the realities of Identity Cards emerge, such Election would likely be lost.

Should the Labour Party succeed in forcing ID Cards onto the electorate, I believe they would be deposed at the next General Election by those committed to cancelling them.

It is counter-productive to have aggressive personalities in charge of Home security because those who are always baring their teeth invariably lack integrity and good judgement. What is needed for this most difficult of roles is less Rottweiler, more sheepdog.

Security services generally, currently have huge technical capabilities at their disposal and quite rightly so. They must be given whatever state of the art equipment is available in order to counter the increasingly sophisticated operations of organised crime, in which I include planning or executing acts of terrorism. That said, no arm of any security service should willy nilly be given carte blanche to raid premises, tap phones or hack into computers etc. without securing a warrant from a Judge, who would have to be provided with good cause for any clandestine invasions of property and privacy. All security services should, of course, keep suspects' movements under observation, recording and photographing their whereabouts, activities and contacts.

Evidence gained by such pre-authorised methods should, of course, legitimately be available for any trial jury to consider. What should not be permissible under any circumstances are invasive fishing operations without prior warrant from an independent Judge having been granted. That is the direct route to Police States which regrettably some countries, Russia and America included, have already taken. All security services should be accountable and when they are, they should be properly financed.

I do have concerns though, about the expectations from techniques such as telephone bugging by whatever means, nor am I happy that terrorists and organised crime have so openly been warned about the fact that Governments have them on their radar screens by highly-sophisticated surveillance systems. To me, this is a remarkable under-estimation of our adversaries, which is always a mistake. Very few of those involved in either organised crime, terrorism or both, are stupid. None are likely to go into a bank, pull a gun on a bank teller and in a low voice say "Air in the hands – this is an upstick".

Foolishly, politicians never stop talking about the fact that Governments' security services have the most sophisticated secret surveillance equipment. Being forewarned, I would be amazed if the seriously bad guys – be they terrorists or international counterfeiters - any longer use their own telephones or computers which could possibly convey anything of significance to the security services. To believe otherwise is frankly naïve and a serious misreading of the threats which face us.

I regret to say that too many of our politicians mistakenly believe that spending billions on trawling the bank accounts, phone calls and internet use of millions of their law-abiding citizens is likely to end terrorist attacks. It will not. It is a misapplication of resources which would be better spent on other security measures more likely to identify and track real suspects.

America's Homeland Security Administration supposedly has the tracking and arrest of terrorists as its primary objective but that is not correct. Fortunately, even amongst those who operate the U.S.A.'s infamous "no-fly" list, there are those who are so disgusted with it that information about its use leaks out on occasion.

The U.S.A. is, in fact, engaged in that most dangerous of games – the identification of President Bush's political and social enemies. Of the approximate 45,000 names on "the list", my information is that 99% have never had any connection whatsoever with terrorism and most of that 99% have done nothing worse than speak out against the ghastly Baby Bush. So afraid of truth is America's pathetic President that he insists that his Homeland Security Gestapo spends hundreds of millions of dollars of his citizens' taxes trawling through billions of fragments of their personal data - which should have nothing to do with politicians - just to find out sufficient about their opinions to put them on the supposedly secret "no-fly" list. This spiteful individual has no qualms about using such quite legitimate opposition to his incompetence to cause serious travelling problems to those who dare to challenge him.

I and others have long been advising people not to travel to scary America and it seems that I am not alone in seeing the dangers. No need to take my word for it. Geoffrey Freedom of the Discover America Partnership has remonstrated with Washington because visitor numbers are down 17% since President Bush's war on terror. Mr. Freedom has called upon his Government to stop treating international travellers like criminals – "we are making them feel uncomfortable, so not surprisingly they prefer to go to other countries". Typically, the U.S. administration has dismissed the concerns of the Discover America Partnership as being no more than the greed of their travel industry. At what percentage drop in visitor numbers, I wonder, will someone in the White House realise that foreigners do not wish to spend their money in a country which treats them in such a high-handed and abusive manner.

In Britain, the two Blairs managed to hike up the spend of London's Metropolitan Police Force to an astonishing £3.2 billion! with an unhealthy amount of this protecting "important" people. The budget for this in 2006 increased by an amazing £100 million to £500 million, whilst that for routine police work dropped significantly. Such misallocation of funds is just one of many reasons why Tony Blair's Government has failed so miserably to make serious inroads into crime.

But what can one expect from the then Deputy Commissioner Ian Blair, who played a major role in a supposed corruption enquiry in which he authorised the secret and illegal phone-tapping of one of his own officers, Chief Superintendent Dizael. At the Old Bailey trail, Mr. Dizael was completely exonerated. He was also awarded £80,000 compensation. The UK taxpayers were not so lucky. They had to foot the £7 million bill for the whole spurious enquiry in which the Metropolitan Police were found to have acted unlawfully. Incredibly, it cost Deputy Commissioner Ian Blair nothing. In fact, he was subsequently promoted and knighted and is now Sir Ian Blair, Commissioner in charge of Britain's Metropolitan Police Force.

No other Commissioner of the Met. has made the blunders which have been features of Sir Ian's reign, so questions must be asked. Is he just leading a charmed life or is there more to his Houdini escapism than meets the eye?

Not surprisingly, more than 400 complaints against Commissioner Blair's Force were upheld in 2006 and the Met. spent a staggering £29 million on the investigations of a 35% increase in accusations brought by the public against the Force controlled by the accident-prone knight.

"Security Services" is a term which should be used with care because it is not just a question of goodies versus baddies. Sadly, because the risks of suffering serious consequences are so low, the baddies occasionally kill police officers, but disturbingly, the police kill a far greater number of completely innocent citizens. According to the I.P.C.C. Report, incidents involving police vehicles in Britain resulted in the deaths of 48 people last year, which puts rather a different slant on the words "Security Services".

On the 3rd November 2006, Inspector Paul Gee, Head of the Police Force's driving school, was caught doing 118 miles an hour in a dangerous location where a number of serious accidents had occurred. He had not followed "on-duty" procedures and his excuse was that he was carrying out risk assessment for the training school. Pull the other one, Inspector. You deserve to be charged, but it seems that arms are being twisted.

Like Britain, Ireland is seriously short of Garda evident on the streets. For its level of crime, it could do with at least 17,500 officers but it was promised only 14,000 by Minister McDowell who, in the end, failed to provide even 13,200 in 2006. The Force is also abysmally organised, ill-equipped and desperately short of specialist units, all of which means that in many areas, gangs rule the streets in the knowledge that the Garda are too over-stretched to cause them any serious problems.

In all high-crime nations, re-appraisal of the Security Services is one of the necessary first priorities. They must be sufficient to get more than just a small percentage of crimes solved and the villains brought to justice. Currently this is a pathetic 2 to 4%. They must be better trained and better equipped. They must spend far more time on their feet, out amongst the public. They must also significantly reduce the time they spend interfering with the privacy and liberties of the law-abiding sector of society and concentrate first and foremost on catching the serious criminals.

My New Sentencing Solutions, two chapters on, will both assist and encourage them in going after the bad eggs.

CHAPTER 9

DRUGS – TIME TO GET REAL

Now for one of the biggies in the crime scene.

Far and away the greatest crime-related problem the world has, is the use of – and much more significantly, the trade in - recreational and/or addictive drugs. By comparison, the damage suffered from acts of terrorism, fraud, speeding motorists, people-trafficking etc. pale into insignificance.

In America, Britain, Ireland, Canada, France, Italy, Spain, Australia, etc. etc. etc. ***between 60% and 75% of all crime is drugs-related***, yet none of these Governments have been prepared to either acknowledge the seriousness of this, or grasp the nettle and take the necessary corrective counter measures.

I could write (and may well) a book on the subject of drugs alone and quote chapter and verse about how various politicians have allowed, or even helped today's dreadful drugs/crime relationship to develop, but for now, I will cut to the quick and limit my conclusions at this stage, to the essential elements, including just a few examples (out of millions) to illustrate where current practices are failing.

Humans have taken narcotics in varying forms more or less forever. Throughout history, mankind has experimented with, enjoyed and suffered alcohol, opium, heroin, tobacco and many other substances to alter their moods, temporarily replace boredom, reduce or eliminate inhibitions, give them Dutch courage, or as a statement of rebellion etc. A complicating factor is that most drugs affect different people in a wide variety of ways. The same few whiskies which put one guy into a relaxed sleepy mood will cause another to break a bottle and smash it into the face of a total stranger for little or no reason, or rape any vulnerable female within reach. How ironic that the nation which is famous for its whisky, tops the league as the most violent (per capita) in the western world. Most of this violence is alcohol or other drug-related, so obviously the Scots (generalising) cannot hold their liquor. According to a United National Report, people in Scotland are three times more likely to be assaulted than those in America.

Another crime-causing drug is the highly-dangerous methamphetamine which is stated by some U.S. Police Departments to be responsible for 40-50% of all arrests and in States such as California, Nevada and Arkansaw, "meth" has already overtaken alcohol as the number one cause of admission to substance abuse treatment centres.

Very few countries have managed to avoid serious drugs-associated crime, although several, including Singapore and Thailand, have had *some* success in containing drugs activity by using draconian measures of control.

Thailand, for example, executed more than 2,000 "alleged" drug dealers in 2004 alone, but whilst this appears to keep the lid on drugs use in that country, it is self-evident that there are still sufficient people there who are prepared to take their chances and risk their lives solely because dealing in drugs can be such a lucrative business. They would not be doing this if there was no demand for their products, nor would they be defying the law if Governments had not forced up the value of low-priced drugs by factors of ten or more by criminalising them.

Ireland's President, Mary McAleese, has angrily hit out at the irresponsibility of both the middle classes and that country's supposedly highly-educated young generation. She blames them for encouraging the drugs dealers by buying from them and thereby fuelling the whole crime scene which goes hand in hand with illegal drugs. In a radio interview, she told Marian Finucane that she was sick with worry and considered the well-heeled, socialising users to be as guilty in Ireland's murders as the feuding drugs gang lords. She claims to be unable to figure out why Ireland's best ever educated generation has no standards when it comes to drugs, alcohol or driving. Surely she too should accept some responsibility because she has been around for many years. Hopefully she will read this book and find some answers which it seems have eluded her until Christmas Eve 2006.

Most western countries have, themselves, caused their own high crime levels by taking a middle-of-the-road stance on drugs, thereby guaranteeing that their populations suffer vastly more drugs-related crime than is necessary. On one hand they condemn drugs use but

166

fail to impose sentences sufficient to deter millions from breaking the law. On the other hand they ride roughshod over the freedoms which all individuals should have, to take such risks as they wish with their own bodies, provided that they do not harm any other person.

No Government - despite decades of escalating "wars on drugs", despite throwing countless billions of pounds/dollars/euros at the problem - has succeeded in preventing very substantial proportions of their citizens from taking "illegal" drugs. They have, in fact, fallen into the trap of creating a worst-of-all-worlds scenario.

According to the Council of Europe statistics – and yes, I do know how dubious they can be - about 185 million people worldwide are regular drugs users, but many believe this to be a serious under-estimate. In truth, no-one knows. However, even accepting this Council of Europe figure shows the enormity of drugs use which Governments have failed to eliminate, despite decades of horrendously expensive and debilitating "wars" on drugs. Don't senior politicians just love the buzz which they get from these.

Wolfgang Goetz, the Head of the European Union's Monitoring Centre for Drugs and Drug Addiction admitted in November 2006 that however many drugs were seized by the police, Customs or the military, this has had no effect on black market supplies at the consumer end. Indeed, the EU has acknowledged that with drugs seizures neither interrupting supply nor forcing up street prices, the feeling amongst some within the European Commission is that 50 years of the international war on drugs is a failure. Pity they ignored sound advice decades ago, but of course, had they done so, there would have been no need for The European Centre for Drugs and Drug Addiction (based in Lisbon, Portugal) and bureaucrats are not ones to admit their own redundancy.

It is the natural inclination of all bureaucracies to work towards expansion and resist any shrinkage, however unnecessary they may have become.

Given some idea of the scale of the problem, I can tell you that if all these drugs users joined hands, they could encircle the earth at its equator **ten times**. That, dear reader, is a 300,000 (three hundred thousand) kilometre line of regular drugs users. All in the queue for their next fix.

Amongst this 185 million drugs users is a huge range of people, including layabouts, politicians, doctors, nurses, police and prison officers, serial rapists, judges, soldiers, sailors, airmen, prostitutes, bank managers, plumbers, airline pilots, burglars, vicars, business executives, housewives, school kids and school teachers, bricklayers, psychiatrists, university professors, etc. etc. etc. – you get the message, I'm sure. Many of these are perfectly respectable people who can both afford and control their drugs use and who, apart from choosing to take drugs, would not dream of indulging in any other criminal activity. It is the height of folly to drive such people into contact with the underworld, or to criminalise them, or to stuff our overwhelmed prisons with them if personal use is their only "supposed" transgression.

In October 2006, a random testing was done surreptitiously of fifty elected Italian politicians who believed their brows were being cosmetically prepared for a TV programme. They were not. The supposed cosmetic swabs were, in fact, taking perspiration samples for analysis. Almost one third (16) tested positive for having used cannabis and/or cocaine during the previous 36 hours. The survey and its findings were, in fact, part of a documentary film on drugs scheduled to be shown on television, but at the time of this writing, political pressure had successfully prevented the programme from being shown.

At the other end of the scale are those who can neither control nor afford their drugs use, which suggests addiction and/or compulsion. Some of these will have been initially tempted to take drugs by those dealers expecting to profit from selling them the products they subsequently craved and which they cannot, in most countries, buy or use without breaking the law.

Millions of those in these categories have drifted into other crime simply to get the money they need to fund their addiction. At this level, shoplifting, car theft, burglary, mugging and fraud are typical of the crimes committed simply to pay the high prices charged for illegal drugs. It is not unusual for the cost to exceed US$ 850 or UK £500 a week.

The big money, not unnaturally, is where the big crime rules. The growers get a pittance for their produce but the bad guys who take on the world's security systems – either head-on or via bribery – are the ones trading in billions. Threats, intimidation, bribery, torture and murder are the tools of their trade.

So great is the crock of gold which Governments have created by criminalising drugs, that it was inevitable that seriously evil people would be prepared to commit or commission any crime in order to get their hands on a share of this massive windfall which politicians continue to make available to them.

Colombia's Pablo Escobar and friends murdered Colombia's Justice Minister, journalists, the judge who sentenced him to prison, eleven other judges, drug suppliers and hundreds in the dealing chain who got in their way. Nor did he stay in prison for long because his massive profits from illegal drugs were more than sufficient to guarantee his freedom. He was eventually killed in a shoot-out with the authorities who had spent many millions of dollars trying to put Escobar out of business, but the drugs trade was not fazed in any way. Others simply stepped into his space and fought mercilessly to grab the biggest possible share of the market.

It was ever thus. It will ever be thus whilstever there are misguided politicians who believe they can either stop people using drugs by banning them, or win the "war" against those trafficking in them.

I frankly do not concern myself overmuch with those who choose to risk their own health, family lives or careers, provided that they do not mug, burgle or harm innocent people in order to fund their own indulgences. I do though, recommend every Government to run permanent drugs-awareness advertising, education and P.R. campaigns and provide far better rehabilitation and education centres for those wishing to kick their habit, or those offered such help by the Courts as a possible alternative to prison sentences. Such programmes will not be cheap but their costs would be only a small fraction of those currently borne by society due to drugs-related crime. The bottom line therefore, would be *a substantial net gain to the taxpayer*.

Britain, for one, totally misallocates the funds it spends on the drugs issue. It has spent billions trying and failing to catch the suppliers and pushers, but little on advertising their dangers. In 2006, according to Nielsen Media Research, the Central Office of Information's expenditure was only £1.4 million. The prohibition billions can be saved and the educational campaigning aspect upped several fold by the C.O.I.

Courts should not, of course, give lower sentences where actual crimes have been committed under the influence of drugs, be they alcohol, marijuana, methamphetamine or whatever. The freedom for anyone to abuse themselves by doing drugs should not then be extended into an excuse for infringing any law. It should not be an offence to take any drug, but all crimes should be prosecuted and committing any crime under the influence of drugs should never earn any leniency from any court. Driving whilst impaired by any drug should always be considered a serious crime.

More laws, more money, more drugs tsars, more special police, more military involvement, more surveillance ships, more border guards and anti-drugs squads together with their inevitable associated bureaucracies have, for decades, been the typical knee-jerk reactions of most countries' politicians. They have been tried, expanded, refined and tinkered with ad nauseum, but what all of these escalating measures have in common is that *they have all not only failed to rid us of drugs-related crime, but they have caused it to rise inexorably*.

All such methods will continue to fail. They will simply pile billions more expenditure and millions more victims of crime onto an already intolerable situation. We are, in fact, paying through the nose for abject failure, so you should all ask your political representatives why they have persisted for so long with a system which is the main cause of crime and whose principal beneficiaries are the drugs warlords and those over whom they have influence or control

Even tiny New Zealand mistakenly believes that its drugs problems can be solved by committees of supposed experts. Unfortunately, their Expert Advisory Committee on Drugs has had the same effect as all the other bureaucratic talking shops on drugs - *precisely none*.

Many police officers in most of the countries I have visited concur with the views I have been promoting on crime for well over a decade and UK Chief Constable Richard Brunstrom's observations are fairly typical.

"Our policy" the Chief Constable says (on the subject of drugs) "is still crazy, being based on a ludicrous lack of logic and an *unwinnable war*. The Science and Technology Committee demolish the ridiculous claim peddled by some, that the UK is bound by international law." He added – "International Drugs Policy is governed by the United Nations, whose agenda has been very largely that of an American-led global war on drugs with proscription and punishment as its mainstays. A worthless policy based on the fundamentalist creed that drugs are somehow intrinsically evil and that all drug users are damned as criminals – morally and legally."

I live in hopes that this particular police officer will reconsider his excessive faith in speed cameras, but on the drugs issue, we are, to a large extent, on the same wavelength, neither of us wishing to see further billions of £s, $s, €s thrown down the drain in a vain attempt to stop people doing drugs and throwing them in gaol if they don't comply.

Quite simply, most Governments have created a black market in drugs which has allowed some seriously-nasty and dangerous guys to gun their way into riches which would otherwise be beyond either their grasp or capability. It is, in fact, politicians who have put top-of-the-range Mercedes, Porsches and Ferrari cars into the hands of evil people who have never done a day's real work in their lives. The very same people prepared to spend hundreds of thousands of dollars providing their drug-pushing gang members with a wide range of firearms.

It is these same politicians who support their own fancy lifestyles from the huge taxes they impose on drugs such as tobacco and alcohol, without which some of their economies would be in serious trouble, so it should not be overlooked that whilst the smokers and drinkers may be hooked on their chosen poison, the politicians are also hooked on the tax revenues which they impose upon them and which contribute to their own over-generous remunerations.

I point this out not because I favour cigarettes or alcohol, but simply to highlight the holier-than-thou hypocrisy of many politicians. My belief is that the same anti-social Value Added or Sales Tax should be added to all recreational drugs and incidentally, to fuel, cars and other similar products which cause significant damage to the environment. Neither taxes nor laws though will stop drugs abuse and most of those claiming otherwise obviously have their own less-than-honourable agendas.

I have examined masses of information about smokers, drinkers and drug users allegedly costing Governments large amounts of money via their increased use of health services, but this is simply nothing more than a smokescreen. Yes, "some" gaspers and boozers do temporarily use medical facilities beyond the norm – *but*, on their Governments' own claims, these same people are going to die from their tobacco and alcohol use much sooner than they otherwise would.

These supposed millions of early deaths represent a huge windfall for Governments in the form of years of potentially-future healthcare being wiped out, and even more financially beneficial to the State, years of pension payments do not have to be paid to all those who die prematurely from their abuse of drugs. Looked at cynically, Governments should not be pretending that drugs users cost their countries money, they should be happy that so many of them choose to shorten their own lives to the huge financial benefit of their treasuries and their more health-conscious taxpayers. Yet again, I have to say to our politicians – stop lying and cut out the hypocrisy. By dying early, drugs users not only save their countries many billions of pounds, they also make a small contribution to slowing down the world's population explosion, which is in dire need of massive reduction.

I will be telling you later how you and millions like you can wake up your politicians to their responsibilities.

Most countries currently suffer massive crime because of their cowardice or corruption in dealing with drugs and they will continue to suffer this crime burden whilstever they make a cheap range of products vastly more valuable (for the drugs dealers) by virtue of making them illegal. We hear of two/three million pounds or dollars worth of drugs being seized by customs or police from time to time, but those hugely-inflated price estimates are only created by virtue of the drugs being illegal. Such seizure figures are, in fact, wholly fictitious because they bear no relationship whatsoever to the very much smaller price paid to producers who are often third world subsistence level farmers selling their drugs for only a few cents on the dollar, pound or euro which applies only because of prohibition.

On the 10th October 2005 for example, 5 villains were quite rightly gaoled for manufacturing amphetamines (speed) in Merseyside, England. The supposed value of the chemicals seized was less than £200,000, but when processed into the illegal drugs market, this was quoted in the media as being a haul valued at £4.5 million. This typifies the gifts our politicians are handing on a plate to the crooks by creating an irresistibly profitable black market for them to exploit.

In Britain, a Deputy Chief Constable, Howard Roberts, late in 2006 acknowledged that addicts are responsible for around 60% of crimes, right up to murder in his county and he believes the time has come for addicts to be supplied with their drugs needs via retail chemist outlets. He believes that average users need £15,000 a year to fund their habit and all too frequently, they have to steal and sell on goods worth upwards of £45,000 in order to cover the actual amount paid for their fixes.

By mid-February 2007, even the President of the Association of Chief Police Officers, Kenneth Jones, was moving towards my recommendations on drugs decriminalisation. He now believes that having Heroin available on National Health Service prescription to addicts is something about which we should be thinking.

Germany, The Netherlands and Switzerland have all shown that drugs-related crime can be significantly reduced by programmes of making Heroin available at authorised social centres where treatment programmes are also in place for those ready to get serious about trying to overcome their addiction.

According to The Independent newspaper, the medical journal The Lancet believes such centres in Switzerland have brought about an 82% reduction in Heroin use since 1990.

Meantime, most other countries, still stuck with prohibition, are going in exactly the opposite direction and suffering all of the crime which always has and always will go hand in hand with any "war" on drugs.

Politicians obviously have learned nothing from America's early 20th century attempt to outlaw alcohol. Its prohibition did not stop people drinking of course. It just created gang warfare amongst those who suddenly realised that by circumventing the law, they could massively hike up the price of booze which otherwise would have commanded a much lower price. Prohibition of alcohol also resulted in dangerous spirits being produced in thousands of illicit stills operated by get-rich-quick merchants with no concern or knowledge about product quality. They were, in fact, selling poison on the black market to people who could not complain. Ditto for drugs right up to today - 2007

Now, many countries have armed gangs fighting for drugs territory. They have addicts prepared to rob, maim, burgle and even kill to get the money for their next hugely price-inflated fix. They have hoards of people in gaol - many who are not traffickers or dealers and who should not really be there if their only "crime" has been to use or be in possession of a small amount of any drug sufficient only for their personal use.

To rub salt into this running sore, their taxpayers are bearing huge crime costs, masses of wasted police time which is needed more urgently elsewhere, unnecessarily occupied prison places with all of their associated expensive costs – all for absolutely no good reason.

All for zero benefit. Criminalising drugs is, and always will be, a lose lose situation for those countries foolish enough to have it as their policy.

Despite decades of massive expenditure on ever more anti-drugs wars, the end result has, in fact, been the opposite to that sought, because drugs use has not been eliminated. It has not gone down substantially. It has not gone down a little or even stayed on a level plateau. *Drugs use has continued to increase* and those of our politicians who pretend that criminalising drugs will stop or seriously diminish their use are just not living in the real world. In most countries there is scarcely a village, a street, a university, a school or a workplace where no-one is doing drugs, so let us cut out the pretence. This is one of the principle routes into the quicksands of crime, so blocking it off is long overdue.

We should also quit being dishonest about so-called recreational drugs use because the eternal no, no, no uncompromising attitude towards their use has not only failed to stop drug-taking, it has often caused it to increase. Young people particularly, do not buy into this one-sided argument and no amount of regulation can force

174

them into its acceptance. Drugs can be dangerous, but exaggerating their effects is counter-productive. When it is plain to see that many drugs users live normal, productive and often long lives, it diminishes the value of warnings which pretend that all drugs are dangerous to all people.

I believe it unwise to dismiss the use of all drugs out-of-hand, or to ignore the very relevant fact that millions of people experience pleasure, relief, stimulation or other satisfactions from their use. Nor should it be forgotten that many people die or suffer other ill-effects, from prescription drugs given to or forced upon them by the established medical profession. I advocate far more serious education about the real dangers of drugs use, particularly those which are most likely to lead to serious addiction, death or other health problems. Blinkered hectoring though, should have no place in public information campaigns about drugs misuse.

So what do we do about an admittedly serious drug problem?

- Every country which has not already done so should decriminalise all drugs as a matter or urgency, thereby saving endless billions on the unsuccessful drugs wars. This will **wipe out the criminal traders overnight** and within months, their national crime levels will drop dramatically. There is no other single initiative which any country can take which can not only bring about a major reduction in crime, but can do so very quickly.

- Make recreational drugs available at pharmacies and/or medical practitioners, who must source their supplies, perhaps via certified producers or wholesalers, thereby ensuring that those foolish enough to indulge are at least avoiding the even greater damage from impure products which are another dangerous feature of the black market. Each country's Health or Customs Department could purchase the required drugs and raw materials direct from the growers or from authorised and supervised co-operatives in the producer countries. All open and above board.

- Install a system to help those addicts without financial resources to have access to drugs via a medical practitioner to take away the alternative of them continuing to steal or commit other crimes in order to get money to satisfy their need.

- Fix maximum prices at which each drug can be sold, according to their perceived dangers. This too will be a further nail in the coffin of today's illegal drug dealers who only stay in business via the highly-inflated prices created by prohibition. The traffickers would be unable to compete with the lower-priced legal products and in any event, users would have no reason to buy from black market dealers once legal sources were readily available.

- Put relevant warnings on the outside of every package and – as is already standard practice with approved medical drugs – printed warnings as appropriate inside every pack.

- Apply an Anti-Social Activity Tax Rate as either a Value Added or Sales Tax and if none exists, introduce one for all recreational drugs. This measure, added to the enormous savings from scrapping the ineffective wars on drugs, will provide Governments with a huge fighting fund. Use part of this war chest in a constantly-changing drugs advice campaign and for greater numbers of drugs rehabilitation centres for those seeking help with their addiction or referred by the Courts. This will be a vastly better use of resources than current practices which have failed to dissuade millions from stepping onto the drugs ladder and are doing far too little to help those who do fall by the wayside.

In short – **kill the market in illegal drugs**, leaving nothing for the evil drug barons and pushers to exploit. This will wipe out the rivers of blood which we are currently allowing to run from countries such as Columbia and Afghanistan right into the streets, clubs and pubs throughout most countries on earth.

NATO is currently spending massive amounts of money sending troops to Afghanistan and much of this expenditure goes on the losing battle against the heroin warlords who will have nothing to fight over once drugs are legalised and controlled by Governments.

Foolishly NATO, driven by American insistence, is planning to destroy the Afghan farmers' poppy crops by aerial spraying in the ridiculous assumption that this will drive out the Taleban. Not surprisingly, that did not happen. Ordinary produce grown by these subsistence farmers was ruined along with the poppies and the growers were left, at best, with NATO handouts. The Governor of Helmand Province, Engineer Daud and the British were seriously opposed to

176

the crop spraying. The Americans got their bullying way. The British caved in, Governor Daud was removed and the Taleban are delighted because the farmers are now anti-coalition and the drugs barons are well pleased because remaining supplies became more valuable. Did it – will it – decrease the amount of heroin reaching western countries? Absolutely not one jot.

Des Browne, the UK's Minister of Defence, claimed in October 2006 that the Afghanistan Taleban did not hate the British troops and were only fighting them "because they are paid". What Mr. Browne did not have the wit to recognise, was that the money to pay the Taleban comes from the illegal heroin trade. I doubt that Britain's Minister of Defence will read this book, but perhaps one or more of his political opponents will pass on the following advice, which will solve two of his country's most serious problems :-

✓ Decriminalise personal drug use in the UK, thereby lowering crime substantially and releasing many thousands of prison places to accommodate many of the violent criminals who have yet to be caught and imprisoned. Do this now and do not waste time discussing it with other countries.

✓ Buy the heroin output of Afghanistan's farmers at a fair price, i.e. sufficiently higher than that paid by the Drugs Warlords. This will enable the growers to be independent of the black market in which they currently do most of the work, but receive almost none of the financial benefits.

This will pull the rug from under both the Taleban and the Warlords and be a truly major step in winning hearts and minds and it will enable the Allies to return to their original declared mission of rebuilding Afghanistan instead of doing just the opposite and causing ever more collateral damage.

Paul Flynn, one of the all-too-few mavericks in the UK Labour Party has a record of proposing common sense solutions to seemingly difficult problems. In the House of Commons on 27th February 2006, he asked the then Defence Secretary John Reid to consider poppy cultivation in Afghanistan under Government supervision in order to produce Diamorphine from it, Diamorphine being in short supply in hospitals and clinics worldwide, particularly in Africa. Predictably, John Reid was not interested, preferring to send more

British Troops to their deaths in an unwinnable war against drugs. At the time of writing, John Reid is currently Britain's Home Secretary.

Eventually, Ministers such as John Reid and Des Browne will have to start listening to people like Paul Flynn and me because until they do, the drugs-related crime wave will continue at massive cost to everyone except the drugs barons and those whom they bribe.

De-criminalising drugs will instantly make it unnecessary to worry any longer about the current bribery of customs officials, police officers, politicians etc. although I have no doubt that some of the very wealthy drug barons will continue to use their political contacts to try to protect their lucrative trade and keep the status quo. The last thing the drugs pushers wish to see is the de-criminalisation of drugs and they will use people in positions of power to argue their case to prevent this coming about. Incidentally, no-one should give any credence to the argument that those involved would simply move into other spheres of crime because quite simply, there is no other area of crime which can remotely compare with the multi-billion dollars a year sloshing around the illegal drugs trade. Even North Korea's counterfeiting of US hundred dollar bills of excellent quality does not even come close.

Question very carefully any politician who resists the legalisation of drugs. The reason cannot be to save people from using dangerous substances because current restrictions are very obviously not achieving this, nor will they ever.

I am not alone in wanting the Irish Government to tell us why they let a known big-time drugs trafficker off the hook, despite the fact that the Gardai caught him with two million euros worth of cocaine and heroin.

Kieran Boylan boasted that he was untouchable and that he would never stand trial for his latest crime – and so it proved. Despite being wanted for drug-running in Ireland, Britain, Holland and other European countries and being out on bail (why?) for other drugs offences, the well-connected Mr. Boylan does indeed seem to have undue influence in the corridors of power and this is not untypical of the murky world of illegal drugs.

Facing a mandatory ten-year sentence for being apprehended with €750,000 worth of drugs at Dublin Port in 2003, this Houdini inexplicably got only a five-year sentence, two years of which were "suspended" and should have been reinstated in the event of any further transgressions. Now he is to escape further prosecution despite being caught with a €2 million drugs haul and not being one to mince words, I want Ireland's Justice Minister Michael McDowell to find out who Kieran Boylan has bribed and/or threatened. It must be one or more persons in high office, because only such persons would have sufficient influence to protect such a high-profile villain.

Some parents, quite naturally, are hesitant about decriminalising drugs, feeling that putting temptation in the path of their children will increase the likelihood of them experimenting. Many though, have come to share the view that current practices in most countries are not dissuading or preventing anyone from entering the drugs scene, whether via encouragement, curiosity or flawed character. Few indeed are the parents who can confidently and accurately, in 2007, predict that their child will never take illegal drugs.

I of course have every sympathy with the relatives and friends of those who have died or otherwise suffered from their involvement with drugs. Understandably, some of them in their distress, support continued prohibition. Regrettably, prohibition has for 5, 10, 20, 30 or more years caused vastly more grief, more suffering and more crime than it ever did in the hundreds of years before some dim or corrupt politicians were persuaded to ban drugs and create the most lucrative black market the world has ever suffered.

Although drugs prohibition must be ended if overall crime is to be substantially reduced, that absolutely should not mean tolerance of any illegal or irresponsible activity connected with drugs activity.

I would like to see driving whilst impaired by drugs a serious offence and any accidents caused, put into a high crime category. Despite being protective of most freedoms, this does not include the freedom to get into what can so easily become an instant death-machine and drive it around public roads whilst under the influence.

I can see no valid reason why every country should not have random stopping of any vehicle in order to test its driver for alcohol or drugs influence. The police are welcome to stop me for such a test anytime and it would save many lives if all drivers were aware that such stopping and testing, even without obvious cause, was a permanent feature of road use.

As of now, there is no satisfactory roadside test covering all drugs, so I propose that Governments should commission further research to find a drugs test or tests comparable with those used for alcohol. I appreciate the complexities involved, but that is no reason not to search for reliable tests to discourage driving whilst under the influence of drugs. Legalised drugs should, as appropriate, contain warnings similar to those on other medications about driving or operating machinery etc.

I have heard it argued that legalising drugs would increase their use and whilst accepting that in the short-term this *may* be so, it is not a valid reason for continuing to bury our heads in the sand. Were decriminalisation to increase use – and that is not at all certain – this would be a very small price to pay for the massive reduction in crime from which everyone, apart from the illegal drugs dealers, would instantly benefit.

I do not pretend to *know* whether or not drugs use would go up or down as a result of legal availability, but the following are worthy of your consideration :-

- All the "wars" on drugs are costing hundreds of billions of dollars/ euros/pounds/whatever, every year, to absolutely no avail. Many millions of people do drugs regardless of Governments' every effort to stop their supply.

- When legalised, there will be no market to be exploited by the middlemen and their gangs and consequently, there will be far fewer people enticing others to take their first steps into drugs- use. This will mean that some people will not even get drawn onto the first step of the drugs ladder.

- There is always a percentage of any population which will undertake any illegal activity simply by way of protest or to get a buzz from the related dangers of doing something illegal or anti-social. Some of these may well lose their interest when the attraction of illegality disappears. H. L. Mencken recognised this a century ago when resisting attempts by the Society for the Suppression of Vice to make tobacco an illegal substance. Even in 1905, H. L. acknowledged the link between smoking and cancer (giving the lie incidentally, to those who sued tobacco companies 70 years later on the grounds of being ignorant of the dangers) but his stance was one of freedom to choose. Perceptively, Mencken warned that a fierce crusade against children smoking would only pique their natural curiosity, making the cigarette the malodorous symbol of the adolescent outlaw. Would that our 21st century politicians understood, as Mencken did, that the surest way to make a given action attractive is to prohibit it and put a penalty on it.

- Already, many drugs-users give them up or seriously moderate their use, entirely of their own accord and the huge increase in support rehabilitation which I recommend accompanies legalisation will help those finding it difficult to kick any dependency. Another factor in reducing the number of addicts.

- Those countries which have partially decriminalised drugs have already seen significant drops in the levels of associated crime.

Nor should it be forgotten that because of America's F.D.A. denying people perfectly valid medicinal drugs, more people die every week, quite unjustifiably, than died in the 9/11 attack. Author Durk Pearson has a string of Court victories over the Federal Drugs Agency on this issue and his book "Life Extension" is a serious indictment of America's addiction to excessive bureaucracy.

On this subject of whether decriminalisation will significantly increase or decrease drugs use, ask yourself :-

1. If you are already a non-user, are you going to start taking drugs simply because they have been decriminalised?

2. If you are already into drugs, would their changed legal status increase your use?

3. With the whole area being brought out into the open, would you be more or less likely to take advantage of de-tox rehabilitation facilities at some point, if these were readily available to you?

If I have to guess, I would expect William Shakespeare's observation in Twelfth Night may well apply – "If music be the food of love, play on. Give me excess of it that, surfeiting, the appetite may sicken and so die".

In conclusion – and following 15 years' research – I can say quite categorically that the world cannot enjoy low crime whilst ever we keep recreational drugs illegal.

I will be happy to consult on how the necessary change towards decriminalisation can be brought into effect in order to secure maximum crime reduction and provide yet another lifeline out of the quicksands of crime.

Late News. After fifteen years trying to persuade Governments to decriminalise drugs, it seems that the UK Home Office is just beginning to see the light.

Expect by March 2007 to see them take the first tentative steps by making Heroin, and possibly other substances, available to some addicts.

CHAPTER 10

CHAOTIC SENTENCING

Most countries have ridiculous systems of sentencing those found by the Courts to be guilty of crimes. These are crying out for review, for several very good reasons, including :-

- There is an unjustifiable range of consequences which bear no relationship to the severity or triviality of the offence. Often, identical crimes are given two, three, four or more times the level of punishment, on no more than judges' subjective whims, moods or prejudices. Listen to no-one who tells you that our judges and magistrates do not suffer from these (and other) human frailties. I assure you they do, including the more salacious ones. I have masses of evidence from my research showing their wild inconsistencies and, that the personal morality of some Judges does not sit well with their pontificating about the behaviour of others.

- With such a wide differential in the sentences passed for like-for-like crimes, the criminals are ever hopeful that they will get away with the minimum. Inevitably, this leads more of them to chance their arms, hence more crimes committed.

- When Sir John Stevens was Britain's Top Cop as Metropolitan Police Commissioner he had a serious spat with the then Home Secretary David Blunkett. The Commissioner rightly claimed that soft sentencing was responsible for rising street crime and that the criminal justice system is appalling and failing to protect the public from becoming victims. He also echoed what I had been telling Blair, Straw and Blunkett for years, that crime in Britain has become a game of no consequences, with Magistrates letting those accused of muggings back on the streets time and time again pending trial.

Blunkett was frequently at odds with Sir John Stevens and reportedly seriously admonished him in 2002 for warning that London was likely in line for terror attacks. Sir John's warnings proved to be prophetic and as so often was the case, David Blunkett's judgement was seen to be seriously flawed.

All too often, sentencing is nothing more than a loopy lottery. How else can anyone explain why the man who stabbed Dominic Holmes to death was sentenced supposedly to "life" imprisonment yet the Judge told the violent thug responsible that he would be eligible for parole in 3½ years.

It is time to say enough is enough. I want every country to stop abusing language and not to sentence anyone to imprisonment "for life" unless it means exactly that. Life should mean life. Period. If it does not, do not use the word to give the false impression that a most serious sentence has been imposed when all too often, nothing could be further from the truth.

Anyone believing that judicial systems are just fine as they are, should ask themselves :- How would you feel if you were David Siddle, who miraculously escaped death when the young thug, who can't be named for legal reasons, was sentenced to just 2 years in a Young Offenders Institution for driving a knife, without any provocation, into his temple. David Siddle was taken to hospital where he needed a five-hour operation to remove the knife"

- Judges and Magistrates are not God, however much some of them wish us to accord them such status. One only has to visit a range of Courts to see how some of the judiciary consider themselves to be omnipotent. Their behaviour and attitude is often high-handed, imperious, pompous and inconsiderate with both plaintiffs and witnesses.

- Too often the Judiciary is leaned upon by the Executive to impose fewer custodial sentences for no better reason than to match an insufficient number of prison places. The young thug who participated in the murder of jeweller Marion Bates in Nottingham, England, for example, was a known serial offender, let out of prison early, having served less than half his sentence, despite a string of burglary and sex offences. He was freed with meaningless restrictions supposedly enforced by an electronic ankle or wrist tag. What did he do? Simple. He took off his tag, which went unnoticed by the authorities for 3 days, during which time he and his mate held up and shot dead Mrs. Bates in front of her husband and daughter. Little wonder that her husband is calling for criminals to be locked up instead of being given airy-fairy, meaningless sentences. You are not alone Mr. Bates. Many of us are with you.

184

- **Rape** is a most damaging crime, but it varies enormously from excessive persuasion into intercourse between known parties, to serious violent attack resulting in death or near death.

In my next chapter you will see that I have broken down rape into five grades – **A** to **E** – together with proposed changes in sentencing procedures. I would have classified Paul Buckley's rape of a 24-year old woman walking home in Cork, Ireland as a Grade **B** rape, described by Detective Sergeant Cahill as one of the most serious rapes he had been involved with in more than 20 years. The lady concerned did not know Paul Buckley, who viciously beat his victim before raping her. She believed she was going to die and when Gardai saw her, she was bloody, bruised and swollen so badly as to be almost unrecognisable.

Justice Paul Butler obviously would not have considered this a Grade **B** rape on my proposed scale because the sentence this carried would have been from 7 to 20 years – probably close to the top end of the range. Inexplicably, Justice Butler sentenced this brutal rapist to only 4 years in gaol plus 6 months for the assault and, to rub salt in the wound, he pontificated about women who had perhaps been drinking, walking home alone.

Crime will never be seriously diminished whilstever there are judicial systems which have Judges with the attitudes of Justice Paul Butler who hand out excessively lenient sentences for serious rapes. Such sentences serve only to downplay the trauma suffered by the victims and by failing to spell out the seriousness of rape, they increase the prospect of every woman being sexually attacked.

Ireland's justice system seems to be bidding for rape tourism by allowing its Courts to pass some incredibly lenient sentences and almost no serious ones. There is more than one rape every day "reported" in Ireland but due to there being only 4 treatment and forensic examiners in the whole country, less than 20% of the perpetrators are prosecuted. Result – every year 97% of rapists in Ireland never go to gaol.

- Justice Paul Carney seems to have no conception of how rape affects the victims.

51 year old Anthony Prior eventually pleaded guilty to raping a young guest in his home, having originally claimed he had mistaken her for his wife – an excuse he subsequently withdrew. Apparently, with no justification whatsoever, Justice Paul Carney at the Dublin High Court flippantly commented that the victim's suffering resulted from the consumption of alcohol which led to a West End bedroom farce, which the lady in question absolutely denies. Disturbingly, Justice Carney gave the rapist only a 4-year prison sentence but – even worse – ***this was suspended***, i.e. for raping a visitor to his home, Anthony Prior did not have to spend a day in gaol.

• Irish Justice Daniel Herbert also caused outrage when he wished a rapist well for the future and gave him a suspended sentence, saying that "no actual injury was inflicted (on the victim) ***other than rape***".

It is time for Ireland to rid itself of its callous attitude to rape and set an example to all, that this despicable crime should not be tolerated by any civilised nation.

• A 15-year old – unnamed unfortunately, due to his age – threw a 13 kilo battery from a bridge which went through the windscreen of a van. Most of us have been startled by the occasional stone hitting our cars, sometimes shattering the screen, causing us to jump involuntarily. Little wonder therefore, that a battery smashing straight through his windscreen caused driver Chris McCaffrey to instantly lose control and crash to his death. Judge Henry Globe gave the 15 year old lout a custodial sentence of only 4 years but in fact, he will likely spend 2 years only in a "children's" home. Go figure? Throw a car battery through a van's windscreen, kill the driver and all you get is two years in a children's home. Some deterrent eh?

• Andrew Haige should have been locked up long ago, for a long time. He had been ***banned from driving 30 times***, but this didn't stop him from drinking 14 pints of beer, hitting a female student's car, driving his car at a passing helper, knocking him down then threatening to kill him. Nice guy. Just the sort Britain needs driving around congesting its roads.

Mr. Haige has serious previous, including 25 convictions for driving whilst disqualified, assaulting a police officer, affray,

5 drink driving bans and driving without insurance. He told Manchester Crown Court that jail had not helped him in the past, so asked not to be sent back for a 9th time.

The Judge *should* have told him that prison can only "help" those who want to be helped and that the public must be protected from those continually flouting the law. What did Judge Andrew Lowlock do? He gave this seriously dangerous villain yet another chance – a two-year Rehabilitation Order and, can you believe it, another 4-year driving ban to add to his existing collection of 45 offences over a 20-year period. This is why the police tear their hair out. They have been forced to do their job over and over again simply because the Courts repeatedly imposed lenient sentences on Mr. Haige which very clearly were no deterrent to him whatsoever.

Under *my* proposals in the next chapters, travesties of justice such as this cannot happen because the likes of Andrew Haige would be permanently in prison long before the likes of Judge Lowlock could allow him to rack up anything like his 45 convictions.

This book is not the place to go into detail about particular murders, rapes, beatings etc., although I do have masses of information on just about every kind of crime. It is primarily about creating climates wherein far fewer people will risk breaking the law because of the increased likelihood of being caught and subsequently ending up in a Court which has no flexibility to let the guilty off with minimal or slap-on-the-wrist sentences. Repeat offenders particularly, would face very long years in gaol if they refuse to mend their ways. Serial offenders known to the police and the Courts will be a thing of the past once the recommendations in my next chapter, New Sentencing Solutions, are brought into effect.

I will though, touch on a small number of representative crimes by way of shining some light on the associated problems.

Torture has already had a chapter of its own.

Murder, *Burglary* and *Head-butting/Kicking/Knifing* are discussed herein.

Murder falls into the top two of my crime categories, expanded upon in the following chapter, i.e. Categories 9 and 10.

Whether or not any nation has capital punishment as the penalty for murder (or torture) is not for me to decide, nor is it for their politicians.

My recommendation is that each country should decide whether or not to have the death penalty as part of their armoury against the most serious offenders. The State's taking of anyone's life is so serious as to merit its validity being put before the electorate on a regular basis. One way to do this could be to attach one of the two following questions, as appropriate, to each voter's ballot paper *at every General Election*.

Q. Where there is currently no penalty – "Do you wish to see the death penalty for Category Ten crimes made available to the Courts?" Yes or No?

Q. Where the death penalty already exists – "Do you wish the death penalty currently available to the Courts to continue?" Yes or No?

This would be true democracy and would enable any nation to change its mind whenever it felt that their current regime was not working to the best interests of the community.

There will never be agreement between the two main diametrically opposite views on the death penalty, both of which merit respect, but it is the whole population which is potentially at risk of being murdered, so it should be the whole population eligible to vote, who should consider and vote upon the pros and cons of the death penalty.

Any nation opting for capital punishment should, of course, use it only where there is quality evidence of guilt. Fortunately, with D.N.A. and ever more sophisticated forensic science capability, there are an increasing number of crimes where the perpetrators can be identified beyond peradventure.

The evidence is clear, that murders increase significantly in those countries which scrap the death penalty and the reverse is also true. I am no fence-sitter, so I unhesitatingly say that without the prospect of losing their own lives, some seriously evil men and women will risk killing or torturing another in the knowledge that their crime will not result in them losing their own lives. That said, I would accept the will of the people on this very important issue, particularly if the mechanism is in place to reconsider the matter at every General Election. Politicians in some countries, of course, are afraid of Referenda, seeing them as a threat to their own preference for unbridled power. You will find suitable responses to political obstruction in a later chapter.

Burglary. Regrettably, many police officers, judges and magistrates treat burglary in far too casual a manner. They clearly do not fully understand the trauma suffered by many of the victims, or the permanent suffering caused by the realisation that one is not safe, even in one's own home.

Burglary could and should be a very rare crime but unfortunately, in many countries, this is not the case, primarily because of lottery sentencing, the police reacting too slowly to reported burglaries and taking too little forensic evidence at the scenes of crime. Often this is because they know that even if they devote more resources to this crime, their work will be rendered essentially worthless by the law and the Courts passing derisory sentences on those eventually declared guilty.

Ireland, for example, has twenty-five thousand burglaries a year, fifteen thousand of which take place whilst the residents are at home. Farmer Padraig Nally had been burgled many times where he lived alone in his isolated farmhouse and not unnaturally, was somewhat paranoid and overwrought when career criminal John "Frog" Ward was found lurking on his property. Nally shot and killed Ward and was charged with murder. The jury though, found him not guilty of murder but guilty of manslaughter, for which he is now serving a six-year prison sentence.

Anne Mendel, a sprightly 85-year old, was stabbed to death in her own home by burglars. It could have been you.

Alice Parker, a 76-year old lady was attacked with a weapon, beaten, kicked, concussed and left with broken ribs and a mangled wrist. Her burglar stole money she had saved to leave to her daughter and her 4.00 am nightmare left her so traumatised that she can no longer face living alone.

Tony Martin, an English live-alone farmer subjected to repeated burglaries, was gaoled for killing a burglar and imprisoned, despite public outcry.

One case I have on file, but who for obvious reasons wishes to remain anonymous, has been burgled 42 times. Two cars and four motorbikes have been stolen from his garage, yet not a single burglar has been caught.

Robin Baker White and his wife were burgled and seriously beaten on three occasions, the last time being when his assailant smashed him to the ground and drove off in his (Robin's) car. It was no protection that he was the previous High Sheriff of Kent.

John Monckton was stabbed to death by burglars and his wife was repeatedly stabbed at their Chelsea, London home by a seriously-evil guy *let out on early release* from a previous prison sentence for violence. You could be next.

Had the proposals in this book been in force at the time, probably none of these crimes – and many thousands of others – would have taken place. Clearly some systems are very broken and no-one is mending them.

Burglary is a vile, cowardly offence yet it is tolerated by many societies and because of this, some countries have hundreds of thousands of unsolved burglaries, with a goodly proportion of the lives of the victims seriously damaged or even snuffed out. Many people live in fear of that noise in the night or waking up with a knife at their throat. Almost none are left unscarred by their experience

And yet – it is almost unnecessary.

Britain, for example, is the burglary capital of Europe, simply because of the timidity of its politicians – particularly Attorney General Lord Goldsmith, Tony Blair, Jack Straw, David Blunkett, Charles Clarke and John Reid. When did you last hear any of these luminaries campaign against burglary? Probably never, because they are too busy discussing Identity Cards with their business friends, seeking to grab a few more billions from the British taxpayers who fund the companies producing these invasive surveillance systems which put them and political conspirators well into the Fat Cats bracket.

Massive reduction in burglary is so simple.

I have almost certainly talked with far more burglars than any of the afore-named politicians and I know precisely how they can be stopped.

194

Send *every* convicted burglar to prison, for between 3 years to life, dependent upon the seriousness of the offence in accordance with the Crime Categories proposed herein. Britain's Attorney General and former Lord Chief Justice Woolf disagreed and encouraged Courts *not* to send burglars to prison because this would necessitate more prison places. That they are wrong is now self-evident. Britain still suffers many thousands of burglaries ever year – not all of them recorded because some victims have concluded that calling the police is a waste of time. Small reductions from high levels of burglaries are recorded from time to time, but these are the result not of official help, but because homeowners and businesses have felt it necessary to turn their properties into fortresses.

Send another very clear message to every person contemplating burglary by changing the law, which currently puts the onus on the homeowner to determine what measures he or she make take in order to protect themselves and their property.

The law at the moment – like so many lawyer-written laws –was designed to be imprecise and hence, fertile ground for endless legal dispute.

In some countries, the law is, that the victim, i.e. the person whose home is being invaded, may use only "reasonable force" against intruders. This is just what the lawyers love – an area of vague and infinitely variable definition, one person's force being another's excessive violence. Unfortunately, no home-owner can be expected to be able to measure what level of force may be both reasonable and sufficient. There are simply too many factors in the equation and too little time during a break-in, in which to reach meaningful conclusions.

- Victims cannot possibly know the physical capabilities of their intruders. Often, the strength of people who may be prepared to kill you, cannot be determined until it is too late.

- Some home-owners have been brave enough to grapple with burglars, but some of these have paid the ultimate price for misreading or under-estimating their opponents. Being dead is a pretty awful result for making a wrong guess about the strength or vicious intentions of intruders.

- Even a weedy-looking pimply youth can have a knife hidden behind his back and at the time of the burglary, there is no judge, no police officer, no Crown Prosecutor, nor smart-ass lawyer with you in the house to either warn or protect you. You are on your own and faced with a very dangerous situation, you have no choice but to make a split second decision.

- All the odds currently favour the burglar. Surprise, fear, weapons availability, familiarity with violence on one side.

- The knowledge, on the other side, is that the law forbids you, the invaded homeowner, from using more than what is ludicrously called "reasonable force" to protect yourself and your property.

- No property owner, woken in the middle of the night, can know whether there is one, two, three or more burglars. They may believe themselves to be confronting one intruder, only to be smashed over the head from behind by another.

Burglary seriously diminishes the quality of life.

It has forced people to live in fear, move house, suffer serious violence, marital break-up, loss of valuables and items of irreplaceable sentimental importance. The psychological damage can be huge.

Burglary has trashed homeowners' self confidence and replaced this with feelings of inadequacy and guilt.

It has increased the divide between the public and the police, politicians and the Courts, all of whom have failed to deal adequately with burglary.

Nations where burglary is commonplace need do only three things :-

a. Bring in mandatory prison sentences for every person found guilty of burglary, in accordance with my next chapter New Sentencing Solutions.

b. Introduce sentence-compounding for second or subsequent offences, thereby eliminating the serial burglars very quickly.

c. Allow homeowners to use whatever means of protection they choose, without any prospect of themselves facing possible prosecution for harming the burglar(s).

Do these three things and burglary numbers will tumble like lemmings off a cliff.

To those who feel sympathy for burglars or who seek to excuse their cowardly, bullying, greedy attacks on innocent people, I say this. Burglars ***choose*** to commit their foul intrusions into people's homes. No-one forces them. Burglars have no concern for their victims and are completely indifferent to either their physical or mental suffering or their financial loss. They expect either not to be challenged, not to be caught or, if caught and found guilty, to get little more than a slap on the wrist from the Courts.

Failure to implement the above three corrective measures will condemn everyone to the prospect of being burgled, so I recommend, in a later chapter, what you can do to wake up those politicians who, for decades, have very evidently not taken burglary seriously.

Meantime, I am working with others to develop an interesting range of small signs which property owners can display outside their homes or workplaces, designed specifically to discourage burglars. By the time this book is published, these should be available via www.crimedown.org or you can email signs@crimedown.org for information about these signs.

It is worth noting that when Oklahoma, U.S.A. changed its law on defending oneself against burglars, in what became known as the "make my day punk" law, burglaries quickly dropped to around 50% of previous levels. Combining this attitude with mandatory and compounded prison sentences would significantly improve upon even Oklahoma's commendable achievement.

A number of former UK Chief Constables were already on my wavelength about burglary in 2004 and I have the names of several in my research files who are scathing of Tony Blair's Government's failure to permit people to defend themselves against burglars as they see fit.

The BBC, incidentally, conducted a poll of its listeners early in 2004 inviting them to choose five laws which they would like to see passed by Parliament via a Private Member's Bill. Overwhelmingly, the British public wanted a change in the law so that in future, property occupants would have the freedom to resist burglars by whatever means they felt to be appropriate, without fear of themselves being prosecuted.

Following on from the BBC's survey of its listeners, a Private Member's Bill was introduced into the House of Commons, but so undemocratic are the parliamentary processes in Britain that such Bills have almost no chance of becoming law without support from the Government. Tony Blair sabotaged the Bill to remove the prospect of burgled homeowners being charged for misjudging the degree of force necessary to overcome burglars. Another blatant example of the Labour Party's complete disregard for the wishes of its electorate.

What did Blair (he of the "tough on crime, tough on the causes of crime" boast), Blunkett, Clarke and Attorney General Lord Goldsmith do? They denied that there was any need to give home-owners any further protection and they continued to insist that people could only use reasonable force against burglars, *knowing full well*, of course, *that there can be no proper definition of "reasonable force"*.

Another victory for the burglars.

It strikes me as bizarre in the extreme, that on one hand the Blair Government claims that its overriding first duty is to defend its people by whatever means it wishes (against any enemy), whilst on the other hand, it is prohibiting each of its citizens from exercising the same right and duty to protect themselves, their families or their property.

The hypocrisy levels of Blair, Bush & Co. are frankly breathtaking. There is nothing "reasonable" about bombing and shooting up whole villages, including women and children because they suspect the presence of insurgents. Indeed, excessive rather than reasonable comes to mind.

One must question the thought processes and motives of politicians who claim the right to inflict shock and awe in far away lands, but deny their own citizens the choice of defending their homes as they think fit.

To these warped minds it is okay for Governments to deliberately plan massive attacks half way around the world which are certain to result in innocent people being killed, but it is not okay for their citizens to protect their own homes against uninvited villains whose intrusions can be a threat to the lives of the homeowners and their families. Only when a burglar is unconscious can anyone be sure that he or she is no longer dangerous, so talk of reasonable force can only put homeowners at greater risk.

I am quite confident that introducing the various jigsaw recommendations running through my "Quicksands" book can see burglaries down by 80/90% to between 10 and 20% of 2006/7 levels. A target I hope my readers will wish to see achieved.

Head-butting, *head-kicking* and *knifing* have now become common practice in disagreements, mainly because Courts have not attached to them the serious sentences which they deserve. Both can and do cause terrible injury, even death and both are a disgusting and cowardly way of fighting which goes far beyond the fisticuffs which I guess will always be with us and which I have been involved in myself on occasions.

Every day people are being knocked down then getting violently kicked in the head, ribs, kidneys - all parts of the body which, when damaged, can have terrible effects. Despite this, Magistrates and Judges all too often fail to understand the seriousness, even at times when victims are surrounded by what can only be described as vicious, out-of-control morons. Alcohol is frequently involved but that should never be accepted by any Court as an excuse. Only when everyone who head-butts or kicks a floored person is *sent to prison* and only when our schools and our Courts spell out this message loud and clear, will these brutish and cowardly violent crimes become largely a thing of the past. In the meantime, more prison places will be needed to accommodate those who are slow at getting the message. Knives are now ubiquitous simply because when first used years ago, Courts could and often did give sentences which did not reflect the seriousness of the crime. My next chapter shows what those countries, which have allowed knife cultures to develop, must do if they wish knifings to be drastically reduced.

Multiple Crimes. Every crime should be sentenced on its own merits and not lumped together with others. It is ridiculous to roll a number of crimes into one. Rapist Antoni Imiela for example, technically received seven life sentences, so how come, according to one newspaper, he will be eligible for parole after only eight years? This works out at only just over a year's imprisonment for each of the seven women he raped. Another source stated that in addition to the seven life sentences, he also received an additional 29 years for the last crime he committed – the kidnap and sexual assault of a 10 year old girl.

I am not familiar with the details of each of these rapes, but in the next chapter, you will see the Categories into which I propose Level *E*, least serious to Level *A* most serious rapes should be put, together with rising terms of imprisonment.

Mr. Imiela should, in my opinion, have been sent to gaol for an absolute minimum of 21 years in the unlikely event of all of his victims suffering the absolute minimum of trauma and no physical abuse. At the other end of the scale, he could have got sentences significantly higher than 100 years in prison, but I expect the appropriate sentence should have been somewhere in between the minimum and maximum applicable because it is likely that the 7 rapes for which he was convicted, would have involved different levels of violence.

Chaotic sentencing has only developed because over the years, Judges and lawyers have increasingly resisted any questioning of their competence, however justified. Determined to live in a rarefied atmosphere of their own creation, they brook no criticism and react violently to any attempts to connect them to the real world.

If we are serious about making major inroads into crime, an important early step must be to get rid of the chaotic sentences passed by the Courts - like Darren Pilkington who was released after spending only two years in gaol for his part in killing a man. Having received only a four-year sentence for helping his brother to kick Paul Akister to death in Hindley, Lancashire, he was released early after only two years - two dreadful judicial mistakes which were to have tragic consequences.

Pilkington, a man with 23 convictions, was then involved in the death of his girlfriend, Carly Fairhurst, but again saw a murder charge reduced to manslaughter. In December, Judge John Roberts at Liverpool Crown Court gave him an indeterminate sentence but, unbelievably, said that the violent thug could be considered for parole after serving three years.

Using my system of sentencing, Paul Akister and Carly Fairhurst would still be alive.

Another problem with Judges is that they are so arrogant and full of their own importance that they believe that when they issue stern warnings to people in the Dock, the villains will actually take their advice. I don't think so.

200

All too often, Judges believe themselves to be above the law and even on occasions demonstrate the truth of their belief. What other conclusion can one draw when a Judge gets off child pornography charges?

Irish Judge Brian Curtin was charged with having child pornography on his computer, downloaded from the internet, but instead of ending up in prison had he been found guilty, it was proposed that he should stand down – but receive his full salary until age 70, then be entitled to his lifetime pension.

How could such an outrageous situation arise? you may ask. Very simply really - smart-ass lawyers and Judges who care more about saving their own necks than they do for justice. Had Judge Curtin been an honourable man, he would have fully faced his trial but instead, he and his legal team found a **technical loophole** which, after days of legal argument, succeeded in getting the trial aborted with the jury **ordered** to enter a "not guilty" verdict. Fortunately for Crafty Curtin, the Gardai who searched the Judge's home and found child pornography on his computer did so on a search warrant which "may" have expired hours beforehand. There was considerable disagreement about whether a seven-day search warrant was valid for seven days from the "time" and date it was issued, in which case the Gardai were within time, or simply seven days, in which case their own incompetence put them out of time by a few hours.

On this crazy bit of chicanery, the evidence of child pornography found on Judge Brian Curtin's computer was declared by the trial Judge, Carroll Moran, to be inadmissible.

I must repeat what I said earlier. No-one should escape the penalty of their crimes on procedural technicalities of law.

That is not justice. It is a disgrace which must be corrected.

All nations should rid themselves of the chaotic sentences syndrome and to do this, they must (a) return to the spirit and intention of their laws and (b) develop New Sentencing Solutions – next chapter.

CHAPTER 11

NEW SENTENCING SOLUTIONS

Crime can be brought down by better education; by real deterrents; by greatly increasing the chances of being caught; by eliminating chaotic sentencing; and then, very importantly, by ensuring that those found guilty of crimes suffer some meaningful, inescapable punishment.

I am absolutely in concert with attempts to rehabilitate offenders, but this should be in addition to the punishment element of their sentences and not a substitute for them. Criminals are liars almost by definition and many fake contrition in attempts to gain undeserved leniency, but my advice to any society wanting lower crime is to remember how little compassion the criminals had for their victims. Although rehabilitation should be available to all criminals, it is not the Holy Grail and its success rate at preventing re-offending ranges between modest to poor. It is also very labour intensive and hence, very expensive, so I would like to see a shift towards inmates studying to pass a version of my proposed Concern & Consequences examination in their own cells. One-to-one counselling may be desirable, but no prison regime in the world can afford sufficient specialists to devote very much time in face-to-face rehab sessions. Perhaps we should be discussing help from the voluntary sector in this area.

Throughout this book you will see that all of my focus is on the actual and potential criminals and I never support the invasions of the privacy of the law-abiding sector of society. Under no circumstances am I prepared to sacrifice individual liberty in order to hand over more power to Governments. Neither right nor left wing politicians have earned my approval and my sincere belief is that no political party can significantly reduce crime without going back to square one and questioning practices which took root often light years ago. By early 2007, politicians of high crime nations have still not recognised the damage done by existing sentencing procedures, so I have taken up the initiative in their place on your behalf – unasked admittedly and unpaid, unfortunately.

This has allowed me to study all crime-related matters and to exchange views with thousands of individuals without pressure or interference from anyone. I wish to see justice and fairness; laws which cannot conceivably have different interpretations; and sentences which really do fit the crimes, have far greater logic and very importantly, consistency. This way, both the law-abiding and the criminally-inclined will know exactly where they stand.

Following years of research and much serious thought, I am convinced that over many decades, most countries have allowed Judges far too great a role in both directing juries and determining sentences. The result has been increased instead of decreased crime. I propose therefore, a number of radical changes in sentencing and law and I do this notwithstanding the outcry which they will doubtless raise in the obvious quarters.

Where implemented, these changes will :-

- Discourage crime, with a particular emphasis of putting an end to the nonsense of repeat offending. Result – far fewer victims, which is the purpose of all of my campaigning and of this book.

- End the crazy situation wherein equal crimes with very similar contributory circumstances result in widely different sentences, sometimes excessive, sometimes staggeringly lenient. Result – greater fairness and hence, more public satisfaction with, and acceptance of the law.

- Provide, wherever practicable, financial restitution to victims and taxpayers.

- Take sentencing power away from the professional judiciary and put it into the hands of the people (juries). Result – a closing of the growing gap between citizens and the Courts. There is, incidentally, a considerable Body of writing which establishes that the opinions of the crowd are often far wiser than those of the so-called experts and academics.

Combined with other measures recommended herein, I have no doubt that these new principles will bring a major reduction in crime which clearly is never going to happen if those Countries with high crime levels continue with their current failed policies. Over the years, there have been numerous politically-inspired changes to judicial systems but even in total, these have amounted to nothing more than tinkering.

All nations need a legal system for today and one which will best protect their people in the 21st century. This cannot be achieved without scrapping much of the legal garbage which, over hundreds of years, has grown like a cancer and obstructed genuine justice. The judicial systems in high-crime nations have, by definition, failed and what they absolutely do not need is yet more tinkering. They need a total overhaul, so here goes.

Lawyers, for their own financial gain, have cluttered up the judicial process with every kind of device intended to increase their own power at the expense of all others. British Prime Minister William Gladstone saw some of the dangers long ago when he said "*Justice delayed is justice denied*" and boy, do lawyers know how to delay and turn a system which could and should be simple into one of almost unbelievable complexity.

Tony Blair, when seeking another term in Office, promised fast-track justice, particularly for juveniles. Twenty days from charge to judgement was his mantra, but five years later, the average time is still more than ninety days.

Our politicians have chosen to ignore Gladstone's truism but of course, many of our politicians are lawyers, so they would encourage delayed justice and mega-long trials wouldn't they?

I address this problem in greater detail later in the book.

I also recommend serious consideration, including open debate, on another matter which some will prefer to avoid.

Most societies which have high crime also suffer traffic congestion, environmental damage and road deaths/accidents. Well. We can reduce all of these very difficult problems in one fell swoop by changing our attitude to driving. It would be sensible to make Driving Licences an absolute entitlement only to those who are sufficiently socially responsible to appreciate the relationship between aggressive driving and serious accidents.

I propose therefore, that in addition to traffic violations, Courts should use the disqualification of Driving Licences as an adjunct to a wide range of non-motoring offences. Courts should also postpone, for a period, the time when a guilty party may apply for a first Driving Licence. In either case, these sanctions should be backed by mandatory prison sentences and extended bans for anyone choosing to ignore them and drive whilst disqualified.

Driving Licences are *the* most important thing to many people, but they are particularly valued by the young, many of whom have openly told me that they would not have committed some crimes had they been at risk of being banned from getting or keeping their hands on that steering wheel. My proposed curriculum for the Concern & Consequences examination would, of course, ensure that all pupils fully understand that any criminality would delay their eligibility for a Driving Licence by a number of years.

Nothing quite concentrates the minds of many of today's tearaways as the prospect of losing their wheels and I strongly urge all countries suffering high crime to add the confiscation of Driving Licences for non-motoring offences to many of my recommended Crime Category sentences featured throughout this chapter.

Here are my main proposals on sentencing, from which any country can benefit – particularly those sinking in the quicksands of crime.

I have condensed these into *seven principles*, as below.

1st Sentencing Principle - Mandatory sentences/fines/public awareness

2nd Sentencing Principle - Compounding sentences for repeat offences

3rd Sentencing Principle - Up-rating Community Service Orders

4th Sentencing Principle - Juries, not Judges

5th Sentencing Principle - Guilt or Innocence? Add "Not Proven"

6th Sentencing Principle - Scrap all double jeopardy laws

7th Sentencing Principle - The Law can be wrong

I explain on the following pages, the need for these new sentencing principles and the benefits which will flow to the law-abiding citizens of those countries adopting them, without of course trespassing on their rights and freedoms.

One solution I propose is that Governments put every crime into one of a number of categories which, for now, I will classify as Category One, the least onerous, to Category Ten for the most serious offences. Before explaining the system further, I must point out that the categories and sentences which I itemise in this Blueprint are examples for demonstration and consultation purposes only. A starting point for public debate. How each crime (of thousands) is eventually classified – and what the range of sentences within each category should be – is a matter for politicians and more importantly, the electorates of each country to decide.

I strongly recommend each nation to make its own Category allocations and not to try and harmonise these in consultation with other countries. Any attempted co-operation with other countries or groupings would simply open the floodgates through which international lawyers and bureaucrats would pour, with lips smacking. An army of these parasites would form Committees, Working Parties and Instant Experts, all arranging expensive conferences in Geneva, Rome, London, Perth, Vancouver etc.

An army of professional parasites would come out of the woodwork arguing that all nations should put the same crimes into the same Categories carrying the same penalties. That fearful world "harmonisation" would once again be used to open up the permanent talking shops, all substitutes for each nation coming to its own decisions about allocating which crimes to which Crime Categories.

Do not let your politicians go down that road.

Each country has its own particular problems with crime and must come to its own conclusions in order to get maximum benefit from introducing a Ten Categories of Crimes regime. You will find some apparent inconsistencies in my personal allocations because by design, these are not based upon any particular country's needs, so they may not be the best fit to solve the specific crime problems suffered where you live.

For example, gun and knife crime are serious problems in some countries and often, the countries where gun ownership is forbidden by law, see gun crime rise instead of fall. A number of countries have tried to ban the carrying of knives, but try fitting that in with the Argentinean Gauchos, Canadian Eskimos or Finnish hunter culture. Clearly that would not be appropriate and on some crime-related matters, I do not pretend that one size fits all.

In my Crime Categories following therefore, I have no allocations in respect of the ownership or carrying of knives or guns other than taking them into schools. I do, of course, put the *use* of knives or guns, to either threaten or injure, into my recommended high crime categories.

My 'Ten Categories' system also allows sufficient flexibility for those passing sentence - (more about this in my 4th Sentencing Principle) – to make such adjustments as they feel to be appropriate within the mandatory levels laid down by politicians as representatives of their people. This is achieved by having the lengths of sentences designed to overlap with those in a lower or higher category.

For example, a Category Eight crime would merit a custodial sentence of 5 years minimum to 12 years maximum. A Category Seven crime, 4 years minimum to 10 years maximum, making it possible for someone committing a Category Seven crime without any extenuating circumstances to end up with a longer sentence than someone guilty of a Category Eight crime which merited a sentence at the lower end of that range and of course vice versa.

This overlapping principle operates throughout the scale and combined with the other sentencing elements would, in my view, provide the best protection for the public, better justice for victims and the greatest degree of fairness for those guilty of crime.

Not all violent crimes, theft from shops, environmental damage etc. are of equal gravity of course, so to enable these to be allocated to the most appropriate Category and sentence, I propose the creation of five *levels* of severity – *A* to *E*, with *A* being the most serious, for each crime type.

Politicians should introduce mandatory sentences, as soon as is practically possible, which Courts *must* follow. The public is entitled to be protected by a system which, whilst still leaving the Courts with considerable discretion, sends a very clear message to those contemplating crime. That message is that *if you are guilty of any serious crime, you are certain to go to prison*. No ifs. No buts. No maybes.

PUBLIC AWARENESS

It is my belief that we are all entitled to know who, amongst us, has been found guilty of committing what crimes. If we break the law, we are, after all, tried in a Court, in public and the Courts in most countries are obliged to make the outcomes known.

This being so, I propose that each nation keeps *a single, on-line database of every criminal case together with all "not proven" or "guilty" verdicts and sentences*. Such a database, *readily accessible to all*, would give the public enormous protection.

Employers, particularly those charged with caring for children or other vulnerable groups, will have immediate access to the criminal records (if any) of all job applicants. Those where financial honesty or access to cash is a feature will immediately be aware of any theft, burglary, fraud etc.

Other countries, when considering Visa applications, will have a facility for checking which is far more reliable and speedy than is currently available.

I appreciate, of course, that the risk is huge but it would certainly be easier and cheaper than many of today's complex Identity Card schemes. It must though be possible to challenge any incorrect listings and have them removed from the database in the event of any incorrect entry.

There are specialist I.T. firms quite capable of bringing such projects to fruition and from *day one*, every guilty or not-proven Court verdict should go onto the publicly-available database against a named person. Social Security, passport and driving licence details and/or date and place of birth should all feature, sufficient to avoid any chance of mistaken identity.

Making it known that all future criminals will be listed on the National Public Crime Database (N.P.C.D.) from *day one* will also be a powerful deterrent to some potential criminals.

Simultaneous with recording all future crimes, the project should start working backwards in order to record who committed what crimes in previous years. It may, of course, be sensible not to go back too many years for the lower of my recommended ten crime categories because if, for example, someone had been found guilty of shoplifting more than five years ago, but had been found guilty of no other offence in the meantime, it may be considered of little value to record that ten years earlier he or she had broken into a car.

There will need to be considerable debate about possible historic cut-off dates related to the seriousness of the individual crime categories. It is possible, of course, that in some countries, existing police/criminal records bureaux databases can readily provide a short cut to my N.P.C.D. Some adaptation will be necessary, but existing police crime records will prove to give my proposed project a substantial kick-start.

Had Tony Blair listened to The Society for Action Against Crime ten years ago, the National Public Crime Database would have been up and running long ago. I have no doubt that the prospect of having their name on a public register would dissuade many of the criminally-inclined from succumbing to temptation. Yet another piece of the jigsaw puzzle which can help achieve significantly lower levels of crime.

It frankly makes no sense not to have a database identifying those who have committed criminal acts. Nor is there any logic in the information being available only to the police via the Criminal Records Bureau. The public have every right to know what crimes have been perpetrated, when and by whom.

Many property owners let out houses, apartments or rooms, some having complete strangers sharing their homes with them. To me it makes good sense for them to have instant access to a public on-line database and I certainly know of tragedies which occurred when landlords unwittingly let accommodation to persons whom they would not have entertained had they known of their criminal backgrounds.

Expect some of the Establishments already running Criminal Records systems badly, to attempt to denigrate the idea of a database permanently available to everyone. They will, of course, not only lose their current cosy positions, they will lose the control which goes with it and more importantly, their mistakes will be there for everyone to see and challenge.

Those imputing the data will just have to be far more careful and their work must constantly be audited.

Fortunately, most people now realise that those currently in charge of homeland security are a pretty incompetent bunch of bunglers who lurch from one crises of their own making to another, then another, then another. Always with their excuses. Always promising to learn from their mistakes – but never in fact learning anything.

A quite different database should also be compiled which is available to the police but which cannot be accessed by the public. This is to record everyone investigated by police, together with the circumstances, regardless of whether or not this had led to a prosecution. Warnings, cautions etc. should all be logged and had this second of my database recommendations been taken up by Tony Blair in 1997, there would have been far fewer victims of crime.

Ian Huntley, for example, would have been flagged-up and simply moving from one police authority area to another would not have let him escape the surveillance net. The two young girls, Jessica Chapman and Holly Wells whom he murdered by taking advantage of getting a position of trust bringing him close to children, would still be alive today.

Here are the **sentences** allocated to my proposed **ten crime categories**. On the pages following, as a base for consultation, I allocate some specific crimes into what may be considered their appropriate order of seriousness. Many more to be added, of course.

Category One -

Theoretical 6 months custodial but automatically commuted to appropriate Community Service Order/fine sufficient to compensate any victim for double the value of any loss of goods and to cover judicial costs

Category Two -

Theoretical 6 months minimum Automatically commuted to appropriate Community Service Order and/or fine to compensate victims	to	Theoretical 1 year maximum custodial plus driving licence suspension at Court's discretion

Category Three -

8 months minimum custodial or the offer of a Community Service Order in lieu	to	2 years maximum custodial plus driving licence suspension at Court's discretion

Category Four -

1½ years minimum custodial. Mandatory plus fine if appropriate	to	4 years maximum custodial plus obligatory suspension of driving licence for 6 to 18 months

Category Five -

2 years minimum custodial. Mandatory	to	6 years maximum custodial plus obligatory loss of driving licence for 1-3 years

Category Six -

3 years minimum custodial. Mandatory	to	8 years maximum custodial plus obligatory loss of driving licence for 2-4 years

Category Seven -

5 years minimum custodial. Mandatory	to	10 years maximum custodial plus obligatory loss of driving licence for 3-5 years

Category Eight -

5 years minimum custodial. Mandatory	to	12 years maximum custodial plus obligatory loss of driving licence for 4-6 years

Category Nine -

10 years minimum custodial. Mandatory	to	20 years maximum custodial plus obligatory loss of driving licence for 5-10 years

Category Ten -

15 years minimum custodial. Mandatory with obligatory loss of driving licence for 5-10 years	to	Full life in custody or capital punishment in those nations wishing it

Notes on Fines and Sentencing

Fines – The level of fines imposed by the Courts cannot always be mandatory because there are simply too many computations of loss in terms of goods, property and personal injury to be considered. As a general principle though, fines should be sufficient to pay victims recompense equal to twice their actual financial loss or suffering, to compensate for any disturbance, trauma, Court/police attendance etc. plus payment of, or contribution to judicial costs.

I deal later on with fines for speeding only (where no accident is caused), this being a matter which should be dealt with as a special issue.

Custodial Sentences – Life should mean *Life*, by which I mean that those given mandatory life sentences should *never* be released.

Where criminals confess to crimes, thereby negating the need for a full and costly trial, the guilty party/parties should expect the Court to reduce the range of mandatory sentence by approximately 25%.

Examples:- The Category Nine tariff of 7 to 20 years would be reduced to 5 to 15 years. A Category Five tariff of 2 to 6 years would be reduced to 1½ to 4½ years

Prior to the introduction of the Ten Categories of Crimes/Obligatory Sentences System, Governments of course should give maximum publicity to the new Sentencing Regime coming into being.

The publicity for this should also be continued after the start date in order that few people are left unaware of the important changes. Such advertising campaigns will pay for themselves many times over because once the criminal fraternity realises, for the first time, that the Courts can no longer go easy on them, many will decide that the risks are too great and that crime is no longer the easy payday of old.

Category One Crimes

Tariff – theoretical 6 months custodial, commuted to, in one instance only, Community Service Order plus fine equal to twice the victim's loss, plus Court costs plus loss of Driving Licence at the Court's discretion. A.S.B.O. if appropriate.

Included in this Category could be :-

- *Level E* shoplifting of goods worth less than £20 (or equivalent in other currencies)

- Anti-social behaviour without personal or property injury/damage

- Discarding casual litter

- Minor noise nuisance

- Failure to have current Licences – dogs, TV, music etc. as required by law

- Using public transport without payment of fare

- Smoking in prohibited places

- Abusive language or hand signals

- Cycling in pedestrian-only areas

- *Level E* minor environmental damage/pollution (definition to be discussed)

Rationale – These relatively minor offences, though not necessarily an indication of the start of a criminal career, should nevertheless not be overlooked. It sends out all the wrong signals when anyone found guilty of even minor crimes walks away from Court with nothing more than a warning or a suspended sentence. Meaningful

214

consequences should flow from every crime. For Category One to Three crimes, loss of or postponement of Driving Licences should be at Courts' discretion. Provided that it is used from time to time by the Courts, the message will be taken and the prospect of being off the road for a while will deter at least some from becoming or continuing to be criminals.

Consultation – Most countries will wish to consider other offences to go into every Crime Category but I recommend they consult less with professionals and more with everyday people, including crime victims. Supposedly highly-qualified people such as those on Britain's Sentencing Guidelines Council have had their chance, but the fact that the crime problems have not been solved is testament to their failure. If crime is to be reduced significantly, every country should move away from Establishment figures and consult more genuinely with those at the sharp end. Police Constables and Sergeants rather than Commissioners, taxi drivers rather than professors of criminology, ordinary solicitors rather than Judges etc. Prison officers, teachers, doctors, shopkeepers, builders, prostitutes, miners, fishermen and dinner ladies could all make a valuable contribution to the debate on the allocation of crimes to categories and appropriate sentencing.

Category Two Crimes

Tariff – Nominal (suspended) 6 months to 1 year, substituted by Community Service Order and/or fine on the same principle as Category One crimes. Loss of Driving Licence for any Category Two offence at the Court's discretion.

Note: Although the Court must decide upon an imprisonment tariff for 6 months to 1 year for possible future use in the sentencing compounding system, should a guilty party re-offend, it may, at its discretion, substitute or add community service orders, revocation of driving licence, or fines, thereby avoiding actually sending the offender to prison.

Included in this category could be :-

• Level *E* minor fraud

• Level *D* shoplifting of goods worth £20 to £99

- Throwing down or affixing chewing gum in other than proper receptacles

- Driver overtaking by aggressive and inappropriate lane switching

- Owning a motor vehicle *parked* on a public road or place when such vehicle does not have both current regulation Road Tax or insurance paid up.

- Level *E* domestic violence

Rationale – These and Category One and Category Three crimes are the only offences which do not carry an automatic custodial sentence, although repeated offences of even these relatively minor crimes can do so. See my later Sentencing Compounding System. This really is almost the last chance for any budding criminal of any age to avoid entering the prison regime. This starts by committing any Category Four or higher crime, even if it is a first offence.

Consultation – Once any nation determines which crimes it is to allocate to which Categories, this information should be part of my recommended Concern & Consequences examination for schools. Pending this, these Crime Categories and sentences should be taught in every school which, for the first time, will bring clarity to the subject of breaking the law at an early age.

Fraud levels *E* to *A* should be determined following discussion with all interested parties.

Category Three Crimes

Tariff – 8 months minimum to 2 years maximum imprisonment or the offer of suspending this to a Community Service Order, plus loss of Driving Licence for 3 to 6 months - regardless of the nature of the offence – at the Court's discretion.

Included in this category could be :-

- Threatening Behaviour

- Spitting at/onto a person

- *Driving* a motor vehicle on which current road fund licence has not been paid

- Criminal damage

- Grafiti

- Level *C* shoplifting of goods worth £100 to £249

- Level *D* environmental damage/pollution

- Violence with short-term minor injury during sports matches

- Serious noise pollution

- Level *D* domestic violence

Rationale – We are now moving into the area of more serious crime and anyone querying why I have put graffiti into this Category should look at the disgraceful damage caused to visual amenity by acres of graffiti in some areas. It all started with just one guy with a few cans of spray paint and failing to treat this as a serious crime has left societies with clean-up bills of tens of millions of dollars.

Retail theft is even more costly, losing the trade more than a billion dollars (or equivalent) in some countries! You the consumer pick up the tab in the end.

Consultation – We should be developing strategies to catch some graffiti polluters in the act. Send them to prison and take away their Driving Licences. They will soon get the message.

In addition to it being a Category Three crime, spitting at a person should also be outlawed from sport. Any player of any sport spitting at either another player or at any spectator(s) should be banned by their governing Body, for at least a year with the ban doubling for any subsequent offence. It is a despicable practice, made even worse by the terrible example it sets to young people particularly.

I will be pleased to discuss with interested parties how a spitting ban could best be introduced to benefit individual sports.

Category Four Crimes

From this category onwards, the Courts have no choice but to give custodial sentences, between the minimum and maximum allocated.

Tariff – Mandatory 1½ years minimum to 4 years maximum imprisonment, plus mandatory loss of Driving Licence for 3 to 9 months following release from custody.

Included in this category could be :-

• Voluntarily being a passenger in a vehicle known to be stolen

• Level *D* fraud

• Animal Neglect

• Vandalising a vehicle

• Threatening (but not carrying out) attack with any kind of possibly diseased needle or instrument

• Level *E* burglary

• Blackmail

• Level *B* shoplifting of goods worth £250 to £999

• Sports violence resulting in the victim being out of action for *??* months

• Random vehicle damage

• Level *E* happy-slapping

Rationale – Maltreatment of animals is a sign of danger in any individual which should not be tolerated by any civilised society.

From Category Four onwards, withdrawal of or postponement of Driving Licences should be mandatory, providing society with an important tool with which to fight the criminal community.

Consultation – Pending the introduction of my recommended Concern & Consequences subject into schools, it is important that all concerned take initiatives to deal with the alarming development of happy-slapping. The message must be got across that this disgusting so-called game will absolutely not be tolerated and that any low-life playing it will end up in gaol if caught.

Category Five Crimes

Tariff – Mandatory 2 years minimum to 6 years maximum imprisonment, plus mandatory loss of or postponement of Driving Licence for 6 to 9 months following release from custody.

Included in this category could be :-

- Level *D* burglary

- Level *E* people trafficking

- Level *C* Domestic Violence

- Level *E* Corruption

- Stalking/Harassment likely to cause distress

- Driving a vehicle which is in a dangerous/ unroadworthy condition

- Abandonment or other unsafe disposal of any kind of needle capable of transmitting disease

- Driving whilst disqualified or without a Licence

- Level *C* environmental damage/pollution

- Level *E* rape where parties are together by agreement but where advantage has been taken of substance abuse

- Level *D* happy-slapping

Rationale – By progressively increasing mandatory sentences in line with each nation's perception of the seriousness of individual crimes, the hopes that almost all criminals have, of being let off lightly by the Courts, will be dashed.

Once the certainty of a custodial sentence is in place for identified crimes, I have no doubt that the number of people committing them will drop substantially. In one respect, "date rape" is even worse than rape by a stranger because of the breach of trust involved. It is though, an area where Courts are faced with having to consider evidence which is often impossible to prove, so great care must be taken in the handling of this very difficult-to-judge crime.

Consultation – The police should seek authority from a Judge to use intrusive surveillance techniques when investigating reports by third parties into the likelihood of some of the aforementioned and other crimes as appropriate.

Domestic violence and corruption, for example, are particularly difficult to prove, so co-operation between victims, colleagues, the police and the judiciary should be brought to bear to possibly use secretive camera and recording equipment.

Category Six Crimes

Tariff – Mandatory 3 years minimum to 8 years maximum imprisonment, plus mandatory loss of or postponement of Driving Licence for 6 to 12 months following release from custody.

Included in this category could be :-

• Level *D* Cruelty / Sexual Assault

• Level *C* Burglary without violence

• Level *C* fraud

• Level *B* domestic violence

• Level *D* people trafficking

• Soliciting money under false pretences

• Level *A* shoplifting of goods worth more than £1,000

• Affray

• Possession of knife without good reason

- Obtaining money by deception

- Driving a motor vehicle whilst disqualified / Theft of a motor vehicle / Second (or greater) conviction for driving without insurance

- Level *C* happy-slapping

- Possession(only) of child pornography – any media

Rationale - Teaching Crime Categories in schools and publicising mandatory sentences will, I have no doubt, persuade most of those who so recklessly commit these crimes at the moment, to seriously mend their ways. Those who refuse to get the message will, quite justifiably, be put where they can do no further harm, at least for a few years. Any who consider themselves the real hard nuts and who persist with their criminality, will earn themselves even longer periods of imprisonment via the automatic compounding of sentences process.

Consultation – Any nation suffering high crime must start to initiate corrective measures and communicate these to the public at large on a long-term basis.

Permanent anti-crime advertising campaigns should be used to get across the varying solutions to particular aspects of crime being targeted.

Category Seven Crimes

Tariff – Mandatory 5 years minimum to 10 years maximum imprisonment, plus mandatory loss of driving licence for 3 to 5 years following release from custody.

Included in this category could be :-

- Level *B* burglary with threat and/or violence

- Level *C* people trafficking

- Level *B* Domestic Violence

- Level *B* Animal Cruelty

- Level *D* Rape, including threat of violence

- Level **D** Corruption

- Level **B** environmental damage/pollution

- Possession of gun illegally - any age

- Level **C** Cruelty and/or Sexual Assault

- Tampering with or invasion of private mail

- Intrusion into private property/telephone, internet or bank privacy by any public servant without a prior "good cause to suspect" warrant authorised by a Judge

- Using a needle to transmit or create the fear of transmission of disease

- Level **B** happy-slapping

Rationale – No-one committing any of these crimes should have the hope of not going to prison and the combination of a known range of custodial sentences, with the then driving ban, will cause many to re-think their criminal careers. These unavoidable sentences will make almost all parents think far more seriously about what their kids are doing.

Consultation – It will be for the prosecuting authorities to liaise with other interested Bodies to decide the level (A to E) with which each accused should be charged.

Category Eight Crimes

Tariff – Mandatory 5 years minimum to 12 years maximum imprisonment, plus mandatory loss of driving licence for 4 to 6 years following release from custody.

Included in this category could be :-

- Level **A** domestic Violence

- Level **C** rape involving actual violence

- Level **C** corruption

- Level **A** environmental damage/pollution

- Level **B** misuse of Public Office

- Level **B** cruelty and/or Sexual Assault

- Level **B** fraud

- Knowingly and unjustifiably claiming or receiving State benefit(s)

- Drunken Violence causing injury or trauma

- Failure to report actual or suspected torture

- Head-butting, kicking, use of offensive weapon

- Incitement to violence

- Sabotaging a vehicle, rendering it dangerous/not roadworthy

- Taking drugs into penal institutions without written consent

Rationale – Violence against the person will not substantially reduce until there is a certainty of the perpetrators going to gaol. Some countries suffer hugely from crimes in this category and their citizens will continue falling victim to them until some ***certainty*** of loss of freedom is brought to bear on the problem.

Consultation – Those nations smart enough to establish a Crime Category Judicial System with mandatory sentences should run advertising campaigns from time to time in order that everyone understands the risks they are taking if they ignore the law. Together with requiring all children to study and pass an examination in the subject, this will persuade many that the crime route is not one worth following.

Category Nine Crimes

Tariff – Mandatory 10 years minimum to 20 years maximum imprisonment, plus mandatory loss of driving licence for 5 to 10 years following release from custody.

Included in this category could be :-

- Murder following provocation

- Manslaughter without provocation

- Causing death or long-term disability by reckless/dangerous driving (this should also be accompanied by a 5 to 10-year driving ban, to commence upon release from gaol)

- Level *A* Burglary using violence resulting in victim needing hospital treatment

- Armed Robbery

- Witness or jury intimidation or tampering

- Level *B* Corruption

- Level *A* Fraud

- Knowingly risking passing on a sexually transmitted disease

- Smuggling any weapon or escape aid into a penal institution

- Level *B* people trafficking, enslavement, forced prostitution

- Level *A* environmental damage/pollution

- Level *A* money Laundering

- Level A cruelty and/or Sexual Abuse, involving juniors/infants in sexual activity/paedophilia etc.

- Level *B* rape including serious damaging violence

- Level *A* Criminal Negligence resulting in death

- Level *A* Abuse/Misuse of Public Office

- Others to be considered following wide consultation

- Level *A* happy-slapping

Rationale – In some countries, some of the above crimes would be treated much more leniently by the Judges, which is why so many of the perpetrators chance their arms. Only by replacing this excessive leniency with sentences which match the severity of the crimes can any society bring criminality down to tolerable levels.

Consultation – There needs to be open debate on the sexually-driven crimes because sentencing is the easy bit. The problem is the on-going one of what to do with violent rapists and paedophiles come release day. I have some thoughts on this but need more time to discuss the problem with others before refining them into hopefully useful proposals.

Along with the dangers which accompany those with serious mental problems, sexual offenders pose one of the most intractable problems in the entire sphere of crime.

Category Ten Crimes

Tariff – mandatory 15 years minimum to life imprisonment or the death sentence in those States where it applies – see *viable alternative* below. Mandatory loss of Driving Licence for 7 to 10 years for those released from custody.

Included in this category could be :-

• Torture – either actual or pro-actively complicit

• Ordering, authorising or condoning torture

• Ethnic Cleansing

• Murder without provocation, including random or targeted terrorist attack

• Failed terrorist attack which could have resulted in death or serious injury

• Hi-jacking of public service or passenger vehicle, train, plane, boat etc.

• Level *A* rape resulting in serious bodily harm and mental trauma

• Level *A* Corruption

• Level *A* people trafficking resulting in loss of life

• Level *A* environmental damage/pollution resulting in loss of life

Rationale – It must be made absolutely clear to anyone contemplating any Category Ten crime that Courts have no option other than to confine them for a substantial period. None of these crimes are committed accidentally nor can they have any worthwhile motive. Some, indeed, are so appalling as to merit the ultimate penalty in those countries having capital punishment available. The public must have maximum protection from criminals prepared to commit such terrible crimes and severe, unavoidable sentences are a valuable factor in keeping Category Ten crimes to the minimum possible.

Consultation – Capital punishment has traditionally been a hugely emotional subject with some countries using it whilst others will not even discuss it. I propose that every nation should consult with their citizens and a good way to do this is to pose the question at *every* General Election. I would be prepared to assist in the precise question to be asked. This would depend upon the crimes allocated to Category Ten, but it is important that a referendum be used at each Election in order that the voters can regularly re-assess how their early decision had worked out in practice.

Inadvisably, the European Union has a total ban on capital punishment but it is typical of that bullying Body that it seeks to deny freedom of choice to sovereign nations. What was sold to the public as a trading group now interferes in almost every aspect of life throughout Europe.

So serious is crime now in many European countries that the question of capital punishment will keep returning and my forecast is that the subject will still be very alive long after the *EU* has sunk into oblivion.

Viable Alternative

When solutions seem intractable, it is my philosophy to search for solutions which have been overlooked, possibly because of their quirkiness.

One argument used by the supporters of the death penalty is the cost of keeping evil people alive in prison and indeed, the cost can be enormous. As much as £1,750,000 (one point seven five million pounds sterling – more than three million dollars) can be the cost to the taxpayer. The average will be somewhat less, but it is still a very

226

substantial figure which will shock even some of those who disagree with capital punishment.

My solution? Let all those who are vociferous against the death penalty form a charity for each individual person condemned to death. Such person can then stay alive in prison for as long as the charity pays for all of the costs of confinement. This will stop the costs being borne by those who profoundly disagree with certain murderers being kept alive at all and it is particularly distasteful to them when this is done at their expense as a taxpayer. It will also let those of the opposite persuasion show the depth and sincerity of their opinions.

Put simply, it is called putting your money where your mouth is and it will be interesting to see how many killers are kept alive by their charities and for how long.

Minor Motoring Offence Category

Offences such as speeding, where there is no victim and no accident, should not be criminal offences in any country and I advise all to re-structure their penalty regimes to better reflect the degree of seriousness of a wide range of transgressions.

To put the Driving Licences of anyone at risk for a series of incidents of exceeding speed limits by a modest amount is frankly nonsense. As remarked elsewhere in the book, almost every driver regularly exceeds speed limits and provided that those caught are doing so only modestly, their Licences should not be at risk.

There should, of course, be speed limits and those breaching them should be fined.

Fines cannot be calculated on the basis of one standard percentage of any excess of speed because exceeding a 20 m.p.h. speed limit by 30% is nothing like as potentially dangerous as exceeding a 70 m.p.h. limit by 30%.

Where the police have incontrovertible evidence of speeds in excess of those applicable – and where no accident or damage is involved – the police should be allowed to offer fines perhaps as below, without the matter necessarily going to Court. This should also offer offenders the opportunity to accept points on their Licences as per the following table – again without clogging up the Courts at great expense. Where offenders cannot afford the fines, they should have the option of accepting a Community Service Order which, provided that it is diligently complied with, would not constitute part of a criminal record.

The table on the following page is a starting point for discussing the whole area of dealing with non-dangerous speeding. Licences to be at risk if twelve or more points are picked up within any two-year period.

Whilst I have no hesitation in recommending a more relaxed and fairer approach to breaches of laid down speed limits, I am equally enthusiastic about measures to deter and punish motorists who are or could be a danger on public roads. I want to see the police stop any driver or rider in order to test them for alcohol or other drugs. They should be allowed to do this without reason and should do it with sufficient regularity for the word to get around. Targeting venues where people drink and party would be sensible.

Traffic police should change their priorities and use vehicles equipped with quality video recorders used specifically to catch some of the dangerous drivers most of us see every day - the impatient lane-switchers who overtake on the wrong side, then force their way back into the lane they should have stayed in; the lunatic driver who overtakes other vehicles on blind bends in the hope that he or she can force their way back into their proper lane if they meet on-coming traffic head-on; the road-rager who, at what is perceived to be some misjudgement, immediately resorts to abusive hand signals, foul language, physical attack and even murder. These are where scarce police resources should be spent and dangerous offenders should face tough penalties.

Speed Limit	Caught doing	Fine	Points on Licence
30 m.p.h.	Up to 37 m.p.h.	Warning only	None
30 m.p.h.	Up to 45 m.p.h.	£60	None
30 m.p.h.	Above 45 m.p.h.	£70 plus £5 for every mile in excess	2 to 3
50 m.p.h.	Up to 59 m.p.h.	Warning only	None
50 m.p.h.	60 to 65 m.p.h.	£70	2
50 m.p.h.	Above 65 m.p.h.	£100 plus £7 for every mile in excess	2 to 3
70 m.p.h.	Up to 79 m.p.h.	Warning only	None
70 m.p.h.	80 to 89 m.p.h.	£120	2 to 3
70 m.p.h.	90 to 99 m.p.h.	£150 to £250	3 to 4
70 m.p.h.	Above 100 m.p.h.	£250 to £500	4 to 5 and in extreme speeds, mmediate loss of Licence

I also recommend that anyone disqualified from driving should be required to re-take their Driving Test.

Careless or dangerous driving/driving without insurance/road tax or whilst disqualified, must be considered by the Courts and I have put such serious offences into the Crime Categories I feel to be most appropriate.

As stated, it is not for me to decide the prior categories or sentencing tariffs, but for each nation to consult widely and determine their own allocations. My role is to persuade the general public of the merits of establishing *the principle of mandatory sentences* in order to get rid of crazy variations in sentencing and to spell out to those contemplating crime that in future, there will be no chance of them escaping the consequences of their actions which the public deems, via their elected representatives, to be appropriate.

The categories and tariffs, in any event, can always be adjusted by elected politicians fine-tuning the system, if circumstances show the wisdom of amending the original allocations. In the first instance though, you as an individual should write to your political representative supporting mandatory sentencing and perhaps indicating a few specific crimes which you would like to see allocated to which categories.

I of course realise that in creating the aforementioned Crime Categories I am sticking my head above the parapet, but it has always been my intention to convert my years of research to practical purpose. I am not one of the plethora of "experts" making a cosy living out of pontificating on crime. Although not a wealthy man, I have financed all of my research at my own and my family's expense.

Britain, for example, has numerous supposed crime experts; academic professors of criminality at many universities; a grand-sounding Sentencing Guidelines Council comprising the great and the good chosen few; a Home Office stuffed with clever, overpaid know-alls on almost every facet of crime and justice, *but* - what have they achieved? High crime levels – fifty million crimes in Britain still unsolved since Tony Blair Gordon Brown & co. came to power, and an endless stream of tinkering, headline grabbing initiatives which never had any hope (or intention?) of reducing crime by 75%

or more. Why is it that countries such as Britain and Ireland have such high levels of crime – violent crime particularly?

The reasons include :-

Too little communication with the public

Too little social awareness education

Too little imagination or philosophy

Too few prison places

Too few Bobbies/guards on the beat

Too few politicians with crime reduction as their principle concern

Too many wasted resources – Identity Cards etc.

Too many "political" senior police officers

Too many lawyers making big bucks out of crime

Too many tinkering bureaucrats

Too many technical, legal escape routes

Too much sentencing uncertainty and leniency

Too much political sleaze and skulllduggery

It can never be possible to design a Sentencing Regime which would receive universal approval and even in the system I am proposing, I can appreciate how some of you will feel that certain offences should be allocated to a different category. That said, I will be happy for you to support either my outline proposals for a range of mandatory sentences, or adjust these to your own preferences and either way, promote them with those seeking your vote or political support.

I am though, confident that my concept is sound and that few thinking people would allocate any of my Category Ten crimes to Category Three or my Category Fours to Category Nine etc.

It is not of critical importance that every crime should, from the outset, be allocated to any particular category because, with the possible exception of Category Ten crimes, there is no clear self-selecting bracket for most crimes, many of which would sit comfortably up or down one place.

Those countries enjoying low crime levels need do nothing further, but those suffering high crime should open up a wide consultation process with a view to establishing Categories for mandatory ranges of sentences. Combine this with Compounding (escalating) Sentencing and with the decriminalisation of drugs and your country will have crime pretty well beaten within only a few years.

Let's get to it.

However crime categories are finalised, the full information of which crimes earn which sentences should be part of my proposed Concern & Consequences Examination which hopefully will become obligatory in every school.

As of 2007, most youngsters believe they can commit crimes and stand a good chance of escaping any meaningful punishment. The system of mandatory sentences I am proposing, combined with its inclusion in a Concern & Consequences curriculum which they cannot avoid, will make it very clear to both pupils and parents that no longer will they be able to avoid being punished for their crimes.

My recommendation is that throughout their time at school, every student should be taught – and be expected to know via the Concern & Consequences Examination – precisely how crime is to be dealt with in the 21st century.

No pupil should ever be able to say "I didn't know" when it comes to crime and punishment.

They will know with absolute certainty that if they are found guilty of any crime, they will receive certain punishment from which neither their defence lawyers nor the Courts can rescue them.

Even better, they will know that for most of the Ten Crime Categories, a prison or other appropriate detention centre is their unavoidable destination. Again, no ifs, no buts, no maybes. Just the certainty that if you are found guilty of a crime, you will have to suffer the consequences.

Fines – you will have seen from the previous listings of Crime Categories that what I term Restitution Crimes are a feature of my New Sentencing Proposals. There are a number of what I believe to be sound reasons for campaigning for their introduction.

- Most crimes result in innocent parties suffering loss. This may be the victim – financially or via trauma or inconvenience.

- You may be mugged, have your car window smashed, suffer a burglary, be the victim of a dangerous-driver road accident. Your insurance premiums may increase and you may, or be required, to buy additional security.

- Some victims and their families will incur medical and other inconvenience costs.

- You as a taxpayer pay for policing, prosecution, Court and prison services.

Rationale – It makes no sense for either the actual victims, their families or the State representing taxpayers, simply to sit back and soak up these costs. They should be borne not by the law-abiding but, wherever possible, by the criminals committing the crimes or by their families. This will certainly concentrate the minds of those who believe living by the law to be an option, not a responsibility.

Surely it would be far more just for the perpetrators of crimes to be required to pick up the tabs. My proposed Retribution Fines can and should be mandatory but unfortunately, fixing minimum and maximum tariffs are not appropriate because of the multiplicity of factors. Courts therefore, will be required to impose Retribution Fines but, unlike prison terms which can only be within strict minimum to maximum ranges, it will be their responsibility to determine fine levels.

It will be for the Courts to ascertain the level of actual and secondary loss suffered by the victim(s); the amount of trauma suffered by the victim(s); and the costs incurred by the State which is the taxpayer which, in all probability, is you.

There are, of course, huge variables, including the value of losses, the length of trials and guilty parties' abilities to pay. Adding a five thousand dollar fine to someone without means or employment prospects may not be appropriate on grounds of affordability, but to a millionaire, it would be neither of consequence nor a deterrent to re-offending. These are amongst the factors which the Courts will have to consider when determining Retribution Fines and how they should be distributed to the receiving parties.

Footnote – Since the initial writing of this chapter, it seems that Britain may be playing catch-up with me on this subject. On 28th September 2006, at the Labour Party's Annual Conference in Manchester, Home Secretary John Reid announced that a Community Payback Scheme was to be introduced. Whilst welcoming this, the Society for Action Against Crime was concerned that the Government may botch a good idea, as they have another of our proposals – a Concern & Consequences examination taught in all schools. We immediately wrote to the Home Secretary asking how they proposed operating their Community Payback Scheme but as of February 2007, no response has been received to my letter of the 29th September 2006. This can be seen on www.crimedown.org.

2nd Sentencing Principle – Compounding Sentences

Complimenting and strengthening the Categorisation of all crimes in my 1st Sentencing Principle (the use of mandatory sentence brackets) is a further measure which will largely solve the problem of repeat crime, a scourge and hugely-expensive matter which is a major escalator of crime in many countries.

Criminals with a string of convictions will be creatures of the past because Compounding Sentences will cut that string very short.

It is utter stupidity to spend huge amounts of money catching and (if lucky) getting criminals convicted, then allowing them to commit further crime(s) which, if apprehended, will at worst result in a sentence not dissimilar to the first. A truly vicious circle if ever there was one.

Self evidently, the offenders in such instances were sufficiently comfortable with their original sentence to risk getting a similar one, so it makes no sense to continue failing to dissuade them from further crime. My conclusion is that only a system of Compounding Sentences and less comfortable prison regimes will deter the career criminal and protect us from the scourge of repeat offenders.

234

There should be no such animal as a serial offender amongst those charged with and found guilty of crimes and the way to guarantee this is to ***ratchet up sentences for all consecutive crimes***. Any politician disputing this should start looking for another job, preferably one that does not require even basic arithmetic. One does not have to be a statistician to work out that if these guys were in prison for a long time after their first or second offence, crime would drop dramatically by millions.

As of 2006, some countries have people who have been found guilty of crimes by Courts 3, 7, 10, 20 or more times – on each occasion getting only the sentence appropriate to their latest crime, often little more than a slap on the wrist. This is crazy. It is hugely wasteful of expensive police and Court time (taxpayers' money) and it significantly increases the number of victims. It is absolutely unnecessary because the principle of Compounding Sentences for more than one crime can, by definition, reduce repeat offending substantially and quickly, ridding us of those anti-socials who have committed, 30, 50 or more than 100 crimes.

In January 2007, Ireland's most prolific burglar was back in Court having supposedly racked-up a hundred burglaries. The costs to the community of this one offender have been enormous and almost all of these would not have been incurred had my compounding sentencing recommendations been taken up.

Nor would young female thug Colleen McDonald have been out of gaol long enough to be arrested 48 times for terrorising the Newbiggin Hall Estate. Burglary, smashing cars, shoving disgusting things through neighbours' letterboxes, smashing windows and beating up other girls were how this slob got her kicks. With compounding sentencing, callous Colleen would have been stopped in her tracks after her first few offences, again saving the taxpayer a great deal of money and the police and judiciary a huge amount of time.

Had my sentencing principles been in place, 18-year old serial offender Joseph Cummins would not have been around to twice rape then rob a 75-year old lady. Nor would the Gardai and the judiciary have borne the cost of processing his 60 convictions, racked-up in only 2 years.

Nor would evil Rory Griffin have raped a 49-year old married woman, had this high-risk serial rapist not been treated too leniently by the Courts previously and then released 3 years early. Griffin was out on "Licence" less than 2 weeks when he committed his third (at least) rape, plus other offences. In January 2007, the Essex Probation Service, which is supposed to monitor prisoners on Licence, held an *internal* inquiry into the case and cleared its own staff of any responsibility and the Home Office issued one of its trite, standard comments, loftily claiming that the sentencing and supervision of offenders is an important part of the on-going Home Office review.

Unfortunately, there are no analytical thinkers doing the reviewing.

Thomas Grant, a young university student, was travelling on a train from Scotland home to England in 2006 when, without warning or reason, he was stabbed in the heart by Thomas Wood. This social misfit already had 21 convictions, some for serious violence and had compounding sentencing been in operation, Thomas Grant and many involved in other tragic events would still be alive.

Stopping such carnage must be a worthwhile objective.

Many societies are plagued by repeat offenders. It is their own fault or more accurately, it is the fault of their politicians. No-one has to spend most of their life in gaol, of course. The choice will be theirs. Everyone will know that once mandatory and Compounding Sentencing is introduced, repeat crime will inevitably lead to escalating loss of liberty for the criminals. Those *choosing* not to learn from earlier mistakes will have only themselves to blame when they suffer ever-longer prison sentences.

Victims and the public despair when they see that not only has yet another terrible crime been committed, but that the perpetrator has already been caught by the police and been through the Courts on numerous occasions. The victims, not unnaturally – if they are still alive – are furious when they realise that they would not have suffered had the judicial system properly protected them. The public of course, sees itself as the next possible victim and is quite rightly angry that its taxes are wasted detecting and processing the same villains through the Courts time and time again.

Compare Three Systems

A. Current Sentencing in Most Countries

	SENTENCE
• Charles Crook commits 1st offence – burglary	Let off with a warning
• Goes on to commit 2nd offence – burglary	9 months prison (6 months of which is suspended)
• Goes on to commit 3rd offence – grievous bodily harm	18 months prison
• Goes on to commit 4th offence – another G.B.H.	18 months prison
• Goes on to commit 5th offence – violent mugging	24 months prison
• Goes on to commit 6th offence – armed robbery	60 months prison

Summary of System 'A' – By now, Charlie Crook has been sentenced to only 123 months in prison for committing 6 serious escalating offences and with varying paroles, may only have served less than 7 years in confinement.

After his first 4 offences, his sentences totalled just 39 months, of which he may only have served less than 2 years in prison. Clearly, this was no deterrent to him continuing to offend and commit even more serious crimes.

Charlie is, in fact, the typical serial offender and of course, he is likely, during his out-of-prison periods, to have committed other crimes for which he was never caught.

Compare this with Scenarios 'B' and 'C' below.

B.   Using my categories/mandatory sentencing proposal in isolation

Charlie's 1st offence would likely have resulted in the jury giving him, say a mid-way sentence of 20 months in prison.

2nd offence	20 months in prison
3rd offence	48 months in prison
4th offence	48 months in prison
5th offence	60 months in prison
6th offence	120 months in prison

Summary of System 'B' – compared with System 'A', I think it likely that this proposed, more structured sentencing process would result in juries giving Charlie Crook custodial sentences totalling 316 months for the same 6 serious offences. Itself a significant deterrent compared with current practices (123 months).

By the time of Charlie's 4th offence, he would have earned himself custodial sentences of 136 months, thereby keeping him out of circulation for more than 11 years compared with 4½ years with current practices.

Something to concentrate the minds of the Charlie Crooks.

C.   Ratcheting up sentences for repeat offenders – (Compounding)

This is the kicker to largely ridding us of the serial criminals who, for far too long, have put up two fingers to the police, to victims, to the Courts and to the taxpayers who have to keep paying for their multiple crimes and judicial processing.

Without the leverage of imposing higher sentences for subsequent offences, there can be no hope of dissuading the Charlie Crooks of this world to mend their ways. Certainly, throughout my research and consultations, no-one has been able to put forward any proposals which would better deter the serial criminal.

• Charlie's 1st offence would earn him the same sentence as System 'B', i.e.	20 months in prison
• However, his 2nd offence would be subject to a 50% mark-up, i.e.	30 months in prison instead of 20 months
• His 3rd (more serious) offence would also have a 75% mark-up	84 months in prison instead of 48 months
• A 4th offence would have a 100% mark-up	96 months in prison instead of 48 months

Knowing precisely what they face, few criminals will choose to commit these or similar 4 crimes, but those foolish enough so to do will already have racked-up prison sentences amounting to almost 20 years. 20 years of protection for the public.

Those **choosing** to go beyond even this level of crime would earn :-

• For that 5th crime – 100% mark-up	A further 120 months in prison instead of 60 months
• For that 6th crime – 100% mark-up	A further 240 months in prison instead of 120 months

The permutations are, of course, almost infinite. They would vary hugely according to the category of crime(s) in question and the above are based upon juries imposing custodial sentences in the middle of the minimum/maximum range which I recommend be mandated by Government.

With my combined **Systems 'B' and 'C'** in place, even those who shrug off current sentences 10 or more times would find it impossible to do so, even if their crimes were in low categories. **Hence, no more serial small-time crooks**. Problem solved.

Those committing more than 2 high category crimes would be stopped in their tracks at this stage. Result - *no more big-time crooks* and a consequent massive reduction in the dangers which, in 2007, still threaten the public.

I have not the slightest doubt that any country putting my Ten Crime Categories and Compounding Sentencing proposals into effect will see a huge and quick reduction in crime. Initially, this will result in higher prison populations but this will be temporary because all but the thickest of criminals will soon get the message that crime is no longer an attractive career option. A message which has been missing for a very long time, with disastrous results.

If you wish to join me in seeing the end of the serial criminal, this is one of the most important measures you should be persuading your politicians to introduce. Contact **sentencing@crimedown.org** to find out how we can raise awareness about repeat offending, which Governments have failed to address.

3rd Sentencing Principle – Up-rating Community Service Orders

More countries are realising that prison is not necessarily the appropriate punishment for some offenders – a view which I have proposed for many years. Right now, we have many of the wrong people in gaol and too many more serious criminals not in gaol.

The U.K. Home Office is suddenly gung ho on Community Service Orders and Anti-Social Behaviour Orders, but they believe that it will solve the awful problem of re-offending. Certainly, there are numerous offenders in prison who should not be there. Long-term prison should be for those who have used violence in their crimes; for sexual offenders who should be in separate prisons undergoing efforts to rehabilitate them; for those guilty of corruption, witness intimidation, incitement to violence, including terrorism, serious fraud, dangerous driving etc.

No-one should be sent to prison for a term shorter than 6 months because (a) they cannot have committed a crime which suggests they are a serious danger to the public, (b) the processing and recording of prisoners into and out of the system is expensive and not justifiable for minor offences and (c) it frees up prison places for the more serious offenders who may well need to be confined for longer periods.

However, simply transferring people from prison to Community Service regimes is not a magic wand and in itself will not stop re-offending. It is right and proper that those guilty of breaking a law in one of my proposed lower crime categories should be expected to repay both victims and the taxpayer by working for the community in their free time. The success of this aspect will, of course, depend upon the calibre of each Community Service project and its on-the-ground and financial management. These are not areas where many Governments have demonstrated much competence.

There is hope though.

Courts should not give a Community Service Order as a straightforward single sentence. Instead, they should first pass the prison term sentence relevant to the category of offence committed. Then, and only then, the Court could, if it felt it appropriate, offer the offender the option of a fine or a specific Community Service Order. This should, of course, not apply to high category offences and even the failure to comply with the terms and spirit of the C.S.O. should automatically result in the offender reverting to the original prison sentence which had been waived in its favour

Now, here comes the smart bit. In the event of any re-offending, it is the prison sentence tariff which would remain on record which would be used to calculate the compounding mark-up applicable to repeat offending – even though the Court had felt it appropriate to have substituted it for a Community Service Order.

Such a system as I propose, would be a huge incentive for offenders to opt for and abide by any Community Service offered, because each culprit would know that any future sentence would be based upon the original (albeit theoretical) custodial sentence and not the alternative fine or Community Service Order which may have been offered by the original Court. It has the added benefit of discouraging re-offending. It can put an end to taxpayers spending outrageous monies keeping non-dangerous law-breakers in prison. It keeps families together and it frees up scarce prison places to accommodate the really serious or dangerous criminals.

Attaching firm disciplines to Community Service regimes though is, in my opinion, vital if they are to make a serious contribution to the reduction in re-offending.

Again, all of these factors should feature in the Concern & Consequences curriculum, which should form part of every youngster's education. All pieces in the Crimedown jigsaw puzzle which I and hopefully you, wish to see completed without further delay.

4th Sentencing Principle – Juries, Not Judges

Once our elected representatives have established the range of mandatory sentences which must be applied to specific crimes, it should be the responsibility of *juries* – and *not* Judges – to determine the sentence to be passed on whomever they have found to be guilty. This, of course, only in respect of serious offences where juries should always be involved. Probably Category 3 and 4 crimes onwards will be appropriate.

Judges, Magistrates and even jurors are just people with human frailties and prejudices, but if justice for the accused, the victims and their families is to be achieved, it should be at the will of the people. *Sentences* should not only fit the crime, but *should also deter future transgressions*, both by the individual concerned and also all others who may be contemplating a life of crime. The people do not elect Judges, they elect politicians and are entitled to expect those they elect to manage the country's affairs and take responsibility for dealing with those who break the law.

Illogically, Judges have been afforded the luxury of imposing an incredible range of sentences on whim, disguised as wisdom. They pontificate about having to take extenuating circumstances into account, but I have files full of cases which show clearly that they often exercise their responsibilities very poorly indeed. What makes anyone believe that juries would be incapable of assessing extenuating circumstances, I simply do not understand. The sentences imposed by Judges for almost identical crimes and with very similar extraneous factors all too often are amazingly different. That cannot be justice for either perpetrators or victims.

This sentencing lottery is a proven failure. It has produced huge unfairnesses, injustice and, in many countries, it certainly has not produced low levels of crime, hence, the urgency for those countries where Judges determine sentences, to look – perhaps for the first time – at their established judicial processes with a view to introducing

242

alternatives. I can think of no solution more likely to restore justice and deter criminals than to move to a system which removes from Judges the ability to keep handing out slap-on-the-wrist or over-zealous sentences.

Judges have certainly contributed significantly to the creation of "serial criminals" when, in a properly functioning judicial system, there should be no such creature. They have caused huge distress and anger amongst victims and victims' families and friends. They have made law-abiding citizens despair of crime ever being meaningfully reduced and they – the Judges – have seriously damaged both the morale and hence the effectiveness of the police and prosecution services. All too often, I have heard the "why do we bother" lament from officers and officials who have worked long and hard to bring villains to Court, only to see them escape their just desserts, even when found guilty. They can be philosophical about those found not guilty because that must always be the possible outcome of any trial, but nothing causes the police and prosecution services to question the value of their efforts more, than seeing those criminals who **are** found guilty, let off with inconsequential sentences – apart perhaps, from those villains who escape paying for their crimes at all on that ridiculous concept "a technical breach of law or procedure".

So how should the Courts determine what sentence is appropriate?

Very simply. By each juror who entered a "guilty" verdict selecting his/her choice of sentence commensurate with their view of the severity of the crime and taking into account all special circumstances, other, of course, than pleas for first offence leniency, which should always be ignored. Their choice of sentence **must** be within the minimum and maximum for the category of offence in question, laid down by the Government as representatives of the people. The proposed sentences from within these parameters should be written down by each juror, with each recorded paper handed to Court officials then on to the Judge, who would take the average of the total. This should accompany all guilty verdicts and this average of the jurors' proposed sentences should be that passed by the Court. Judges should also be permitted a single sentence input, equal to that of each juror and contributing to the averaging process. At a stroke, this will take away from Judges the power to pass a never-ending stream of nonsensical sentences on both sides of the spectrum. The minimum to maximum sentence range is not a guide – it is mandatory.

A word here about juries. I would welcome consultation on jury selection/duty in order to reduce, where it exists, the lawyer-dominated compilation of juries. Certainly the grounds for objecting to any juror should be very few and pretty obvious. I also think it unwise to force any individual to serve on a jury. Only willing jurors are likely to exercise their responsibilities with maximum impartiality.

Nor should we go down the road of having professional jurors because this would eliminate millions of people with a range of experiences, common sense and concerns. Professional jurors would be paid by the Government and they would be chosen by someone or some process which would inevitably have in-built biases. We already have a plethora of "experts" at all levels of politics, law and bureaucracy and it has served us abysmally by allowing crime to reach wholly unacceptable levels. Creating yet another gaggle of experts would also be extremely expensive and would be a further link between the executive and the judiciary which is always dangerous. The greater the separation between Government, the Courts and the police, the better the quality of the justice and the lower the levels of crime.

This recommended system will contribute much to serious crime reduction in those countries with the foresight to adopt it. It will completely eliminate the subjectivity of single Judges which has served society so badly for so long and, with each juror registering a preference, no individual juror could unduly influence the outcome.

For example, if a given offence comes within a category for the minimum to maximum sentence laid down by elected politicians was, say, 7 to 12 years imprisonment, no single or even couple of jurors could seriously distort the end result. If all but one of the jurors felt that the sentence merited only a 7, 8 or 9-year term, the odd one who may always incline towards the 12-year maximum incarceration would move the average up only from 8 to 8.4 years. With there being no such thing as a proven perfect custodial sentence, such an effect by a single prejudiced juror (or even two) can only be marginal and supportive of my recommendations for a complete overhaul of sentencing in the interest of greater fairness.

Where crimes are tried in lower Courts without jurors, sentences should still be within the obligatory Ten Category minimum to maximum range laid down by the nation's lawmakers on behalf of you and me.

244

The proposals herein are, of course, in outline form only and will benefit from extensive consultation, public debate and fine-tuning, to which I would happily contribute, but the important thing right now is that the *principle* is established as one of the many pieces of the jigsaw puzzle which together can bring about massive reductions in crime.

How the people of Guangzhou in China must wish my proposed system had been in operation there. So lax has sentencing by their judges been, that crime has escalated out of control. Much of this is drugs-related, but so great has been the public outcry that judges have now swung to the opposite extreme and have introduced the death penalty for offences such as bag-snatching, which has become endemic.

Using my proposals, such increases in crime could never emerge, nor could there be any violently-distorted fluctuations in sentencing as has happened in China and elsewhere.

5th Sentencing Principle – Guilt/Innocence Not Proven

A fault in some countries' systems of justice is that plaintiffs can only be found either guilty or not guilty. I believe this to be misguided, because many trials cannot prove absolute guilt or establish complete innocence.

No-one should be found guilty other than beyond reasonable doubt, but there have been thousands of occasions when guilty verdicts have been given simply because the Court was not convinced of their absolute innocence. The reverse also applies.

Under such circumstances, a "Not Proven" verdict has considerable merit insofar as it avoids serious miscarriages of justice, but leaves open the door for further consideration in the future. Not that the door to justice should ever be closed, even where an accused is found not guilty, as can be seen in my 6th Sentencing Principle.

I fully appreciate that inconclusive verdicts may seem to some to be something of an anti-climax, but surely that is better by far than finding an innocent person guilty, or a guilty party innocent.

6th Sentencing Principle – Scrap Double Jeopardy Law

One of many nations' most illogical and dangerous laws is that known as double jeopardy. In essence, this law prohibits anyone being tried again for the same crime, having once been found "not guilty". Another good reason for having inconclusive "not proven" verdicts available to the Courts.

I of course see the danger of the State harassing and re-trying people for its own disreputable reasons, having failed to get a guilty verdict from a public Court first time around. I know too much about how some Governments work to trust them with willy-nilly multiple trials of the same person(s) for the same crime, but it is perfectly possible to safeguard against this potential abuse by putting checks and balances into place to prevent such oppressive tactics.

The important issue is how to prevent the guilty escaping justice forever, simply because of one faulty "not guilty" finding.

Think about this. Your wife/mother/sister/daughter/son is raped but, as so often happens, there is insufficient cast iron evidence to convict the guy who did it. You subsequently learn that the nasty low-life concerned bragged in front of his mates and other witnesses that yes, he had done the dirty deed but nobody could now touch him for it. Why not? Double jeopardy dear reader, double jeopardy.

How would you and yours then feel about that?

There are thousands of villains walking around right now who cannot be tried again, despite firm fresh evidence becoming available. Walking around free to commit further crimes.

The police are also in a dilemma following a single not guilty verdict. Do they spend more resources searching for an alternative culprit to charge, or surreptitiously close the file, being sure that the guilty party had escaped justice but was thereafter untouchable due to double jeopardy protection?

After many years of lobbying on the subject, The Society for Action Against Crime was encouraged that the UK Government in 2005 succumbed to our constant campaigning and decided to move towards our position on double jeopardy. Problem – Tony Blair had already signed the proposed European Convention which included – you've guessed it – double jeopardy protection, guaranteeing that no-one in Europe can be tried more than once for the same crime. Just one more lunatic piece of legislation coming out of Brussels and Strasbourg.

I have sought clarification on this from Tony Blair and Charles Clarke, but many months on, I am still waiting for their reply. They bang on about terrorism but they are sending out contradictory signals about trying anyone more than once for the same offence – even if D.N.A. or forensic evidence proving guilt subsequently emerges. So, how serious are these guys if they are prepared to allow known criminals, including terrorists, to roam around at will because of some hugely-illogical out-dated double jeopardy law?

Footnote:- The UK Director of Public Prosecutions in November 2005 consented to the revised (April 2005) law being used for the first time by authorising an application to the Appeal Court for a re-trial of William Dunlop for the murder of Julie Hogg 14 years earlier. One can only wonder how many villains have escaped and how many victims and their families have been denied justice during the 800 years of this ridiculous law. Whatever the Brussels Bureaucrats try on, no country should prevent anyone facing further trial if significant new evidence subsequently emerges.

Double jeopardy typifies my conclusions that, in the 21st century, we must be prepared to put our existing laws under the microscope and if necessary, scrap or revise them.

Being ancient does not, in itself, bestow merit on any law and Tony Blair and his successors must make it absolutely clear to those in Europe, that Britain will refuse to sign up to any Convention or Treaty which includes double jeopardy protection for criminals.

Consider the following :- Billions are being spent trying to nail terrorists and your Government traces Mr. X, charges him, takes him to Court, which is not convinced that the evidence is sufficient to find him guilty of murder. In the absence of a "not proven" choice, he must therefore be found "not guilty". Subsequently, D.N.A. evidence emerges indicating Mr. X's absolute involvement, but in those countries where no-one can be tried twice for the same crime, Mr. X is untouchable.

C'mon Governments – its time to get real. Scrap double jeopardy protection and do so p.d.q. Tell Brussells' bureaucrats to take a hike.

7th Sentencing Principle – The Law Can Be Wrong

In order to bring law and justice closer to the people, and to put a check rein on control-freak politicians, I believe juries have the moral right and obligation to find an accused to be not guilty if they perceive the law itself to be suspect. Such a finding should only be permissible where the jury was either unanimous or in high majority that the law itself was unsatisfactory.

I am not proposing that a single jury decision should oblige any Government to scrap or amend the law(s) in question, but such jury decision should be taken on board by all politicians. In any event, if repeated juries take issue with a particular law and refuse to convict under it, such law would effectively become worthless by virtue of its continually being ruled against. Another good reason for transferring sentencing to juries, is that they are much less likely to succumb to Government pressure than are some judges, wishing to protect and progress their careers.

Governments can and do pass bad laws. Other laws become outdated or overtaken by events. My proposal is that those countries which do not already accept the principle of innocence by virtue of unjust law, should now do so. The Governments of some countries, whose Courts already have this centuries-old right, disgracefully pretend that they do not. They do their utmost to hide the truth.

America is one such country. Successive Presidents, once elected, have abused their positions and behaved as Dictators, kicking the concept of democracy into the long grass. Once they get into power, they come to believe themselves omnipotent and brook no dissention to their own dictats. Very specifically, they lean on their politicised judges to keep from juries their rights to find an accused person innocent by virtue of the law in question being unreasonable.

This right is guaranteed by the Constitution, the Bill of Rights and by Chief Justice Jay (Georgia –v- Brailsford 1794) and Chief Justice Samuel Chase who, in 1804, confirmed that jurors had both the right and the power to decide the validity of any law.

In 1969 the U.S. 4th Circuit Court of Appeal in U.S. –v- Moylan reiterated the undisputed power of juries to acquit, even where such verdicts are contrary to the law, the evidence, or the direction of the judges. Juries, it was stated, have this power to acquit for any reason which appeals to their passion, logic or conscience and Courts must abide by such decisions.

Every nation should give this right and responsibility to its juries and resist all attempts by their politicians or weak, politicised judges to either remove or hide it.

Democracy should be the will of the people and it is the people who suffer the crime, and it is juries, not politicians, who are closest to the people. Let the people decide.

I come now to William Gladstone's remark that *"**justice delayed is justice denied**"*.

There are, of course, instances where this is not necessarily so, but I do concur with its main sentiment.

Only in the legal profession can procrastination, tardiness, obfuscation, obstruction and downright incompetence not only pass unnoticed, but reward the perpetrators. Lawyers rarely show urgency and are quite happy letting the clock tick at someone else's expense.

No-one should be surprised that tolerating races between snails and tortoises over many decades has led to mega trials and all too often, the huge costs of these are borne by you, the taxpayer. They can range from show trials, such as that of O. J. Simpson in America, to the recent farce of Slobodan Milosevic's trial in The Hague. There was no justification whatsoever in spending millions of euros bringing Milosevic to trail, then charging him with 66 war crimes and still have the case running *four years later*, at the time of his untimely death. The only winners, of course, were the lawyers, the bureaucrats and all of the hangers-on who feed off any lengthy Court case, particularly the high-profile ones.

The lawyers and politicians try to portray such protracted nonsense as being necessary in the interests of justice, but that argument is false.

Presumably, had Milosevic been accused of 600 crimes against humanity instead of 66, his trial would still be going on in 30/40 years time.

Despite his over-long trial, it was never going to be possible to identify precisely which individuals had been killed on the orders or inaction of President Milosevic, so the lawyers' claims that full justice and closure would be achieved by charging him with 66 crimes was a deceit.

It is quite wrong and counter-productive for any case to take more than a year to come to trail, or to take more than one calendar month to resolve when it does reach Court. Sorry lawyers, but you have been taking us all for a ride for years and the game is up.

Solution? Take a chainsaw to log-jam Court cases. Prosecution and defence should, pre-trial, offer their best evidence to the judge, who will allocate a reasonable amount of equal time for both sides to present to the Court their principle arguments. This may be as little as one hour each side, to several days, or in complex cases, perhaps several weeks. Such limitation is eminently reasonable. It would wake up both prosecution and defence lawyers and concentrate their minds upon the most compelling arguments they believe they have and stop them trawling through mountains of secondary irrelevances, the main purpose of which is to puff up the pockets of procrastinating practitioners in law.

Example. Slobodan Milosevic's prosecutors could have been given up to 4 weeks to present their most damning evidence of 3 or 4 of the ex-President's alleged most obvious and serious crimes to the Court. He or his defence would also be given up to 4 weeks to try to disprove the charges against him.

Result? *All done and dusted* in less than 3 months, instead of the case never being resolved, even after more than 4 years' tinkering by an army of lawyers, judges and legal-process associates.

No-one will ever be allowed to know the full cost of this or other Court farces, but of one thing I am certain, they are astronomical, they are unnecessary and they clog up the entire judicial system.

Had my system of time-limitation trials been operative, Milosevic would either have been found innocent or 'case not proven' and he would have been freed – or the Court would have found him guilty and passed an appropriate sentence. *All within 3 months*. Many millions of euros would have been saved and justice far better served.

Would this not have been immeasurably better than no resolution after years? and although this was a high-profile case, the same principle would be beneficial for all Court cases.

Lawyers, of course, are highly skilled at furthering their own financial interests and over many years they have developed procedures to stretch Court cases way beyond reasonable bounds.

I have more to say about the legal profession as an unhealthy Establishment in a later chapter, but for now, suffice it to say that their slowing down of judicial systems to a snail's pace is both hugely damaging and very costly as a direct result of the International Brotherhood's skills of procrastination.

For an example of legal sloth, judicial and political incompetence, massive waste of time and money, and pure farce, one need look no further than the trials of Saddam Hussein and his cohorts in Iraq.

His trial was a disgrace throughout and whilst the guilty verdict was certainly correct, the time taken to reach it and the quality of the judicial process were deplorable in the extreme. Whilst I acknowledge the right of any nation to have the death sentence as an option for very serious crimes, when used, it should be with as much dignity and solemnity as possible and Iraq should be deeply ashamed at the conduct permitted at Saddam Hussein's execution. I also believe that, however bad the villain, any man or woman condemned to death should be permitted the civilised gesture of being offered their own choice of method of final dispatch.

CHAPTER 12

PENAL INSTITUTIONS

Every country should have sufficient prison capacity to confine every criminal for a time commensurate with the sentence which a public Court has considered to be appropriate. Many have not. Britain, for example, has only 77,000/80,000 prison place s (2006/7) yet since Tony Blair's Government came to power, *it has more than 50 million unsolved crimes*. Prison capacity there is already over-stretched to the point that Judges must not send criminals to prison unless absolutely necessary ….. Did they ever?

So, if just a tiny percentage of these "on-the-loose" criminals are caught and convicted, what do Tony Blair and his succession of Home Secretaries think should be done with them? If not sent to prison – for those deserving it - what would be the point in spending billions of pounds bothering to catch them and put them through the judicial process? This is a question so often asked by the police themselves.

Britain, of course, is only one of many countries with too many unsolved crimes and too few prisons and this is primarily because politicians have believed them to be too costly. At a supposed £37,000 per inmate per annum, the cost is far greater than it should be and this is a separate issue which needs addressing urgently. However, even at this high price, it is still cost effective to keep serious and would be serial criminals in gaol rather than having them on the loose. Confining serious criminals in prison is one of the most profitable measures which any Government can implement, having a wide range of both financial and lifestyle benefits to society at large. These benefits far outweigh the necessary investment.

Before prisons come into the equation of course, offenders have to be caught and convicted and The Centre for Crime and Justice Studies in London on 15th January 2007 reported that only 3% of reported crimes in Britain currently result in a conviction. They also accuse the Home Office of spinning statistics in order to make it seem that the fight against crime is being won. It isn't.

Having 50 million crimes unsolved since he came to Office, Tony Blair has made no impression on crime. The number of police stations *closed* since he promised to be tough on crime, tough on the causes of crime, is more than 800 and even with new ones opened, the net loss is still more than 500. How is that for policing at local level? Seems the Home Office is incapable of making the connection between 50 million unsolved crimes and the net loss of 500 police stations.

I believe it is Tony Blair and his inappropriately-chosen Home Secretaries who are "unfit for purpose" as John Reid so succinctly put it in a moment of panic.

California's Governor, Arnold Schwarzenegger, in 2006 called for swift and dramatic action to deal with the dangerously jam-packed prisons in the State. One of the problems of course, is that drugs-related crime in America – mainly victimless possession – has risen in 30 years from less than 20% to around 60%.

In May 2006, the UK's previous and current Lord Chief Justices, Lord Woolf and Lord Phillips, came out with public comments that too many criminals were being sent to prison instead of being given community service orders; that politicians should not criticise individual Judges; that overcrowded prisons prevent prisoner rehabilitation; and that there should be fewer mandatory sentences and more discretion for Judges. Let me deal with each of these misconceptions.

Too many criminals sent to prison. You are both right and wrong, my Lords.

Yes, there are too many petty offenders clogging up British and other gaols and it is encouraging that such senior Judges have so recently woken up to this fact. What have they been doing for the past few decades? Society would be better served by such minor, non-violent criminals being ordered to more productive community service, allied to a rehabilitation programme.

Yes – overcrowded prisons are unlikely places to minimise re-offending, although one should not deduce from this that there are any affordable external rehab programmes proven to be very successful. I can find no evidence of any system which would reduce re-offending on a large scale to below ten percent.

On the subject of re-offending, there are many airy-fairy claims that this or that rehab programme reduced re-offending rates by 'x' or 'y' percent. This is arrant nonsense of course, because their figures can only be based upon those who have been ***caught*** re-offending.

254

Are these people really asking us to believe that none of Britain's 50 million unsolved crimes (since 1997) have been committed by ex-prisoners or ex-Community Service Order participants? Of course they have. It defies logic, common sense and statistical probability to believe otherwise, but conveniently, those making claims for their rehabilitation programmes forget the fact that some released prisoners commit further crimes but *do not get caught* for them. Someone, of course, is responsible for these 50 million unsolved crimes and no-one with an ounce of savvy could believe that they were all committed by virgin criminals who had never been to prison. You should therefore understand that *all* statistics on re-offending rates seriously understate the reality and are invariably slanted to promote the agendas of those operating anti-prison regimes.

Individual Judges should not be criticised. How very cosy!

This kind of arrogant remark by Judges demonstrates very clearly the gulf which has grown between the judiciary and the public. Just who do these guys think they are, that this puts them beyond comment or criticism? Both of which you and I have been subject for most of our lives.

"Yeronners" already live in ivory towers which take them out of touch with the realities of life. Now they want immunity from being criticised for their mistakes. Sorry my Lords, but it is time you came back into the real world, dragged and screaming, if necessary.

Fewer mandatory sentences. Absolutely not.

We need almost all crimes to carry *inescapable minimum and maximum sentences*, set not by Judges but by the people's elected political representatives, as already outlined in my New Sentencing Solutions chapter.

What Lords Woolf and Phillips are doing in rubbishing mandatory sentences is blatantly trying to protect the power and exclusivity which the legal profession has so assiduously built up for itself over generations. Their protests have little if anything to do with justice. They have everything to do with trying to hang on to over-complex legal systems operated by themselves and their elitist brethren. Just another over-opinionated Establishment desperately trying to cling to powers and privileges which should have no place in the 21st century.

Back to overcrowded prisons. Yes, I have already agreed that most prisons are overcrowded and I have been saying for many years that our Courts have sent many people to prison who should be in community service programmes.

However, this does not mean that other, more serious offenders should not be apprehended and given custodial sentences.

Nor does it mean that American, French, British and Irish prisons could somehow end up with adequate prison places simply by kicking out offenders who may well be better doing community service or other suitable reparation.

What it does mean is that we have too many petty offenders in gaol and too many really dangerous criminals out of gaol. Unfortunately, in many countries, the latter group is much larger than the former group. This would lead rational people with no axe to grind, to the inescapable conclusion that in order to best protect the law-abiding sector, we need not less but more prison places, at least until we have in place more effective measures designed to deter many more individuals from turning to crime.

In countries such as Britain, the judiciary and the executive conspire to keep the need for more prisons from the public, though each does so for very different reasons.

Note how Lord Chief Justices Woolf and Phillips conveniently overlook the fact that since Tony Blair came to power in 1997, Britain has built up a staggering fifty million unresolved crimes. They, and all of us, should think about that. 50,000,000 crimes for which no perpetrator has been found and punished. Apparently our most prestigious Judges attach no importance to this amazingly high level of unsolved crime, nor have they asked themselves what should be done if the police – as they should – become more successful at catching another few hundred thousand of the more dangerous offenders.

Where would our Noble Lords have them go? No wonder Lord Chief Justice Woolf wanted ***murderers*** who pleaded guilty to serve ***only ten years in gaol***.

The answer, my Lords, to overcrowded prisons is very simply the one which inexplicably you prefer not to address. ***Building more*** *prisons* is the answer, then none would be overcrowded and staff could then concentrate more on rehabilitation.

Insofar as one can rely on the relevant official figures, my calculation is that it costs the public ten times as much to leave criminals on the loose than it does to keep them in gaol. This of course varies country to country, according to their very different per-prisoner confinement costs.

A major study in America revealed that confinement costs were $25,000, whilst the average criminal unrestrained piled costs many times greater onto the population at large.

In the UK, Dr. David Green, Director of Civitas, showed prison costs at £2.2 billion a year to be tiny when compared with the £60 billion cost of crime. I believe the cost of crime to be in the region of £100 billion but no matter – all available evidence shows, to anyone prepared to examine the facts, that it is vastly cheaper and more effective to keep serious criminals in gaol than it is to have them roaming around outside.

The Howard League for Penal Reform has seriously lost its way and refused to acknowledge the clear evidence. The Howard League, in its determination to be limpy liberal, continually lobbies for fewer prison places and this has resulted in many more people becoming victims of crime. It is a disgrace that this organisation pays its Executives handsomely to spout absolute nonsense about prison not working. I know far more on this subject than anyone at the Howard League and I know without question that Britain and Ireland have far too few prison places and that building many more would save those countries a fortune in hard cash and save millions of people from becoming victims of crime.

The Howard League for Penal Reform would have my support if it confined itself to working against prisoner abuse instead of campaigning for the closure of women's prisons. I don't know about you, but if my daughter had been beaten and kicked unconscious by a gang of girl thugs, or my grandparents tricked out of their life savings, I would not want those responsible to be doing community service – I would want them in prison for quite a long time.

If you support the Howard League, whose efforts *increase* crime, you may care to contribute instead to The Society for Action Against

257

Crime (**www.crimedown.org**) who are planning a major campaign to *reduce* crime dramatically. More prison places are part of the solution and the Anti-Prison Brigade should note that :-

- Crime in Britain began falling in 1995 when Tory Home Secretary Michael Howard's "tougher sentences and prison works" regime began to pay dividends and had Tony Blair built upon Michael Howard's philosophy, crime in his country would be around half of what it is today.

- Had Mr. Blair worked with The Society for Action Against Crime since 1997, I have no doubt that crime – particularly violent crime – could today be 60 to 80% lower.

- More than 90% of the young offenders in David Blunkett's non-custodial flagship scheme went on to re-offend in 2005. No-one can ever know, of course, how many crimes they actually committed whilst on these "alternative" programmes, but what we do know for certain is that no crimes would have been committed on the public had the offenders been in prison.

- Of those criminals convicted and put onto non-custodial drug treatment programmes, 90% went on to commit further crimes. Almost all of these crimes will be eliminated when the hopeless war against drugs use is ended.

Prison Regimes

Prisons should be run on a carrots-and-sticks, snakes & ladders basis, rewarding good behaviour and punishing every infraction of prison rules. Any Governor pontificating that prisons "cannot be run without the consent of the inmates" should be fired. Such an attitude is an open invitation to subversion.

Whether or not drugs are illegal in any given country, *there should be no recreational drugs in any prison*. Full stop. Prison is a place where you forfeit your freedom, your preferences and your pleasures. They are there for criminals to be punished for their crimes and - if the prisoners wish - to rehabilitate them with a view to preventing re-offending and helping them qualify for a more positive role in society.

It is a disgrace that some prisons have to admit that they have a drugs culture. Always, this has come about by weakness, bribery and on occasions, by threats made against the families of prison officers and some prison visitors. This should be dealt with by raising the sentencing level for such threats. The offence of witness or jury bribery or intimidation should be lifted into a very high level category with appropriate obligatory sentences. These offences strike at the very root of any civilised society because if evil thugs can prevent justice being done, or decide how prisons are to be run, then we lose the battle against crime and consequently leave ourselves at the mercy of the bullies and the evil ones.

No-one should be able to enter or leave any prison without the likely prospect of being searched and/or scanned. After all, you and I have to turn up hours early just to get on an aeroplane, even if we are completely law-abiding citizens on our way to visit other law-abiding friends or relatives.

Equally, sophisticated search equipment should be in use at all prisons and everyone going into a prison should be made very aware of what is likely to happen to them if they are caught smuggling anything into or out of a prison which is against regulations. You will have seen in Chapter 10 that I put this offence into my Category Eight, which carries a mandatory prison term of 5 to 12 years. Once criminals realise that they can have their drugs on the outside but never on the inside, many, I believe, will stop seeing prison as a soft option.

Prisons, above everywhere else, should be drug-free environments and this should be the case regardless of the prevailing drugs regime – illegal or permitted – outside of prisons. Drugs apart, every prison should have available a range of privileges which can be awarded to those who earn them by their faultless behaviour. None of these privileges though, should be given before the passing of an initial 9-month period in a very basic and mainly boring regime. This will help discourage those serving short sentences from perceiving prison as a soft option to which they would not be too concerned about returning.

All prisoners, of course, must be treated humanely and with respect, but at the basic level, the only stimulation available should be that associated with attempts at rehabilitation. Quite properly, the United Nations severely reprimanded Huntingdon Prison in Pennsylvania, America where prisoners had been seriously abused over a long period and I am well aware that many prisons around the world fall far short of acceptable standards. Only by having civilised standards ourselves are we entitled to expect them of others.

Some prisoners, of course, are evil characters who make themselves a serious handful for the prison staff and for these, there must be a sub-basic level of detention, including necessary restraining and calming procedures to counteract violence, but not, of course, any physical or mental torture or abuse of any kind.

Rehabilitation attempts have, in most countries, been pretty dismal failures and this is certainly no surprise to me. By definition, with more than half of current released prisoners re-offending, prison has not been a sufficiently disagreeable experience to deter them from going back there. To start with, the entitlement to better than basic facilities available at 9 months for good behaviour should not be available to those returning to prison, not having learned their lesson. Inmates should understand that if they choose to commit crime which results in their being given a further custodial sentence, they will not be allowed to join the ladder-section of the prison's snakes and ladders regime for 18 months – instead of the 9 months on offer during their first term. Their choice.

Without more serious consequences for bad behaviour, no amount of counselling and in-prison education will seriously reduce re-offending.

In addition to a carrots-and-sticks approach, I also would like to see specially-written education programmes developed for in-prison use via television and, in the classroom/workshop, via computer. I see a ***Concern & Consequences Examination*** as being an important element in all school curricula and I believe an adaptation of this for use in prisons would be a valuable tool in changing attitudes. Its study and proof of understanding should be obligatory for any prisoner applying to be released before serving the full term of their sentence. There should however, be no full and open access to all TV programmes for any prisoner. No Eastenders, no films glorifying violence or anti-social behaviour, only programmes considered suitable by the prison authorities and controlled centrally. There can be no doubt that some people are only in prison anyway because they foolishly aped the more surly, violent and foul-mouthed low-standard characters portrayed in a range of dumbed-down television programmes and films.

It is not surprising that the weaker-minded in society so readily identify with the nasties, so feeding them such garbage via TV whilst in custody is the height of irresponsibility and foolishness.

Many of our civil servants purport to be clever people, yet we pay them handsomely for doing little more than shuffling papers around, creating meaningless Reports, Counter-Reports, kite-flying and attending meetings and conferences.

I know this from years of direct experiences.

Small Government has been promised to us for decades, usually in the run-up periods to elections, but we never get them. Almost all Governments just grow and grow and grow, with those employed having their own financial gain as their prime objective. Some admit to, joke, and even boast about their cushy lives, high salaries and unbelievable pensions. Surely it must be possible to switch some of these public employees to more worthwhile work. If they are as bright as they claim to be, why cannot they develop computer and video programmes designed for prison use aimed at rehabilitation?

Why does it need me, or anyone else, to spell out that there should be *no drugs in prison?* And why haven't these numerous parasites in the Home Office not already organised worthwhile sticks-and-carrots regimes in all of our gaols?

Most countries are adding to crime levels by having far too few prisons which politicians seem to see as an embarrassing failure to control crime. There is some truth in that, where UK prisons, for reasons which are unclear to me, cost far too much – a claimed £37,000 per inmate per year. I would like to know why this is so high. A breakdown of the costs should be made available for public scrutiny and open debate started about how costs-per-prisoner can be slashed.

Whatever the cost of keeping prisoners securely confined, a meaningful proportion of this should be offset by prisoners working, and again, some of the brain-power currently vegetating in Government Departments should be brought to bear on this aspect of prison life.

In western countries, the days are long gone when trades unions can prevent prisoners from doing work on the basis that this takes work away from union members. This argument never had validity of course, but it held sway in some countries for many years.

Now though, in 2007, such objections to prisoners working in commercial activities have been blown out of the water by a more competitive global environment. There can now be no excuse for preventing prisoners from working in competition with the Asians, South Americans and East Europeans who are quite happy to sell their labour at a fraction of the cost of that prevailing in most "western" countries.

I would like to see a new drive to help prisoners earn money for prison services (and for themselves and their victims) and I welcome hearing of any entrepreneurial initiatives to achieve this end. These could be in manufacturing, bearing in mind the restrictions on certain tools in prisons; processing and computer work and for non-dangerous prisoners, outside contracting and community clean-up work.

It should not be forgotten that there are also many good brains amongst the inmates and I believe it would be sensible to invite *their* suggestions for prison-based work or businesses. I would though, be somewhat concerned about any proposals involving 3-slide ladders or mountaineering equipment.

The European Court of Human Rights which sits in Strasbourg, France showed itself, in October 2005, not only to be undemocratic, but devoid of either wisdom or commonsense.

By a majority of 12 votes to 5, the Grand Chamber agreed there had been "a violation of Article 3 of Protocol No. 1 (right to free elections)" in the case of Hirst -v- The United Kingdom and that criminals in prison should have the right to vote in elections. John Hirst had been given a term of discretionary life imprisonment after he pleaded guilty to manslaughter on the grounds of diminished responsibility and as a convicted prisoner, was barred by section 3 of the Representation of the People Act 1983 from voting in parliamentary or local elections.

Mr Hirst issued proceedings in the High Court, under section 4 of the Human Rights Act 1998, seeking a declaration that section 3 was incompatible with the European Convention on Human Rights. On 21 and 22 March 2001 his application was heard before the Divisional Court but his claim and subsequent appeal were both rejected.

An application was lodged with the European Court of Human Rights on 5 July 2001 and subsequently referred to the Grand

Chamber who, by a majority of 12 votes to 5, agreed with Mr. Hirst. They also, incidentally, awarded him 23,200 euros for costs and expenses. Your money, of course.

Well, I don't know about you, but I for one do not want any Government to be chosen by criminals, but that is precisely what the E.C.H.R. decision is now trying to make possible. Elections are won by one or more votes and very small majorities can determine which Political Party is afforded the responsibility of governing the country for some years. Handing the balance of power to criminals in prison seems to me to be a decision of staggering stupidity.

I have read all of the arguments about inclusion in society and "possible" rehabilitation of prisoners but they pale into insignificance compared with the prospect of criminals affecting the outcome of elections. Bear in mind that in most countries, their elections could, at some point, be very close indeed, America, Puerto Rico and Germany being recent examples.

You need only to ask yourself these questions :-

• Would most criminals be more likely to vote for those candidates with lenient views about crime – or those who are tougher on crime?

• Are criminals more likely to support those politicians offering to make prison life more comfortable, or those believing that prison should concentrate upon re-education, devoid of luxuries?

• In those electoral areas with prison populations sufficient to possibly affect the outcome of elections, does this not create the prospect of candidates courting the criminals for their votes at the expense of abandoning their principles? If they have any, that is.

• Do you think that murderers, terrorists, paedophiles, rapists, burglars, muggers, fraudsters, people-smugglers etc. should have the same rights as law-abiding citizens in choosing your Government?

In my view, diminution of the punishment element of prison in some countries has already been complicit in failing to deter many from committing crimes and giving prisoners voting rights will simply add to crime. The European Court of Human Rights clearly attaches more importance to the interests of confined criminals than it does to those of the law-abiding, victims or potential victims of crime.

The term **Human Rights** in the title of "The European Court of Human Rights" is, of course, deliberately misleading, inviting as it does, everyone to believe that it exists to protect the human rights of all where prior courts may have failed so to do. The reality, of course, is that this is not always possible because protecting the rights of one person or group can often only be achieved by trampling on the rights of another person or group.

Increasingly, The European Court of Human Rights is meddling in the affairs of individual nations to their serious disadvantage. It is, in fact, yet another layer of international legal bureaucracy. More jobs, for ever more lawyers and more money for more eurocrats to spend. Our money, of course.

I recommend you to register your objection with any politician who supports giving votes to prisoners and withdraw your support from any Government if it fails to disassociate itself from this ludicrous E.C.H.R. decision.

As at the end of 2005, many countries do deny voting rights to prisoners, including 13 Member States of the Council of Europe and it will be interesting to see which, if any of these are prepared to bend the knee to the barmy bureaucrats of Brussels by abandoning their sovereignty and the protection of their own citizens.

Ireland's prisons are frankly in meltdown and crime is running rampant due to grossly insufficient capacity. In the Celtic Tiger's headlong pursuit of growth, it has overlooked the fact that too few police officers, too slow a judicial system and too few prison places and prison staff are a certain recipe for high crime. Mountjoy prison, for example, is a disgrace. It is seriously over-crowded and in the summer of 2006, three inmates died there as a direct result.

The Irish Prison Service mistakenly attempts to run its prisons on the basis of not daring to upset the prisoners. They are afraid that the inmates will protest – as they have done – about family visits and being allowed recreational drugs. It is this craven attitude that has resulted in Irish taxpayers stumping up more than two million euros since 2002 to pay for prisoners' out-going telephone calls. All but the most urgent calls, granted on compassionate grounds, should be paid for by either the inmates or their relatives or friends. All calls should be a privilege attached to good behaviour – not available as a right.

Pathetic Justice Minister Michael McDowell went berserk at Inspector of Prisons and former Judge Dermot Kinlen's pronouncements about Ireland's prisons. Ireland's Justice Minister was outraged when the Sunday Times reported upon a European Union Report showing Ireland to be on top of the crime league and he lashed out at his Inspector of Prisons for exposing the serious situations in Irish prisons. Bully that he is, Minister McDowell attempted to censor ex-Judge Kinlen's Reports on prisons, delayed their publication to limit debate on them and went to great lengths to denigrate the man commissioned to produce them.

Minister McDowell seems to have taken lessons from British Home Secretaries – when in trouble, use the possible introduction of Identity Cards as a diversion. He should not be surprised therefore, that Dermot Kinlen described him as a frightening fascist whose Department of Justice considered transparency and accountability as dirty words.

I spend a lot of time in Ireland. It is a delightful country in many respects, but its successes, brought about principally by its foresight in bringing in a low tax regime for businesses, have resulted in money becoming God, family values diminished and law and order being overlooked. Fortunately, many Irish people are beginning to be uncomfortable with "keeping up with the Quinns" and it is to be hoped that their numbers will increase and prevent their country's more civilised standards from being swamped by excessive credit-driven consumerism.

The alternative is that today's high crime will get worse.

Finally, there should be fewer freedoms for criminals and more freedoms for the law-abiding. Oppose any politician who gets this the wrong way round by allowing the former to have drugs in prison whilst forcing ID Cards on the rest of us.

How long, I wonder, before the prison incapacity situation becomes so serious that instructions are given by the UK Government to its Crown Prosecution Service to reduce prosecutions? And when that bit of further tinkering doesn't work, the police will presumably be told to stop trying to solve serious crimes because there is nowhere to put the criminals.

On this issue I have some sympathy with Home Secretary John Reid because it is his predecessors and Tony Blair/Gordon Brown who have dumped this huge problem in his lap. They all failed to respond to our big, big questions :-

Do you want to catch and convict a substantial number of those responsible for more than 50 million unsolved crimes (since 1997)?

If the answer is no – why do we need a police force?

If the answer, hopefully, is yes – Where do you propose putting another 50,000 to 150,000 serious criminals when the current prison capacity of 80,000 is already over-subscribed?

It has fallen to John Reid to take panic measures, including using police cells, open prisons, women's prisons and army barracks. Hopefully you will join me in refusing him the use of your garden shed. It was not until the 4th October 2006 that the British Government woke up to the fact that its prisons were being swamped and by Jan./Feb. 2007, it was apparent to all but those who were determined to keep their head in the sand, that Tony Blair had negligently ignored the need for a major increase in prison places throughout his premiership. Even the Labour Government's own Inspector of Prisons, Anne Owers, described the service as being in crisis and Home Secretary John Reid pathetically tried to defend his decision to "communicate" to Judges the inescapable fact that there was no room at the prison inns.

Perhaps by the time you read this, Tony Blair and his successor will have asked the Queen if she could take some overflow in Buck House or, as Britain is being forced back onto a war footing, the Government might add to its Identity Cards nonsense by forcefully billeting criminals on householders. Oh, and by the way, if you refuse to take in your share of criminals, you could go to prison. Someone mention Catch-22?

Some considerable leeway could be most quickly created by releasing from prison those whose only offence is the possession of drugs for their own use. Rather than waiting for the penny to drop about the de-criminalisation of drugs for personal use, those currently in gaol solely for this offence should immediately have the remains of their sentences commuted to suitable Community Service Orders.

266

The police should also be told to concentrate on more serious crimes, a sensible move to take the pressure off both the Courts, the prison services and the taxpayers' pockets.

Foreign criminals should *all* be sent home, preferably to their own prisons, but if their countries will not imprison them, send them back anyway with restrictions preventing them from ever returning to any host country whose hospitality had been abused. No country should be obliged to pay for the long-term care in detention of any foreign criminal.

One of the most difficult decisions facing society concerns the release of sex offenders when their sentence has been served and I have agonised long over this seemingly intractable problem. Psychiatrists have been unable to devise any tests which can reliably determine whether or not a particular individual will re-offend and that is no reflection on the psychiatrists – it is simply an acknowledgement of the complexity of the conundrum.

When considering sex offences, it has to be acknowledged that we are dealing with a contradictory phenomenon which cannot be compared with any other crime, because what most of us do for pleasure as a consensual act becomes a seriously repugnant crime when consent is absent. This of course becomes worse when violence is added to rape or when children are sexually assaulted, some of whom will have little understanding of what is happening to them, or why.

With every other crime I have been able to gather information, talk to victims, perpetrators and many others, then think my way through to what seem to be the most appropriate solutions. Not so with paedophiles, rapists or the range of sex offenders in between. All I can offer right now are some thoughts for consideration:-

- Is it possible to determine the level of compulsion which drives sex offenders? and what measures are available to diminish these?

- Can a way be found, enabling offenders to be released following some years in prison without undue risk to the public?

- Assuming that at least some sex offenders are beyond control, perhaps even to their own distress and revulsion, can we not move away from simple knee-jerk condemnation and search for ways to help those who may actually be desperate for understanding?

- Probably like you, I have an in-built abhorrence of rape and child abuse and am tempted to throw those responsible into gaol and throw away the key. However, following much reflection, I have to ask myself – "What if I had been born with uncontrollable sexual urges or deviations?" "Had I even been forced to forego one of life's major pleasures for too long, might I not have ignored one of society's principle taboos?" I like to think not, but it does give me pause for thought and make me realise that this is not a black or white issue.

- We will get nowhere on this very difficult issue if we are not prepared to address some of the traditional no-nos, so should we not be considering castration and/or permanent incarceration of the most difficult cases.

France has a particularly serious problem with sex offenders, seeing those in gaol rising from 4% to 25% in recent years. So concerned are some about this increase that Justice Minister Dominique Perben authorised scientists to begin laboratory trials of drugs designed to eliminate the sex drives of paedophiles and serious sex offenders. Doctor Serge Stoleru, at the French National Institute for Health & Medical Research, was hopeful that sex offending could be reduced almost to zero in any man. Problem is, that such drugs would need to be taken regularly and I believe it is naïve in the extreme – and very dangerous – to put any faith in sex offenders keeping themselves under control by voluntarily taking drugs for the rest of their lives. Perhaps the French should dust off their ancient guillotines and re-direct them to solving one of the numerous crime problems on a more permanent basis.

- Perhaps we should be creating a new type of confinement facility where those who have served their prison term, if any, can be accommodated, instead of being launched into a revolving door scenario with ever more victims left in their wake.

- Whilst a firm opponent of the storage of data about law-abiding citizens, I have fewer reservations about appropriate information on known and proven sex offenders being recorded and made available to those with the responsibility of trying to protect innocents from becoming victims. Some countries already operate Sex Offenders Registers but those on them can usually move to another country in order to avoid their consequences. This is a matter which must be addressed.

- Could charity groups be set up to try to help paedophiles re-integrate into society and what would be their likely prospects? Maybe. In the absence of any obvious solution to this most difficult of problems, it is an avenue worthy of consideration.

A less complicated area of penal institutions concerns those where people are kept imprisoned without charge. Take Guantanamo Bay, America's toe-hold in Cuba, for example. This and similar clandestine facilities have not protected America at all. They have, in fact, had precisely the opposite effect. By October 2006 the U.S. Government was beginning to realise this and blustered that the world should stop calling for the closure of the infamous Guantanamo because, after detaining some prisoners for more than 5 years, they were trying to send them back, but were having difficulty because some countries would not accept them. They did not name either the prisoners or their countries of origin.

Well, Messrs. Bush, Cheyney, Rumsfeld, Rice & co., I can solve your problems for you. You lifted these individuals via clandestine and strong-arm methods, so simply reverse the process if you cannot put your suspects on public trial. Just take them back from whence they came or ask Amnesty International or the International Red Cross to take them into their care. Alternatively of course, you could just open the gates of Guantanamo and let out your prisoners. I doubt they would have much difficulty finding their way to Havana for a chat with the Brothers Castro.

An excellent example of an Establishment going to disgraceful lengths to protect even its own criminal hierarchy, is the way the Roman Catholic Church covered up their sex crimes.

Trying to hide the sexual misconduct of some of its priests, Pope Benedict XVI set in train a cover-up operation intended to keep the sexual abuse of (mainly) children away from the public gaze. Bishops throughout the world were instructed to do everything possible to keep known sex abuse cases in-house and shamefully, victims, witnesses and offenders were encouraged to keep quiet, on pain of excommunication.

Typical of Establishments, the Catholic Church's priority was its own protection and in attempts to secure this, some victims were paid silence money and paedophile priests were moved on to new parishes. Not having been reported to the police, these abuser priests were not, of course, on any Sex Offenders Register, so their new parishioners, sometimes in other countries, were kept in ignorance of the dangers introduced into their midst at Rome's instigation. There was allegedly a seven million dollar budget allocated to concealing information about priests' involvement in sexual abuse. The drive for this suppression of uncomfortable truths came more from the top than the bottom and it was today's Pope, at the time Cardinal Joseph Ratzinger, who ordered that the facts about Father Oliver O'Grady's sexual offences against children should be hidden. Canon Lawyer Father Tom Doyle confirmed this when he publicly declared that his Church's hierarchy was only interested in damage control and not exposing and punishing those guilty of criminal acts.

I have not the slightest doubt that most Catholic priests are a great bunch of guys who give up much to care for their parishioners. Indeed, the initiatives to expose the sexual abusers eventually came from parishioners, priests and bishops mainly in America and Ireland who were angry and ashamed, not only about the offenders, but also about what some of them described as their hierachy's Mafia-type culture of secrecy.

This book is not the place to rake over decades of dubious practices within the Roman Catholic Church, but in the context of who will resist the introduction of serious anti-crime measures, it is important that everyone understands that even Establishments as venerated as religions, will go to extreme lengths to protect their own advantages. This chapter, therefore, is simply to alert you to the advisability of asking why particular groups may wish to keep the status quo for reasons which may well be less than altruistic.

The place for those in any religion who betray the trust of their followers is not a new, far away parish, it is a prison cell.

More, serious problems exist with the half-way houses used to accommodate those newly-released from prison but not yet ready for total, unrestricted freedom. Bail hostels and other such institutions for temporary use are currently between a rock and a hard place. They get often violent, dysfunctional people dumped on them sometimes whose release from prison has been authorised by psychiatrists who have not even seen them.

Dennis Finnigan was stabbed to death in Richmond Park, London by such a schizophrenic who was known to have stabbed three people previously.

Anthony Rice, a life-sentenced serial rapist was released early into a low-risk hostel. He very quickly strangled and stabbed Naomi X.

Many of these time-bombs are seriously into drugs which had somehow been available to them in prison but incredibly, the half-way hostels *are not allowed to search their "residents" for drugs!* Why? Human Rights legislation dear reader. Human Rights.

David Charles had already committed violent crimes whilst in a hostel but their request for him to be returned to prison was refused. He hailed a taxi and for no reason, murdered Colin Winston who had picked him up as a fare.

Seems to me that the Human Rights of innocents are being forfeited in favour of those of the criminals and I for one wish to see this changed.

The Human Rights of criminals should be restricted to ensuring that they are not abused, but they should not be used in any way which can trash the Human Rights of innocent, law-abiding citizens.

Time for some serious re-thinking.

We can start by making far better use of the BendyProbe Cameras, searching for drugs and other unlawful materials in all prisons and all half-way house hostels.

CHAPTER 13

BEWARE SELF-PROTECTING ESTABLISHMENTS

Having read so far, it will be clear to you that I am not courting popularity with the great and the good, many of whom will perceive my research and conclusions as seriously threatening. For some, that may well be true, but given time to think, most of the apparent losers from my proposals will also be beneficiaries from significantly lower crime. It was Dr. Albert Schweitzer who, on winning the Nobel Peace Prize said ... "The single biggest problem with the world is that *people do not think!* because thinking requires one to come to conclusions and very often, the conclusions are uncomfortable".

Cartels, monopolies, establishments – call them what you will – exist in many spheres of life and invariably they resort to devious and dubious practices in order to protect and perpetuate themselves.

Crime is one such area and there are organisations and professions who, perhaps secretly, do not wish to see major reductions in crime. Some of these will surprise you because of the cloak of apparent respectability which they have woven for themselves, sometimes over more than a hundred years.

Before addressing the crime establishments who can be expected to resist measures designed to reduce crime, I will paint you a picture to assist your understanding of how others may well view the likelihood of major crime reduction with alarm.

Imagine that a natural product or combination of products was discovered which prevented heart disease, strokes, kidney or liver failure, multiple sclerosis, Alzheimers etc. and cured those already suffering their effects - a miracle alternative cure-all which people had used and found to be unbelievably effective.

Now you may think that such a wonderful discovery would receive universal acclaim, but I promise you it would not.

- Most of the medical profession, which is a very closed establishment, would see it as a threat to the jobs of tens of thousands of their members. High-flying doctors would weave a web of dire warnings about the miracle product not having been subject to years of double-blind trials. Learned and confusing papers would be written by consultants scaring people about appalling consequences, perhaps if not now, but for future generations.

- Powerful drug companies, seeing the markets for most of their products disappearing before their eyes, would massively expand their existing lobbying against natural products. They already conspire with the medical profession and with Governments to suppress "alternative" natural treatments, so it requires little imagination to realise the lengths to which the drug companies would go if 80% of their lucrative business was about to become redundant.

- The Drugs Licensing and Supervision Bodies, comprising scientists and bureaucrats, would also join forces with the above, seeing their own comfortable jobs about to disappear overnight.

- Private health insurers would be appalled at the prospect of losing most of its customers and closing its hospitals.

- Hospital builders and companies making the wide range of diagnostic and treatment equipment would also face liquidation and ally themselves to the other Establishment interests.

- Governments would simply crunch the numbers, weighing up their own personal benefits and the pros and cons of supporting the cheap unpatentable natural miracle cure. Their treasury computers would calculate the enormous immediate savings in health care expenditure on the one hand, with the nett costs of people living another 20 years on the other. They would also factor in the prospective permanent loss of millions of well-paid jobs which would see positive tax flows replaced by negative Social Security payments.

This little parable is simply to demonstrate that even the most respectable Establishments will seriously consider resisting even clearly beneficial changes when they see them as posing a threat to their own status or financial interests.

You may think that, criminals apart, almost everyone will see the commonsense and value of the initiatives recommended in this Blueprint to secure serious reductions in crime but be warned – there will be some serious resistance to driving down crime. Some of this obstruction will be apparent, some will be mounted surreptitiously behind closed doors, but forewarned is forearmed.

Potential Establishments who may resist crime reduction

The criminal fraternity is my number one target, being by far the greatest losers from better law and more efficient law enforcement.

Strictly speaking though, it is not a single Establishment and it was Mark Twain who said "In America, there is no distinctive criminal class – except Congress." In most countries because many criminals are individually-driven opportunists who expect not to be caught, nor to suffer any serious consequences if they do end up in Court, these guys and dolls have no usable voice and if my proposals are put into effect, they can only either mend their ways, or suffer more certain and more serious consequences. However, they would become an Establishment Body of sorts if given the right to vote whilst in prison. Inevitably, such a retrograde step would lead prisoners to become "organised" in the most dangerous sense of the word – a Criminals Union, no doubt headed by imprisoned Mafiosa.

Some countries are already at risk of the outcome of their elections being determined by the votes they permit to the criminals in their prisons. This is bizarre and I made this very clear to Mark Oaten, the then UK Liberal Democrats' Home Affairs spokesman prior to the 2005 General Election, who promoted this dangerous notion. It did not, in the event, feature in his Party's manifesto and it was not long before Mr. Oaten's sexual conduct resulted in his judgement in other areas being shown to have been seriously lacking. Even so, some misguided countries still persist in promoting this crazy idea.

Organised crime, on the other hand, which includes international smugglers, drug barons, people traffickers, protection racketeers and terrorists, is of a different order and is certain to increase its current practices of bribing and/or threatening those in positions to protect or help their illegal operations. Anyone believing that such corrupt practices are not common in all high-crime countries is dangerously naïve and should think again. They would educate themselves better by reading John Simpson's book "*A mad World, My Masters*" (Pan Books, MacMillan). Along with journalist Robert Fisk, he has a track record of putting himself at considerable personal risk and he has first-hand experience of how the villains of our world operate. There is no Camp David, Chequers or Elysse Palace for these guys, nor any reliance on dodgy intelligence. They get off their butts and take serious personal risks to find out for themselves, as journalists, what exactly is going on around the world, often in theatres of hot war. The world needs more John Simpsons and Robert Fisks.

Politicians are responsible for high crime both directly and by default, which is to say, they have watched crime rise enormously but have failed miserably to restore law and order. Together with their bureaucratic masters/conspirators, they prefer tinkering and shuffling about meaningless Reports and wasting masses of money on endless meetings, conferences, treaties, partnerships, pilot studies and quangos instead of bringing simple, commonsense solutions into effect. The words 'simple' and 'commonsense' of course, strike fear and dread into the hearts of politicians, civil servants and lawyers, in the same way that flat taxes send revenue collectors, treasury mandarins and their hoards of parasitical bureaucrats into convulsions.

The Political Establishment will rant long and hard against my proposals, openly and behind closed doors, because 'simple' solutions are as dangerous to them as cryptonite is to Superman. *Their* food and drink is complexity, quantity, obscurity, endless debate, hundreds of academic Reports, conferences, luxury travel and hotels, supposed "research" trips and power games. The very thought of fewer, more straightforward laws and judicial systems, will send many of our political grandees into apoplexy and it will be interesting to see who comes out of the woodwork trying to justify the status quo of high crime. We will then see who is in public office for the public good, and who is only there for the easy life, for their own financial gain and for the ego-trip of wielding power – all, of course, at the taxpayers' expense.

Ask any politician why they want political office and invariably they say it is because they want to make things better and the breed has been trotting out this facile mantra for generations. So, how come we still have so much crime, so much unfairness, so much debt, such poor health care and so much regulation of, and interference in, our lives? How come our politicians are too craven to vote according to their consciences for fear of being pushed off the political career ladder? And why do our elected representatives spend most of their time trying to ensure that their particular Party remains in, or gains power, instead of reducing crime and protecting their citizens' liberty and privacy?

The motives and methods of the political class are so central to the whole issue of high crime as to merit a chapter of its own later in "Quicksands".

Media – I have yet to reach a conclusion as to whether or not the various media will combine as an "Establishment" to oppose attempts to bring crime down hugely. What I do know is that newspapers and broadcasters have studiously avoided the research and the initiatives of The Society for Action Against Crime, despite being regularly updated about its work. I am also aware that if I am successful in persuading the people that matter - i.e. the public – that crime can be largely overcome and political shenanigans greatly simplified, then our news media will have huge holes to fill. That would not, of course, put them out of business, nor should it, but it will necessitate change, the prospect of which some media owners may prefer not to have to face. To most people, the idea of apparently respectable businesses not wanting to see crime and political incompetence almost disappear would seem ludicrous. However, when one realises that so much of what these media groups trade on is the reporting of crime and pontificating about it, the question which arises is "What would our newspapers, TV and radio stations do without this huge chunk of their staple diet?"

I don't pretend to know what the media's reaction to the prospect of major crime reduction will be, but bearing the foregoing in mind, I speculate that its support or rejection of the proposed solutions herein will not be unanimous either way.

All will be revealed shortly. Just be aware.

The Judiciary as an Establishment will be one of the main Bodies facing change if we are to be successful in winning the battle against crime.

Few lawyers can be expected to welcome my exposure of the legal profession, which has been responsible for increasing, instead of reducing crime. Even fewer Judges will initially accept that there are better ways of running our Courts in order to ensure justice for crime victims and less wildly-fluctuating sentences for those found guilty of crimes. They love the power and prestige which they have cornered for themselves over generations. When it comes to sentencing criminals, Judges just love being the only game in town and no-one should be surprised to see this particular Establishment fight tooth and nail to keep it that way. I wonder though, if a few may be sufficiently enlightened to acknowledge the need for change.

More likely, there will be huge resistance from the legal cartel to many of my proposals – an indication of the extent to which these vested interests attach far greater importance to their own ambitions and financial rewards than to the public good. It is hardly surprising that so many people from all walks of life hold lawyers of all grades in low regard - *including Judges* - and some of the reasons for this are explained elsewhere in this book.

By cornering the market in practicing law, the club which affords itself the title of the legal profession has hi-jacked the laws of almost all countries in order to prevent competition from outsiders and to earn themselves huge fees, even on the all-too-frequent occasions when their legal opinions are proven to be wrong. I guarantee that if lawyers had to forego their fees *and* had to pay half of the other costs associated with losing civil court cases, we would have a huge reduction in litigation, thereby freeing up Court time for the more serious matter of dealing with criminals much more promptly.

Such wise solutions and others proposed herein, will doubtless be belittled by the Judiciary and strenuously resisted. That is the automatic knee-jerk reaction of Establishment cartels the world over, *but changes are necessary and changes will come, with or without the co-operation of the protectionist legal profession*. I look forward to learning whether or not there will be members of the legal profession with the wit and courage to acknowledge the merits of at least some of the solutions I propose herein.

In their determination to protect their own Establishment, lawyers have insinuated themselves right into the hearts of many Governments, which enables them to have an undue influence on those nations' affairs. From deep inside the corridors of power, these legal termites can and do trash simple, commonsense laws and turn them into inscrutable legalese gobbledegook. They write laws specifically intended to be capable of a range of different interpretations, some of them absolute opposites. Such unnecessarily obscure laws are fertile ground for lawyers to argue about, invariably at someone else's expense, of course.

Juries in America are already entitled to throw out any case if they believe the law in question to be faulty, but Judges are so worried that this diminishes their authority, that they have conspired to hide this option from everyone since 1895.

In a highly-contentious split decision, the Supreme Court that year ruled that although juries did have the right to declare any law as faulty, the failure of the Judge in Sparf & Hansen vs. U.S. to advise the jury of this power was not sufficient cause for a mistrial or appeal. From that day onwards, Judges have routinely decided to chance their arms by not telling jurors of this very important option which had previously been so successfully used by juries to end slavery in many States even before the Civil War, and many other injustices.

The pressure applied in Courts by Judges determined to avoid jurors knowing they can override any law they believe to be bad, is a disgrace. They lie by telling juries they can only decide on the facts. Individual jurors who know of this law are always excluded. Self-defenders are slapped down by Judges if they try to introduce it and the few lawyers who have dared to raise it have even been threatened with contempt of Court. Judges will go to almost any lengths to prevent even the slightest threat to their almighty power.

In 1771, U.S. President John Adams stated very clearly that even though in disagreement with the Court and the Judge, it was a juror's right and duty to declare a verdict according to his personal judgement and conscience.

U.S. Supreme Chief Justice John Jay (Georgia vs. Brailsford) was equally unequivocal when he said that juries have every right to judge not only the facts of a case but the merit of the law itself.

President Thomas Jefferson considered that trial by juries is the only anchor yet devised by man whereby Governments can be held to the principles of the Constitution.

Since then, the legal profession has completely lost its way until now, in the 21st century, it is just another grubby, self-serving Establishment interested only in increasing its own power and financial benefits.

The Legal Profession has been instrumental in creating a monster of complex laws and regulations designed specifically to be incomprehensible to those who are expected to abide by them. That is absolutely unnecessary and I make an offer to any English-speaking Government - give me any current law and tell me what it seeks to achieve/prevent, and I will convert it to a form of words which anyone with an I.Q. of 100 or more could understand without the help of someone with a mop on their head and wrapped in an over-large black sheet.

My offer does not extend to tax law in the U.S.A. which extends unbelievably to more than *13 million words*, many of which cannot be accurately understood. Even their own Internal Revenue Service frequently misinterprets their tax laws and the time is long overdue for the complete overhaul of this imbecilic nonsense, compliance with which costs the citizens and corporations of America huge fortunes year after year after year.

Every country should override their lawyers, simplify all of their laws and scrap their unbelievably complex tax systems and replace them with either a flat rate income tax and/or an adjusted Value Added or Sales Tax and of course, green taxes. This would free up major amounts of revenue, some of which could go to reducing taxes, some to crime reduction and some to other social benefits.

I would guess that less than 1% of the world's population knows the basis from which the Legal Establishment has spread its cancerous cells into every organ of society, so I will bring it out into the open in the hope that some sunlight may begin to reduce the mould.

The Legal Establishment is not based upon any publicly-owned or Government-created Body. It is not a Body whose prime function is justice, nor is it a Body which is there for the protection of the individual. The Legal Establishment does not exist to protect liberty, freedom or privacy. What it is, is a private club to provide its members with a climate based upon thousands of unnecessary laws and regulations, out of which its members and only its members can then earn huge fees arguing about different interpretations of laws which were purposely written by the lawyers to invite dispute.

So – what is this private club? It is the **BAR** Association, which is the only route to becoming a Barrister or Judge.

So – who is the BAR Association? This is likely to cause you to question either my learning or my sanity, because the answer truly does approach the unbelievable. The BAR initials are, in fact, those of the British Accredited Registry headquartered in the City of London, England and the American BAR Association is simply the U.S.A. branch of the London-based international network.

280

It gets worse. The **BAR** incredibly, is controlled not by any public or independent Body, *it is controlled by the Rothschild banking cartel!* and apart from themselves, it is accountable to no-one.

From very early on, the BAR had a grand plan to inveigle its own (lawyers) into positions of power within the politics of as many countries as possible. This would allow them to promote ever more laws, virtually guaranteeing that many citizens would break or misinterpret them.

America now has – wait for it – more than 60 million statutes on its books, a wonderful trough of law available to the snouts of an ever-growing army of BAR brothers and sisters. The evidence that this means mega bucks for the lawyers and bankruptcy or serious financial loss for millions of individuals and corporations is before us every day. This particular Establishment has corrupted politics, spread its deadly influence into international affairs and trade, secured important positions in most bureaucracies and turned common law into a minefield of excessive regulation, through which only lawyers can walk and not only survive, but come out smelling of roses.

My advice – never vote for a lawyer at Election time because we have the evidence before us of the mess in which most countries find themselves, largely as a result of having too many lawyers in high political office. The BAR's gain is always the people's loss. How else do you think lawyer Lord Falconer managed to conspire with lawyer Tony Blair to secure preferential tax treatment for the UK's Judges? This was nothing more than a blatant and corrupt misuse of power by lawyer politicians.

Ban the rights of lawyers to be the only ones permitted to represent clients in Court. This right should be open to any individual chosen by any client.

Lawyers should be banned from Tribunals and only the parties concerned should be allowed to present their evidence, because once lawyers become involved, they pretend to investigate every microscopic detail they can either find or dream up. This would save many many millions of dollars, euros, pounds etc. Apart from anything else, expect to see the numbers of Tribunals drop significantly once lawyers are prohibited from them and more of the contenders reach far cheaper accommodations between themselves.

Ireland particularly, has wasted huge sums of money on Tribunals which have benefited lawyers immensely, to the great cost of all others, mainly the Irish taxpayer. Tom Gilmartin, Taoiseach Bertie Ahern, Padraig Flynn, Michael Lowry and those called to the Barr Tribunal about the Gardai shooting of John Carthy, are just a few of those who could attest to the cost, both in financial and energy terms of inquiries which so very rarely get to the truth. John McGuinness, Vice Chair of Ireland's Public Accounts Committee claimed in 2004 that Tribunals may be costing more than a billion euros to "no good purpose" but 3 years on, nothing has changed. Cut out the lawyers and let us find better ways of resolving disputes.

Time was then the French had a grip of things when, in the late 1700s their most brilliant lawyer Monsieur de Malesherbes represented King Louis XVI at the Tribunal considering charges of treason. There were no great financial pickings to add to the fortunes Monsieur Malesherbes had previously screwed out of the legal system this time. He not only lost the case, he, the king, the queen, their children and their grandchildren also lost their heads. Anyone mention poetic justice?

Lawyers, particularly ruthless American lawyers, make obscene amounts of money from class actions which invariably result in little or no financial rewards to any individuals. They, for example, went after Citibank, who had allegedly overcharged their customers by treating payments due by 10.00 am as late. Such is the level of fear of litigation costs in America that Citibank chose to amend the due payment time from 10.00 am to 1.00 pm and to "settle" for 18 million dollars. The amount each Citibank customer received out of this $18m was, on average, *less than one dollar*. *The amount received by the lawyers was $7.2million*.

This was by no means an unusual case – there are many class actions which have produced far worse results, with the vulture lawyers being the only real winners. This pity is that not only are lawyers ruining America by involving individuals and corporations in unaffordable litigation – and the hugely costly insurance premiums which flow from this – they are spreading their cancers to other nations.

David S. Casey Jnr., President of the Association of Trial Lawyers of America, not surprisingly claimed in 2004 that there is nothing wrong with the class actions system. Now there's a surprise.

Hopefully juries everywhere will soon re-assert the principle of personal responsibility and start throwing out class actions and stop awarding millions to someone who spilled coffee, which they were told was hot, onto themselves.

Smokers and drinkers have known forever that their habits were harmful and it is not the fault of any food manufacturer if people eat some of their products to excess whilst slumped in front of the telly.

Trial lawyer John Banzhaf is now so wealthy from targeting companies such as McDonalds that, for the time being at least, he is untouchable because of America's out-of-control legal system. America must choose. Either change the system or let the likes of David Casey and John Banzhof cost corporate America hundreds of billions of dollars. These huge and unnecessary costs can only come from two sources – the shareholders of the stung businesses and the consumers, faced with the higher costs needed to recover the money which the lawyers have so easily pocketed.

Professor Ferdinand von Prondzynski (love the Irish name) of Dublin's City university clearly sees the dangers of Ireland following America's traumatic addiction to litigation. He quotes American academic Richard Posner's assertion that history shows that all branches of the legal profession conspire together to secure a lustrous place in the financial and social status sun.

It is also true that the more per capita lawyers countries have, the lower they are in the rate of economic growth.

The good Professor also reflects my own view that we should have a debate about the legal profession and we should be seeking ways to avoid many of the pitfalls involved in resorting to law and search for other ways to resolve disputes. Even some Judges such as Mrs. Justice Baron have become concerned at the hugely disproportionate amount of money taken out by many lawyers in divorce cases. Stringing out cases is a typical lawyer tactic and Senior UK Costs Judge, Master Hurst, is on record saying that solicitors have a vested interest in maximising the costs recoverable from paying clients.

The Joseph Rowntree Foundation is also very sceptical of allowing lawyers any say in how long children of divorced parents should spent with each parent.

This then is certain to be one of the Establishments which I expect to use its undoubted political clout to resist any of my anti-crime proposals for no other reason than that some of them will reduce both the power and the earnings of lawyers. Robert Ringer's words on lawyers is pretty succinct – "I abhor over-generalisations" he said. "Fairness compels me to point out that only 97% of attorneys in America are lazy, incompetent, negligent and greedy – yet they give the entire profession a bad name."

The words of poet Alfred, Lord Tennyson are appropriate for the Legal Establishment to take to heart, viz-a-viz - "And may there be no moaning of the bar".

Few people, of course, realise the extent to which cartels have inveigled themselves into our lives. Let me give you one further example of the secrecy of cartels and the damage they inflict upon us all.

The Federal Reserve Bank of America impoverishes everyone by its manipulation of interest rates and by its complicity in the continual printing of ever more U.S. dollars and releasing them onto the market via preferred banks. This, of course, has built a massive debt bubble; inflation hidden by statistical manipulation (lying); and of course, it impoverishes everyone who either holds U.S. dollars, dollar assets or is paid in this nonsensical fiat currency.

It gets worse.

Most people throughout the world believe that the Federal Reserve Bank is a Government entity, but nothing could be further from the truth. It is, in fact, nothing more than a cartel of well-connected but highly-secretive *private* banks which very deviously chose to put the word "Federal" into its title precisely to create the impression that it is a Government Body, which most certainly it is not. Not many people know this.

You can decide for yourself, dear reader, whether or not you believe that this misleading and secretive cartel is using the word Federal in its title without a nod and a wink of approval from the U.S. Government itself.

My advice? Ditch those U.S. dollars before they lose the rest of their value and leave you seriously impoverished, possibly even bankrupted. U.S. dollars are backed by nothing. They are simply

I-O-Us – just pieces of paper with a promise of payment from a Government drowning in debt.

Religions have, for centuries, been amongst the world's most powerful establishments and it is depressing that some religions have misused the powers they gained, in manners which have resulted in the violent deaths of millions of people. Many members of most religions are kind, humane, charitable and forgiving, but unfortunately, they all too often find themselves in bed with fanatical bigots purporting to be of the same faith.

Regardless of the origin of their beliefs, too many faiths believe that *theirs is the one and only valid religion*. This self-delusion is fine by me, provided that they do not seek to force their views on others, because this is the root of so much crime and tragedy throughout the world.

My personal opinion is that structured religions are run by the powerful – usually academics – wishing to exploit the vulnerable and gullible. If the masses are prepared to subject themselves to such control, that is their affair. I have no wish to persuade them to forsake their faiths, many of which are based upon mainly worthwhile principles which provide good spiritual guidance.

One does not, of course, need to belong to any religion to have high standards of behaviour., nor to have an inner awareness of some indefinable spirituality.

The problems, including death and destruction, which have been caused by the religious Establishments for centuries are still with us today, but of course, we never learn from history. The world is awash with academic historians and in my view, they should all be fired (dismissed, that is, not put to the torch). By all means let them study history as a pastime, but they should do so in their own time and with their own money – not mine and yours. It was William Shakespeare who said "what is past is prologue". How right he was, but what a tragedy that we never learn from history.

For centuries, major religions have been in conflict and each has its rump of fanatics beyond the control of their mainstream members. Unfortunately, even these normally sober mainstream members are all too easily whipped into frenzies of hatred by either the fundamentalists or the high priests of their religions. One moment these individual members are lauding high moral principles, the next, they become part of the howling mobs threatening and sometimes succeeding to kill people and destroy property. Invariably, this rage is triggered by perceived insults which most sane people would regard as trivial or of little consequence.

Staking out a claim as **the only true religion**, whichever it is, is provocative and aggressive and such claims can only have one result – conflict.

Some other religions claim the same ground, believing or claiming that they are the "only" true religion, thereby inevitably creating head to head clash scenarios.

Not all religions, of course, are so dogmatic or grandiose in their claims, but even these tend to defend their own spiritual territory.

Then there are the millions of freedom-loving individuals who think for themselves, which is anathema to those in the religions which demand that their believers hand over their own minds and believe in masses of dogma supposedly handed down by God to some chosen individuals.

We do not yet live in a civilised world and religions share much of the responsibility for this. My book is a genuine attempt to move us towards a more caring society and I do not shrink from ruffling the feathers of any Establishment, even knowing the power they currently wield.

Although it saddens me to see religions controlled by hierarchies of cardinals, bishops, imams, priests, rabbis etc. who all too often have vastly more interesting and financially comfortable lives than do their flocks, I have no wish to outlaw any religion. I just wish them to be seen for what they are – Establishments which survive by preying on the weaknesses in human nature.

Religions are simply props upon which some people will always seek to lean. Little different really to other forms of dependency, such as lifetime employment, drugs, Political Party membership etc. – all part of life's rich tapestry and all fine by me, until they lead their followers into crimes of violence.

A good example of the dangers of religion is the saga of the publication of the cartoons by the Jyllands-Posten newspaper in Denmark which resulted in deaths which, at the time of writing, has already seen people killed and buildings burned in a number of countries.

Religions, by the very nature of their claimed certainties, particularly those with extremist views, leave themselves open to ridicule and satire and many within those religions have sufficient humanity and sense of humour to take this on the chin. Of course, the lines between humour, political comment, distaste or offence are unclear and beyond precise definition and I see nothing but serious dangers if we listen to those demanding restrictions on freedoms of expression. I for one have no wish to insult any religion, but I will never dilute my honest opinions for fear of upsetting any over-sensitive feelings – real or contrived.

Incitement to violence, of course, is quite rightly an offence in many countries but that apart, it is simply not possible to define what is offensive. On the subject of blasphemy, this should be a matter only for those claiming to be of the faith in question and should not apply to outsiders.

One has to ask why such a furore was raised months after the September 2005 publication of the cartoons in Denmark. Hardly anyone in the world would either have seen or heard of these cartoons but for the actions of certain Moslems. It was they who massively increased the exposure of the cartoons and by so doing, inflicted suffering – if suffering there was - on their fellow Moslems, some of whom, they must have known, would easily be roused to anger and mob violence. I have no doubt that many Moslems – even when faced with material which they found offensive – would not see such material as justifying the kind of mindless rage which was orchestrated by what (hopefully) was a minority of fundamentalists. This appears to have been nothing more than an opportunistic attempt to attack the freedoms of anyone prepared to express anything questioning the Islamic religion.

My advice to all Moslems is – "subject yourself to the disciplines of your religion as you wish. Many of your laws have much to commend them and indeed are shared by millions of non-believers. You do though, inflict considerable harm upon your own religion when you attempt to force your opinions and your interpretations of its restrictions on everyone else".

Unless anyone libels or slanders me – in which case I could seek redress in a Court of Law should I so choose – they can say what they will about me or my work and I will not kill, threaten to kill, or incite others so to do in retaliation. There are far better ways of dealing with adversaries.

At various other times, most of the world's major religions have committed appalling crimes under the pretext of righting wrongs, revenge, call it what you will. I have to smile whenever I see people whose supposed sensitivities are so easily offended, suddenly become capable of the most barbarous and uncivilised violence. The amount of crime associated with religion, defending democracy, recovering territory etc. is enormous and trying to prevent it has become prohibitively expensive.

It is not, of course, those who are responsible for the bloodshed who suffer the consequences. It is the minions under their control who are the victims and I would welcome receiving proposals from any quarter, including the religious themselves, concerning the problems associated with religion and crime. The best I can hope for right now is that more of us think very carefully about the negative forces abroad which are constantly exhorting us to anger and vengeance for their own unworthy purposes.

Lovers of freedom and peace should be ever vigilant and they should resist all attempts by either Governments or religions to threaten or diminish those freedoms which, to me, are our birthright. We do not "belong" to any State and however much one may feel affinity with a particular religion, that should not automatically align you with everything done by others in the name of that religion. Religious leaders are, after all, only men and women with their own subjective views and interpretations of someone else' scriptures.

Think for yourself.

I have no particular expectations about the reactions of individual religions to the recommendations contained herein. They have certainly failed to deliver non-violent societies themselves, but as only some of the religious fundamentalists can be expected to suffer any consequences from my proposals, I would like to think that mainstream religions will see the need for change and support my anti-crime campaigning.

Other Establishments likely to resist any efforts to resolve conflict and reduce crime are the arms industries of the world, without whose products there would be only a tiny fraction of today's crime. They have a vested interest in conflict and very little in peace.

America is at the forefront of negative self-protecting Establishments yet again, dragging or forcing other nations along with them.

In 1998/9 there were only 9 corporations in the U.S.A. with Homeland Security contracts, but by 2006 there were an amazing thirty-three thousand, eight hundred and ninety (33,890) as politicians and corporation executives conspired to create and milk a worldwide terrorism panic.

Creeps such as Attorney General John Ashcroft were quick to spot the opportunities for making money. He cynically extended America's laws to spy on its own citizens, then silkily slipped into the private sector, setting up the Ashford Group Corporation to exploit the very federal security contracts area which, as a member of the Government, he had helped create.

It is depressing in the extreme, that the American public tolerates the corruption spewing out of Capitol Hill and allows it Presidents such dictatorial powers. No-one should be surprised, therefore, if the Establishments which benefit from war oppose any measures likely to make the world a much more peaceful place.

The Do-Good-Brigade – Whilst not a single Establishment with a single purpose, there are charities – usually run by overpaid executives/officers – whose jerking knees can be heard clicking from afar whenever they read the two terrible "*P*" words – prison or punishment. Some believe in neither. Others grudgingly accept that anyone guilty of the most vicious murders should spend some time in prison. Prison though, should be neither uncomfortable nor - heaven forbid – boring.

The Do-Gooder groups have more or less held sway in most western countries for more than fifty years and I am in no doubt that their misguided influences have contributed to high levels of crime. Their interest is in protecting the criminals at the expense of the victims. By constantly badgering Governments to go easy on punishment, and by lobbying for capital punishment to be abolished and replaced by life sentences, they succeeded only in driving up murder rates. Not satisfied with this disaster, the Do-Gooders then set about attacking life sentences, persuading the judiciary to qualify these by offering release, even for murders, to 20, 15 or even only 10 years served. Any kind of Detention Centre employing strict discipline was anathema to this bunch of airheads, the same Do-Gooders who attacked and got rid of discipline in schools decades ago – and we all know where that led; teachers facing stroppy, abusive youngsters physically attacking teachers and those of their peers who actually go to school wanting to learn and disruptives who know how to play the politically correct system and who prefer the easy profits from crime to the prospect of working.

The Do-Good Brigade bangs on about alternatives to prison, but having examined most of these, I despair that these supposedly intelligent people can be so naïve as to believe that such schemes will ever persuade some of the disgusting criminals I have encountered to alter their ways. Yes, Community Service Orders have a role to play, but it is small. They are not, though, suitable to either dangerous or repeat offenders.

I am well aware of the damage which this loose Establishment has caused and that they will resist many of the anti-crime proposals contain herein. My advice to them – stop treating prison and punishment as dirty words and wake up instead to the reality that without them, the criminal classes would become ever more cavalier in their disrespect for the law.

Cherie Booth Q.C. (Mrs. Tony Blair) is, according to the Sunday Times of 18th January 2004, on record as claiming that there is an urgent need to "find" alternatives to prison. Now, I wonder if the fact that hubbie was running out of prison places had anything to do with Cherie's need to find alternatives. Certainly, three years on, alternatives have not been "found", but I have no doubt that the Do-Good Brigade will continue pontificating about them to the detriment of all but the criminals.

Long after I had written this chapter, the **UK** Independence Party is getting a serious taste of the Establishment's Dirty Tricks Department at work.

According to Nigel Farage, **UKIP** had inadvertently accepted a contribution of £367,697.00 from a supporter, but some Establishment ferrets had discovered that although Alan Bown had been on the Electoral Register for the years prior to making his gift - and the year following – critically, he was not on it during its actual year. Unlike Tony Blair's received gifts disguised as loans, or vice-versa, **UKIP**'s was not hidden and whilst I disagree with any Political Party receiving large contributions, I deplore even more, the behind-the-scenes collusion which resulted not in **UKIP** having to return the gift to the donor, but to hand it over to the Labour Government's Treasury.

More about this will emerge after Quicksands has been published, but knowing what I do about Establishments, I already see their devious minds behind this attempt to cause **UKIP** serious financial problems.

My later recommendations about Political Party funding will, if adopted, put an end to all of these eternal rows about who have given what; to whom; and under what circumstances.

CHAPTER 14

UNFAIRNESS & INJUSTICE LEAD TO MORE CRIME

Before I progress to explaining why this chapter heading is valid, let me clarify my own position and philosophy.

I am no dreamer looking for a completely fair world.

I am not seeking to bring about a world where everyone is equal and I not only accept that life is not fair, I do not understand the frequently-quoted, trite mantra that all are born equal. Human nature, genes, where we are born, whether or not our parents have passed Aids or other transmittable disease onto us, financial inheritances, the proximity of clean water etc., etc. all mitigate against this facile cliché that we are all born equal. Nor should we overlook the part which Lady Luck plays in so many lives.

Theoretically, if all of the world's riches were equally distributed, there would be no crimes committed with injustice as their cause, but what a depressingly dreary world that would be. Certainly not one which I would wish to see.

Unfairness and injustice are simply a part of life and within reason, accepted as such by most of us. ***The problems, including those associated with crime, come about when excesses of power and obscene greed come into the equation***. When individuals or groups find themselves in situations over which they have no control and where society at large has no roadmap for redress, or escape from tedium, poverty and oppression, that is when society breaks down and when crime comes into the equation.

Whatever the real or perceived discrimination, people will react to it differently. Some will simply be resigned; some will suffer stress and ill-health; some will try and find a positive solution; some – and I have been told this numerous times – will lash out in various directions, seeking revenge, or at least the satisfaction that they did something to address their plight.

Many many crimes have been committed due to anger and frustration and whilst few of these can be condoned, many of them can be understood when they were triggered by abuses of excessive power or exploitation of the powerless by the manifest greed of a (relatively) few individuals.

Even in supposedly rich countries, poor people, including those on basic State pensions – not the bureaucrats of course – have been and are still, in 2007, seriously conned by politicians of all Parties.

Real prices, as opposed to the bent indexes used by Governments, are rising very much faster than the pathetic State pensions. So great has the disparity become between the incomes and unavoidable day-to-day living expenses of basic State pensioners in Britain for example, that some have died from malnutrition, hypothermia or stress-related despair. For many there is a stark choice – *eat* or *heat* – because they cannot afford to eat healthy meals and pay to keep warm in their homes. And all the time, Tony Blair, Gordon Brown & co., who live in the lap of luxury, lie to their electorate by telling them that the gap between rich and poor is closing, when the truth is, the gap has become wider year on year. Every time those at the top become wealthier, this makes those at the bottom of the income ladder relatively poorer.

Faced with the prospect of dying from either lack of food or from cold, is it any wonder that some are driven to crime? and would any British Home Secretary be prepared to see such desperate pensioners sent to gaol for stealing provisions or warm clothing in order to stay alive?

No-one should be surprised that gross unfairness leads to crime, when the wealth of the three richest families on earth is greater than that of the combined assets (sic) of the world's poorest billion citizens.

Bearing in mind that the fortunes of these three mega-rich families would not have been amassed without recourse to bribery, law-breaking and creative chicanery, it is inevitable that some of those at the opposite end of the scale see nothing wrong with turning to crime in order to improve their own circumstances, albeit only fractionally.

Ask yourself – How would you feel if you had been sent to gaol on perjured evidence?

How would you feel if you were one of the small percentage of people brave enough to bring a rape charge, only to see the perpetrator found not guilty and walk free?

How would you feel if an innocent loved one had been killed or injured by your country's supposed security services?

294

How do you feel as you witness your elected political representatives spending a hugely disproportionate amount of their time progressing their own careers and living luxurious lives - at your expense?

How do you feel when out-of-touch Judges give derisory sentences for serious crimes?

How do you feel when you see or hear your President or Prime Minister give fatuous answers to serious questions?

How do you feel when you see Boards of Directors ripping off their shareholders and demeaning their employees by taking huge amounts of money as salaries, over-generous expenses, share options, "golden hellos", mountainous "goodbye packages" and obscenely generous pensions?

Pleased? I think unlikely.

Resigned? Angry? Depressed? Vengeful? Frustrated? Spurred to action? – Very probably and with good reason.

When disrespected or disadvantaged, most people will experience one or more of these reactions and simply bottle up their feelings. Others will be spurred to action. Some, including myself, take the legal route of campaigning via writing, speaking to various groups or resorting to other tactics, some subtle, others less so.

This leaves a group whose reaction is to resort to violence, destruction or fraud and whilst no society should pander to these people, who often have serious personality defects, it does behove us all to keep unfairness and injustice to the absolute minimum possible. This is both a moral imperative and sound practice to help keep crime down to reasonable levels. History shows that greed and power go hand in hand and the avaricious resist any limitations to their ambitions until such time as the underdogs decide to bear it no longer. France is currently a prime example of a country beginning to suffer the effects of mis-Government having, for decades, neglected those with nothing, whilst providing millions of bureaucrats with cosy, lazy lifestyles. The result of this lunacy has caused entrepreneurs to leave in droves, whilst a serious underclass is left behind, close to revolution.

Countries which restrain unfairness and injustice, such as Denmark, Switzerland, Austria, Norway, Luxembourg, Canada and Andorra are, according to surveys, near the top of the scale whose people feel themselves to be happy and content. They are also low down on the recorded crimes per capita scale and from this, most people will draw the obvious conclusion.

Those living in countries which suffer high crime need not despair though, because there are things we can all do to reduce levels of unfairness and injustice and hence, curtail those crimes committed as a result. Crimes which some commit specifically to redress a particular problem, or simply as a lashing out against oppressive societies in general, can best be eliminated by minimising obscene levels of wealth and/or power. Every day of every week, cars are set alight in France, even though the Government tries to suppress the fact. What a tragedy that a country with so many natural advantages should diminish them by failing to realise that unfairness and injustice inevitably leads to serious discontent, which just as surely leads to serious crime.

To overcome these problems will require politicians to reduce unfairnesses, judicial systems to be adjusted, Boards of Directors/ Executives to significantly reduce their greed levels and Governments to significantly reduce their interference in people's lives. This, of course, will not happen without pressure being applied from a variety of sectors of society in all of those nations suffering unfairness, injustice and high crime.

The first two of these aspects are dealt with elsewhere in this book and further recommendations are covered in the later chapters, particularly related to how to deal with those politicians choosing to resist change and live permanently with high levels of crime. This leaves arguably the single most damaging element of unfairness and injustice – the outrageous level of financial rewards which top company executives have manipulated for themselves, particularly in the last thirty years.

Let me be quite clear. I have no problem with people being rich and but for the wealthy, there would be no fine yachts, no Ferraris, no private planes, no beautiful houses, nor the employment which produces them. A very grey prospect indeed. Gone also would be huge funds which some of the well-heeled sector generously give to Charities and other good causes.

The following clearly shows how Corporate Executives in America have progressively grabbed an even bigger share of company remunerations and regrettably, certain other countries are trying to emulate them. According to the Institute for Policy Studies :-

In 1982 executive pay at more than 350 large companies was 42 times that of the average production worker. Unbelievably high, you may well think

BUT hold it – it gets worse, unless of course you are one of the devious ones on the receiving end

By 1990 it was 106 times that of the average production worker

By 2003 it was 300 times that of the average production worker

By 2004 it was 431 times that of the average production worker

It is higher still in 2006/07, confirming my research findings that for some, greed knows no bounds. However much they grab, they always push for more.

Even worse, the average earnings of more than twenty of America's top Hedge Fund Managers exceeded $350 million (each) in 2005.

Two of them (I have their names) coined in more than $1 billion each, all by gambling, not with their own money but that of other people.

Running a UK Building Society, particularly in the rising housing bubble of recent years, has been one of the easiest of corporate jobs. Almost all of those managing these easy-money operations are there via a huge slice of luck and an equal measure of cunning. Only a financial fool could fail, so how do these guys con their businesses owners into paying them from £300,000 to more than £1.3 million a year? Quite simply, they take the credit for the success which in fact is earned by those working beneath them and by being part of a hugely-rigged Remunerations Cartel.

The problem is, of course, that Executive greed knows no bounds because each exaggerated payment gained by these ruthless, selfish individuals is used by others in a continually rising game of money leap frog. Onwards and upwards they go and nothing demonstrates this better than the Walt Disney Company's stuffing of its shareholders.

Disney's Board of Directors voted their out-going President, Michael Ovitz, an amazing severance package of more than $140 million – for only 14 months in the job. Well, Disney's Mickey Mouse Board would do that, wouldn't they? They are already screwing their shareholders and doubtless look forward to using Ovitz's hundred and forty million dollars as a benchmark come their own remuneration revision time.

Forget any ideas you may have that Directors of major corporations necessarily get their positions on merit, or have skills guaranteed to make money for the owners of their companies. All too often they get on the gravy train via the 'Old-Boy' network, by lying, by fraud and frequently nothing more than good old fashioned luck. Top Investment Banker Sir Derek Higgs believes that only 4% of Directors have achieved their positions on Boards via a hiring process, which is obligatory for all other positions. Unbelievably, most are appointed to run multi-billion dollar international corporations - Sir Derek Reports - with less due diligence than is applied when appointing even the lowest grade employee. Once in situ however, their principle skills kick in – fooling the company's auditors and banks; misleading the media; obstructing and sidelining their shareholders; firing their workers; and clinging onto power like clams.

Renowned management guru Peter Drucker sums up Board Directors very well. Boards have one think in common, he says – "they do not function".

How, for example, did Bernie Ebbers ever become the outrageously overpaid C.E.O. of WorldCom, which he and others – Skilling, Lay, Fastow and Sullivan - milked into extinction via an $11 million accounting fraud?

At his trial, he admitted that he had dropped out of two colleges, worked as a basketball coach for a minor team and had been a milkman and a delivery driver. His knowledge of telecommunications (WorldCom's business) was minimal and he confessed to not understanding accounting nor being up-to-date on technology. He left such matters, including WorldCom's revenues and other necessary financial information to others, he claimed. So, what was Mr. Ebbers doing which entitled him to rake in hundreds of times more pay than the employees to whom he actually delegated the work? And how come Mr. Ebbers' C.V. was kept hidden until he fessed-up at his trial? One might also ask what part the company's Remuneration Committee had played in this fraudulent fiasco.

Collapsed UK Company Farepak, which collected the Christmas fund savings of tens of thousands of ordinary people on a supposed piggy-bank basis, typifies the contempt which many Board Directors have for those who give them their lavish lifestyles. The punters, with savings of between a few hundred to more than a thousand pounds, suddenly found, just before Christmas 2006, that all or most of their funds had disappeared. Chairman, Sir Clive Thompson was okay. He had already been paid more than £½ million and was living in his luxury £2.2 million home in Kent.

At one time, this corporate creep was the FTSE's highest-paid executive, earning more than £800,000 a year plus bonuses. That did not stop him being complicit in a disastrous company takeover – buying DMC for £35 million only to see it tank and subsequently sold for only £5 million. He and other Directors, George Pollock, Nicholas Gilodi-Johnson, Chris Hulland and William Rollason had all pocketed huge six-figure sums from parent company EHR and/or Farepak. Their skills? Getting onto company Boards and nest-feathering, even whilst they were screwing those who had trusted them.

One of the problems with trying to rein-in Fat Cat incomes is that politicians are generally not interested, either because they are seeking donations; greedy themselves, or are looking for Fat Cat positions in the private sector for when they either retire from politics or are kicked out by the electorate.

I will cover this sector in my later chapter on politicians.

The shenanigans of State Bodies also should come under greater scrutiny and control. Ireland's Aer Rianta gave Margaret Sweeney an €800,000 Golden Handshake after being the **Acting** Chief Executive of the State-owned company for **less than a year**. Ms. Sweeney's severance package would have been subject to Department of Transport scrutiny, but she skilfully resigned, having formerly been the Deputy Chief Executive, a position which was not subject to Government involvement. Such exploitation of technical loopholes amounts to defrauding the taxpayer and gives a green light to others to find their own ways of enriching themselves.

Who could fail to be angry when they see themselves being taken for a ride by the Eurocrats.

Take failed UK Labour Leader Neil Kinnock, for example. He probably never did a useful day's work in his life, but he and his family certainly knew how to exploit the political machine. Exiting the profitable House of Commons, he picked up a sinecure as EU Transport Commissioner (don't ask me how) then became Vice President in charge of eliminating corruption. For this, he was paid £142,000 a year – "justified" claimed an EU spokesman, because the EU faced heavy competition in trying to attract "the most talented" to be Commissioners. An EU spokesman would say that, wouldn't he?

Most talented? I do not think so. I would not pay the guy in washers. His only skill is in manipulating his way into good bureaucratic positions, but once there, he fails. Not surprisingly, the corruption in the EU that Mr. Kinnock was paid handsomely to stamp out **doubled** during his period of office.

Knowing how to milk the system though, for his failures, Neil Kinnock received a **tax-free** "transitional stipend" on leaving Office, reported to be worth £270,000 over 3 years. From 2004, age 62, he enjoys an ex-Commissioner's pension of £63,900 a year for life, on top of his other pensions (House of Commons, more than £25,000 for life and State pension). It would be surprising if he also did not have other streams of easy money coming in, because political operators of Kinnock's ilk spend much of their time in Office ensuring that their future nests are fully-feathered. These, then, are the State Fat Cats riding on the backs of ordinary pensioners getting £5,000 a year – if they are lucky. Socialist – Capitalist – what's the difference? Not bad, for someone who almost single-handedly lost his Labour Party the General Election in 1992 and saw EU fraud and corruption double during the time when he was paid to eliminate it.

Such people are, quite simply, robbing their hard-working taxpayers, many of whom end up on paltry State pensions, having had far too much of their small incomes taken in taxes to support the luxury life-styles of the likes of Neil Kinnock.

When they see such terrible behaviour by those who gain privilege and power by devious means, many decide to turn to crime, when they realise that those whom they have elected to political office have

304

been conning them for years in their scheming to get salaries and pensions many times larger than the average.

Each current EU Commissioner now costs in excess of £400,000 in salaries, expenses and perks. I have no figures for how much the numerous "retired" Commissioners are costing their taxpayers, but would welcome any verifiable information.

London City Consultants Towers Perrin were claiming that UK Civil Servants earning between £125,000 and £300,000 a year should have a **90% pay increase**, confirming the incestuous links between the public and private sectors which are designed simply to create an elite class, at the expense of the working and middle classes striving to produce the nation's wealth for moderate rewards at best.

A direct connection between excessive wealth and crime was established at the 2004 trial of Joyti De-Laurey, a secretary at Goldman Sachs U.S. Investment Bank in the city. It took Goldmans 6 years to realise that this smart cookie had glummed more than $6 million out of the personal accounts of three of the company's excessively-paid Directors. Joyti De-Laurey saw all of this easy money sloshing around and decided to help herself to part of the action by forging cheques and money transfers. A London Court found her guilty on evidence that was damning, like buying a half-million dollars worth of jewellery, a million dollar villa in Cyprus and generally living it up like the Fat Cats she saw all around her.

Now I don't know about you, but I would pretty soon know if a few hundred, let alone a few million dollars were missing from my bank account.

I have a massive file on overpaid C.E.O.s, far too many to list in this book, which only covers the Fat Cats situation because of its relevance to crime. The following though, are just a few examples of which many readers will be unaware.

In a year when the company of which he was C.E.O.

LOST 60% of its share value,
James Morgan (Applied Materials) got $48 million

LOST 78% of its share value,
William Esrey (Sprint Fon) got $49 million

LOST 83% of its share value,
Wilf Corrigan (LSI Logic) got $83 million

LOST 87% of its share value,
Joe Nachco (Quest Communications) got $97 million

LOST 81% of its share value,
John Chambers (Cisco) got $157 million

LOST 99% of its share value,
Jeffrey Skilling (Enron) got $84 million

Welcome to the world of Fat Cat remuneration.

The above are by no means rare. There are tens of thousands of Directors/ Presidents of companies using their shareholders' funds principally to line their own pockets and as already shown, their greed knows no bounds. The unfairness and immorality of doing this; of putting endless people out of work; of wiping out small shareholders' savings or condemning them to lives of poverty whilst they themselves enjoy luxuries and security beyond most people's wildest dreams, has no place whatsoever in their world of total selfishness.

No-one seeing these annual payments of millions of dollars, euros or pounds should fall into the trap that this makes payments to C.E.O.s of hundreds of thousands reasonable. Only very occasionally, when the personal and unique efforts of a particular executive result in significant and identifiable benefit to the shareholders and company employees, should any officer be paid more than ten times that of the corporation's lowest-paid worker's remuneration.

By 1980 though, the "average" C.E.O. remuneration had become an outrageous 42 times that of their average employee and by 2002 (source: Fleet Street Letter) this had risen to a difficult-to-comprehend 475 times. No wonder America is the most dysfunctional nation with the greatest debt and crime burden the world has ever seen. A country with such structural unfairness is, I forecast, headed for serious civil unrest because all Ponzi schemes inevitably collapse, leaving a heap of furious victims seeking revenge.

In an attempt to head this off, I would like to see ordinary people take steps to redress the crazy imbalances and hopefully this book will open sufficient eyes for corrective action to begin. A huge task,

306

to be sure. Trying to take money from the grasping fists of those who have convinced themselves that they are entitled to plunder the resources of corporations which they do not own is not going to be easy. Right now they have the power. They have the contracts. But what they do not have is the moral justification for their never-ending greed. Nor do they have the approval of the majority of their shareholders, although they are likely to be propped up by a small number of institutional investors who, in turn, cast their votes without the permission of their own clients.

So – what to do?

First, let me repeat that I have no problem with anyone becoming wealthy by their own initiatives, inventions, hard work and risk. My beef is with the culture which an elite group of sly operators has developed, mainly by establishing as a norm, a system of hire by the most disgusting type of one-sided contracts imaginable.

It may be that some of these contracts could be overturned at Law, but that is not my expertise and there are far cheaper and more direct and effective remedies. Here are some suggestions - I have others for later use :

If you are a shareholder,

- Ask the Corporation/Company for details of the total remunerations and contract details of each Board Member plus any other employee paid more than five times that of the average employee. Attend company meetings and ask embarrassing questions.

- If you do not get a satisfactory answer, or if you are not receiving a dividend at least 3% above central bank base rate, **sell your shares**, buy gold, silver, platinum, copper or uranium, then write again to the company telling them why you are no longer prepared to leave your money just to support the excessive greed of its executives. Do this now, before those in charge off-load any of their own shares, leaving their ordinary investors in the lurch. Directors have a nasty habit of selling shareholdings when they see problems ahead for the companies paying them.

- Invite other investors to join you in securing major reductions in Executives' pay.

- Ask the Company Secretary or Chief Financial Executive how much theft or fraud it has suffered in recent years.

- If you contribute to a pension fund, write to its controllers and ask them not to invest in companies who pay their Directors too generously and not to vote any shares they may hold to support excessive remunerations.

- Contact the media and ask them to recommend their readers to take similar action. Mainstream and internet publications regularly expose Fat Cat Executives, so are a good source of information.

- Start your own internet campaign against identified Fat Cats and the companies indulging them. Blogging can be very effective.

- Write to, or visit your political representative expressing your concerns. Email **fatcats@crimedown.org** with any responses and your comments.

- In summary, take a far more pro-active interest in any company using your money and regularly ask why dividends to shareholders are so abysmal, or even non-existent.

If you are job seeking,

- Keep away from the greedy-Director companies and don't be fooled by suggestions that it may be you getting the top job one day. You won't, you stand more chance of winning the lottery, which would be a more honourable way of becoming rich anyway.

- Apply only for jobs with those companies who pay their controllers well but not excessively.

If you are an employee in a Union,

- Ask your Union to find out the remuneration disparity level between yourself and your bosses and seek explanations if they are paid more than you can earn in a week/month/year – whatever. Leave your Union if it cannot satisfy you. Ask first though, for your own remuneration to be doubled or trebled to bring you just a little closer to the rewards being enjoyed by others and in the likely event of this being refused, start looking for another job where pay differentials are significantly fairer.

- Consider strike action if your company will not significantly reduce the remunerations of its overpaid Executives.

If you are a consumer

- Boycott the products or services of those companies who pay their Directors more than 5, 7 or 10 times what they pay their average employees, dependent upon the size of the company. Write to such companies and to the media, telling them what you are doing and why.

- Switch your banking, insurance and mortgage business to whomever pays their Directors the lowest remunerations. Ignore the glib "pay peanuts, get monkeys" gibes. Even the lowest paid bank, insurance, mortgage, savings and loans executives are wildly overpaid. By no means are any of them paid peanuts and in any event, monkeys are usually much cleverer than gorillas. You will often find anyway, that switching to a financial services company which does not line its Directors' pockets as excessively as others will give **you** a better deal.

Unions and shareholders

- Wake up and realise that your interests are common insofar as neither wages nor dividends can be maximised whilst overpaid Directors are bleeding dry companies which they did not start up, did not invest their own cash in, work no harder in than most of their co-workers, but expect to get paid extra hundreds of thousands – or millions – even when they leave, often after performing abysmally and failing to produce satisfactory incomes for either their workers or investors.

- Unions' and shareholders' representatives should get together and use their joint clout to bring excessively-paid company bosses back into the real world and they can do this in the knowledge that reducing unfairness and injustice will be making a contribution to lowering a wide range of crimes.

The members of the Chelsea Building Society may or may not envy former boss Michael Bage who somehow contrived to be paid £500,000 in 2003 and when he retired, aged 60 in 2005, he reportedly left with an annual pension starting at £300,000, despite having made no contributions for at least five years.

Not surprisingly, his abuse of his privileged position caused outrage amongst the Society's members and employees, whose best course of action should be to remove their investments and labour from such a deviously run Society.

Michael Casey got it just about right when he wrote in the Irish Times Business News – Why do shareholders never question these galactic salaries? – because most of the shareholders are institutions whose Senior Executives live in the same kind of rarefied financial world.

Are these salaries the result of market forces? Michael Casey asked. Absolutely not. Running a business is not rocket science, he said, and with tongue only slight in cheek, he went on :- Indeed, banking used to be called the 3, 6, 3 business. You took in money at 3%, lent it out at 6% and were on the first tee by 3 pm. The only difference now is that you take in the money at less than 1%, lend it out at 7% but the tee time is still the same.

A not untypical example of inappropriate Executive rewards was Roy Ranson who, as Chief Executive of the infamous Equitable Life Insurance Company, ran it into very serious financial difficulties. The UK House of Lords was eventually brought into the debacle and Scottish High Court Judge, Lord Penrose, lay the blame for a billion and a half pounds (sterling) black hole in the Accounts on Management's culture of secrecy and manipulation. "Ranson" said Lord Penrose, "was obstructive, manipulative, autocratic and dismissive of regulatory restrictions", but that did not prevent Roy The Rich from adding to the sufferings of Equitable's policy-holders by trousering a lifetime pension of at least £149,000 a year, into which he had paid nothing. What was "equitable" about that, you may wonder?

By contrast, I have nothing but praise for Harry Potter's creator J. K. Rowling, reputed to be worth around £500 million. Only 10 minutes' bus ride from the wealthiest part of Edinburgh - which she described as a world of cashmere and cream cakes – she lived in an area of near squalor where drugs and violent crime were ubiquitous. Admirably, J. K. has not forgotten the desperation of those suffering the unfairness and injustices which drove or contributed many of those around her to vandalism, burglary and drink. Despite having suffered personally from the deprivations of her early days in Leith, a part of Edinburgh, she has not forgotten her early sufferings there and is now striving to make the area more inclusive and less damaged by crime.

By contrast, C.E.O.s Michael Mahoney (Viatel) and Kevin Ryan (DoubleClick) seem to have had no social conscience when they made, respectively, $6.5 million and $16.8 million by exercising share options, then quickly off-loading them. Can it be coincidence that very shortly after taking these astronomic gravy train gains, Viatel had to claim the protection of Chapter 11 bankruptcy and DoubleClick's shares **dropped** by around 85%?

It is the cream which gets to the top, the C.E.O.s tell us. Well – not really.

The cream contains thousands of bacteria which, if left in-situ for long, turn sour and ruin everything with which they come into contact.

Perceptively, Agora Publishing's Daily Reckoning commented that as wealth becomes concentrated, the living standards of the other three classes progressively declines into the "haves" and the "have-nots", resulting in crime, poverty and malaise and eventually the revolution of the masses.

According to CCN Group Research, more than 10% of Company Directors are serial failures. Almost a million UK Directors (more than a third of those on file) had been involved with at least one failure and 300,000 with multiple collapses. More than 3,000 men and 400+ women somehow managed ten or more company failures, clearly demonstrating their inability to succeed at what they were paid to do.

So much for the cream coming to the top.

Company Directors may claim to be the cream, they may even come to believe their own rhetoric as to their colossal worth but – only those in the "Club" go along with them.

The BBC reported that a Financial Times survey revealed the public's view that 80% of top Directors are both grossly overpaid and untrustworthy. Had those questioned seen the evidence which I have on this level of greed and unfairness, I believe that the 80% findings of the F.T. would have been well above 90%.

Here are some suggestions about reducing the injustices of the Fat Cats incomes:-

Scrap all share purchase option schemes, signing-on bonuses, leaving bonuses, retention or death-retention bonuses (Mrs. Fat Cat often joins the gravy train). Without either the knowledge or approval of the shareholders, Cablevision Systems took this fraud even further, by giving favourable stock options to a dead Executive, back-dating a stock options package in order to enable a C.E.O.'s heirs to cash in, to the disadvantage of the corporation's shareholders.

Pay good salaries – say 5 to 10 times that of the company's lowest paid worker *plus* bonuses directly related to declared dividends, *not* to share price because that can too readily be manipulated via lots of clever manoeuvres.

No Executive should be *given* shares, although they can always buy them at the going price, should they so choose. Their employment terms should simply agree performance bonuses over and above their salaries, accrued from the dividends of a notional agreed number of shares, but which in fact they do not own.

This would introduce some measure of fairness between Board Members and shareholders and prevent the latter being ripped-off by the former. No dividends for shareholders – then no bonuses for employed Executives. Such a system would also encourage some other employees to buy shares in the company, thereby improving company morale via greater inclusiveness. In other words, pay for performance – not promises.

On 8th April **1998**, in response to my questions to Tony Blair about (amongst other things) the effects of the widening gap between rich and poor, the UK Home Office wrote to me claiming that the introduction of the minimum wage would play a part in reducing this gap. Of course it did no such thing. The remuneration gap between average incomes and those at the top – politicians, senior civil servants, company Directors etc. has widened exponentially since 1998.

The Home Office also told me that it was concerned (whatever than means) about the effect which seemingly (whatever that means) over-generous remuneration can have on a company's reputation and on the morale of its employees and warned that the Government will consider taking action if companies did not adopt a more responsible approach. Of course Tony Blair's Government did no such thing. Quite the opposite, in fact, because six years later, Trade Secretary Patricia Hewitt announced that *no legislation is planned to tackle excessive Director remuneration*, not even where the Fat Cats have caused their companies to perform abysmally, to the serious detriment of their workers and shareholders. By then, of course, Tony Blair was toadying up to the Fat Cats, hoping to hop from one gravy train onto another before too long. Echoes of Neil Kinnock, me thinks.

So much for the Government's "concern" expressed to me in 1998. I had, in fact, asked Tony Blair several very specific questions, which of course he ducked – getting the Home Office to send me a smoke and mirrors reply which the years have shown to contain nothing but falsehoods.

As at October 2006, the *average* income of the Senior Executives of a hundred of Britain's public companies was up 28% at £2.3 million each, which was 90 times greater than that of their companies' average worker.

Whilst the UK Labour Party was reneging on promises to reign in Fat Cats' salaries, it was screwing its State pensioners into misery. No 28% increase and £2,300,000 incomes for them. For the lucky ones, it is £4,800 a year, upped by a miserly 3% with the Government using its fictitious cost of living index. Nor would swapping the percentage increases of the two groups help reduce this particular unfairness because giving pensioners a 28% increase would still leave them poor, whilst giving the Fat Cats another 3% would further increase the rich/poor gap, by adding another £69,000 a year to the F.C.s' already obscene incomes. I chart this arrant and dangerous nonsense later in this chapter so graphically as to make my case against Fat Cats' salaries irrefutable.

At the time of this writing, Mr. Blair is still dangling Britain on his piece of elastic, so we may not yet know the extent to which his networking and giving honours to wealthy Labour Party supporters opens which doors for him into Fat Cats Fairyland.

What we do already know though, is that he has no interest in ridding Britain of either unfairness, injustice or the high level of crime which flows from these poisons.

I am writing this section of my book without knowing what Tony B. will do when he is no longer Britain's Prime Minister, but I doubt he will work for Green Peace, The Society for Action Against Crime, Age Concern, Oxfam or Amnesty International. More likely, he will do a Kinnock and negotiate a bureaucratic or quango sinecure, or he may go to America where manipulative spin doctors make huge amounts of money which Bush's poodle clearly believes himself to be entitled. The term 'hypocritical socialists' comes to mind.

He and Cherie could, of course, start their own law firm – Blur & Blur perhaps.

All of this extravagance started, as do many damaging trends, in America where people are now living in a fantasy land, floating on clouds of debt stretching up to the stratosphere. Paul Krugman confirmed this in October 2006 when writing on the subject for the New York Times. "Like the Hedge Fund managers", he said, "C.E.O.s have rigged up a 'heads I win, tails you lose' pay scheme" he wrote "with C.E.O. remuneration soaring from 44 times that of their average worker to 367 times that average." At 44 times the average income of $34,268 a year, i.e. more than $1.5 million, these Executives were already massively overpaid. That they then pushed, stabbed and connived their way to getting this increased to more than $12.5 million a year confirms my accusations that the greed of these despicable specimens is so manifest that they will never voluntarily agree to their rewards returning to the perfectly generous levels of 5 to 10 times that of their average worker.

There are, not surprisingly, other injustices which are so unfair as to cause some to seek redress by turning to crime.

The U.S. Civil Forfeiture laws allow the police to seize any citizen's property without accusing them of any crime. If they claim that a crime has been committed connected to your house, your car, your boat – even by someone without your knowledge or consent – any property can and often is seized. 'Grab it first' is the State's motto, leaving even totally innocent parties to either lose their asset(s) or resort to law in an attempt to recover them and we all know the costs of litigation in America. The Authorities have made huge profits out of this immoral activity and some other countries have already seen the attractions of introducing similar laws. Assuming guilt, is not a principle upon which any civilised country should base its law. They should find the evidence first, take any suspect to Court and then – and only then – should any State consider asset seizure, assuming of course that guilt had been established and that the seizure was consistent with the crime. Abuses of these asset-grabbing laws is a certain way to produce home-made terrorists. I want to see criminals caught and convicted – not created.

Eminent Domain (E.D.) laws in America are another misguided way of turning perfectly normal, law-abiding citizens into State-hating renegades. All countries have to have laws permitting the compulsory purchase of land and property from private owners when railroads, motorways, free-ways, prisons etc. are authorised. This is fine, provided that a proper planning process has authorised the project and when fair compensation is paid to the displaced. Unfortunately, Eminent Domain has been used mischievously by some Local Authorities who have connived with private developers to compulsorily purchase individually-owned homes and small business properties, not for any community need but to demolish them in order to make way for private developments – shopping malls, office blocks etc. which, surprise, surprise, would pay the Local Authority far more money in property taxes.

This abuse was not just in isolated instances, because more than 5,700 properties across America have been threatened or taken over in the last 12 months. Many, including The Society for Action Against Crime, supported serious objection to the practice and Organisations such as The Institute for Justice and The Castle Coalition went much further and have had some considerable success in persuading 45 States in America to change their stance.

The House of Representatives was eventually persuaded to pass the Private Property Rights Protection Act in November 2005 but legislation at the time of writing is still stalled in the Senate, so any representation which individuals can make is still very welcome. The pity is that the bullying Local Authorities have caused and continue to cause huge resources to be applied defending properties which should never have been threatened in the first place.

The Institute for Justice/Castle Coalition (**www.ij.org** email: **general@ij.org**) work against a whole range of officialdom's malpractices and are worthy of the support of all who are concerned about Big Brother in America.

I am now going to expose another very long-established practice as being not only outrageously unfair and unjust, but a major contributory factor in creating an ever-widening gap between the haves and the have-nots. A certain recipe to drive some to resort to crime. I – and I doubt you – have never been shown the effects of this disgraceful practice and as a researcher, the only explanation I can offer is that the elite sector of society has conspired to censor out any discussion of the subject. Examination of the following tables shows very clearly that the elitists have, for years, been perpetrating a huge confidence trick on the have-nots and to a lesser extent, the middle classes.

The con-trick? Across-the-board percentage pay or pensions increases.

Sounds fair, doesn't it – giving everyone the same percentage pay or pension increase each year. But hold it just one cotton-picking minute. Let me show you some of the consequences of this devious ploy and to do this, I am presenting you with the figures in slow sequence rather than just giving you beginning and end results. This may seem a little tedious, but it will give you a better understanding of how gradual progression of an apparently fair annual percentage increase is, in fact, anything but equitable.

Here are some figures using Britain and a 3% annual increase as an example.

A State pensioner starting at £4,800 a year in 2007

After 1 year
will get an increase of   £144.00   Total for year   £4,944.00

After 2 years
will get an increase of   £148.32   Total for year   £5,092.32

After 3 years
will get an increase of   £152.77   Total for year   £5,245.09

After 4 years
will get an increase of   £157.35   Total for year   £5,402.44

After 5 years
will get an increase of   £162.07   Total for year   £5,564.51

After 6 years will get an increase of	£166.93	Total for year	£5,731.43
After 7 years will get an increase of	£171.94	Total for year	£5,903.37
After 8 years will get an increase of	£177.10	Total for year	£6,080.47
After 9 years will get an increase of	£182.41	Total for year	£6,262.88
After 10 years will get an increase of	£187.88	Total for year	£6,450.77
	£1,650.77		£56,677.28

So here we have it. If we continue with percentage increases for most, over the next 10-year period anyone living only on the UK State pension will have incomes averaging £5,667.72 a year with the 3% annual increases averaging a miserly £165.07 a year.

I do not understand how any politician can expect any pensioner to live anything approaching a reasonable life on such an income. To make matters worse, the true cost of living is always greater than that used by Governments when adjusting pensions. Think heating; lighting; the fruit, vegetables and fish we are all told to eat; think Council Property tax – come back Poll Tax all is forgiven.

Beyond a 10-year period, the situation for pensioners will progressively get worse, with Governments "pretending" to be concerned by making pathetic, papering-over the cracks gestures via tax credits or other near-worthless handouts to those negotiating the bureaucratic minefield with their begging bowls. All the while, that deceitful duo Blair and Brown have smugly boasted that pensioners are being well cared for and that the gap between the haves and the have-nots has been closing year on year during their (almost) 10-year reign as Prime Minister and Chancellor of the Exchequer. Crap!

These guys are either outright liars, financially illiterate or both.

The following tables are irrefutable evidence of this :-

I move now to a comparable table for a low wage worker earning say £10,000 a year rising by the same 3% per annum. This worker :-

After 1 year
will get an increase of £300.00 Total for year £10,300.00

After 2 years
will get an increase of £309.00 Total for year £10,609.00

After 3 years
will get an increase of £318.27 Total for year £10,927.27

After 4 years
will get an increase of £327.81 Total for year £11,255.08

After 5 years
will get an increase of £337.65 Total for year £11,592.74

After 6 years
will get an increase of £347.78 Total for year £11,940.52

After 7 years
will get an increase of £358.21 Total for year £12,298.73

After 8 years
will get an increase of £368.96 Total for year £12,667.70

After 9 years
will get an increase of £380.03 Total for year £13,047.73

After 10 years
will get an increase of £391.43 Total for year £13,439.16

£3,439.14 £118,077.93

Now Chancellor Brown, I don't have the facility of the hugely expensive computer models which your overpaid treasury bureaucrats have available, courtesy of the taxpayer, nor am I an economist - I have more sense than to waste my life on such worthless financial quackery which in fact is nothing more than guesswork dressed up in fallacious theories. I can though, still do the basic arithmetic which I learned before my teens, the lack of which seems to have been missing from the educations of those getting degrees in economics at top universities.

The above shows that the minimum wage worker has an average income of £11,807.79 throughout the 10-year period including 3% annual increases averaging £343.91 a year. At year one, the low wage-earner was receiving £5,356 a year more than the basic State pensioners. Difficult enough itself you may think, receiving less than half the income of even the lowest paid worker, **but** – and here is the crippler – by year ten, the pensioners have fallen behind even further, earning an average of ***£6,988 less than the lowest paid worker*** each year. Add more years and the gap grows ever larger.

I, and hopefully you, will be interested to hear whatever waffle Blair and Brown come out with to try to portray this serious falling behind of basic State pensioners as just the opposite. Pray tell us gentlemen - How can you possibly construe these very straightforward figures as a "catching-up" when, every time you give the same percentage increase (whatever it is) to different income groups, you make those at the top richer and those at the bottom poorer by comparison?

The injustice gets worse

I move now to someone earning say £30,000 per annum after tax and national insurance. They :-

After 1 year
will get an increase of   £900.00   Total for year   £30,900.00

After 2 years
will get an increase of   £927.00   Total for year   £31,827.00

After 3 years
will get an increase of   £954.81   Total for year   £32,781.81

After 4 years
will get an increase of   £983.45   Total for year   £33,765.26

After 5 years
will get an increase of   £1,012.95   Total for year   £34,778.21

After 6 years
will get an increase of   £1,043.34   Total for year   £35,821.55

After 7 years will get an increase of	£1,074.64	Total for year	£36,896.19
After 8 years will get an increase of	£1,106.88	Total for year	£38,003.08
After 9 years will get an increase of	£1,140.09	Total for year	£39,143.17
After 10 years will get an increase of	£1,174.29	Total for year	£40,317.46
	£10,317.45		£354,233.73

By year seven, not only has this group of earners started off with incomes six times greater than that of the basic State pensioner, their *increase* via their 3% increments has **risen by more than the entire annual income of the pensioners**. So much for closing the gap between the rich and the poor.

The total 10-year income increases for the pensioner amount to £1,650.77.

The total 10-year income increases for this next group amount to £10,317.45.

It is time for the British Government's claims to have created a fairer society to be exposed for what it is – a sham. A confidence trick. A downright lie.

I accuse Tony Blair, Gordon Brown and their lapdogs of grossly deceiving their pensioners, both current and future, and of insulting their intelligence. On average, the 3% per annum increase produced each State Pensioner an additional £165.07 a year. The same increase gives those in this £30,000 income group an additional average raise of £1,031.74 a year. Justice? Fairness? Give me a break.

And how about these for hypocritical villains

History confirms that British Members of Parliament continued stuffing their basic State pensioners by ensuring that the income gap between the two groups grew wider – not closer as claimed.

320

In 1997, when Tony Blair conned his way into power by promising a fair and more equal society, bog standard MPs – and most of them are dismally bog standard – were paid **£40,000 a year more than the basic rate pensioner**, i.e. twelve times as much. Additionally of course, they get "expenses", allowances, perks and pensions to dream of.

Now you would think that those Members of Parliament would be more than happy with such monetary advantages, perhaps even a little sheepish about ditching the pensioners who voted for them on the promises of a fairer society. Not a chance dear reader. Not a chance.

By 1ˢᵗ November 2006, the MPs' advantage over the pensioners had risen from an already high £40,000 a year to **£57,277 a year**. The following Table shows what will happen to income of ordinary Members of Parliament if it is increased by 3% a year – making an assumption based upon previous practice. Based on the current 2007 salary of £60,277, they :-

After 1 year
will get an increase of £1,808.31   Total for year   £62,085.31

After 2 years
will get an increase of £1,862.56   Total for year   £63,947.87

After 3 years
will get an increase of £1,918.43   Total for year   £65,866.30

After 4 years
will get an increase of £1,975.99   Total for year   £67,842.29

After 5 years
will get an increase of £2,035.27   Total for year   £69,877.56

After 6 years
will get an increase of £2,096.32   Total for year   £71,973.88

After 7 years
will get an increase of £2,159.22   Total for year   £74,133.10

After 8 years
will get an increase of £2,223.99   Total for year   £76,357.09

| After 9 years | | | |
| will get an increase of | £2,290.71 | Total for year | £78,647.80 |

After 10 years			
will get an increase of	£2,359.43	Total for year	£81,007.24
	£20,725.23		£711,738.44

Cabinet Ministers have an even greater opinion of their own worth. Their ministerial entitlement at April 2006 was £75,651 per annum, which is more than £70,000 more than the basic State pensioners' incomes of £4,800.

That, regrettably, is only part of the picture, because on top of this £75,651 a year ministerial entitlement, these hypocrites still keep their ordinary salaries as constituency MPs, bringing up their total income, before allowances and perks, to £135,337 a year, which is more than £130,000 higher than the basic rate pensioner. This is 28 times the incomes of the pensioners.

I can see no justice whatsoever in a Minister being paid to run both a Ministry and his/her Local Constituency because they cannot possibly do both jobs satisfactorily. Either being a British Member of Parliament is a full-time job, in which case it couldn't possibly be done alongside any other; or it is a very undemanding job, in which case why are the taxpayers forking out more than £60,000 a year (each) to 646 MPs for doing a cushy part-time, undemanding job?

This chapter gives every reader an understanding of greed and unfairness. Internationally, there is an on-going leap-frogging system wherein elected Members constantly point to their counterparts in other countries who may be paid more than themselves. They never mention those who are paid less than themselves.

This is dangerous and erroneous because the fact that the French are stupid enough to allow Jacques Chirac to behave like an old-style Russian Tsar in no way is a measure of his worth. In fact, being responsible for France's runaway crime, social division and bureaucratic overload, Chirac really is not worth paying at all.

No-one looking at the figures can any longer accept any politician's claims that they have made society fairer and more equal. Many people have suspected that they were being ripped off, but the facts

I give you here are evidence of how widespread greed has become and how most people are falling way behind in incomes received. Everyone can now see why their politicians never follow up on their promises to do something about the Fat Cats. They will never voluntarily do anything about the Fat Cats because politicians are already Fat Cats themselves and seeking to become ever fatter, which is a personality defect of the breed.

It is Tony Blair, of course, who hammers on about a fairer and more equal Britain, but he is a seriously dishonest man whose main skill is in evading truths. I have been inviting Mr. Blair to address crime-related issues since long before he became Britain's Prime Minister but without success, which in part is why I am now converting my research into book form.

Not unnaturally, there is a growing number of people disillusioned with Blair and his band, having discovered that trying to get truthful responses from them is more difficult than trying to pick up a bead of mercury wearing boxing gloves. I recommend you not to ask Tony Blair about his income because all you will get is spin and waffle. What I can give you here though is information about just his Parliamentary entitlements, which again give the lie to his claims.

In 1997 Prime Minister Blair's Parliamentary income, i.e. not including huge perks, exterior earnings and lifestyle advantages – which for any other taxpayer would incur benefits-in-kind charges – was outrageously high. His ministerial entitlement was £100,000 a year plus his salary of £43,860. That was disgracefully higher, by more than £140,000 a year, than the paltry less than £4,000 received by basic State pensioners.

Every pensioner should write to Tony Blair, whether or not he is still in Office, asking why he felt himself entitled not only to be in such an elevated income bracket in 1997 but why he did nothing to moderate such huge differentials.

In fact, by November 2006, his ministerial entitlement had risen to £126,085 a year *and* his second Parliamentary salary upped to £59,686. *Total – a cool £185,771* a year for Tony Blair, which is now more than £180,000 a year greater than the pittance on which Britain's pensioners are expected to exist – plus allowances, plus immensely valuable lifestyle benefits – Downing Street/Chequers/luxury travel/holiday hospitality etc.

Only those near the top of the world's hypocrisy league have the gall to look us in the eye and tell us what they know to be untrue. Only the Tony Blairs and Gordon Browns have the brass neck to indulge in the old propaganda trick of repeating big lies over and over again in the hope that they will take root. Anyone who bangs on about narrowing the gap between the rich and the poor in the knowledge that he has seen his State pensioners' pathetic incomes rise to only £4,800 a year whilst his own astronomic income has risen to more than £185,000 a year is a fraud and a mountebank. My hope is that this book will help history accord Tony Blair the contempt that he deserves and acknowledges the damage which he and his cohorts have done, not only to socialism but to politics in general.

The foregoing shows Tony Blair's official income details 1997 to 2006.

The following shows what will happen to Britain's Prime Minister's income if it is increased by 3% a year – making an assumption based upon previous practice. Based on a starting figure of £187,771, he/she :-

After 1 year
will get an increase of   £5,573.13   Total for year   £191,344.13

After 2 years
will get an increase of   £5,740.32   Total for year   £197,084.45

After 3 years
will get an increase of   £5,912.53   Total for year   £202,996.98

After 4 years
will get an increase of   £6,089.90   Total for year   £209,086.88

After 5 years
will get an increase of   £6,272.60   Total for year   £215,359.48

After 6 years
will get an increase of   £6,460.78   Total for year   £221,820.26

After 7 years
will get an increase of   £6,654.60   Total for year   £228,474.86

After 8 years
will get an increase of   £6,854.24   Total for year   £235,329.10

After 9 years
will get an increase of   £7,059.87   Total for year   £242,388.97

After 10 years
will get an increase of   £7,271.66   Total for year   £249,660.63

UK Prime Minister's income
Increases & totals   £63,889.63   £2,193,545.74

By comparison, that of the poor
State pensioner   £1,650.77   £56,677.28

This then is the **Big Con** of percentage increases which I am exposing.

Few of the **have-nots** have previously understood the magnitude of the deception being forced upon them.

None of the **haves** controlling politics, big business and the media want to see the subject discussed at all.

The figures in these Tables say it all. The **haves** are quite happy to see any of themselves increase their huge wealth exponentially whilst throwing bones worth a measly £165 a year to those at the bottom of the pile. Then they wonder why there is so much crime.

I have more to reveal about politicians and democracy a few chapters further on.

The Corporate Fat Cats. Let me show you the comparison between a 3% annual income for a Fat Cat earning (what they claim) a very modest after-tax income of £250,000 and our much abused pensioner – not that any of the Fat Cat greed-balls would ever be satisfied with a measly 3% increase, of course.

The Fat Cat

After 1 year
will get an increase of   £7,500.00   Total for year   £257,500.00

After 2 years
will get an increase of   £7,725.00   Total for year   £265,225.00

After 3 years
will get an increase of   £7,956.75   Total for year   £273,181.75

After 4 years			
will get an increase of	£8,195.45	Total for year	£281,377.20

After 5 years
will get an increase of   £8,441.31   Total for year   £289,818.51

After 6 years
will get an increase of   £8,694.55   Total for year   £298,513.06

After 7 years
will get an increase of   £8,955.39   Total for year   £307,468.45

After 8 years
will get an increase of   £9,224.05   Total for year   £316,692.50

After 9 years
will get an increase of   £9,500.77   Total for year   £326,193.27

After 10 years
will get an increase of   £9,785.79   Total for year   £335,979.06

£85,979.06   £2,951,948.80

Now we have moved into the rarefied atmosphere of the Fat Cats where the F.C.s' first year 3% is 4½ times greater than the pensioners' total increases over 10 years. The pensioners' income, after 10 years, has risen to a pathetic £6,452 a year whilst that of the Fat Cats has risen by £85,000 to a gargantuan £335,979.06.

One must ask what the Trades Unions have been up to all these years because they have been either asleep, incredibly complacent or complicit in this so damaging use of across the board percentage income increases. It was inevitable that this process would fuel inflation and significantly favour the rich to whom inflation is of no consequence whatsoever. Rising prices, in fact, impact only on those with either average or low incomes and the longer this continues, the greater will be the anger and frustration amongst those on the receiving end. Do not expect to climb out of the quicksands of crime whilst these appalling injustices continue.

Many people realise that any system which keeps a proportion of its pensioners living hand to mouth at best, must be broke and where such poverty exists, indeed it is broken.

It is natural and proper that some people's incomes are significantly greater than others and I am quite comfortable with that. What is not acceptable is that some societies have introduced into their financial rewards culture, a virus which doesn't simply maintain differentials, it guarantees to increase them to the huge additional benefit of the wealthy, and the dreadful disadvantage of the needy and impoverished.

Arguably the sneakiest and most disgusting Fat Cats are those working in the public sector, pretending to be caring for the general public whilst in fact they are screwing them blind.

In Britain, more than 40 of these Fat Cats have, over the years, wound up their pay to over £¼ million a year.

Fourteen of them "get" – I can't bring myself to misuse the word "earn" – more than £½ million a year and 3 get more than £1 million a year.

Richard Granger, for being in charge of the N.H.S. failed I.T. project, managed to trouser £285,000 so is constantly responsible for two drains on the public purse - his own outrageous salary and the appalling value for money in the Department some had mistakenly believed he could run effectively.

Sir Andrew Turnbull, an ex-Cabinet Mandarin ended up, according to Liberal Democrats, with a pension pot of more than £2½ million. Not bad for a supposed civil **servant**. Wouldn't mind doing a bit of serving myself, with that kind of moolah sloshing around the system.

There are controls, of course, but these are not exactly under the auspices of representatives of the normal hard-working taxpayers who pay these Public Fat Cat Servants.

In a totally rigged establishment cartel, the Government appoints an Actuary who "advises" on the pensions of public sector workers. He is just a regular guy called Chris Daykin, whose own pension pot is supposedly already almost £2 million and rising.

Just another way of reducing the gap between the haves and the have-nots, of course.

This over-paying goes on right throughout the public sector whose employees work far fewer hours than almost anyone in the private sector. They generally retire 5 years earlier and when they do, their pensions are invariably final salary schemes, a benefit enjoyed by less than 20% of workers in the real world.

Again we are sold the myth that these Fat Cats are highly-paid because they are in demand, but all of the evidence suggests otherwise. I am quite willing to find high calibre replacement personnel for any of these Fat Cats claiming to be in demand and I would expect their cost to be 25 to 50% lower than the incumbents. According to the Taxpayers Alliance October 2006 Report, public sector pay awards rose 8½% in 2005 and that on top of already excessive incomes.

The EU's Single Farm Payment Scheme is another example of the complicity of bureaucrats in directing the big money not to the small struggling hill farmers trying to scrape a living on a few thousand euros a year, but to the likes of Ireland's Larry Goodman. This multi-millionaire Fat Cat's company, Irish Agriculture Development, reportedly leeches €10,000 *a week* out of the Single Farm Payment Scheme for which all he is supposed to do is keep his farm in good agricultural condition – whatever that means. This crazy EU handout-scheme is scheduled to continue until at least 2013, by which time Larry Goodman's company is expected to have received more than €4 million for doing precious little.

For this we have France to thank. Its politicians and bureaucrats never saw a subsidy it could resist and the Irish hierarchy are not ones to miss a good loophole waved in front of them.

This killer virus is the across-the-board percentage pay/pension increase and the higher the percentage figure, the greater the injustice to those at the bottom of the pile. One does not need a Government enquiry to understand the effect which such injustice has on crime. Unfortunately, it is not possible to find out who originally conspired to introduce the highly-damaging principle of percentage income increases but what I can say with certainty is that for many years it has been used by elites to further enhance the benefits which they already enjoyed. Some of the elitists will identify themselves by openly resisting any changes to percentage increases. Some will simply keep their heads down, hoping that necessary changes will never see the light of day. Others may see the wisdom of tackling this virus before its effects move on from debilitating to disastrous.

This book is not the place to propose corrections to all of the world's ills, although for any interested, I do have suggestions for improving the lives of the poor and installing an inflation adjustment system designed to save them from falling behind in the future.

Inevitably, this necessitates more than simply containing current income differentials. There has first to be a serious shrinking of all remuneration gaps which will only come about when the full extent of this particular aspect of unfairness becomes public knowledge. From this hopefully will come an awakening of conscience and a change of heart about excessive greed.

There are, of course, plenty of other unfairnesses and injustices which result in crimes being committed and many of these will be addressed following the publication of this book as part of a major and on-going anti-crime campaign planned in conjunction with others.

January 2007 Update – David Cameron

Two days ago, the Leader of the UK Conservative Party announced that, starting in 2007, his Party was to be that of the ordinary working people of Britain and not the wealthy privileged elite.

Setting aside the fact that the United Kingdom is now governed by Scots, and that we now have Labour Leaders to the right of the Tories – and vice versa – Cameron's pronouncement is welcome, *if it is genuine*.

You and I will know this when we see how the well-heeled, overpaid, upper-crust Conservative Leader reacts to the unfairnesses addressed in this book.

I will be delighted if David Cameron contacts me with a view to discussing any crime-related matters, but in view of his claim to now be Robin Hood, I particularly wish to hear what proposals his Party have to really reduce the gap between rich and poor, and not just sound off about it. Lower salaries and expenses for politicians and top civil servants will be an excellent place to start David.

British Members of Parliament at the end of 2006 were calling for their already over-generous salaries of £60,277 to be upped to £100,000 a year. Many have written to the Senior Salaries Review Board proposing such an increase on the basis that top civil servants earn more than they. The old catch-up and leap-frog routine used forever in the determination of elites to wide the gap between the poor and the wealthy. What is the betting that there is not a single person on the Senior Service Salaries Review Board whose only income is the State pension?

I wonder how many taxi drivers, police constables, warrant officers, school teachers, nurses or deep sea fishermen are on this S.S.S.R. Board or what the individual incomes are of that illustrious Body, both from their role on that Board and from other of their interests.

What should be happening – if the gap between the haves and the have-nots is to be reduced just a little – is for the salaries of the M.P.s and the upper-crust civil servants to be substantially reduced. If they fail to do this, they will simply be putting up two fingers to everyone, from State pensioners to the middle classes.

In the same vein, in January 2007, Ireland's seven university Presidents are seeking an increase of €135,000 a year to bring them at least €320,000 a year. They trot out all the usual garbage about comparing themselves with other better-paid groups and needing to pay top dollar to attract candidates of high calibre - themselves, of course. No wonder higher education is so expensive and so many students leave university with mountains of debt. Time to cut these already overpaid creeps down to size.

Ireland also seems to lack Government Auditors capable of keeping their elected members' expenses under control. The T.D.s' expense claims very widely from zero (Noel Treacy, Fianna Fail, Galway East) to €85,998 (Noel Davern, Fianna Fail, Tipperary South). Only 10 T.D.s submitted expense claims below €10,000 for December 2005 to December 2006 whilst 83 claimed amounts between €50,000 and €85,998.

Even top churchmen in Ireland are beginning to see the connection between burgeoning greed and criminality. In Christmas 2006 messages, Church of Ireland's Dr. John Neil and Catholic Archbishop of Dublin Dr. Diarmuid Martin warned against the emptiness and despair which now afflict even those who have secured financial benefits by trying to hang on to the tail of the Celtic Tiger. The Archbishops confirmed my own research and findings by relating insatiable greed and manic spending to a huge increase in gang crime.

Dr. Martin sees terrible violence on Dublin's streets and a disregard for the value of life which, he says, haunts him and fills him with a sense of horror.

Speaking on the subject of Fat Cat incomes and City bonuses, Northern Ireland Secretary of State Peter Hain said the gap between top and bottom incomes is just indefensible. He finds it offensive that some company bosses earn three times their staff's incomes. Three times Mr. Hain? What planet are you on? Try ten/twenty/fifty and more times, then you are beginning to understand the scale of the unfairness.

Roger Jenkins, for example, whose work in "structured finance" for Barclays Capital doesn't add one jot to mankind's well-being, reportedly trousered between £30 million and £60 million in 2006. By my calculation Mr. Hain, that works out at around 1,500 to 3,000 times the UK's average wage, but I have not come across a single complaint about this outrageous payment from any politician – even those of the supposedly Socialist persuasion.

And they wonder why we have crime.

Whilst Peter Hain expresses anger about the Fat Cats' incomes and claims, quite rightly, that it is a sign of a society which has lost its moral compass, his only solution is to "have a debate about it and a genuine dialogue with the City" and senior business executives.

That a senior politician can be so naïve as to believe that talking to the City (whatever that means) can make the slightest difference, is worrying in the extreme. Sure, these greed-balls will talk to you, but what they will not do is voluntarily and significantly agree to reducing their own huge incomes. It is not in the nature of the beast and Peter Hain has been part of Government which, for ten years, has aided and abetted the Fat Cats, so it ill behoves him now to be feigning concern, unless he has some serious proposals to deal with the issue.

Should he have, he can contact me any time at **pancho@crimedown.org**

CHAPTER 15

LESS FREEDOM = MORE CRIME

Now I come to one of my driving passions. **FREEDOM**.

Freedom. The very word which has provided succour, hope and the courage to withstand adversity, to many in their darkest days.

There can, of course, be no universal definition of freedom and it certainly does not bestow the right to do whatever we want, whenever and wherever we want.

Even many criminals accept that society has the right and duty to remove their freedom if they have committed serious crimes. The converse is that some of those mistakenly judged to be guilty, who know themselves to be innocent, take a conscious decision to seek revenge – if necessary by subsequently breaking the law, perhaps for the first time. Insofar as it is humanly possible therefore, it behoves us all to ensure that our laws are fair and that the due process of law avoids denying anyone their freedom without just cause. Regrettably, too many of today's gung ho politicians attach little or no importance to freedom. The UK's Chancellor of the Exchequer, Gordon Brown, supported detaining suspects for ninety days without charge or trial in order for the police to "interview" them, as he so euphemistically put it. Detaining people in a high security prison for up to ninety days confirms how little importance he and the UK Labour Party attach to freedom. How would they like to be deprived of their freedom, I ask myself?

There are, of course, grey areas of freedom too numerous to list and like many of you, I am ambivalent on some of these and may even change my views on some from time to time.

Just a few examples :-

- When I judge it safe to do so, I exceed the speed limit. Just like almost every other driver who has ever used a motor vehicle in fact. Step forward any off-duty police officer, judge, magistrate or pontificating politician who claims never to have exceeded the speed limit (assuming regular road use).

The truth is that in any given week, most drivers exceed speed limits so many times that if caught each time, they would lose their licences. Only good fortune in the ridiculous reverse lottery of road traffic regulations saves them from this fate. Others, of course, are not so lucky. This makes an absolute nonsense of traffic laws which can result in potentially 99% of absolutely average drivers losing their licences for offences which had no suggestion of dangerous driving.

• As a pedestrian, I will cross the road when the red signal is telling me not to, if there is no traffic whatsoever in sight. Those who do not do this are taking a first step in giving up their freedom and accepting that a Government machine is entitled to enslave them.

• Should I ever be asked by a loved one suffering unbearable terminal illness, to help them end their life and suffering, I cannot be sure how I would respond, but I hope I would have the courage to concur. Certainly I believe that anyone faced with such a terrible choice should be free to come to their own decision without risk of prosecution. Brave, retired medical doctor, Michael Irwin, now awaits the prospect of prosecution for accompanying Dave Richards on his suicide mission to Switzerland from England. Mr. Richards, a sufferer from incurable Huntingdon's disease simply did not wish to await the final indignities of his condition at home, where he was denied the freedom to seek assistance to end his suffering. That any State should deny any individual or their compassionate helpers this ultimate freedom is oppression at a truly inhumane level, particularly when anyone offering assistance may find themselves charged with a crime.

• I would refuse (now) to serve in the armed services again unless I personally believed in the war in question. I should be free to decide whether or not I concluded that my country was under serious threat and I am, incidentally, neither an automatic conscientious objector nor a pacifist. It is just that as a free person, I am not prepared to allow any power-crazed politician, be they President or Prime Minister, to send me around the world on a kill or be killed mission with which I may profoundly disagree.

What this chapter is mainly about though, is the *basic, fundamental freedoms* which I consider belong to every human being and which, if abused, refused or oppressed, may well lead the victims to seek redress, revenge, compensation, whatever. Such attacks on freedom have resulted in some of those aggrieved resorting to crime and there can be no doubt that many acts of terrorism over centuries had their origins in the denial or oppression of basic freedoms. Getting even; "tit-for-tat" revenge; an-eye-for-an-eye; have been features of human nature since time immemorial and are not about to go away any time soon.

I was born a free person. I "belong" to no State nor did I ever "belong" to my parents, or to the religion into which it was assumed I could be directed, even before I could speak. I have never been a member of any Political Party because they all consider freedom to be some kind of dangerous disease. Nor have I any wish to become a Freemason, which is, in fact, a serious misnomer because applicants to this secretive order, in the expectation of pecuniary advantage, are required to swear away their personal freedom.

Freedom is allowing people to do what they want provided that others do not suffer as a direct result. By "suffering", I do not mean taking offence or feigned offence at the written or spoken word claimed by those with apparently incredibly thin skins.

Freedom should mean that you cannot be arrested or confined by any Government for more than 3 days without being charged with a specific offence, then being tried in a public Court.

Provided that I am not **known** to be involved in any criminal activity, freedom should mean that my telephone calls, my computer-use, my relationships with my bank manager, lawyer, doctor, accountant, business contacts, friends and my mail, should be confidential. They are no business of Governments. Nor do I want my taxes to be wasted on officials and their surveillance system monitoring trillions of bits of absolutely innocuous information.

Freedom means travelling where I wish without my every movement being tracked or recorded on any Big Brother database. I do though, see nothing wrong with the police being empowered to stop my car and require me to take an alcohol or drugs test, any such substances having the ability to reduce my driving competence, thereby putting the freedoms and safety of others at risk.

The creeping step-by-step dismantling of individuals' freedoms is spreading around the world, led by those who have hi-jacked America – Land of the Free. Until the 23rd January 2007, Americans could travel to, and return from most other of their neighbouring countries with almost any kind of photo I.D. – driving licence etc. They could visit Canada, most Central and Southern American countries, Bermuda etc. with almost no formality, but now at all airports, a passport is a must and will soon also be a necessity at land and sea points.

To turn the screw, passports can now be denied without tax clearance and for other dubious reasons. America is also trying to strong-arm other countries into taxing those of their citizens who have lived abroad, even for decades.

A further attack on the right to privacy and the freedom to travel, is that any laptop computer can now be seized at any airport, seaport or land crossing in the United States *without cause, suspicion, or without judicial authority*.

Susan Gurley, the Executive Director of the Association of Corporate Travel Executives wrote early in November 2006 to the U.S. Department of Homeland Security, wanting to know the parameters of such seizures. It seems that there are no restrictions on how long you can be denied your own computer, nor are you entitled to know if its contents have been copied or who may have access to what may be very secret and valuable commercial information.

Had I been foolish enough to visit America with much of the contents of this book on my laptop, (a) it may never have been published and (b) I would personally have suffered some serious consequences.

Almost everyone travelling anywhere connected with America is now having information secretly stored about them for at least 40 years, as the U.S. trawls billions and billions of pieces of information even about completely innocent, law-abiding people. Any of the information about you, on this Automated Targeting System (A.T.S.), can be made available to numerous other bureaucracies around the world. Stephen Yale-Loehr at the Cornell University Law School summed the situation up very succinctly when he concluded that "everybody else can see the A.T.S. information – except you".

Freedom means absolutely no all-encompassing Identity Cards. A Driving Licence – fine, if I want to use a motor vehicle. A Passport

– fine, if I need one to visit other countries, but what should be an absolute no-no is an Identity Card which *either now or in the future* could contain mountains of information which would go far beyond proving my identity. *I warn every reader now.* If you allow your politicians to force through supposed ID cards with such capability or potential, *you are volunteering to become a slave – to be controlled and exploited by the worldwide Brotherhood of Bureaucrats.* You are giving away not only your own, but also your children's freedoms and these are easier to lose than they are to regain.

The Bushes, Blairs, Clarkes, Chiracs and Putins of this world are pulling out all of the stops to strip away ever more of their citizens' freedoms. Make no mistake, these power-crazed morons are determined to know and record every aspect of your life and to keep it all on their universal databases, which eventually will be available to every little tin-pot bureaucrat on the globe. No such multi-capacity Identity Card should be imposed upon the citizens of any nation without their prior approval by referendum and this would need to be based upon known and inviolable boundaries, limiting and defining precisely what such ID cards could contain and to whom such data would be available. Even that, of course, would still be no guarantee that in their traditional manner, politicians will not simply ignore the law and authorise the addition of more information about us, step by step. Do you really trust any politicians who allow the likes of George Bush and Tony Blair to ride roughshod over America's Constitution and Britain's Magna Carta?

America superficially had a freedom-embracing Constitution and Bill of Rights, but any study of these shows them to be very limited in restraining Governments' attacks on freedom. In any event, once in Office, most of its Presidents then applied huge energies and resources to trashing their own Constitution in order to further diminish its citizens' freedoms and increase their own power. I can quote masses of evidence to prove this, should anyone care to dispute the issue.

In their determination to force Identity Cards onto the British public, Tony Blair and his then Home Secretary Charles Clarke, soon put their dirty tricks departments into gear in order to rubbish the Cost Report of the London School of Economics and to inflict serious financial damage on the L.S.E.'s visiting fellow, Simon Davies, who had been hugely critical of the Government's cost claims. So concerned was Sir Howard Davies, a former Chairman of the Financial Services

Authority about the brutal personal attacks on Simon Davies (no relation), that he is said to have complained to Tony Blair. He was, of course, ignored because this is Tony Blair's standard practice when confronted by uncomfortable facts, as I know from long experience in trying to persuade him to get serious about crime.

Tony Blair lets the cat out of the bag

At Prime Minister's Question Time in the UK House of Commons on 08 February 2006, Tony Blair thought he was being clever accusing David Cameron of flip-flopping. He quoted supposed remarks made by David Cameron, the Leader of the Conservative opposition, claiming to be a "Liberal Conservative" and "a Conservative to the core of my being" – "no wonder he is against Identity Cards" smirked Blair.

I seem to be the only commentator who has noticed that Tony Blair connects Identity Cards with recording individuals' political persuasions thereon. In making the connection, Tony Blair's slip has simply confirmed what many have been warning about for years.

Stealth has always been the tactic of the bureaucrat and politician and introducing oppressive laws, initially in their least onerous form, is a typical ploy. From day one, they have a plan to add more draconian measures whenever there is an event with which they can scare the public again, in order to steal more of their freedoms. Prime Minister Blair, in his eagerness to ridicule David Cameron, let down his guard by giving us a foretaste of what the UK Labour Party has in mind for ID Cards in due course.

I and many others have long concluded that some politicians wish to have almost every aspect of our lives on a single Government database for purposes which are against the best interests of all individuals. More and more information will be added to this record step-by-step and some of this will, of course, be wrong, either by accident or malice. Many Governments already demand to know far too much about you than is necessary, but ID Cards, combined with modern technology, now represent a truly fearful weapon of oppression.

Tony Blair's attack on David Cameron can only be interpreted as meaning that with ID Cards in place, our political persuasions would be on record. His remarks could not, in fact, have meant anything else, because it was he who linked political allegiance to Identity Cards and but for the intention I have identified, the Prime Minister's Freudian taunt would have been devoid of either substance or meaning.

I strongly urge you **_never to vote_** for any politician prepared to impose Identity Cards upon your nation. If they are already in existence, do not vote for any candidate who is not committed to working positively towards having them removed. Passports and Driving Licences are the furthest intrusion we should tolerate and neither of these should contain any information about us other than that which is absolutely necessary for their purpose, which must never go beyond simply identifying us.

When any nation continually strips away the freedom of the individual, it becomes dangerously powerful because inevitably, this results in those on it's payroll or seeking its patronage, to further enslave their own citizens – all allegedly in the national interest, of course.

Were American citizens ever asked if they wanted people scooping up in Afghanistan and elsewhere and given the cynical label of Enemy Combatants? Of course not, because the question would invite a likely "no" response.

Did the American or British people know that the U.S.A. had a disgusting detention centre in Cuba? No. Well, not until it was too late, that is.

Did the countries used by the Americans to kidnap then transport foreigners from place to place, have the permission of their people to involve themselves in this slimy trade? Absolutely not.

Did you, dear reader, expect your Government's military to abuse, debase and torture people who became their prisoners? I sincerely hope not.

Do you approve of anyone being held captive for months or years without legal representation, without visits from friends or family, often without outsiders' knowledge of their whereabouts and without charge, without evidence of guilt, without public trial and without any end in sight? Most people tell me "no way", but Bush, Blair & Co. think it is fine that those in their employ should commit such crimes and make a mockery of the freedom they cynically pretend to want to spread around the world.

Well, I for one am not beguiled by the mesmeric Tony Blair, nor am I stirred to accept dirty, back-alley crimes by Mr. Bush's supposedly rousing "save our nation" speeches. Their kind of spoof freedom and rigged power politics democracy, the world can well do without.

Again, it is America driving global anti-freedom measures, encouraging puppets like Tony Blair to add repressive laws in their own countries.

Then come the International Treaties with each Police State agreeing to allow others to share all known information about everyone. Using organisations including FATF and the IMF, Governments worldwide are being arm-twisted into putting everything they know about everyone onto computer databases, to which Washington demands access at all times without the need to provide any justification. Most of this information is completely benign, but some of it is open to serious and damaging misinterpretation. Some is plain wrong and the consequences of these bureaucratic mistakes can be horrendous for the innocent individuals concerned. All of this global surveillance is because the U.S. Department of Homeland Security cannot keep its nose out of matters which should be none of its concern. Terry Jones, actor, film director and of Monty Python fame, writing in The Guardian, summed it up beautifully, offering President Bush a membership to the World League of Despots for his outstanding human abuses and destruction of freedoms.

If Bush and Blair genuinely believe in democracy, they should go and study it in Switzerland, where freedom and privacy still exist and where no Political Party, Language Group or Religion can get their hands on the levers of power. In Switzerland, the Government has to do substantially what the citizens want – not the other way around. *That* is democracy. That should be spread around the world, but of course, the Swiss would never think of attacking other countries in order to do it. They quite properly mind their own business.

The personally wealthy Bush, Blair & Co. by contrast, are trashing their own citizens' rights whilst charging around the world murdering 50 innocent men, women and children for every possible insurgent they manage to kill? All hypocritically in the name of freedom, which their own citizens no longer have. At the time of writing, the number of civilians killed in Iraq seems to be somewhere between 250,000 and 600,000 and with no end in sight. All the result of the decisions of supposedly educated men.

340

Those who claimed that education is a search for truth were seriously misinformed or perhaps just naïve in believing that education results in civilised behaviour.

It is tempting to conclude that our politicians do not understand the meaning of the word "Freedom", but that would be a dangerous misjudgement. They understand freedom only too well. The problem is that it is a concept which scares the pants off those who have gorged themselves on the drug of power for so long that they need ever more power in order to confirm their omnipotence. Power and freedom are, in fact, incompatible.

The irony is, of course, that Blair, Bush & Co., in further encroaching on our centuries of traditional freedoms, are also doing exactly what a small number of terrorists wish them to do. They are complying with the Taleban's and Al Quaeda's plans to see ordinary people throughout the world become subjugated and kept under the strict control of an elite. Western countries are not, of course, as blatant as the Taleban in the suppression of their citizens, but in a way, their cunning step-by-step salami-slicing of freedoms may, if not stopped, become even more dangerous. If you have not read George Orwell's book 1984 I recommend you to do so now.

The truth is that Bush, Rumsfeld, Rice, Blair, Straw, Blunkett, Clarke, Reid, the Taleban, Al Quaeda et al, are all enemies of ordinary people. They all want the same thing – control. It is just that they offer different excuses for taking away our freedoms in order to get the control they crave.

It may be that in the short-term, either or both will succeed in imposing ever more regulations upon their own and other people and force them to pay ever more taxes enforcing them.

There is hope though. Whilst ever the internet stays relatively free from Government control, I fully expect the influence which politicians have gained over the main-stream media to diminish. This will give greater voice to independent bloggers and whistle blowers prepared to expose the greedy machinations, corruption and incompetence of their current political masters.

The very freedom of the internet is already causing Governments to dream up excuses to begin to control it and we allow this to happen at our peril. I believe an independent internet to be vital to freedom and it may well prevent at least some unjustified armed conflicts by virtue of its capacity to disseminate widely, information which the power junkies have previously been able to distort or keep completely under wraps. If we lose this freedom to communicate with each other internationally, without interference, it would then be very much more difficult for ordinary people to prevent their Governments from running amok. China, France and the U.S.A. are already amongst the countries interfering with the freedom of the net and one must conclude that any nation so doing must be considered a dangerous Police State.

Few Americans and almost no foreigners are aware of how George Bush's Government is planning to further restrict the freedom of the Internet. He and his cohorts are determined to restrict open blogging by riding roughshod over a First Amendment clause which guarantees the right of every citizen to petition the Government to seek redress for any grievance.

In a typical step-by-step anti-freedom programme, the American political elite are so alarmed by seeing the general population able to express itself via blogging on the "net", they want it stopped/controlled. The first step in this planned sequence of invasive controls has already been taken, with paid lobbyists being required by law to register and provide Congress with quarterly Reports itemising their activities. Attempts have already been made to widen the scope of lobbying control by using Section 220 of 2007's First Order of Senate Business which, on the face of it, was simply one step up from the above, but the proposal was so cunningly written in typical lawyer-speak, that it could have hogtied every individual blogger. Go to **www.grassrootsfreedom.com** to learn more.

At the time of this writing, Proposal 220 has yet to be adopted, but rest assured, it has not gone away. Being America, there will be attempts to get it through clandestinely by tacking it onto some totally unrelated Bill.

I have no doubt that many politicians, particularly in the U.S.A., have plans which could allow them to classify every individual blogger as a lobbyist, forced to register and forced to submit regular Reports to some Government bureaucracy, paying a licence and submission fee most likely.

342

Exposing such plans in this book and elsewhere will hopefully encourage others to be more aware and this, in turn, could make it more difficult for those wishing to gag the internet.

Protect the independence of the internet with vigour because without it, the prospect of taking back lost freedoms will be seriously diminished and as freedoms are dashed, crime inevitably increases.

Bush, Blair and cohorts jump on every chance to close down more of their citizens' freedoms and thought themselves such clever people, forcing their banks to disclose even very modest and completely innocent amounts going into or out of their customers' accounts. This, of course, imposes huge additional costs on the banks and most of us know what banks do with such extra costs – they pass them on to us, their customers.

How many terrorist attacks have these ridiculous controls on millions of innocent transactions prevented? None.

What they have succeeded in doing, is making some countries develop alternative ways of transferring money without involving American or British banks at all. Result - loss of throughput of funds for the legitimate banks; the cutting of connections which could really have been useful in tracking terrorists; the souring of relationships between banks and their law-abiding customers; more cynicism of politicians and victory to the likes of Venezuela's President Chavez who, with the help of Ricardo Fernandez Barrueco, has simply by-passed the US/GB banking systems by either buying or doing deals with banks in countries which quite properly respect their clients' confidentiality provided that there is no suggestion of money laundering.

I very much doubt that the bank accounts over which President Chavez now seems to have total control – more than 25 billion dollars – are untainted by criminality, but Bush and Blair seriously miscalculated if they thought that they could prevent countries such as Venezuela, Cuba, Iran, Russia, China, Lebanon and Bolivia from moving massive amounts of money around the world at will.

They would have achieved far more by letting the terrorists "think" they could use the American and European banking systems with impunity, but of course, Bush and Blair could not resist the temptation to tighten the screws on all of their own citizens and grab a few TV soundbite opportunities. Now we will know far less about what these freewheeling countries and criminals are up to. How clever is that?

Another serious mistake which our political masters are making is research into identification and tracking-chips which, step by step, they intend introducing as an implant system into humans. The system is already in use by City-Watcher in Ohio and initially is put into the muscles of workers on a voluntary basis for the apparently benign reason of enabling access to a secure area. One maker of these chip-implants – the Verichip Corporation – envisages numerous uses for these radio frequency identification chips, but as of now, they are only naming their innocent-seeming purposes, available to be used on an entirely voluntary basis. A bit like the way in which the proposed UK ID Cards were originally portrayed in fact.

In the short time since Big Brother Blunkett proposed voluntary ID Cards, things have already moved on and a Home Office Minister's leaked letter let slip that the proposed Identity Cards are, in fact, planned to have radio frequency identification and tracing-availability chips and I can tell you now that these will, in future, be loaded with more information about you than you know yourself and of course, being a Government computer programme, it will be in a permanent state of dysfunction and error. The consequences of these "mistakes" for those individuals on the receiving end can be extremely serious.

Tony Blair is trying to sell Identity Cards employing the same dishonest techniques used by a succession of Governments to bamboozle their electorates about the European Economic Community. Have a less-than-honourable control system as the final goal, but sell the early stages as something far less complex in the meantime. The oft-used "step-by-step" scam. It was how 25 countries have been tricked into handing over most of their sovereignty to a bunch of unelected bureaucrats in Brussels and Strasbourg.

No-one should trust any Government to keep any ID controls in their original form because the nature of the beast is always to add to their powers. Nor can any Government be relied upon to accurately record personal data, nor to keep it confidential. Look no further than Tony Blair's Criminal Records Bureau which, only when caught out, had to admit that it had listed 2,700 perfectly innocent law-abiding Brits as paedophiles.

This can only lead to a widening of mistrust between the executive and the people and some who suffer as a result will seek redress by whatever means is available to them. When individuals' lives are blighted by mistakes on Governments' data records, it is inconceivable that some will not seek redress by illegal routes if they cannot get or afford satisfaction at law.

Even more worrying is the secretive programme being set up by The Welsh Development Agency, Ceredigion Country Council and the European Union to research unmanned aerial vehicles (UAVs). These tiny flyers, only a few centimetres long, are designed to eventually be able to read the chips which Tony Blair wants us all to have to carry around with us as a supposed simple Identity Card.

Trust him – he's a Prime Minister. Yeah, right!

Almost a hundred years ago, when crime in the US and most other countries was much lower but rising, H. L. Mencken wrote:-

"This gradual (and of late, rapidly progressive) decay of freedom goes almost without challenge; the American has grown so accustomed to the denial of his constitutional rights and to the minute regulation of his conduct by swarms of spies, letter-openers, informers and agent provocateurs, that he no longer makes any serious protest."

All of my research shows that in the intervening century, freedoms have continued to be battered. Mencken's spies are today's bureaucrats; his letter-openers have added unwarranted phone-tapping and internet surveillance to their armoury; his informers are now banks, building societies, car distributors and librarians. And all through these perpetual attacks by States on the freedoms of their citizens, crime has risen in concert with the thousands of new laws, edicts and regulations.

America has led the way in the destruction of liberty and its famous statue of that name has long been a sick joke.

In Mencken's day, the police would never have broken down an 84-year old's bedroom door at two o'clock in the middle of the night looking for drugs.

In modern-day America though, Annie Rae Dixon was lying in bed with pneumonia when she was shot dead by a police officer who cynically asked us to believe that his gun was accidentally discharged when he kicked this old lady's door in. There were no drugs in the property.

Freedom, and the low crime which accompanies it, are possible in some countries, even today, but America last enjoyed a good measure of these in the period 1865 to 1895 and it has been downhill ever since.

With more than 200 Federal laws and thousands of State laws permitting police to seize private assets with neither evidence of crime nor Court warrant, the State has become the criminal.

From motorists alone, the police in Volusia County, Florida stole more than eight million dollars between 1997 and 2001. They stopped motorists not because of any traffic infringement, not to breathalyse them, but simply to ask "How much money do your have?" If it was several hundred dollars or more, the money and the car was confiscated and the owner left to mount a Court battle to prove that the money and car were untainted by crime. Only problem – the legal costs, at $10,000 to $100,000 would often be higher than the value of the car and forensically, well over 50% of US dollar bills currently have traces of illegal substances on them – even though they may have been accessed through the owners' banks.

Many would believe that America would be satisfied with the 70% of its citizens' incomes it takes in direct, indirect, compliance and stealth taxes, but as I have shown elsewhere, power and greed know no bounds. Perhaps one day though, Americans will wake up and demand a really serious down-sizing in Government. Perhaps.

European Commission Chief, Manuel Borroso is, quite rightly, critical of Turkey's restrictions of freedom and their charging of Author Elif Shafak with insulting "Turkishness" – whatever that may be. What a pity though, that Mr. Borroso does not campaign to allow home-schooling in Germany or for workers throughout Europe to have the freedom to work however many hours they wish, rather than following the lazy French into global uncompetitiveness. If the European Commission truly believed in freedom for its citizens, it would have learned the lessons of history and not allowed America to force countries in Europe to pass dangerous, Nazi-type laws to repress even their law-abiding citizens.

In 1933, the Germans sat back and saw the seeds sown for that country's disastrous growth into Dictatorship and tragedy. Mesmerised by those claiming the Fatherland to be under threat from outsiders, the German people failed to see the dangers of President Hindenburg's involvement in allowing what, in effect, authorised the Nazis to override existing laws and democracy. We all know what happened next and yet ..... both America, with its 2001 Partriot Act (sic) and Britain, with its 2004 Civil Contingencies Act failed to learn the lessons of history. It was ever thus.

Neither of these plunderings of citizens' freedoms were fully explained. Both were supported, often sight unseen, by craven politicians. Both were sold like deodorants, based on exaggerated fears and both have put massive power into the hands of the Executive. Now, I don't pretend to know when the next Adolph will come along, but George and Tony, who brook no opposition, are certainly showing dangerous signs in that direction. Already they have stolen most of our freedoms and they, and probably their successors, plan to steal more.

This they will continue to do until we, the people, stop them and put their power-grabs into reverse. Meantime, in the same way that many ordinary people create a black market in trade when their Governments over-tax and over-regulate them, many people turn to crime when they perceive their over-large Governments as being hell bent on enslaving them. Presidents and Prime Ministers may not like this, but that's the way it is.

It is time Governments stopped telling us all how to lead our lives, not only because hectoring people all too often turns some of them to hit back, but because it is incredibly bad form to keep insulting everyone who doesn't conform to the do-gooders ideas of correct living.

Retired Alan Treece now has no faith in either the police or the judiciary, having suffered incredible attacks on his freedom. Over a period of seven months, he was dragged through three Hearings in two Courts and fined £450 for breaching new Health & Safety Regulations. His offence? He had dived into the deep end of his sports centre's swimming pool, something he had done for years without harming himself or anyone else. Believing in freedom and commonsense, Mr. Treece had declined to gently lower himself into the almost empty pool – as ordered by some stroppy rule book attendant. As a result, and because he had tried to register a complaint against the Erith Sports Centre's attitude, the police turned up at his home and arrested him, setting in chain a nonsensical series of events which can only be described as a huge waste of time and money, at a time when both the Courts and the police are failing to catch and convict more than 3% of the really serious criminals.

Freedom – I doubt some politicians have any true understanding of its meaning.

It means that if you choose to eat junk food and drink fizzy drinks, that is your business. If you choose to enjoy tens of thousands of moments of pleasure which eating burgers, chips, sweets and TV meals give you, that is your absolute right. You may be happier doing this even though your weight may go up and you may prefer this even though it *may* shorten your life. A visit to a few old people's homes may also cause you to question why anyone would want to forego any pleasures simply to suffer a few more years as a skeletal zombie, slumped in a chair staring uncomprehending at Friends or Eastenders on TV.

What you do not want are Government spokespersons banging away via the media, telling you that you are fat-obese, as though you were not aware that you were not a size 8.

Smokers have always known their habit to be unhealthy and addictive, as have those seriously into booze or other drugs, but some of those who kick their habits become the most sanctimonious bores on the planet. Fate, of course, often takes a hand when, having given up their pleasures, they get run over by a bus, die following a plane trip from deep vein thrombosis or get murdered by a burglar after having gone to bed early to get the prescribed healthy hours of sleep.

I for one do not want a world populated by people conforming to what their Governments portray as best practice. Sure, I love to see beautiful and healthy people, but my life – and I am sure, many others – would have been considerably impoverished had there been no Winston Churchill, Burl Ives, Tessie O'Shea, Ernest Hemingway, Boris Johnson, Richard Harris, Clare Short, Bob Boothby, Robert Mitcham, Chuck Berry, Luciano Pavarotti, Geoffrey Barnard, Edit Piaff, Orson Wells, Louis Armstrong, Vitas Gerulaitis, Peter O'Toole, Judy Garland, Geoffrey Archer, Bessie Smith, Alex Higgins, Freddie Mercury, Felix Dennis, Marlon Brando – and many others.

Love them or loathe them, politically incorrect with each having one or more of the "differences" which Nanny States are trying to make us all feel so guilty about – obesity, smoking, doing drugs, philandering, enjoying fish 'n' chips, mars bars and a wonderful variety of alcoholic beverages – without such freedom lovers, what a dismal place the world would be.

It was Peter O'Toole who proudly stated that the only exercise he takes is following at the funerals of friends who were regular exercisers.

Perhaps, like me, you have such characters within your own circle of friends. They are to be treasured and Governments' attempts to force them into a one-size-fits-all straightjacket will do far more harm than good. Depriving anyone of the freedom to be themselves, likely triggers psychiatric problems which, not surprisingly, causes some to venture into crime. Not for the first time in this book, I not only question the assumption that everyone wants to live as long as possible, I point out that those who die early make a huge contribution to their country's Exchequers and the taxpayers left behind who no longer have to pay their pensions or healthcare costs.

We should all celebrate the passing of those who brightened our lives by treating political correctness with the contempt it deserves. My son Cass, for one. Smoker, big-time drinker, non-exerciser, seriously overweight, he died aged 53, but his funeral was testament to the huge love which his irreverent lifestyle generated in a wide circle of relatives and friends. By common consent, his funeral was the most amazing mixture of tears and laughter any of us had ever seen.

Political Correctness is, in fact, the antithesis of freedom, a subject about which U.S. Founding Father and President, Thomas Jefferson, was a passionate believer.

- "Honest payment of our (U.S.) debts."

- "Freedom of the press and freedom of all persons under the protection of Habeas Corpus."

- "Trial by impartially-selected juries."

- "Peace with all nations but political connection with none, with little or no (international) Treaties or Diplomatic Establishment."

- "Relieve commerce from the shackles of piles of regulating laws, duties and prohibitions."

These were ***all principles espoused by Thomas Jefferson***.

How tragic that his teachings have been so foolishly ignored, resulting in American Governments no longer adhering to any of his beliefs. This is why Americans no longer even understand freedom. This is why America is despised the world over and why its discomfort with itself has caused so many of its citizens to resort to crime, whilst others simply leave to live in more civilised countries. This will not change until that sickest country of the western world reverts to Jeffersonian principles.

Many Americans, unfortunately, have a ridiculous and unhealthy respect for their Constitution, either because they have not studied it or not understood it. It is, in fact, a document permitting politicians to plunder the right of every citizen to control his own life. Only the Bill of Rights (the first ten amendments) originally bestowed any protection for the individual against the State, but unsurprisingly, the State did not like that one bit. Result? Appoint Judges to the Supreme Court who will, at the bidding of the Executive, overturn those "rights" to freedom which were an obstacle to the power ambitions of the politicians and their wealthy lobbying support groups.

Before anyone decides to challenge me on this, I strongly recommend them to read Lysander Spooner's expose "No Treason: The Constitution of No Authority" and Sanford Levinson's "Our Undemocratic Constitution: Where the Constitution Goes Wrong and How We The People Can Correct It" – Sanford Levinson is a law professor at Austin's University of Texas.

Another reality check which is worthwhile is to compare the U.S.A. with its northern neighbour.

- Canada has only a normal number of laws and regulations whilst America is overwhelmed by them.

- Canada has a small population and contributes little to global CO^2 emissions whilst America has a massive population and is the world's largest producer of damaging greenhouse gasses.

- Canada has almost no debt. America has trillions of dollars of debt which it can never repay.

- Canada has no overseas bases, has never started a war and sends it military abroad only under the auspices of the United Nations whilst America has military bases in more than a hundred countries and has a record of starting wars and generally interfering in the affairs of other nations.

Where has all this led by 2007?

It has resulted in Canada having a modest per capital crime level with almost no-one murdered by guns, even though many Canadians legally own several firearms whilst in America there is high crime and more than 11,000 are murdered by guns every years.

Less Freedom – More Crime! More Freedom – Less Crime!

Be very sceptical, dear reader, whenever any politician suggests that "we" must strike a balance between this or that, because invariably they are promoting something drastic when, in fact, there is no true relationship between "this" and "that".

On the 29th September 2006, at the Labour Party Conference, Tony Blair wowed his selected, mesmerised, brain-dead delegates, asking how do we reconcile liberty and security. Pity he hadn't listened to me, because I have written to him repeatedly, pointing out that liberty and security are not mutually exclusive. The honest answer is to leave liberties and freedoms strictly alone and concentrate on catching, convicting and confining the law-breakers. There should be no compromising of freedoms, and pretending that trading these away will give us greater freedom is false.

Tony Blair pompously stated, in order to make the case for Identity Cards, that when crime goes unpunished, that is a breach of victims' rights. Whilst as a soundbite that sounds great, because it is true, it is hypocrisy in the extreme coming from the politician whose regime has already racked-up more than fifty million unsolved crimes, not because the perpetrators could not be identified, but because they knew that the chances of being caught and suffering serious consequences were minimal.

With only 3% of crimes leading to a conviction in Blair's Britain, it ill behoves him to be rabbiting on about balancing liberty and security. This delusional control freak is quite simply a fraud and I for one am not fooled by his mock sincerity.

Richard Thomas, Britain's Information Commissioner, has stated that *he knows* that Government databases are insecure and accessed by private investigators, as are those of corporations. He has issued warning after warning about Government's storing, misuse and lax attitude towards personal data, the latest raid on which is the proposal for soon-to-be Stalinist Britain to have every scrap of private information between you, the patient and your doctor and hospital transferred instantaneously to a central, leaky database which can never be free of serious errors. The UK Labour Party proposes that no individual shall have the right to refuse to have their personal health concerns entered on what is to be the world's largest database.

Watch out for the step-by-step tactic to kick in, with P.R. firm Porter Novelli having been given a million pound contract to soften up the public by hiding the full extent of this massive assault on your privacy and freedom. The outrageous and unbelievable expense, to create and run this scheme, has nothing to do with delivering better health care. That is simply the façade used to sell yet another piece in the total-control jigsaw.

The negatives, on the other hand, are numerous and they include:-

• The destruction of generations of trust between patient and health practitioner.

• Giving criminals and numerous other interested parties, access to information about you which you may not even wish your nearest and dearest to know, perhaps even to save them distress.

• Information Commissioner Richard Thomas already knows more than three hundred media personnel who have bought supposedly confidential information from databases and he has called – so far without success – for today's paltry fines to be replaced by mandatory prison sentences.

• An increase in blackmail crimes as sensitive information about health matters, pregnancies, abortions, mental health problems, sexually transmitted diseases etc. gets stolen for criminal use.

• Many people, unhappy about being forced into such an anti-freedom database without their consent, will simply stop going to their doctors and some will go abroad to seek advice about their medical concerns.

All because of those politicians who cannot bear the thought that we are sovereign individuals who are entitled to our privacy.

The British Medical Association has stated its opposition to any database which includes information without patients' consent. Well – let them refuse to operate any such system. Let them defy the control freaks and let them demonstrate to us all that they have the backbone to defend patient/doctor confidentiality.

The UK Government's tame Chief Medical Officer, Professor Liam Donaldson, has already been triggered into spin/bullying mode and he has warned General Medical Practitioners to rat (my word) on those patients who wish not to have their health records transferred onto any central computer database. He has allegedly "instructed" G.P.s to forward any letters of objection to Britain's most insensitive Health Secretary ever, Patricia Hewitt. Anyone remember how Dr. Goebbels began his campaigning in Nazi Germany, with lies about non-existent threats and step-by-step removals of citizens' freedoms?

CHAPTER 16

THE POISON OF SECRECY

As with good bacteria, bad bacteria; good cholesterol, bad cholesterol; good stress and bad stress; there is good secrecy and bad secrecy.

It is of course right and proper that Central Governments should try to protect sensitive information about their military weapons capacity and operational plans etc. Few people, myself included, have a problem with that.

No-one can reasonably object to business corporations wishing their development and marketing information to remain confidential until such time as they deem to be appropriate.

Every individual has a perfect right to the privacy of all of his or her information and transactions provided, of course, that they are legal.

Unfortunately, I can state quite categorically that it has become the practice of many politicians, bureaucrats, quangos, corporations etc. to confuse the good secrecy with the bad.

Think again if you believe that the welfare of mankind is the prime motive of most drugs manufacturing corporations. It is absolutely not. It is profit, and drugs companies use secrecy to hide any negative, even dangerous effects which their products may have on some of their users. Glaxo Smith Kline is not alone in hiding information about its products, which only serious legal action managed to partially bring out into the open. In order to prop up their profits on their adult anti-depressant drug SeroxaT, G.S.K. decided to market it aggressively to under 18s and they kept secret any information about their drug possibly inclining young takers towards suicide. At the time of this writing, Glaxo Smith Kline are being pursued in the Courts and whilst the outcome is not yet decided, what is known is that the company used secrecy to keep uncomfortable information from the medical profession and the public. But for some diligent legal work, this would never have been revealed.

A culture of excessive and unjustified secrecy is now commonplace amongst control freaks seeking ever more power, usually in order to achieve their own personal aims. Such unnecessary secrecy is a major contributor to crime and/or unfairness, injustice and, all too often, corruption. Invariably, secrecy turns out to be a cover-up for sleaze.

The ladder to Party political progress has numerous rungs of secrecy designed to prevent the public from knowing what those seeking or holding public office are really up to. It has become standard practice for those in power to use secrecy to hide or cover up their mistakes, incompetence, fraud, corruption or even straightforward crime. When attempts are made to call them to account, their chosen escape route is invariably to shield themselves by claiming that they cannot respond because this would involve revealing "classified" information.

Very, very rarely are such claims either true or justified.

Try getting the truth from Bush, Chirac, Blair (Tony), Putin, Straw, Clarke, Blair (Sir Ian), Rumsfeld or window-dummy Rice about torture, extraordinary rendition, detention without trial, the killing by the State of innocent people – or about the extent to which you, as a supposedly free law-abiding citizen, are being surreptitiously spied upon by your own Government.

Try finding out who authorised faceless bureaucrats to continue for decades with their devious step-by-step plans to move 25 countries into a *Federal* Europe with a common high level of taxes, without the permission of the electorates of the countries concerned. Ted Heath, the then UK Prime Minister, lied and conspired with others for the whole of his 50 years as a Member of Parliament. They agreed *in secret* to hide their true intentions – the creation of a *Federal* Europe. Instead, they used secrecy to pretend that Europe was to be a loosely-linked single market trading of Nations. Not surprisingly, only 34% of the British, by December 2006, considered membership of the EU as a good thing, according to a Euro Barometer Poll conducted for the European Commission.

Try, as an existing or potential shareholder, finding out what each Member of a publicly-quoted Company Board really receives as a total remuneration, including benefits in kind and expenses and ask who valued their services at 5, 10, 50, or more than 100 times that of the average employee, without whom there would be no Company. You will find that the Directors of most companies are highly-skilled at secrecy and stone-walling. Far more skilled, in fact, than they are at delivering decent dividends to their shareholders who employ them, or benefits for their employees who make their firms tick.

Try finding out from your Local Council what early stage development plans they have which may affect your area or why they throw away valuable Business Rates revenue by issuing Discontinuance Notices against fully-legal billboards which have often been in situ for decades without a single complaint from the public ever having been registered. Ask Humberside UK, Derby and Lincoln City Councils why their Planners meet in secret to develop policies without public consultation and why they persecute legal advertising whilst turning a blind eye to blatantly illegal examples. I declare an interest here because I have suffered serious financial losses due to Local Authority secrecy and unacceptable bias.

Try going regularly to your Local Council meetings which purport to be public but from which, all too often, the public is excluded in whole or in part.

Invariably you will get no further than "sorry, such information cannot be given to you. It is classified" – i.e. secret. Almost never is this either necessary or in the public interest.

Anyone interested in learning more about how politicians hide behind secrecy will find the following revealing.

House of Lords
European Union Committee
40th Report of Session 2005-2006
Behind Closed Doors :
The meeting of the G6 Interior Ministers at Heiligendamm
37 Page Report with Evidence   HL Paper 221
19 July 2006

Steve Peers, Professor of Law, Human Rights Centre at the University of Essex is also knowledgeable about Freedom of Information (not) in the EU and organisations such as Statewatch, EU Observer and the Cato Institute struggle valiantly to get behind the bureaucratic mask of secrecy.

An excellent example of unacceptable secrecy interfering with justice is the attempts of the U.S. Military to prevent the UK Coroner's Court, and the bereaved families, to have access to vital evidence in the case of British Solider Lance Corporal Matthew Hull who was killed, presumably accidentally, by American Forces. Such tragedies do regrettably occur in battlefield conditions, but instead of apologising and perhaps offering some compensation, the Americans refused to allow the video information to be made available to the Coroner's Court, the Coroner being the legal entity charged with establishing cause of death.

How typical, that instead of assisting the British Court in its enquiries, they resorted to their usual obstruction and secrecy, pretending that their military would be giving away some earth-shattering information which would cause them serious problems. Garbage. Despicable, disgusting, insulting garbage which simply adds to the suffering of the friends and relations of Matthew Hull, for whom the Americans' misuse of secrecy affords neither compassion nor respect. At the time of reviewing this case on the 7th February 2007, it seems that the outcry, not against the accidental killing, but against America's intransigence about releasing the film of it now known to exist, to the British Court, is likely to persuade the U.S. military to back down on the issue.

Most Governments require most or all of their employees to sign some kind of Official Secrets Act which is all encompassing and designed to ensure that the public, which pays for the service, cannot be given information about even the most grotesque or trivial matters which have nothing whatsoever to do with national security.

Governments take us into wars, supposedly to defend our freedoms, but they forbid any member of the armed services from talking to the media about anything without prior consent. So, soldiers cannot speak out about any bullying, atrocities they may have witnessed against innocent civilians, the Colonel's clandestine affair with a best mate's partner, gross waste of money or inadequate equipment. They cannot talk to outsiders about it without formally seeking permission, which is invariably denied. Secrecy, apparently, is more valuable than the freedoms for which we purport to ask our military to risk their lives.

Why so much secrecy if these Governments have nothing to hide?

What do they fear? – public anger? – ridicule? – exposure of incompetence? - having to be accountable to their taxpayers or rate-payers? – less elbow room for corrupt gains?

When it comes to corruption, the entire system of Government in America, for instance, is worse than that in some of the third world countries of which they are so hypocritically critical. They pass thousands of laws and regulations which almost no-one, in either Congress or the Senate, has prior opportunity to even read, let alone debate. Most of these involve billions of dollars of taxpayers' money being distributed to vested interests in secret deals between Senators, Congressmen and the lobbying groups offering support at the next-up Election. This is criminality at a very high level, made possible only by Government secrecy.

Under this veil of secrecy, millions of dollars are being pocketed by individuals with good political connections. Inevitably, this gives some of those outside of this magic circle an excuse to justify moving into criminal activity themselves – "If those in power can enrich themselves by abusing their positions, why should I not get some of my taxes back by any means available to me" – is a sentiment we come across all too often.

Germany too, is suffering from years of corporate corruption, much of which has been permitted in collusion with senior politicians. Eventually, a number of Siemens' Senior Executives were arrested in an investigation into millions of dollars being paid as bribes to Nigeria's disgusting Dictator Sani Abacha. Chairman of Siemens Supervisory Board, Heinrich von Pierer, admitted that he had failed to fight corruption, but I doubt we have heard the last of that Corporation's involvement with corrupt practices.

Several (at least) Volkswagen Senior Executives were also allowed to use secrecy to line their own pockets at the expense of their shareholders and workers. Their one-time Personnel Director, Peter Hartz, eventually confessed in Court to bribery and corruption on a serious scale. Questions still need answering about how he was elevated from being a lowly-paid union worker to being a Board Member with a six-figure income, which then allowed him to pay around ten million euros (equivalent) in bribes to Klaus Volkert, the former top man of the Volkswagen Works Council. Expensive holidays, high-class hookers and connections with politicians such as former Federal Chancellor Schroeder, were also part of the mix of sleaze, secrecy and crime and there is ample evidence that such practices have become endemic.

There are, of course, anti-corruption groups such as Transparency International who try to bring focus to bear on these crimes, but so expert at secrecy are some of those with their sticky fingers in the corporate tills that, like myself, T.I. has serious problems getting to the truth.

This book is the essence of 15 years of research into crime and by publication date – hopefully early 2007 – it will have been around two years in the writing. My main difficulties have not been what to include, but what to set aside (+95%) and how to keep to a minimum, whatever included information may be overtaken by events between completion of my book and its publication.

As of April 2006, George Bush, Jacques Chirac, John Howard, Vladimir Putin, Silvio Berlusconi and Tony Blair still lead their respective countries, but the latter two at least, may not do so for much longer, although I expect Tony Blair to guarantee Labour's continued unpopularity by dangling his Party on a yoyo about his departure date well into 2007.

If anything is going to hasten Prime Minister Blair's early demise, it will be his propensity for secrecy and distorting the truth. His prime interests are maximum power, financial gain for himself and his family and retaining the UK Labour Party in power – in perpetuity if at all possible. The people of Britain are way down his list of priorities and he believes his rhetoric will always be swallowed by a gullible public.

Secrecy and Goebbels-type spin have been his principle weapons.

He used the secrecy of many millions of pounds of "loans" from a handful of wealthy business people to the Labour Party because he sought to hide the fact that Elections in Britain were not the result of the electorate's preferences, but of an ego-trip battle of those whose patronage he sought - the mega rich.

So secretive was he – as written up in another chapter – that he kept any knowledge of these huge loans not only from the public, but also from almost all of his closest colleagues. Watch your back Gordon. With friends like Tony, who needs enemies.

Secrecy, of course, requires effort. It needs cover-up plans, clandestine meetings and negotiations, avoidance, obfuscation, arm-twisting, time, energy and misuse of taxpayers' funds. Whilst Tony Blair has wasted years on these negative and unnecessary secretive machinations,

360

the number of unsolved crimes in Britain has risen inexorably and by 2004/5, this was fifty million since he came to power. It continued to rise throughout 2006, with violent crime increasing most significantly and most worryingly to the British public.

This poisonous secrecy is deeply entrenched throughout most political and corporate regimes.

The Bank of International Settlements, for example, which serves as a bank for central banks, secretly manipulates the price of gold in order to prevent it from finding its natural level in the world market place. It secretly conspires with the International Monetary Fund to funnel huge amounts of money around the world, much of which ends up in the palaces and South of France luxury homes of African Dictators.

If you or I did anything even much more modest we would, quite rightly, be arrested for money-laundering and have our assets confiscated.

Unknown to the American taxpayer, the I.M.F. used taxpayers' money under the pretext of shoring up the economic collapse in Brazil, but the reality was that they were secretly bailing out major U.S. banks such as Morgan Chase, who had made some injudicious loans in that country. Not only is the B.I.S. incredibly inscrutable, it is also completely free of any kind of oversight, with all of its archives, data and documents guaranteed to be - quote "inviolable at all times and in all places".

Thank goodness for whistle-blowers, but we should not have to rely on such brave souls – we are entitled to a much higher level of transparency from organisations which can create huge injustice, all by secretly manipulating money which does not even belong to them.

Without secrecy, it would have been far more difficult for America to fly people around the world in order for them to suffer what, in my opinion, is one of the worst of all human crimes – *torture*. Secrecy, of course, is central to this disgusting practice.

Terry Davis, the Council of Europe's Secretary General, in February 2006, left the media in Strasbourg in no doubt about his disappointment in the response from the Council's questionnaire about assistance given to the C.I.A. and other Secret Services in respect of individuals being flown around the globe on "extraordinary rendition" programmes.

Sir Christopher Meyer was vilified by the Political Establishment in Britain for revealing (after his retirement) matters which came into his orbit as the UK Ambassador in Washington. His book *'D C Confidential'* brought Labour M.P. Gordon Prentice – at a Commons Public Administration Select Committee session – close to apoplexy. His concern was not with the validity of what Sir Christopher's book revealed, it was simply that everything undertaken on behalf of Governments should be kept secret. ***Yuk!***

That is not how the public sees it Mr. Prentice.

The UK Home Office is a perfect example of how its secretive practices, obstruction and obfuscation prevent crime being discouraged and adequately punished. The problem is, that a succession of Home Secretaries have been toy tough-guy types but missing any of the ideas or imagination needed. Minus some lateral thinking and a willingness to deal with some sacred cows, neither Straw, Blunkett, Clarke or now Reid were, or are ever going to bring serious crime down in Britain by 15 to 25% year on year for a few years.

Had Tony Blair been serious about being tough on crime and tough on the causes of crime, the level of crime there would, by now, be less than half of that currently suffered. Instead, he and his Home Secretaries have managed to destroy the morale of the police, prison, probation and immigration services. Some legacy.

We want much less secrecy. We want far greater transparency.

One huge contribution, which I recommend all Countries claiming to have respect for their citizens should put into effect, is to get rid of the appalling practice of hiding official documents for 10/20/30 or more years. Reducing this ridiculous level of secrecy will have considerable benefits, including :-

- Reducing suspicion and increasing the trust which the public has for its Government, be it national or local. Currently, this trust is at a probably all-time low level, having gone down dramatically as secrecy has gone up.

- Greater transparency will also make it possible to correct serious mistakes which right now, many Countries allow to remain hidden in the archives for decades.

- Most importantly, by opening up all but the most sensitive military and security information to public scrutiny within 3 to 5 years would actually reduce the number of political dalliances with projects which should never gain public approval

The knowledge that senior politicians and bureaucrats can commit and hide their most damaging mistakes without ever being accountable during their period in Office – and sometimes even within their lifetimes – has cost many Countries dearly.

Conversely, knowing that what they are being paid to do will be available for inspection within, at most, a few years will concentrate the minds of all public servants and dissuade them from their more disastrous actions and promotions of white elephants.

When one examines much of the information which has not seen the light of day for decades, it is easy to see why the original perpetrators of events would wish to see them buried. Most information should never have been - or be – kept secret at all, but unfortunately, allowing bureaucrats to get away with a limited amount of secrecy leads almost inevitably to further abuse.

As I explain elsewhere in my book, it is an unfortunate characteristic of the type of person who seeks political or bureaucratic office that once they gain power, step by step, they manoeuvre to increase it. They are exactly the same with secrecy. Allow them a little – which may be justified – and there is no limit to what these manipulators will try to hide.

Many illegal acts have been hidden from the world in the certainty that those committing them would never be exposed in their lifetime. Thousands have suffered and died unjustly and unnecessarily as a direct result of this cult of bureaucratic secrecy.

Let us put all of those who are paid to work for and protect us, on notice that whatever they do in that role will be open for the public's consideration, either immediately or certainly within 3 to 5 years. Hopefully, long before they retire, get promotion or die. Only then will they be accountable to those who pay their wages.

End the secrecy. Open the records.

American politicians and their cohorts are particularly addicted to secrecy and use it to cover up their own criminality. Confronted with a growing mountain of debt, they foolishly decided to hide some of the facts by stopping the normal practice of reporting the M3 money supply numbers. This was done for no other reason than to keep secret the amount of new U.S. dollars being printed.

Printing new money, not backed by gold or silver, is in fact nothing more than theft because it immediately devalues all of the money (which originally was asset-backed) already in circulation.

It is bad enough that America has indulged in this sleazy practice over many years, but at least when M3 money supply figures were published, holders of U.S. dollars could see the extent of the thievery. The subsequent hiding of M3 figures is nothing short of fraud which of course is a crime always committed in secrecy.

In Britain in July 2005, Tony Blair's group of lawyers, the Civil Procedure Rule Committee, working for the Department of Constitutional Affairs, *secretly* passed a new rule into law which trashed one of the important pillars of British justice. This bunch of legal lepers, determined to enhance the power of their own profession – Tony Blair included – surreptitiously slipped a new measure into the statute book preventing either the media or the public from having access to details of writs issued in legal cases.

Now, only lawyers, that ugliest of Trade Unions, with a long history of resisting freedom of expression, have the right to see the details of issued writs. This is a serious breach in Britain's long-established policy of justice being seen to be done in public at all stages and as a result, some facts will never reach the Courts because the public will be kept in ignorance of the cases. Such failings can only benefit the wealthy and their lawyers at the expense of justice and those with shallower pockets.

The culture of secrecy pervades all levels of Government, from Local Authority to international shenanigans. When asked by Statewatch for what should have been public information about formally-adopted policies related to the G8 Ministers of Justice and Interior meeting in Moscow on June 16th, 2006, the UK Home Office flatly refused. The information was declared to be "exempt from disclosure" by the Home Office. In other words, the public cannot be told what its representatives have agreed to *in secret* because this would "prejudice relations" between the UK and the G8 nations. Quite what "prejudice relations" means and why John Reid is so secretive about what his Home Office is up to is impossible to say. What it does demonstrate is a remarkable arrogance and a distrust of the public's judgement, which not surprisingly is fully reciprocated.

The EU, driven principally by France, has in fact become expert in secretly getting serious changes written into stone, by which time neither individuals nor nations can amend or veto them. Members and prospective Member countries of the EU naively underestimated France's ability to set agendas in the jungle of bureaucracy and as a consequence, the European Union is now in serious trouble.

Even without knowing one percent of one percent of what the European governing Bodies and their army of bureaucrats is really up to, the citizens of most countries have come to realise that the secrecy, corruption and shady compromises are not delivering what they want. Europe has become a byword for subsidies, hidden agendas, obstructions to free trade and the over-regulation of both businesses and individuals.

One encouraging sign is that Britain and the Netherlands are at least trying to get some transparency introduced into the accounting procedures of the European Union budget where secrecy has reigned for years. They called, in November 2006, for each country to come clean about how they spend EU money and if successful, there may be some embarrassing disclosures by 2008 about some of the beneficiaries. More open disclosure may also help those auditing the EU's books, which have been so unsatisfactory as to cause the independent Auditors to refuse to sign off their acceptance for twelve successive years.

French Governments have, for decades, stubbornly refused to moderate any of the numerous advantages they conned out of other nations and may well continue their intransigence, causing the collapse of the entire EU project within the next 5 to 7 years. Remember, this is a country whose Government is still paying every one of its nationalised railway workers - clerks included - "dirty work" payments negotiated more than 50 years ago when fireman had to stoke coal into the old steam trains' boilers. All French Unions pride themselves on never giving up any gained benefit, no matter that their relevance disappeared decades ago. Their Government operates on the same nonsensical basis of taking the maximum out of any situation and giving nothing in the way of quid pro quo to its European partners. It is as a result of this arrogance, unwillingness to adapt and highly secretive bureaucratic determination to insulate France from the global marketplace and protect its privileged elites at the expense of its growing number of disillusioned citizens, that by 2006, more than seven hundred vehicles are being torched *every week* and crime levels are constantly rising, despite secretive attempts by officials to cover up the extent of the unrest which is no longer confined to the Muslim ghettoes around Paris, despite Chirac's claims to the contrary.

Undoubtedly the most scary and dangerous secrecy is that surrounding certain Governments' investment in and with terrorists. By its very nature, this is very difficult to pin down because those involved are a clever, devious, totally unscrupulous group prepared to do anything to enhance their own power and personal financial benefits. Using carefully screened intelligence personnel, this fascist cabal has been destabilising world order for a very long time, using a range of techniques so appalling that many people will have difficulty taking it in.

Military/security exercises – some public, some highly classified – are morphed into apparent terrorist attacks.

Ask yourself – Is it a coincidence that Peter Power (ex-Scotland Yard), as head of a private security firm, was running a practice exercise in the London Underground involving a thousand people on July 07, 2005? His company, Visor Consultants was, Peter Power told the BBC, simulating bomb explosions on the same day as the "London bombings" as part of Atlantic Blue, a British, American and Canadian mock exercise.

It gets worse.

Visor Consultants' mock bombs were not only on the same day as the London bombings, they were *in the London underground at the same time and at the same stations as the actual bombs which were exploded.*

This raises some very serious questions. Was Peter Power's company innocently involved, or were they part of the same devious

Government plot? Was the Atlantic Blue mock operation nothing more than a genuine exercise? Were that the case, I can only conclude that details of it must have found their way to those who planned to and did explode the live bombs in the London underground. One must then ask "Were the bombers simply terrorists working completely in isolation, or did the security service have some involvement with the perpetrators, whoever they are?"

There are many such "coincidences" in most supposed terrorist attacks, including lots of very worrying aspects of 9/11/01 which were kept from the attention of the subsequent Commission of Inquiry into the tragedy.

I have asked myself repeatedly since 9/11 why Osama Bin Laden has not been killed or captured, despite America, Britain and others being prepared to borrow and spend many billions of dollars on wars in Afghanistan and Iraq. Could it be that Bin Laden is more useful as a bogeyman, with Al Quaeda blamed for terrorist acts committed clandestinely (I hope) by fascist elements inside western Governments?

It stretches credulity that with all its might, all its supposed wealth, all of its high-tech surveillance capability and firepower, America has been unable to arrest or kill just one man with a huge price on his head.

It further defies belief that Osama Bin Laden, supposedly skulking from cave to cave to village to village can be controlling a worldwide terrorist organisation whilst on the run and without any secure means of communication.

Could he already be dead, but that fact kept from public knowledge, either to keep him as a bogeyman or to prevent a Muslim backlash?

Could Bush and Blair not want to bring him to justice for fear of exposing matters which they wish to keep secret?

Is he being hidden and protected by Pakistan?

Is he in one of America's secret prisons already?

I do not pretend to know which, but what I do know is that he could not have evaded capture or death if America and Britain had seriously wished him dead. Who knows? Perhaps he has been given a new identity in America where it was reported that President Bush ordered the F.B.I. to end its surveillance of the Bin Laden family members living there, despite some of them being suspected of terrorist organisation connections.

We are all now constantly bombarded with warnings of terrorism but so secretive are those flying these kites and so untruthful are they in other areas of life, that we should all be very sceptical about everything they ask us to believe.

Secrecy and surveillance have long been bedfellows and Tony Blair and his Ministers have turned Britain into the most spied-upon nation on earth and in the more than nine years this has taken to build up, unsolved crimes have risen to fifty million.

In 2004, Richard Thomas, The United Kingdom's Independent Information Commissioner warned that the country was sleep-walking into a surveillance society.

Two years on, in November 2006, this Commissioner acknowledged that his warnings had gone unheeded and that the surveillance society is now already all around us.

Nor is it just the *four million spying cameras* which have destroyed the trust between citizens and Government. Professor Nigel Gilbert reached the same conclusion I have been warning about for years. Heading a Royal Academy of Engineering Study into surveillance, he confirmed that there will shortly be so much data on the internet that it will be possible to find out what individuals are doing anytime, any place.

No Government will/can ever guarantee to protect your data and just the latest confirmation of this was the 9th February 2007 admission by the UK Department of Work & Pensions, that *twenty-six thousand* of those on its database had their personal, sensitive records *sent out to the wrong people*. People who had no rights to it whatsoever and only time will tell how much of this misdirected information is used by the unknown recipients for mischievous purposes. Just more proof that no "official" records are ever either accurate or secure, whatever the storage method, but particularly when computers are involved.

So you see – if we want to live in a civilised society, where we trust everyone unless they betray our trust, we have more than just the muggers, burglars and murderers to discourage and re-educate.

368

We have those equally dangerous villains secretly working through every kind of bureaucracy to stick their Pinocchio-sized noses into every aspect of everyone's life. That is not the kind of country in which most people wish to live.

Britain, under the Blair Government, is by far the most intrusive country, with only Austria, Germany, Luxembourg, Liechtenstein, Andorra and Switzerland in Europe offering their citizens any worthwhile privacy protection. It is not as though Blair's 4.2 million spy cameras have done more than catch the occasional criminal and brought recorded crime down to low levels. They have, in fact, had almost no measurable effect and despite taking up a huge proportion of the Home Office's crime prevention budget, crime in Britain remains at an amazingly high level. A 2007 European Union Report confirmed my own long-held conclusions that the United Kingdom and the Republic of Ireland are Europe's highest crime countries by some considerable margin.

Note. Readers in America, Mexico and Canada should contact investigative journalist Jerome Corsi or Canadian Mary-Sue Haliburton at the Centre for Research on Globalisation. They have uncovered a secret bureaucracy working on an EU-type Federation and hoping to get their project well-advanced well before the publics of each country become aware of them. You have been warned. President Bush is involved and has already signed up without the authority of either the U.S. Congress or the electorate, thereby contravening the U.S. Constitution.

It is, I suppose, a statement of the obvious that most of the bad things which happen to us are first planned in secret. All the more reason to have more open Government, because whenever officials are able to operate behind closed doors, unfairness, corruption and other forms of criminality are all too often lurking in the wings.

Governments have, for years, been conniving to achieve the perfect system for controlling all of their citizens and monitoring your every movement and they have done this in secret and in most countries, in direct defiance of their authorised remit.

Already, airlines are having to submit 34 pieces of information about every passenger flying from Europe to America. The former have spinelessly caved in to this American-dominated International

Civil Aviation Organisation and the only debate now, is for how long this data can be kept? The EU wants this to be 3 years but America wants 40 years, but who is to know? Read into this what you will.

Next Election? Vote only for candidates promising to work towards abandoning secrecy, supporting privacy for the law-abiding and serious consequences for the law-breakers. See later chapters to find out more.

CHAPTER 17

CRIMES WITHOUT NAMES

My definition of crime is not the narrow one of simply breaking a written law. Such a diminished meaning, self-evidently, cannot be universally correct because what is often a crime in one country is not necessarily a crime in another and I would not have it otherwise.

It should be up to each community to set its own laws in order to address its own problems, which may be very different from those of other nations. There are though, some crimes which merit and should suffer universal disapproval, protest and retribution.

This chapter is less about statutes which already define what is unlawful, it is more about crimes mainly against humanity and what should be our wonderful planet. Some of these crimes have yet to be identified as such, but that is insufficient reason not to give them exposure in this book.

I offer some examples which hopefully will give you food for thought.

- Is it a crime that we spend hundreds of billions of dollars on space exploration *before* we have dealt with the urgent sufferings of the millions of poor people, many of whom live in appalling health and circumstances?

  To me, it is morally criminal that we further enrich the directors of already wealthy military arms companies (with taxpayers' funds), but allow millions of unfortunates to live without clean water and die from malnutrition, malaria, Dengue fever and numerous other diseases.

  On reflection, the word "unfortunates" gives the wrong impression, implying that they are the recipients of unavoidably difficult circumstances. The truth is that the poor of the world do not suffer misfortune to anything like the extent to which they suffer **neglect and corruption**. Neglect and corruption are not accidental – they are caused by people, usually fascist elites posing as respectable politicians or major corporation executives.

- Is it a crime that Governments and the Airline Industry conspire to deny or play down the serious health risks of flying? Our politicians grasp every possible excuse to take away more and more of our liberties under the pretext that their first duty is "to protect their citizens". Why then, do they do nothing to protect these same citizens from the damaging effects of flying in pressurised planes, at incredible altitudes, breathing re-cycled germ- and virus-laden air, in the most ridiculous and unhealthily cramped conditions?

The lid is kept tightly closed on the number of people who die or become ill as a direct result of flying in planes which Government-controlled Air Safety Bodies allow to be designed for maximum passenger numbers and minimum passenger health protection.

Certainly, there is a far greater threat to your life and health just being a passenger in today's planes than there is from terrorism. It may not be as dramatic as a terrorist act or a crash caused by systems failure, but it is even more dangerous for that very reason. Hiding or minimising the health risks of flying has resulted in people dying or suffering serious long-term health disability.

Just another crime without a name.

It is a crime that our politicians are too cowardly to impose serious taxes on flying and these should be on a per mile basis with a substantial minimum which would often be greater than the low-cost flight ticket. Serious damage has already been done and the world simply cannot afford willy nilly flying just to indulge the saddos looking for ever more places to ruin with what they call partying, holiday homes etc.

Nothing wrong with having fun or seeking new experiences, of course. I love both, but I acknowledge that it cannot be without limits because of the serious consequences. Sooner rather than later, restrictions will have to be imposed on flying if irreparable damage to our planet is to be avoided. Educating the public about the dangers of casual flying and confirming this by meaningful taxes to discourage it is, in my view, an urgent first measure which any responsible politician should promote or support. It is vastly more important than restricting smoking, because cigarette smoke poses no permanent threat to the environment. Though not yet named as such, hurtling our planet towards extinction, for humans and many other species, is, in my book, a crime of major magnitude and I expand upon this in my next chapter.

Slavery is another crime and one which, typically, our politicians generally ignore. Some were not only extremely vocal about the suffering of the people of Iraq, they decided to invade that country under the pretext of freeing them. Getting control of Iraq's oil via an installed puppet Government was, of course, just a happy coincidence and how fortunate that it also scuppered Saddam Hussein's plan to sell that country's oil in euros instead of US dollars.

Quite why Bush and Blair chose not to free the people of Zimbabwe, Burma, Sudan etc. I leave you to decide. Nor did I hear a word about slavery raised by President Bush when he visited India in March 2006.

I accuse many of the world's politicians of criminal neglect by not addressing the dreadful plight of those living in slavery. Compared with today, the number of slaves in the $17^{th}/18^{th}/19^{th}$ centuries was peanuts.

There are now 27 million people living in absolute slavery and *250 million pittance-pay wage slaves, mostly between age 6 and 12*, from which there is no escape without political intervention.

It is two hundred years since the tenacious and courageous William Wilberforce succeeded in outlawing slavery in Britain. This was after being mocked and reviled for more than a decade by his fellow Parliamentarians who were as sanguine about the loss of freedom as are many of today's Government Ministers in the House of Commons. Wilberforce was a man of very short stature, around 5'3", but compared with him, the likes of Tony Blair and Gordon Brown are the Pygmies.

What record does *your* President, Prime Minister or Foreign Secretary have on campaigning to free today's millions of slaves?

Answers please on the back of a postage stamp.

- Is it a crime that America and Britain used depleted uranium shells, bombs and missiles in Kuwait, Iraq, Afghanistan, Croatia and elsewhere causing thousands to die, not only from direct assault, but from the inevitable long-term consequences of serious exposure to radiation?

- Is it a crime that power-crazed politicians authorised the use of these disgusting weapons without a care, not only for the civilians caught up in war, but not even for the welfare of their own troops, who were kept in ignorance of what they were handling or how they were being ordered to participate in rendering the environment dangerous for many generations

- Is it a crime that Defence Secretaries/Ministers etc. with the approval of George Bush, Bill Clinton, Tony Blair & co. have conspired to deny or belittle the terrible effects caused by using depleted uranium munitions? Included in these are leukaemia, cancer, infected soil and very long-term pollution of water courses. Thousands of men, women and children are today suffering pain, despair and the breakdown of their immune systems. Some are passing symptoms onto subsequent generations and sadly, many have already died.

I say, to those denying Gulf War Syndrome – a term which can justifiably be used for other war theatres – Are *you* prepared to accept long-term exposure to these depleted uranium materials yourself? Unless you are, you have absolutely no right to deny the problem or to deny your victims, whatever their nationality, such help with their suffering as can possibly be provided.

- Is it a crime, that more than 4 years after the invasion of Iraq, and having sequestered 30 billion dollars of Iraq's oil money for reconstruction, there are now thousands of Iraqis suffering and dying because their hospitals are being starved of equipment and medicines which were available when Saddam Hussein was in power?

- Is it a crime that any Government can permit the sale of disgustingly violent computer *games* – not just to our kids, but for anyone? It undoubtedly is.

Although there *may* not (yet) be empirical evidence linking specific games to particular crimes, I have not the slightest hesitation in supporting Giselle Pakeerah's campaign to have these hideous apologies for entertainment banned.

Her lovely, caring son – 14 year old Stefan – was attacked with a knife and a claw hammer in a seemingly motiveless murder by his supposed 17 year old "friend" Warren Leblanc who inflicted 60 wounds on Stefan. Leblanc owned, and was believed to have been playing, the rated 18 video game *Manhunt* "all week" prior to killing Stefan. I have not seen this video nasty because there is a limit to what I am prepared to do in my crime research, but the police say *Manhunt* is gratuitously gory. In this 'game', the player takes on the role of a convicted murderer, earning points (rewards) for killing people. Machetes, a garrotte and shards of glass are, I understand, just some of the available weapons and the game even portrays the victims' agonies, including – sickeningly - the breath of a victim inside a plastic bag as he was dying of suffocation.

It is a major crime for any Government to be side-lined by those producing this foul stuff into allowing it with age-to-buy or age-to-view limits. If it is available, there is nothing which can prevent these dangerous "games" falling into the wrong hands. Our politicians know this and it is a crime that they are too craven to stop this filthy trade which can do no good to anyone playing such violent garbage and it can seriously affect the mental states of some. Is this really what we want vulnerable youngsters to be doing with their lives.

Crime is crime and this book is about opening eyes and opening minds and it is not enough to concentrate on exceeding speed limits if we ignore the massively greater crimes authorised or committed by Governments.

The U.S.A. Patriot Act is a crime, in it's own right, both legally and morally. It was rushed and forced through following 9/11 in typical opportunist manner by George Bush. Quite how it can be "patriotic" to trash your own citizens' freedoms, Constitution and Bill of Rights beggars belief, but America's cowardly politicians in both the U.S. Senate and Congress either buckled under their Dictator's bullying or sucked up to him in the expectation of future favours. All but a handful conveniently "forgot" that they had sworn an oath to uphold the Constitution, which certainly precluded secret surveillance of any citizen by any means, without just and specific cause being authorised by the judiciary.

Even President Lincoln was found guilty by the U.S. Supreme Court of violating the Constitution when he suspended habeas corpus in the Civil War and subjected his political opponents to unlawful trial by military tribunals.

Unlike today's puppet judges, the Supreme Court, in Lincoln's day, was comprised of honourable men – real patriots – and they told President Lincoln in no uncertain terms that he had exceeded his authority. Quote – "The Constitution of the United States is the law for rulers and people, equally in war and in peace and covers with the shield of its protection all classes of men, at all times and under all circumstances". Prophetically, the Court also recognised and warned that the nation "has no right to expect that it will always have wise and humane rulers sincerely attached to the principles of the Constitution". How right they were.

Wake up America. You are walking blindly into Dictatorship. By allowing *your* Constitution to be salami-sliced, you already live in a Police State in which numerous Government entities can and do maim, kill and steal from their citizens, sometimes by mistake, more often using bully-boy tactics in the prosecution of minor or even accidental infringements of unbelievably oppressive and nit-picking regulations.

Perhaps tens of millions (of the 350 million) Americans already understand the dangers, but the rest, as in Hitler's Germany and Stalin's Russia, prefer to look the other way. *That* is one of the greatest crimes of all which, if allowed to continue, will turn America into just another third rate country with zip freedom. Don't say you were not warned.

The deceit of disguised taxes – and the astronomical amounts of money spent (wasted) on collecting and accounting for them - is certainly one of the major unnamed crimes. These stealth taxes are simply theft. They understandably create huge resentment amongst the victim populations who suffer them and the assertion that some of them may be technically legal does not make these hidden taxes any less of a crime. It ill behoves politicians to be lecturing others about stealing, whilst simultaneously being clearly addicted to the same deplorable practice themselves.

Transparent flat taxes combined with Value Added Taxes are the answer. Properly constructed, it is well-demonstrated that they can generate a larger pot of revenue for Governments at significantly lower cost to taxpayers, be they companies or individuals.

Only the vested interests of bureaucracy are preventing some countries from enjoying the huge benefits of simplified tax regimes.

- Max Valentina, German U-boat commander in WW1, sank the first passenger vessel R.M.S. Falaba without warning. He went on to sink many other merchant ships, as well as Royal Navy vessels and after the war, he was put on trial for the random slaughter of civilians (ships' passengers)

Was he guilty of committing crimes?

Absolutely yes.

Unfortunately, he was acquitted, which was not only a serious miscarriage of justice, it lead, from that day onwards, to "open season" by the military against innocent citizens being declared.

Had Commander Valentina been found guilty, millions of lives would subsequently not have been forfeited. U-boats and allied submarines would, or should have restricted their activities to attacking military targets. The random killing of civilians, euphemistically referred to now as collateral damage, would have remained, as it should have, a dishonourable practice.

There would have been no London Blitz.

No fire-balling of Dresden.

No Hiroshima or Nagasaki.

No napalming of entire villages in Vietnam.

No massacre of the Moslems by the Serbs in Bosnia.

No killing of hundreds of thousands of civilians in Iraq.

These all took place because the indiscriminate killing of civilians in time of war has not been unconditionally condemned by the international community as a crime. Bloody lawyers again.

Attempting to excuse the murder of civilians in order to accomplish supposed military or political advantage should not be acceptable in any society claiming to be civilised, whether named or not named as a crime.

- Is it a crime that Drugs Manufacturing Corporations are permitted by politicians to bribe healthy people to be initial trial-users of their unproven drugs?

Accepting that all new drugs must, at some point, be tested on humans for a first time, I have (as usual) a better solution.

All first trials should be carried out on those individuals whose bank balances or reputations stand to gain most when (if) the drug(s) in question prove safe and efficacious. This used not to be rare practice amongst research scientists many moons ago, but today's drug manufacturers have conveniently slid out of such responsibility.

The Directors and scientists of the Corporations seeking to profit from any drug should be required to submit themselves to supervised trials of their products over a period of time. Should they be unwilling to do what they are bribing others to do, consent for their drug(s)' further use should be denied. They may not, of course, be suffering the particular condition targeted by their proposed drug but it would seem sensible as a first step to ascertain what, if any, side effects may be suffered by volunteers.

Such a system would not only be fair, it would more greatly concentrate the minds of the drugs Corporations on safety and would also enhance their standing with the public.

My belief is that it is immoral for anyone to invite others to take risks with an unproven drug which they are unwilling to test themselves.

Most, probably all drug companies have Executives and researchers who travel globally, including to countries where malaria and other dangerous diseases are a problem and it is a crime that so little has been achieved in their eradication.

A major reason for this is the disgraceful and criminal way in which the R.B.M. (Roll Back Malaria) programme, the United Nations, the Global Fund to Fight *Aids*, *TB* and *Malaria*, *U.S. Aids* and the World Bank and the United Nations have misspent allocated funds.

These puffed-up Bodies have spent 90% of budgets on talk shops, consultants, so-called technical advisers and ridiculous Public Relations campaigns. Only 10% of funds have been spent on the direct measures which actually save lives, such as education, mosquito-netting, insecticide spraying and drugs. Cynically, just sufficient of these serious anti-malaria tools are available to create TV P.R. opportunities, but they are just a drop in the ocean in tackling disease which, after years of yak, yak, yakking, are still rising.

Forget "halving malaria by 2010", the supposed aim of the R.B.M. Consortium because no-one – and I mean no-one – can ever know if this has been achieved because there are no reliable figures against which the "halving" forecast can be measured. Today (January 2007), the published numbers of deaths from malaria – or survivals – are nothing but the wildest guesses. This of course is just the sort of vagueness which the bureaucrats love because it allows them to make false claims based upon completely fictitious numbers. Yet another crime without a name.

Bureaucrats of course, are experts at pretending to solve the world's problems, but how strange that they choose to fly around the world just to talk about them. This they could do just as effectively via video-conferencing instead of criminally adding to the world's pollution and wasting their taxpayers' monies flying to exotic places, staying in luxury accommodation and generally living like rich tourists.

In November 2006, 60/70 European Members of Parliament jetted off to meet other world parasites to talk about EU trade policies, water shortages and aid. Quite why these problems are still with us when these same people have been pontificating about them for years is not clear. Nor is the reason for holding this cosy get-together in exotic Barbados with delegates staying at the exclusive Colony Club, described as a perfect venue for wealthy honeymooners, or hotels such as the Amarylis Beach, Turtle Beach or Tamarind Cove – not exactly places to learn about real poverty and water shortages first hand, particularly when some of the socialising was scheduled to take place on a luxury 30-metre floating entertainment palace.

The assembled group, the African Caribbean Pacific EU had no shortage of water, having a 20-metre water slide on hand, which must have helped their purpose, which was to chat about democracy, Human Rights and trade. The ACPEU Body has no executive authority of course, which is both a good thing and a bad thing. Good, because having such no-hopers actually able to turn their chatter into practical measures would be a disaster. Bad, because the money wasted on such nefarious projects by people unable to actually put proposals into effect could and should have been put to far better use. Who was Co-Chair of this luxury living group? None other than that bureaucracy-addicted M.E.P. Glenys Kinnock, wife of the Welsh windbag Neil Kinnock, failed UK Labour Leader and ex-EU Commissioner who also failed to reduce EU corruption – the job for which he was handsomely paid.

That we have such people living and working in luxury whilst more than half of the world's population still has no access to electricity is, in my view, a crime, albeit one which has avoided the Statute Books and is not, therefore, so readily identifiable. Unless we deal with such unnamed crimes simultaneously with the more conventional ones, we will not convince enough of our populations to stay on the straight and narrow.

Is it criminal that the European Parliament steals money from taxpayers to continue the farcical musical chairs of switching the running of its affairs from Brussels to Strasbourg several times a year? Damn right it is.

For those of you not aware, twelve times every year, all these crazy bureaucrats pack up their offices, lock, stock and barrel, load them into removal trucks and ship them off from Brussels, Belgium to Strasbourg, France. A few days later, they and the employees reverse the process. More accurately we, as taxpayers, pay others to do the actual work and no-one should be surprised if there are a few brown envelopes involved in giving out the profitable logistics contracts involved. This means paying for two hugely-expensive, large and luxurious office facilities in high-cost cities hundreds of kilometres apart. At any one time, one set of offices remains essentially unused.

A group of M.E.P.s headed by Sweden's Cecilia Malmstrom, has collected more than a million signatures via their on-line campaign **www.oneseat.eu** in an attempt to end this lunacy and there is no doubt in my mind that the electorates of most countries would vote overwhelmingly to end this massive waste of taxpayers money and M.E.P.s' and their staff's time. The reason this out-dated nonsense continues is that nothing can be changed without the consent of all Member States and France, being one of those States, is not interested in saving taxpayers' funds.

Government debt can and usually is a terrible no-name crime inflicted on all citizens in countries which are too weak to balance their budgets. The monies borrowed are rarely for sensible purposes, they are almost always used to finance unnecessary cancerous bureaucracies which demand ever more money; wars which literally just set fire to billions of dollars, pounds, euros etc. No other word can better describe America's creation of debt than criminal. Profligate and stupid do not do justice to the scale of irresponsibility of George

Bush's six-year reign in the White House. America's current account losses in 2006 were continuing to *increase* at the mid-boggling rate of *seventy million dollars every hour*.

This is so alarming and is such a criminal theft of its own citizens' and foreigners' funds, that I must repeat – America is spending, every hour of every day of every week, year in year out – seventy million dollars which it does not have. Seventy million dollars which, every hour, it borrows, mainly from foreigners.

It is a crime for anyone to borrow money with the intention of never paying it back in currency of equal value, yet this is a scam which America has somehow managed to pull off for many years. It sells treasuries and bonds in the full knowledge that it will regularly print millions more dollar bills and allow its currency to de-value against those from whom it has borrowed. This appears to be a crime without a name but in fact, it is called theft.

American Governments and George Bush's in particular, have been skilful in keeping its true debt level from the world at large, but even they have had to fess up to owing an alarming eight to nine trillion dollars, plus future commitments of tens of trillions for unfunded, promised, social programmes. Smart analysts, such as Outstanding Investments, calculate the Dis-United States of America's debt to be more than seventy-six trillion dollars.

Do they intend paying their debts? Well, put it this way. If they paid back a dollar every second of every minute of every hour of every day of every week of every month of every year, it would take them 272,523 years to repay (without interest) the 8/9 trillion they are admitting to and between 2 and 3 million years to repay their true debt.

Readers can work out for themselves how many dollars per second America would have to pay in order to repay their debts by the end of this century. This will simply confirm that the land of the free is actually the land of the free-loaders.

Not many have yet named this crime, but borrowing without the intention or means of paying off your debts is fraud, pure and simple.

So what happens now? The money cannot be paid back unless the U.S. dollar is massively devalued; American citizens even more highly taxed; and Government expenditure slashed by more than 70%.

A hundred years ago, Americans made the mistake of not calling its Government to account for incurring a debt of two billion dollars – the very thin end of a very thick wedge. At that time, the total Government tax take was less than 10%, but even though this had increased to more than 40% by 2005, plus a substantial percentage conforming with and accounting for business and personal taxes, this has still failed completely to pay for America's huge extravagances. This is, in fact, the world's largest ever fraud amounting to a staggering tens of trillions of dollars – a fraud committed against foreigners, against Americans and depressingly, Americans who have yet to be born, because the moment they come into the world, they inherit a huge burden of debt and before too long, the American State and its numerous tentacles will be taking more than $70 for every $100 of earnings.

I call that criminal.

Millions of people have used the Belgian Company, SWIFT, to transfer money electronically from one account to another.

In its usual belligerent manner, American Intelligence demanded that SWIFT hand such data over to them. Cravenly, the Belgian company did the bully boys' bidding and passed over data which they were supposed to be processing in confidence. Users' names, addresses, account numbers, bank addresses and amounts of money transferred say from Germany to Spain, are still meekly being given to the Americans without any satisfactory protection as to whose hands it will pass through, or what use or misuse to which it may be put.

This is criminal. The European banks have their own money-laundering protections and it is criminal of both American Intelligence and SWIFT to subvert these and put innocent bank customers at risk of having information about themselves being illegally used to their serious disadvantage.

Crimes against the vulnerable elderly seem to be on the increase by late 2006, but much of this is based on second or third-hand accounts of paid carers abusing their charges. Occasionally though, hard evidence does surface, as in the case of a disgraceful record of neglect and abuse at a Dublin, Ireland nursing home, Leas Cross.

382

Professor Des O'Neill, a specialist in geriatrics, was commissioned to enquire into allegations and concluded that there was institutionalised abuse at Leas Cross and that the care was substandard. The Government and the Area Health Authority were roundly condemned for inspection failures which resulted in patients suffering excruciatingly painful pressure sores, inadequate staffing and poor training. Typically though, the Health Service Executive, whose oversight allowed the abuses, wriggled off the hook, as did the actual abusers.

That old and infirm patients – your mammy or granddad perhaps, or you one day, maybe – can be treated so cruelly and disrespectfully behind closed door is, itself, a disgrace, but of equal concern is the lack of serious consequences, even when evidence does emerge, as in the case of Leas Cross. That there was an official enquiry which failed to roll management heads or result in prosecutions of the cruel incompetents was surely criminal.

Two related un-named crimes are those connected with excess population and rape of the environment, which politicians have permitted to progress without challenge for generations. They are not on the statute books for the simple reason that no-one has assessed the damage they cause or the benefits of addressing them. So serious are they though, that they deserve a revealing chapter of their own, which follows.

CHAPTER 18

ENVIRONMENT – THE CRIMINAL DAMAGE

I know of no Government getting serious, by the end of 2006, about the protection of even their own environments, let alone that of the whole world.

I do know plenty though who very recently have been spewing out nonsense about problems which they should have been addressing 10, 20, 30 years ago.

Right now, Governments continue to be conniving with big business to pretend they are going to deal with the world's environmental difficulties by restricting everyone's attention to the question of CO_2 emissions.

Without question, CO_2 emissions pose a grave danger to the survival of mankind, but they are but a small part of the equation and it is criminal that our dishonest politicians are running major public relations campaigns on this issue alone, whilst ignoring more serious threats. These campaigns, including Kyoto, (a) put far too much emphasis on CO_2 emissions, to the exclusion of other dangers and (b) have incredibly low and distant targets even for the reduction of CO_2.

Carbon trading proposals are nothing more than a sham – just smoke and mirrors designed by bureaucrats to mislead the public into thinking that it is a substitute for real and urgent reductions. On the CO_2 front, every day when emissions are not reduced significantly is a further nail in mankind's coffin.

Kyoto's targeted 8% reduction by 2012 is ample demonstration of the lack of serious concern or intent because such a limited slow-down will not prevent the disastrous effects of global warming. Northing short of a 15% reduction by 2012 and 90% reduction by 2050 will prevent a catastrophic tipping of earth's finely-balanced ecosystems.

Anyone (including politicians) who has studied the science knows this only too well and it is indicative of their cowardly short-termism that they refuse to set the necessary targets. Notice how Tony Blair, Gordon Brown & co. studiously *avoid setting annual targets* for CO_2 emissions or other pollutants because these would make them accountable in the near future, something which makes them very uncomfortable.

You should put no trust in politicians who are not prepared to set annual targets which, if not met, would show their proposals to have been ineffective and misconceived. *Only annual targets*, with serious consequences for failure, have any hope of success and only well-publicised annual targets will concentrate the minds of all concerned.

America, for starters, should have a long-term aim of reducing its massive use of the world's total energy from its current 22% closer to the 4% appropriate to its population size and it should do this starting now – 2007. By the end of 2007, its share of global energy use should drop to 21%. For each of years 2008 to 2012 it should drop by a further 2% each year, which will still leave the U.S.'s 4% of world population using 11% of global energy. Thereafter, it may only be possible to effect very small reductions in energy use on an annual basis.

Even the laggards at the European Commission had, by the end of 2006, begun to realise the weaknesses in the Emissions Trading Scheme, such as the crazy decision not to include the hugely-damaging emissions of the Airline Industry. EU Environment Commissioner Stavros Dimas recognises a few of these problems but has no plans to take early counter-measures.

I will come to my own practical measures for the better protection of the environment later in the chapter. For the moment, I will look at where we are now, early in 2007.

Many of us have been warning our various Governments about environmental damage for many years but criminally, too many politicians have used what they claim was the lack of empirical evidence to stall year on year. It seems that they have neither common sense nor eyes to see or noses with which to smell.

Mankind has killed off thousands of species of flora and fauna; seriously polluted the air, soil, rivers, lakes and seas; produced masses of unnecessary waste; depleted both finite and potentially renewable resources; and created millions of unsanitary slum dwellings – all without any serious intervention by those paid to run our affairs and those who never stop pontificating about how their first priority is to protect their citizens. Bit of a credibility gap there then.

They lecture us to eat more fish, but if we all heeded their advice, there would be no fish left to eat. Fish farms have been encouraged, but so carelessly-controlled have these been that they have become a danger themselves. In many locations, they have wiped out 95% of the young wild salmon making their way out to sea. America's National Academy of Sciences has warned that some farmed salmon are host to harmful levels of cancer-causing toxins.

Ireland once had a healthy and thriving wild salmon/trout fishing tourist industry but no longer. The Independent Salmon Group's science shows clearly that pollution, habitat interference, declining water quality and an excess of driftnet fishing have decimated Ireland's fish stocks by 70% and wiped out most of the associated tourist income. Many scientists believe that only drastic measures can prevent the almost complete wipe-out of the world's fish stocks within just a few decades, but our politicians still co-operate with the vested interests who are now virtually hoovering up our waters.

The International Council for the Exploration of the Sea saw its October 2006 Report recommending a moratorium on fishing the North Sea for Cod ignored by the politicians who cravenly caved in to threats from the owners of huge trawlers using practices which are guaranteed to prevent the healthy recovery of stocks. Is such wanton abuse of our environment a crime? It certainly is.

For years we have witnessed the annual destruction of more than 150 million hectares of agricultural land, the conversion of another 6 million hectares into desert and the loss of 20 billion tons of valuable top soil. We have seen farmers encouraged to use manmade pesticides and herbicides, resulting in the serious pollution of water courses and in some areas, a reduction of top soil depth from 40 to below 5 centimetres. Hardly surprisingly, Lord Martin Rees, Astronomer Royal and author of 'Our Final Century' puts humans' chances of surviving at only 50-50. He is an optimist.

Unless we effect some very serious changes, starting today, I believe that our abuse of the environment will result in a massive increase in crime as factions increasingly steal or fight for diminishing resources. Without the implementation of drastic measures beginning 2007, it will be surprising if a billion people survive the 21st century. For the long-term future of mankind, that would actually be a good thing.

Remember that 70 years ago we discovered 10 billion barrels of oil but used only 1.5 billion barrels of it, leaving a surplus for future use. 45 years later, discovery peaked at 48 billion barrels, of which only 12 billion were used, leaving a surplus of 36 billion for the future. By 1988 things were getting dodgy, but still our Governments stuck their heads in the sand as consumption and new discoveries were equal at 23 billion barrels. "Where's the problem?" they asked. Our politicians were warned of the dangers at every stage but true to form, they failed to address the facts, so by 2005, less than 6 billion new barrels of oil were discovered but we consumed 30 billion barrels, eating into declining reserves by a frightening 24 billion barrels in one year. In only one year since 1988 did we consume less oil than we discovered and apart from that, we have been consuming our reserves and new discoveries at an alarming rate. There may well be some small relief via shale oil sands, mainly in Canada, but these will be overwhelmed as China and India get seriously into car ownership.

Make no mistake, we are running out of oil. That is why Tony Blair and George Bush invaded Iraq and are cosying up to other Middle East countries. Nor are there any viable alternatives to oil because all of these are so energy-hungry in their production as to render them pointless for a fast-expanding vehicle market. The principle answer to this and other environmental problems will be explained later in the chapter.

Scientists, the Oil Industry, academics, Governments and the media pontificate ad nauseum about *when* the world will run out of oil. What a fruitless waste of time and energy. No-one can *know* when oil discoveries will be no more than an inconsequential trickle and I have certainly seen credible research suggesting years from 2030 to 2050, dependent upon who has guessed best about a large range of variables.

I have news for all of these experts - *it doesn't matter* precisely when we run out of oil because we *are* going to run out. What we should be doing is buying some time by reducing our consumption now and concentrating far more on researching alternative energy sources and educating people to the reality that a century of criminal profligacy is drawing to a close. Don't get me wrong, I enjoyed the ride as much as anyone, but as I travelled the world I became appalled at the remorseless damage so-called civilisation has inflicted on its beauties and most of its population. Now its payback time.

Another unpalatable truth is that we will not avoid serious environmental damage unless we ***massively reduce flying, starting now***. Off-setting/carbon trading are worthless – no better than putting a sticking plaster onto a multi-fractured skull. We now have irrefutable evidence that flying is a huge pollutant, not only due to its high contributions to destroying the ozone layer and global warming, but on the damaging particles spread around the earth's surface from engine exhausts. Unless we reduce flying down to 15 to 20% of current levels, then we will not even begin to restore our world to good health. This, of course, means a huge change in our lifestyles, but if we fail to grasp the nettle, how can we expect the billions in China and India, who cannot yet afford to fly, to forego the same extravagances which we have permitted ourselves for decades.

Tony Blair should stop using the argument that Britain or any other country would be wasting its time by acting in isolation. Whilst it is true that no single nation can solve all of the world's environmental problems, every little helps and it is timely to set an example if one is serious about the problems – and not just spouting about them, as Britain's Prime Minister has been doing for years.

Kyoto's and other world conferences will never reverse or even contain environmental damage, especially if delegates are flying to different venues around the plant - like the UK's Department of the Environment, Food and Rural Affairs, which is supposed to be leading Britain's climate change programme, but has increased its own expenditure on flying 5-fold within one year.

According to Oxford University's Environmental Change Institute Report 17 October 2006, it is absolutely vital that air travel is cut down significantly and with 20% of all flights worldwide being to or from the UK, Britain is the number one place to start this reduction. The party's over, dear reader and there will be no evading that very uncomfortable fact.

It really makes no sense whatsoever to be flying plane-loads of yobs from London or Dublin to Budapest or Ibiza just to be vomiting and urinating in a different place. That this is made possible by ridiculously low air fares is frankly crazy and because fuel consumption is greatest at take-off and landing, I think there should be a take-off tax equivalent to between £30 and £60 ***per seat capacity*** whether each seat is occupied or not.

In addition, there should be a serious tax on all aviation fuel, which will ensure that the super-rich flying the world in their private jets cannot disproportionately pollute the environment. Right now, we have planes jetting hither and thither, often for trivial reasons and with only one or a handful of passengers, when almost the same amount of fuel would have transported between 20 and more than 100 people. Currently, the tax on car fuel is too high in countries such as Britain, whilst that on aviation fuel is ridiculously low. The former should be reduced a little and the latter increased a lot.

I make such recommendation with great sadness because by inclination, I am a believer is allowing the market to decide. I am philosophically opposed to most taxes and I attach considerable importance to freedom. However, my definition of freedom is that it should not harm others and flying does this in several ways.

Reversing more than a century's profligacy and environmental damage is vital if civilisation is not to deteriorate even further. It is going to be an extremely difficult, uphill task and we are all going to have to ditch many of our long-established comfortable but hugely wasteful practices – starting right now.

We must, of course, make sure that aviation taxes go towards subsidising more environmentally friendly energy production systems and research for alternative sources. They absolutely must not be scooped up into general treasury maws. Expect howls of protest from O'Leary, Branson & co., but we cannot prevent environmental disaster without impacting upon those who have profited from contributing to poisoning our planet.

This will pretty well stop planes flying around half empty because the airlines will be paying for all seats, empty or occupied. At the moment, people are booking peanut-price tickets and just not bothering to turn up. Flying has to become much more costly, far less frequent and it must be taxed sufficiently highly to contribute to the development of less-damaging alternative energy projects.

Millions of business flights are already undertaken unnecessarily, including many by bureaucrats who look for any excuse to arrange conferences and meetings in desirable locations around the world. These jollies all need a serious level of axing and most of the other business flights can now be avoided – thanks to *CISCO*.

Hypocrisy is every evident in Irish politics and the CO^2 footprints of its Government Ministers are a disgrace by any standards.

Fifteen of them in 2006, despite lecturing everyone else on the subject, managed to produce almost a thousand tons of the damaging stuff just via their use of State cars, commercial flights, private jets and helicopters. That is 3½ times the national average of 16.8 tons which itself is disgracefully high.

The Ministers pretend that their profligate misuse of energy is to fit their briefs but of course, these are written by Government and include numerous engagements which are quite unnecessary. Much of their travelling has little to do with managing the nation's affairs but a lot to do with their permanent electioneering and their wish to keep high personal profiles.

Disgracefully, Taoiseach Bertie Ahern spewed out ten times the national average of CO^2 using jets and helicopters in the most cavalier fashion, which demonstrates his complete lack of concern for the environmental consequences.

How on earth do such Ministers think Ireland is ever going to convince their population that major pollution reduction should be right at the top of every country's Agenda? Setting the worse possible example, Dirty Bertie causes major pollution by his incredibly wasteful use of the two Government jets, forcing them into numerous unnecessary take-offs and landings simply because he prefers to use Dublin airport, 10 miles from the city, rather than Baldonnell airport where the Government jets are based – also 10 miles from the city. Many of these ridiculous and expensive close-to-home journeys can and should be taken by car in around half an hour but so important is this pathetic man that he has to have taxpayers' jets using disproportionately high amounts of fuel at by far their least area of fuel efficiency - taking off and landing.

No-one who uses Gulfstream jets to fly just a few miles can have the vaguest idea about the dangers of environmental damage, but what can one expect from a man who cost his taxpayers more than €160,000 on a St. Patrick's day jaunt by jet from Baldonnel to Dublin to Winnipeg to San Jose to Washington to Dublin to Baldonnel. Time to wake up Ireland. You are already amongst the worst of the European dirty polluters, despite having little heavy manufacturing and your politicians are setting the course for gaining the top spot.

CISCO to the rescue

The introduction, in October 2006, of CISCO's mega video conferencing system, *Telepresence*, is a major advance in internet-based video, bringing a facility which has been around for years to a completely new level. Doubtless others will join what is likely to be a hugely-growing market and drive down costs even further.

I would like to see the emergence of *Video Conferencing Centres* available for small companies and Government Departments who cannot justify the cost of installing such high-end facilities in-house. Sorry ladies – no more shopping sprees in Dubai or Rodeo Drive. Sorry guys – no more high-class hookers in Budapest or Bangkok, but we are talking here about the avoidance of some disastrous outcomes and reducing flying significantly is just one of many measures which must be taken if we are to have any hope of saving our seriously neglected environment.

Interestingly, HSBC, which was London's first bank claiming to be carbon neutral, believes it can reduce its business flying by almost 70% and that video conferencing will have a significant role to play in achieving this.

Unless we acknowledge past mistakes, I forecast that we will surely make ones of similar or worse magnitude in the future. "Mistakes", in fact, is not really the appropriate word to describe the criminal negligence of those responsible.

Take polychlorinated biphenyls (PCBs) for example. These manmade chemicals were developed by supposedly clever researchers; more clever people found ever more uses for them, sticking them into a whole range of everyday products including packaging, a range of lubricants, insulators, paints, pesticides and preservatives to name but a few – all without a whimper from either the regulatory Bodies concerned or the thousands of politicians supposedly caring for their citizens during the several decades when PCBs were so freely used.

Unfortunately – unfortunately, in order to kow-tow to big business, none of the very clever people involved bothered to ask if PCBs were safe and fit for purpose. Typically, it was not until it became clear that PCBs were damaging to human endocrine systems did alarm bells sound loud enough to wake up those who had been caught asleep on guard. By then, of course, it was far too late. In excess of three billion pounds weight had been produced and used and today they are ubiquitous. Nowhere is now free from PCBs – not either pole, not our rivers, lakes or seas, not any plant or animal species. Shrimps, plankton, whales, human beings, polar bears and algae all now carry some level of these dangerous manmade chemicals with the highest levels being found in remote areas which had never used these products directly. Too late, our scientists and medical researchers realised that PCBs are responsible for serious damage to the immune system, dreadful birth defects, deformed sexual organs and a range of cancers, the causes of which all too frequently go misdiagnosed. Already they have contributed to crime by causing brain damage, decreased intelligence, the inability to handle stress and attention deficit disorder.

My point being – treat the advice and claims of all experts with considerable suspicion and the cleverer the supposed experts, the greater should be your scrutiny of their motives.

As at the end of 2006, the battle is still going on about the proposal to create **REACH** in Europe – **REACH** being a Body for the Registration, Evaluation and Authorisation of Chemicals. Already diluted because of joint pressure from some politicians and monster chemical companies, REACH seems in danger of either being stillborn or so neutered as to be an ineffective waste of taxpayers' funds. The chemical giants seem already to have protected 80% of dangerous substances from scrutiny, including some known to damage hormones and cause birth defects, liver and kidney damage and cancer.

Despite protests from the medical profession, Greenpeace and even responsible companies such as Marks & Spencer, Addidas and Nokia, it looks like the anti-control lobbyists have won the day. Disgracefully it has taken eight years of negotiations even to get **REACH** close to "possible" launch in 2007, albeit in pretty toothless form. It would not then be in full flow until 2018, which is a nonsense. **REACH** should either be given maximum freedom to protect the environment – and quickly – or it should be aborted now, before it starts gobbling up money to no measurable benefit.

Waste has also become a huge problem and Stavros Dimas, the EU Environment Commissioner acknowledges that the Ivory Coast deaths caused by the dumping of toxic waste by a Greek-owned, Dutch-chartered vessel is just the tip of the iceberg, with Africa being used as a dumping ground by wealthier countries. This is criminal both in respect of the deaths caused and the cavalier attitude to the protection of the environment. According to the EU, 51% of waste shipments in 2005 were found to have been illegal, but they are coming up against serious resistance in trying to criminalise those responsible.

Politicians and bureaucrats in Malta have, for years, ignored the warnings about what they have allowed to become what is possibly the world's largest and most dangerous rubbish tip. There is a very real risk that at some point, the methane gas pockets will ignite in one almighty explosion which, on such an over-crowded small island, would be catastrophic. As a matter or urgency, the Maltese politicians and bureaucrats should take the measures necessary to rid their island of this danger and if they fail, they should face criminal charges.

In his speech on 25th September 2006 to the UK Labour Party Conference, Gordon Brown bizarrely said that the Labour Party does not want our children to say that it knew what was needed to protect the environment but did not have the will to do it.

What gall. Our children and many generations beyond, absolutely can accuse today's and yesterday's politicians of all parties of outrageous short-termism and allowing massive, worldwide pollution and the reckless use of irreplaceable resources. Come off it Mr. Brown. Scientists have been issuing dire warnings about environmental damage for decades and those of us with little more than common sense could see the evidence with our own eyes.

Only fools and mountebanks claimed that without empirical proof, nothing should be done, but that has been the delaying tactic which our politicians have employed because they have been too embedded with big business and too afraid to tell their citizens the uncomfortable truths about environmental damage.

On the 27th September 2006, Richard Branson claimed that until 12/18 months previously, he did not know about the seriousness of environmental damage. Really?

There are none so blind as those who do not wish to see.

Perhaps Mr. Branson has been too busy with his business dealings to look up to the sky on a clear day. Try it Richard. You will often see a lot of nasty white stuff being excreted by your flying toys.

The Taboo Subject

One problem above all others is responsible for just about *all* of the manmade damage to the environment. Had this one problem been acknowledged and tackled a century ago, we should now still, in 2007, have more than three hundred years of oil-based motoring and flying ahead of us. That is more than two hundred years in which to develop alternatives to getting our energy from fossil fuels. It is criminal that Governments have failed us all by being too cowardly to address this problem at any time in the past hundred years. Had they done so, we would now suffer millions of fewer crimes every year.

Had this single taboo subject not been so studiously and foolishly ignored for generations, we would now have far fewer prisons and there would be no people anywhere in the world living in poverty or unsanitary circumstances.

Had our political representatives tackled this problem head-on, instead of caving in to, or conspiring with, big business, we would not now be suffering global warming.

Dealing sensibly with this one problem area would have left us with unpolluted air, rivers, lakes and oceans.

It would have ensured that fish, fruits and other foods would always be in plentiful supply.

I am not unique, of course, in identifying this single most important factor in our known universe. Others have tried, over the years, to point out the wisdom of dealing with this issue and exposing it to scrutiny and debate. Ignoring them has brought our world to a pathetic state of disrepair, criminality, gridlock and squalor for all but a fortunate few, but even the elites will find it increasingly difficult to escape the consequences of avoiding just this one taboo topic. Perhaps this is cause for optimism, because when the rich discover that their money cannot buy them protection from rampaging criminal gangs, or buy them clean air and water, something may be done.

I am talking about the *grossly excessive population* which we suffer in the 21ˢᵗ century and started to suffer in the 19ᵗʰ century.

Earth would be a beautiful place for around one billion people to live in harmony with each other and with nature. It currently exceeds six billion and is forecast to reach an obscene nine billion.

This is the single most important reason for almost all of the world's problems and it seems, yet again, that as with prison places and percentage income increases, our politicians and economists simply cannot do basic arithmetic.

Clearly, had we kept our population at one billion, our oil and other finite resources would have lasted 4, 5, 6 or 10 times longer.

Fish stocks would never have been under threat.

Pollution and waste would have been easily manageable.

Global warming due to CO_2 emissions would never have happened.

Okay, okay, okay. We didn't take the sensible route a hundred years ago; what's done is done; 20-20 hindsight; blah, blah, blah. Such comments are fine. They are perfectly valid, particularly if they come from today's youngsters. However, if we are to move forward now, we must understand that there was never any justification in **not** containing population growth and we must realise that the same categories of people who promoted population increases a century ago are still around today in 2007.

So yes – we are where we are, but that is no reason to keep making the same mistakes just to make a tiny elite even wealthier.

We must stop falling for the con that growth is either necessary or beneficial.

We must resist the mantra that businesses must always be growing because the concept is garbage. Big Biz, unfortunately, has far better access to Big Gov. than you and I have and between them, they connive to sell "growth" as a good thing. One of their favourite tactics is to promise more jobs and that this must be beneficial. Wrong. The truth is that these two major establishments have vested interests in having more people than jobs because this gives them greater control over the workforce. Huff and puff as they do, neither Big Biz nor Big Government really wants full employment because that would bestow freedom to those who are currently bullied, exploited or even enslaved. The prospect of more jobs – sometimes real, sometimes not – is in fact a red herring, as are almost all of the claims to sell growth.

I have a very simple question which exposes the cancerous nature of growth - "What possible benefits can there be in providing millions more jobs whilst simultaneously allowing an addition of one and a half million population growth for every million jobs created?"

Yes, the Big Biz and Big Gov. spin doctors can claim that there are now more people in work than ever, but the reality is, that every further half a million people not only increases the pool of the global unemployed, they add to the existing six plus billion who are already gobbling up ever more of the world's resources and adding to the devastating pollution of our already damaged environment. So much for the supposed benefits of growth.

Many businesses, in fact, would be of far greater value to their workers and their shareholders if they shrank somewhat but provided better dividends for their shareholders and higher wages for their employees.

Beyond a certain size and level of profitability, bigger is not necessarily better. Ditto for a nation's population.

No country needs more people – period. New Zealand is roughly the same size as Britain, but with less than 10% of the UK's population, it has a higher and more civilised standard of living. The Kiwis very sensibly are not bemoaning the fact that they do not have Britain's 60 million people

Not for a moment do New Zealanders feel deprived by not having an extra 50 million plus bodies cluttering up the place and they still manage to beat England at cricket and rugby. They demonstrate admirably that one does not have to be a yob to be tough.

Nor would many Canadians change places with their neighbours in overcrowded America. Canada is still self-sufficient in energy and water and can remain so for many generations longer than most countries. Had America not so foolishly allowed/encouraged massive population growth, it too could have enjoyed a happier and healthier future similar to that of Canada and New Zealand. Regrettably, big business led it astray and although smaller than Canada, America has ten times it population and is now in serious trouble with huge energy deficits, an unrepayable level of debt and the high level of crime which inevitably accompanies these three extravagances.

Cyprus, or more accurately, the Greek sector of that sadly-divided island, is currently in danger of making a serious miscalculation.

Not recognising the advantages of low population, there are serious proposals to pay £23,000 for every third and subsequent child produced by any couple in order to boost population. They could, of course, do this by taking in some of the surplus people from overcrowded countries, but the intention seems to be to increase the number of *Greek* Cypriots for political reasons.

The proposal could, in fact, backfire because some couples will surely elect to stop work and spend their time producing ever more kids – one of the main things our world absolutely does not need. Quite how Cyprus's citizens could afford to pay for the baby-making sausage machine, when it apparently cannot afford to care for or employ its older people, the proposers have not explained.

This is not, by the way, just a feature of individual countries' population density because some countries with low populations suffer some serious urban overcrowding and/or deprivation.

Statistically, for example, each Australian has five times as much land as the New Zealander, but that will not help the millions living in and around Sydney when the oil runs out and the water becomes even more of a problem. The distorting factor is that most of Australia is desolate and cannot sustain agriculture, whilst in New Zealand, the reverse is the case.

Brazil is another distortion, with a population density below 30 inhabitants per square mile, which is seemingly quite modest. Unfortunately, Brazil also has Rio de Janeiro and Sao Paulo, where millions live in squalor in cardboard and plastic-sheeted shanties with neither running water, electricity, proper sanitation or law and order.

Anyone doubting that high populations lead to disproportionately high levels of crime should see the organised gangs at work in Sao Paulo dragging 10 year old girls into prostitution and robbing at gun or knife point being daily occurances. Not surprisingly, this has resulted in police death squads taking the law into their own hands, knowing that the judicial system is too overwhelmed or corrupt to ensure that the rapists, murderers and drug dealers get their just desserts. How much better if the world's unfortunates had never been born. There are now more people out of work – always a dangerous situation – than was the entire world population only a hundred or so years ago. Such are the dreadful effects of growth.

Similar problems are replicated around the world. China is already a basket case. Its air, audio and water pollution are horrendous; its mega cities a perfect blueprint for "how not to" develop a living environment and much of its countryside is now an unproductive dustbowl.

Even in tiny Ireland, with a relatively low population density, it is possible to see the correlation with crime. County Leitrim, for example, had only 12 people sent to prison in 2005, none for high category offences. Dublin, in contrast, had 3,478 sent to prison out of 8,686. Although County Leitrim has Ireland's lowest population, its crime level is still disproportionately low and Dublin, with 29% of the country's people, contributed 42% of those sent to prison. Cork and Limerick, both with large populations, are Ireland's crime black spots and interestingly, of the 906 women sent to gaol, not one was from County Leitrim.

Here we are then, in 2007, with a massively over-large population of six billion people (still rising) and with only a small percentage of these living healthy civilised lives. We have inflicted huge damage on our world and now we have to pay the price. If we fail, mankind will perish and deservedly so.

So – what now?

- The immediate need is to de-bunk the myth that the world can only operate via growth. Remember, growth is another word for cancer and neither companies, national economies nor individuals are long-term winners if we allow the cancer to continue spreading untreated.

- Whilst much of the Stern Report quite properly warned of grave environmental damage, it saw a 20% contraction in the global economy due to climate change. Unfortunately, the Report misses the point. We certainly do not need the climate change that is hurtling towards us, but we absolutely do need a massive reduction in the world economy and long before 2050. It was a hugely-missed opportunity that the Stern Report failed to address the world's number one, fundamental problem – *excessive population*.

- We must remove the taboo of addressing population and agree initially to stop its continuing expansion as a matter or urgency.

- Debate should be opened up in each country which has a population of more than 50 people per square mile of land, about how to secure reductions year or year. There can, of course, be no perfect ratio because countries vary enormously and I am certainly not suggesting that Japan should reduce its population-to-land ratio to that of Australia, Norway or Canada.

- Each country should set its own realistic targets and shun any talking shops seeking global agreements because these would be dragged out for years. International agreement will never be reached but, as with CO^2 emissions, those who wise up first will not, in fact, be disadvantaged – they will get enormous benefits which the slow starters will eventually have to follow.

Easier said than done?

Absolutely. We are taking on a small number of wealthy and powerful people who prefer to have a pool of billions of poor virtual slaves to exploit.

Politicians want more subjects because that necessitates more politicians. It also gives them greater tax revenues to play around with, which adds to their power and self-importance and all too often, it affords politicians with a larger pot of money to plunder which would shrink along with smaller populations.

There are also ethical and practical issues to be addressed and I do not underestimate these for a moment, but if we fail to significantly reduce populations, as fossil fuels and other energy sources fall to zero, the results will be nothing short of catastrophic. Like it or not, six or more billion people cannot continue today's lifestyles for much longer and Mother Nature will force us to accept this unpalatable truth. It would be wise to give her a helping hand and hope that we have not already left it too late.

Here, then, are some openers for discussion. If you have more, do please email them to **populations@crimedown.org**.

1. Stop paying anyone for having children. No more family allowances, no more tax credits for kids. The world

doesn't need children being produced at current levels. If individuals want children they should, as used to be the case, be the ones responsible for caring for them.

2. Consider giving tax breaks to those couples who do not have children.

3. End all public funding for fertility treatment. In October 2006, a woman in Yorkshire, England was seeking treatment, against her doctor's advice and the British taxpayers' cost, to have fertility treatment *in order to have her 14ᵗʰ child* at the age of 45. An extreme case maybe, but what's the betting that most of Mrs. Broody's first 13 kids would never have been born if she had not been subsidised so foolishly by the State. Even crazier, on January 1st, 2007, a Spanish woman – seemingly with an eye to selling her "story" – had fertility treatment in order to give birth to test tube twin boys. *She was 67 years old*. What is the world coming to?

4. Consider significantly greater controls/prohibitions on a range of fertility treatments even if paid for privately. No more frozen eggs/embryos/sperm because what Nature is telling us is that not all of any species can or should be expected to produce offspring. There are, in any event, numerous babies and disadvantaged youngsters desperately in need of fostering or adoption. We should stop putting so much faith in science because almost all of their positive advances are followed by extremely negative consequences. Not so long ago, scientists gave us the contraceptive pill, which allowed us to have sex without producing babies. Now, science invites us to manufacture babies without any sexual involvement.

5. Mount population problems awareness campaigns.

6. Remove all taxes from birth control products.

7. States to pay for abortions for those who choose them.

8. Population damage to the environment to be a feature of my recommended Concern & Consequences Examination subject to be compulsory in all schools. Ditto teaching youngsters of both sexes that if they make babies, *they*, not other people, will have to pick up the tab.

9. Permit/encourage same sex marriages and allow suitable responsible couples, under strict terms, to foster or adopt children in need of parents. Before making this proposal, I admit to having had to overcome some deeply held prejudices. Same sex or opposite sex; married or not married; all couples should have the same rights and responsibilities.

10. Stop badgering everyone to stay alive as long as possible. If people want to take drugs, smoke, overeat, laze or drink themselves into an early grave, let them.

"Here lies the bulk of Gloria Gannet
She over-ate to save the planet"

And

"Smoker Sam deserves a mention
He never lived to draw his pension"

11. Nor should we shy away from the really tough life/death issues. With people in many countries naturally living longer, can we continue wasting huge resources artificially keeping alive those who have no hope of ever again living a life of quality?

Even worse, some countries force people to suffer agonising pain, mental torture and gross indignity by denying them the mercy killing they desperately ask for and deserve.

12. I have already recommended that every country should have the right to end the lives of certain categories of criminal where their guilt is beyond doubt and where the electorate of those nations have voted to make capital punishment available to the Courts.

There should also be discussion about the use of castration/sterilisation as deterrent, punishment and protection of the public because right now, violent and vicious rapists and even murderers are being released from prisons following completion of their sentences. Often they have incurable mental health problems resulting in them assaulting or killing more innocent victims once they are freed. Time and tragic events have taught us that no-one, including specialist psychiatrists, has any way of knowing which, if any of these proven criminals are safe to be let loose. The Probation Services are between a rock and a hard place – they cannot legally or operationally hold the hands of released villains 24/7 so they are damned if they try and damned if they don't.

We either forsake future victims and allow them and their families to suffer unnecessary sexual/murderous attacks, or we cut out the taboos and start talking about how the use of castration or sterilisation may prevent some tragedies and as an additional benefit, stop the potential perpetrators from having children who may be similarly dysfunctional. In an already seriously over-populated world, it makes absolutely no sense to avoid talking about this subject, uncomfortable though some find it – myself included.

Incidentally, it is simply not true that we need to keep increasing birth rates to avoid a decreasing number of workers having to support a growing number of oldies. There are perfectly good counter-balancing alternatives available, including better utilisation of labour, shortening university courses, discouraging perpetual students, lowering consumption, better small scale land use, reducing high level pensions and advancing retirement ages in line with continually increasing natural longevity averages.

Lower birth rates will also rid those countries smart enough to achieve them, of almost all of their current costs associated with unemployment because more than 99% of those willing and able to work will have jobs.

Religion has also been a major factor in driving up world populations with little responsibility for the inevitably damaging outcome. Competition is at the heart of those religions encouraging their flocks to go forth and multiply and to make sure they do, some even declare birth control to be a sin.

Religions' true reasons for pushing over-population are no different from those of big business and big Government. The greater the glut of gullibles, the greater the pickings and the greater the "perceived" need for more bishops, mullahs, rabbis, company executives, generals, political leaders and their trains of hangers-on.

They all pontificate about the environment but stop short of actually protecting it. Apparently these guys can't count. They pretend not to have worked out that halving the population would:-

Halve CO_2 emissions and delay global warming considerably

Halve the amount of other toxins produced by or on behalf of you and me

Halve the volume of rubbish we create

Reduce crime by more than the 50% reduction in population

Eradicate poverty and hunger

Allow the detoxification of our rivers, lakes and seas

Slow down our fatal effects on other species, including allowing the recovery of fish stocks

Slash airplane pollution and restore the world's forests to sustainable levels

Eliminate traffic congestion

Delay the run-out-of-oil date from around 2035-2045 to perhaps almost into the 23rd century, giving us far more time to develop more environmental energy sources.

Smart Tips

Simply by not following the herd and questioning your own habits, you can both save money and reduce environmental damage. Just a few small examples - no-one needs shampoo or hair conditioner and very few people need deodorant – just water and a little soap are more than adequate, but big business has scared people into thinking that our hair will fall out or we will stink like a skunk if we don't use their wasteful products. I am living proof that this is not so. Nor do we need either shaving foam, brushes, oils or after shave. Although I have a tough beard, I long ago discovered that washing with just a little soap and water produced a shave just as comfortable and long-lasting as any of the proprietary products I had used over the years.

I have no idea how many billions of bottles, spray cans and tubes corporations such as Gillette and Wilkinson Sword produce each year but what I do know is that we don't need them. They all need transporting around the world, they use up valuable resources unnecessarily and nearly all are disposed of in environmentally damaging ways. Try it. I think you will be pleasantly surprised and you are under no obligation to keep the executives of major corporations living the life of Reilly at your expense.

Big business generally, has been criminally cavalier with our environment and it is up to all of us to change this. Waiting for the disasters which will inevitably come if we continue on our present path is not a sensible option.

Ever more people chasing ever fewer resources is already a major factor in crimes ranging from single persons prepared to steal or kill in order to survive or advantage themselves, to serious wars. The 1958 film "The Big Country" tracked the scenario with great perception. Get a copy if you can, because its main theme is playing out on the global scene right now. Threaded through this are also some moral philosophies from which all of us can benefit and both acting and directing are of a very high standard.

No-one should think that only countries in Africa and Asia will have problems such as water shortages because already supplies in California, Arizona, Nevada, Florida, Spain, Mexico etc. are under threat and Canada and several of America's Northern States have already reached agreement to stop fresh water being diverted from the great lakes to the drier States in the South. All very sensible, but not many countries have similar options.

Time to wake up and smell the coffee.

Steven C. Amstrup, a Research Wildlife Biologist with the Unites States Geological Survey at the Alaska Science Centre tells us that the measured melting of the Artic sea ice is responsible for the decimation and poor health of our polar bears which have now been put on the World Conservation Forum's Red List of threatened species. At the opposite Pole, Emperor Penguins' breeding numbers on the Western Antarctic Peninsula have dropped from 300 pairs to just 9.

Within only a few years there will be no Snows of Kilimanjaro and according to the World Glacier Monitoring Service, 103 of their 110 glaciers recorded by them every 5 years are in serious retreat.

However, we should not get enmeshed into the argument that earth was perhaps warmer hundreds of thousands of years ago because that would certainly have taken tens of thousands of years to develop. Today's problems are almost all down to changes which we humans have caused in one century. Nor should we be sidelined into thinking that global warming is our only environmental challenge, because we have allowed, and continue to allow our planet to be raped unmercifully in so many venal, money-grubbing ways. A perfect example is that of the European Union's proposal to revive electric fishing in 2007, a deplorable practice which was banned 10 years ago. Instead of adopting periods and areas of zero fishing for cod, whiting, plaice and haddock, the nutcase bureaucrats at the EU are going in the opposite direction of sending electronic shocks to force up fish from the seabed in order to facilitate their easier catching. To make matters worse, they are doing this without any knowledge of the disturbance effects of using these clever toys.

My belief that our world would be a wonderful place for its occupants if its population dropped from six billion (and rising) to around one billion, is based upon my own observations, travels and considerable reading and what I hope is a huge slice of common sense.

When I was in Cortijo Grande, a beautiful part of Andalusia, it was my practice, during my daily walk, to pick up all of the litter and take it home for proper disposal because I was appalled that people could so randomly discard not only bottles and cartons, but far worse, particularly in such lovely surroundings. Friends used to congratulate me for creating what was likely Spain's only litter-free 3-kilometre stretch of road, but some would tell me that nothing I could do would stop people throwing litter from their cars. My response to such comments was that whilst I could not stop people discarding their litter, nor would those doing so stop me picking it up.

Very few countries are now mainly litter-free and will continue to suffer the blight until the crime is taken more seriously. Litter also seems to increase disproportionately to population density. Whilst my conclusions about one billion humans being best suited to them living civilised lives on our planet are not empirically based, it is worth noting that a far greater expert than I on population and the environment, has come to an even more serious conclusion.

Professor James Lovelock, who has directed his fine mind to studying climate and its effects, believes there is nothing we can now do to prevent global warming and that the hotter earth which results will permit the survival of little over 500 million people. Tony Blair, on the other hand – he who knows little but pontificates relentlessly – told the European Leaders at the November 2006 Summit meeting in Finland that we still have a 10 to 15 year window in which steps can be taken to avoid the tipping point into catastrophe. It is worth noting that Professor Lovelock has spent much of his life warning of the imminent environmental dangers, whilst Tony Blair has spent most of his life ignoring such warnings. Exactly the same as he has ignored warnings about crime-related issues from myself and many others.

It is sensible never to take Government pronouncement at face value because they are all too often misleading, at best. Greenpeace recognised this with Tony Blair's promised "fullest possible public consultation and information provision" on the subject of next generation nuclear power development in Britain. Absent more detailed data, and because the United Kingdom has recklessly allowed itself to become hostage to dangerous foreign oil and gas suppliers, it is easy now to see that nuclear power must be a front-running option. That said, Greenpeace were right to go to Court to challenge the Government's abysmal consultation process. They won their legal action, with Mr. Justice Sullivan ruling that the supposed consultation was "seriously flawed, wholly insufficient".

Like so many Blair-inspired public consultation promises, that surrounding the nuclear option was a sham which Judge Sullivan, by declaring it illegal, has made the Government go back to square one and start the whole process from scratch. Particularly, Greenpeace has forced them into a position of having to provide serious additional information, specifically about the economics of new nuclear power stations and the storage of their waste products. Whether or not Greenpeace's views of nuclear's future prevail remains to be seen, but they deserve a big thank you from us all for successfully challenging Big Government's failure to properly consult.

I have tried many times to discuss a range of subjects with Government Ministers but found their consultation processes to be controlled by selected establishment figures expert at side-lining new ideas. That is why the House of Lords will not be allowed to become a truly democratic Chamber, as I have proposed. That is why our schools, through no fault of their own, are turning out anti-socials by the thousands. That is why we have too many serious criminals and too few prison places and why, without genuine consultation, we will continue to trash our environment beyond the point from which it can ever recover.

CHAPTER 19

POLITICIANS. THE WEAK LINK IN THE CRIME CHAIN

What every high-crime nation now needs is a new breed of politician. Without these, crime will continue at dangerous levels; global warming, pollution and excessive population will increasingly be allowed to destroy our environment; the liberties and freedoms which should be an absolute right of every law-abiding man, woman and child will be further stolen from us all; we will be forced by misinformation and blatant lies into ever more unjustified wars; we will fail to eliminate world poverty and millions will die from unnecessary diseases such as malaria, cholera, dengue fever, hospital super-bugs etc.; we will continue running crazy economic regimes staggering under massive Government debt, whilst escalating controls, and interference in everyone's lives, will continue stifling initiative but encouraging inertia and criminality.

Power is the problem because our political representatives see themselves not as managers but as controllers of those who voted for them.

It takes a particular kind of warped personality to ask for your vote then, once elected to Office, use it to take away your freedoms, increase your taxes and impose a never-ending stream of regulations designed to control almost every aspect of your life.

Invariably, the kind of person who wants power over you is also the type to work towards improving their own status and particularly their own and their friends' financial benefits.

Dr. Ron Paul, a Texan (Republican) Member of the U.S. Congress is one of America's few politicians prepared to speak out about corrupt pork barrel politics which has led to its Government's horrific immediate debts of 8.2 trillion dollars, which equates to $26,000 for every man, woman and child. An even more alarming scenario is the M. W. Hodges report which cites America's total time-bomb debt as being 40 trillion dollars and soaring. All such figures, of course, depend on what is included and the time-scale, but whichever one chooses, the U.S. debt is astronomical and unsustainable.

Ron Paul well understands the abuses of Party political power and is outspoken against America's mega, meddling, profligate Government and quite rightly would love to see it seriously down-sized. All high crime nations need many more politicians of Dr. Paul's calibre and I show you later how we can have them.

Put bluntly – we need politicians honest enough to admit to decades of serial incompetence and come up with genuine solutions to all of the above failures, instead of an endless stream of meetings, conferences, training courses, treaties, inquiries, partnerships, pilot studies, research projects, secret or sexed-up Reports – all of which are nothing but delaying tactics and jollies used by cancerous bureaucracies to increase their own parasitic mini empires. High-crime countries desperately need people who can cut through all of the current crap and actually get things done. They need people who, *for moderate personal remuneration*, will devote their energies to serious crime reduction and to the general welfare of all people everywhere. This is currently not possible in America, Australia, France, Great Britain, Ireland, Italy etc. where, over decades, a culture has developed in which almost all of those supposed to be representing their electorates do no such thing. Instead, more than 90% of their time is spent playing Party Politics, which means concentrating on either gaining power, holding on to power or jeering and sneering at those whom they consider opponents. This lack of consensus politics pervades all levels of political activity in these countries which is why so little of value has been achieved in the last 50 years. It is a disgrace. If Switzerland can do so much of benefit to its citizens by avoiding these ridiculous yah-boo circuses, so can all others – if they have the will.

With the exception of Andorra, Belize, Botswana, Canada, Panama, Switzerland, Uruguay and the Scandinavian countries, I know of no Government which right now (2007) is not wallowing in swamps of inefficiency, patronage, corruption and rule-bending, devoid of either wisdom or common sense. Regulation after regulation, and tinkering with past tinkerings is the current name of the game, with politicians and civil servants pretending to be so terribly busy and important whilst in fact, they are usually doing far more harm than good.

One only has to see the huge hurdles which face any individual politician wishing to introduce a new law – however much public support it may enjoy – to realise why most countries are in such a mess. The whole political system is one of unnecessary complexity

410

and obstruction with most politicians spending an inordinate amount of time protecting their own Parties and trying to promote their own personal careers instead of pursuing the best interests of their electorates.

Tony Blair, Britain's Prime Minister, is a perfect example of the kind of politician his country does not need. He promised, in order to gain Office in 1997, to be "tough on crime, tough on the causes of crime" – he was neither. His legacy, by 2007, is that Britain now has more than *fifty million unsolved crimes since he came to power*. That is almost one unsolved crime per head of population. Notwithstanding this, and the fact that only 20% of the population voted for his "New" Labour Party, instead of ridding Britain of its own runaway crime, Blair struts around the world invading other countries which are no threat whatsoever to Britain, pontificating about democracy which he makes absolutely sure is not enjoyed by his own population. Tough on crime? Tell that to the Brits, the Afghans and the Iraqis Mr. Blair.

No-one could have summarised his view of being Prime Minister better than the man himself. Touring New Zealand at the end of March 2006, Blair is quoted by the New Zealand Herald as saying, about his job "you get a lot of brickbats, but so what. It beats working for a living". Surely the perfect motto for most Party politicians. Neil Kinnock obviously taught him well.

Blair is a showman, a sham, an arch user of words calculated to mean quite different things to different people. He is a lawyer. He pretends to oppose torture but never takes the steps which I know can lead to its demise. Instead of condemning Egypt, for example, for its use of torture, he accepts that country's hospitality and takes luxurious holidays there. He could and should have told George Bush years ago – "close down Guantanamo and other such detention centres, or Britain will no longer support you in Iraq/Afghanistan etc.", but he prefers instead to be flattered by association with the world's most powerful 21st century Dictator and to misuse his own position to try to have suspects held in police custody for up to 90 days without charge. His obfuscation about Extraordinary Rendition is a disgrace.

When it comes to the black art of the misleading use of statistics, Tony Blair, the UK's sub-Prime Minister takes pride of place.

Whenever he is faced with uncomfortable facts or with embarrassing questions, down goes one shoulder, off come the specs, on comes the triumphal stare and up goes the voice pitch as he launches into his mirror-rehearsed misleading mantras. Most on the receiving end of these ear-bashings are bored rigid with Blair's childish parroting of what only he, his slavish Ministers and a diminishing band of gullibles consider to be his Party's achievements.

I have looked at these claims with the same scrutiny which I have applied to my years of crime research, so here then are my analyses of Tony Blair's defence mantras.

A.	The Soundbite	The Reality
	There are now more people in work than ever before	Possibly true as a statistic, but a misleading half-truth missing out more important facts which are that:-
		Hundreds of thousands of those in work are now immigrants, so Britain is adding to its already-overcrowded island simply to create jobs for foreigners.
		More people now have to go out to work. Time was when one person's income was sufficient to support a family, with mortgage lenders needing a 10% deposit and offering loans limited to 2½ times annual salary.
		Under Blair's version of a better Britain, lenders are now forced to offer 4/5/6 times joint salaries. It is called slavery and it is worth noting that in 1990, 5 million work days were lost in Britain due to stress, depression and other mental illness. By 2006, this had risen more than 300 percent to 16 million lost days – far greater than can be accounted for by the modest additional increase in people in jobs. Just another of the negatives associated with driving everyone into the workplace

| **B.** | **The Soundbite** | **The Reality** |

B. **The Soundbite**

More people are now in education, passing exams and going to university to get degrees

The Reality

How come then our schools are churning out ever more foul-mouthed yobs?

The facts are that Blair's highly-structured education system has completely failed to get over to our youngsters that getting out of their heads on drugs or booze and spending huge amounts of money just to throw up are not very clever things to do.

If Blair's education is such an achievement, how is it that employers in 2007 are constantly complaining that so many young people cannot add up, spell, write sensibly or put a few understandable sentences together?

Blair's education system has left our teaching profession seriously demoralised and it has caused those going to university to accept that there is nothing wrong with starting life with more than £10,000 of debt.

Education has become a numbers game instead of a system of enlightenment and an awareness of social issues.

C. **The Soundbite**

We now have more children in nurseries, crèches and with pre- and post-school facilities than ever before in our history

The Reality

Absolutely true and an absolute disgrace. By escalating Central and Local Government debt, mortgage and credit card debt, Tony Blair's warped version of socialism has resulted in an economy where most parents are forced to go out to work.

Instead of parents spending more time with their kids therefore, they now spend much less, so the guidance which youngsters should be getting from mums (mainly) and dads has been seriously diminished.

Children in Britain have spent too long at school for decades but Blair & co. have compounded this crime-producing misjudgement, then they turn around and blame irresponsible parenting for the huge rise in out-of-control youngsters.

In many countries, including Russia and Scandinavia, schooling doesn't even start until age 6 or 7, but this has only beneficial effects on their education and behaviour. Whilst we should do nothing to stop both parents going out to work, if that is what they wish, we should not be selling such a prospect as some kind of ideal life.

Some countries have had the trial for a few decades now and it has led to disastrously high crime and a disconnection between the generations which is both sad and dangerous.

More crèches, nurseries and more time spent in schools or associated clubs are nothing to be proud of, they are simply pouring petrol onto a fire.

Blair's repeated parroting of "education, education, education" I have long held to be no such thing. It is, in fact, all about egulation, regulation, regulation".

D.	The Soundbite	The Reality
	Under Labour, we now have more police and more prison places than at any time in history	True, but grossly misleading, because Blair is pretending that the higher numbers mean that Britons are well-protected.

The reality is, that even these higher numbers of police and prison officers are needed in Blair's Britain. Indeed, so bad is the situation following four disastrous UK Home Secretaries, that many more police and prison places will be necessary in the short-term if future crime is to be reduced by something like 15% to 25% year on year for a while.

Blair's mantra on this subject never mentions the fact of the fifty million crimes since he became Prime Minister which remain unsolved.

E.	The Soundbite	The Reality
	This Party has spent umpteen billions on the National Health Service and has met this, that and the other targets for waiting lists etc.	Substituting the word "wasted" for "spent" would be a more accurate portrayal of the statistics. Anyone can spend money, but it needs skills to spend it to maximum benefit.

Morale at the caring end of the N.H.S. is at an all-time low and massive funds have been wasted by their bureaucrats pushing everyone to meet centrally-imposed targets and at almost every level, personnel are now spending far too much time filling in forms, inputting information into computers and juggling the selection of patients just to avoid missing "the targets" and whilst all of this clever management is gobbling up those unaccountable billions, ever more patients are dying from a range of deadly diseases which they did not have until they went into one of Tinkering Tony's supposedly well-funded hospitals.

F.	The Soundbite	The Reality

Pensioners and those on low incomes are now better off than ever before

If lies were in league tables, this one would be right up with the front runners in the Premiership (the soccer, not the political one).

The gap between the wealthy and those trying to survive on the basic UK State pension or low wage has never been wider, as proved elsewhere in this book.

Whilst Blair is rolling out such ridiculous nonsense at Prime Minister's Questions in Parliament, those of his countrymen at the bottom of the pile are literally having to fight to survive. Not all of them do.

Noticeably, we never see the P.M. make such outrageous claims face to face with an audience comprised of absolutely ordinary people - not the tame media figures he selects, but a room full of State pensioners whom he could not fob off. I challenge him to participate in such an event.

So next time you hear Blair, Brown, Prescott, Reid and colleagues trot out their mantra of spoof successes, I recommend you to think about the reality of their effects.

Ask them why, in the February 2007 UNICEF Report, Britain came bottom of the 21 industrialised nations surveyed, for young people to be brought up and its mentor, America, was placed 20th, next to the bottom.

The immediate response from the UK Government was to deny the validity of years of survey work – probably without reading all but a synopsis - and ignoring the fact that the same methodology was applied to all of the 21 countries. Strange, is it not, that a Labour Government which loves applying targets and league tables to all and sundry, seeks to denigrate those which show the reality of their own poor performance?

Quite why David Cameron has not exposed them in the British House of Commons long since is also worrying, implying that the Tories are equally devoid of sound policies and have been bamboozled by the great snake oil salesman.

No country needs politicians whose intentions are to become wealthy, if necessary by allowing their spouses and friends to capitalise on the standing and power of the partner who had somehow managed to manipulate him/herself into Political Office.

Over the years, any Government could have significantly reduced crime by introducing the measures I propose in this book, but that of course assumes a level of analytical ability, creative thinking and common sense, which simply does not exist in the type of snakes who wriggle their way up the party political candidate selection process.

Party politics, in my view, is *the* single most damaging factor at the heart of dysfunctional Government.

Mistakenly, the idea still lingers on, that most western countries enjoy that much vaunted concept – democracy, which to me means citizens having a real and free voice in who represents them in Government to do what is best for their country and not just what gives the greatest perceived advantage for one or other Political Party.

If only.

Democracy, the will of the people, is no longer, if ever it was. Quite simply, apart from in Switzerland, partisan *Party* politics has completely hi-jacked democracy and turned it on its head in order to take power away from the people and lock it into the sticky and grubby hands of a select group of Party elitists.

To compound the problem, the *choice of Party* has become irrelevant in most countries, and certainly in America, Australia, Britain, France, Germany, Ireland and Italy.

a. Because there is so little difference between Right, Left or Centre Parties. They are all constantly moving into the territory of their opponents whenever they perceive it to be in their interests so to do. Their original ideologies, which rightly or wrongly may have resonated with millions of supporters in by-gone days, are cynically dumped for every short-term gain which crafty Party politicians may spot. It matters not that some of these opportunities mean abandoning firmly-held principles which got them elected in the first place.

b. All Parties now operate on the principle that anyone voting for them or being a Party Member, automatically accepts the Party's "Manifesto" in its entirety and from that moment on, must toe the Party line. Very few intelligent people reading any of these Manifestos could possibly agree with all the aims stated therein, so how come they keep quiet about those aspects with which they may profoundly disagree?

c. No *Political Party* in any of the major western countries has ever had programmes which have *succeeded* in eliminating poverty, reducing total Government tax-takes, *increasing* the freedom of its citizens, eliminating debt, or bringing crime levels down below two per hundred of population. *Never*.

Opposition Parties would rather be in opposition than not be there at all. They are also aware that what goes around comes around and they expect their next turn at the steering wheel to be never more than one or two elections away. In order to keep this cosy power-sharing arrangement to the exclusion of independent candidates, the major Political Parties allocate themselves considerable amounts of money to campaign for their re-election. This, of course, is not their own money – it is stolen from all taxpayers, even from those who have no wish to see any of the Political Parties misappropriating their funds to stay in or achieve power, or it is gifted or loaned by the wealthy, most of whom hope for– or have been promised – some status reward or other for their contributions. If you or I indulged in such practices we would, quite rightly, end up in Court charged with fraud or corruption.

The shabby UK affair of cash for Honours, honed to the nth degree by Tony Blair's New Labour Party, is a disgrace, but nailing the slippery customers involved – some of them skilled lawyers – will not be easy.

It may be that those responsible for soliciting/accepting millions of pounds as gifts or loans to enable the Labour Party to buy Elections were smart enough either to leave no traces or get them covered up. The true perpetrators may yet evade justice, but I find it inconceivable that just by coincidence, almost all of those who gave huge amounts of money to Tony Blair's Labour Party ended up being made Knights or Lords. It is, regrettably, the Prime Minister's decision which finally decides who receives such Honours and, typical of the man, he now, after 10 years enjoying this power, is recommending its removal.

I would have been more impressed had Mr. Blair foregone this power privilege on first being elected.

Monopolies & Mergers Commissions, Offices of Fair Trading and Anti-Trust Departments **should** be investigating Political Parties, but how likely is this when they themselves are Government-controlled? The question "Why is there only one Monopolies & Mergers Commission?" is not as flippant as it may seem.

The principle aim of almost all of those gaining Political Office is to turn it into a lifelong sinecure. Having got the cushy number, their next goal is to hold onto it and set in motion a system to guarantee themselves semi-permanent tenure and ever-increasing pensions *as their reward, even when they fail* to solve their countries' problems. When they leave Government, they expect to further cash in on their contacts by calling in favours which they granted when in Office. There is a long list of ex-politicians gaining overpaid positions in the real world which they would never secure in the open market if they had to rely on their own limited talents.

Welcome to the dirty world of *Party* Political Democracy.

Inevitably, this has led not to true democracy but to the concentration of massive power and wealth in the hands of the few, whose interest in such mundane subjects as ridding us of crime, vanishes once they achieve electoral success.

Effectively, George Bush and Tony Blair are Dictators who do not hesitate to trash the rights and welfare of their law-abiding electorates in their determination to increase their personal power and show that they are in sole command.

How about this for sheer *"I am God" arrogance*?

President George Bush – not content with the renewal of his unconstitutional anti-freedom U.S.A. Patriot Act – decided he did not like some of the checks and balances, limited though they are, which Congress had written into the law. Specifically, Congress wrote in a number of oversight provisions requiring Justice Department officials to more closely monitor how the F.B.I. uses the new powers afforded it under the disgraced Patriot Act. On the 9th March 2006, Bush made a great show of signing the renewed Act at the White House, but what he did not tell the media was that in fact, he had surreptitiously added a personal addendum, claiming that he does not feel himself bound by the protections which Congress had passed as part of its allowing the renewed Patriot Act into U.S. Law.

Even this Draconian Act however, does not go far enough for George W. though. Oh no. His "Signing Statement" declares that if *he* wishes, *he* can by-pass the law if *he* thinks using harsh interrogation techniques are necessary to protect national security, impair foreign relations, the deliberative process of the Executive or the performance of the Executive's constitutional duties.

If this is not dictatorship, what is?

Senator Russell Feingold has proposed that Bush should be censored for breaking wire-tapping laws.

Senator Pat Leahy has had a Statement put into the record of the Senate Judiciary Committee objecting to Bush's attempted, but as yet unresolved, bizarre interpretation of the infamous Patriot Act.

Neither these objections, nor the President's insertion of his Signing Statement accompanying the Act, seem to have been covered by America's mainstream media. I wonder why?

David Golove, Professor of Law at New York University, believes this Statement of Bush's illustrates the Administration's mind-boggling expansive conception of Executive power and Bush's low regard for the elected legislature. Amen to that.

Again, I compare this to Switzerland, where no individual would be allowed to worm, threaten or bribe their way into a position of effective dictatorship.

For those readers unfamiliar with Switzerland's vastly more truly democratic system of Government, the following is its essence:-

In my research, which has included visits to very many countries, I have found none where the population at large holds its politicians in such high regard as do the Swiss. Nor am I speaking of the sycophantic sucking-up to the powerful as in America, France and Britain, because Swiss politicians neither seek nor could gain power to anything like the same degree. They are, in fact, just everyday men and women, which is why they are looked upon with fondness.

They have no hugely impressive (and costly) Government buildings from which to discuss and manage the nation's affairs, so they suffer no delusions of grandeur, as do Parliamentarians of most countries. Their facilities are modest in the extreme, totally without airs, graces or palaver and there is virtually no security and no searching of people going into the Swiss *Bundeshaus*. All very civilised. All very refreshing. Try getting into the American Senate or British Houses of Parliament where, even after being processed like criminals, the British Public are treated with such suspicion and contempt by their politicians that a multi-million pound impenetrable barrier has been erected to keep them apart.

No-one seems to ask why the politicians of most western countries who deny their citizens guns, feel the need to protect themselves by every conceivable security measure, sealing themselves off from those whose votes put them in power.

I would also like to know why Tony Blair thinks his wife Cherie is entitled to a high-powered full-security car at the taxpayers' expense when the King and Queen of Norway move around at will, just like the rest of their citizens.

American Presidents please note that had you been successful in seriously diminishing crime, you too would be able to walk amongst your people without layer upon layer of security personnel, all paid for by your taxpayers.

Before forcing all of those expensive protections onto their electorates, why did these politicians not visit Switzerland? I guess it is because they don't want to know that politicians do not **need** elaborate protection if their citizens are fond of them and can remove them almost at will if they start stealing their freedoms or getting too big for their boots.

Foreign politicians visiting Switzerland would also learn that crime is very much lower than that in their own countries. They would also discover another truth which they would find unpalatable, which is that a nation with the lowest number of gun crimes actually has, by far, the greatest number of guns in the hands of its citizens. There are assault rifles in most households – at least 500,000 – and Swiss youngsters are taught how to respect and use a range of weapons from an early age and are required to demonstrate their marksmanship on a regular basis. This – not invading countries around the globe – is the way to minimise terrorism. Notice the similarity between the Swiss approach and the **original** American Constitution. Both majored on the freedom of the individual and keeping Government out of their lives. Regrettably, these laudable principles have now been well and truly trampled into the dirt in America by both Republican and Democrat Presidents.

On the subject of guns, I did forecast, long before the British Government decided to take away legally-held guns from its citizens, that gun crime would go up and not down as a result. Now, I was not particularly intuitive in so forecasting, I was simply going on the record of those States in America (and other countries) which had made the same mistake. Those States which took away from its people the Right to Bear Arms, which was written in the U.S. Constitution, all suffered increased gun crime as a direct result.

Quite simply, when the bad guys know for sure that they cannot come across a law-abiding citizen capable of defending his/herself (or other members of the public) with a gun, they can use their own illegal weapon of choice in complete safety, without any risk of being confronted by someone else on equal terms.

This is what has happened in Britain. Only the criminals (and the Government) now have guns – unregistered of course – and gun crime is much higher in 2007 than it was when more ordinary people could have guns under Licence a decade ago. This, surely, is the height of folly.

Just one more warning on guns. Every instance of tyrannical, iron-fisted rule which has resulted in the genocide of millions of innocent people, has been set up by the Governments concerned first passing laws making it illegal for their citizens to own guns for their own protection. Simple really. Take away their weapons of self-defence and you can then enforce any law and turn your citizens into slaves. Your papers please.

It was precisely to avoid such suppression of the citizenry that the Founding Fathers' "Right to Bear Arms" in the American Constitution makes clear, is not something which the Government could "permit" or refuse or suspend. It was and still should be *a right*. No ifs, no buts, no maybes.

Nor do the Swiss see the need to be introducing and arguing about a constant stream of new regulations. To a degree this is because most decisions are not only taken at Canton (local) level, many of them are the product of the people's direct wishes, often expressed by Referendums, which are far more readily available than in those nations suffering *Party Political* as opposed to *representative* democracy.

Nor have Parliamentarians in Switzerland distanced themselves from their electorates by constantly increasing their own salaries. According to O.E.C.D. statistics, Swiss Legislators' salaries were only 55% of those in Britain or France and 40% of those in America, yet they achieve far more for their people than any other nation. Being by far the least expensive Legislators, this gives the lie to the ridiculous "pay peanuts, get monkeys" argument which most politicians (and businessmen) trot out in their constant holding out of their begging bowls, through the windows of their luxury cars. Swiss Parliamentary sessions though, are not as long as some and many Legislators substantially keep up their day jobs as housewives, doctors, union officials or business people.

I am far from being the only one to recognise the poor value of UK Members of Parliament of course. None other than overpaid *Home Office Minister Charles Clarke* hit the nail on the head when he said – and I heard him say it – that those Labour MPs who challenged him and Tony Blair were – quote "*ne'er-do-wells*". Well, if Charles Clarke admits that those of his colleagues with a modicum of conscience are ne'er-do-wells, he should not be surprised that we attach even lower value to the Government Ministers trying to bully them. Incidentally Mr. Clarke, if your memory is not so good, I have the time and date of the opinion you expressed. You may also care to explain why British taxpayers are being charged £60,000 a year to fund each of your ne'er-do-well colleagues.

By contrast, the unwillingness to allow bureaucracy to dominate, flows smoothly through all aspects of Swiss life. The police are controlled by and responsible to the people, largely at Cantonal level and this feeds through into low crime. Similarly, Education Administrators are few in number and they operate from extremely modest premises – unlike their American, British and French top-heavy bureaucracies with their lavish offices and lifestyles.

Rarely in my many years of research into crime have people spoken well of politicians and many, having seen through the myth of democracy, no longer vote at Election time. They see all too clearly that despite the mock sincerity, most politicians as individuals are far more interested in their own careers and the financial rewards and opportunities which this opens up, than they are with the problems of either their electorates or the world's welfare.

The road to power in "Party" politics is paved with scheming, deceit, treachery, corruption, secrecy, conspiracy and low-down back-stabbing – and those are just the best traits. What we need to do is to create a route into politics for those individuals who genuinely wish to serve – not to gain and misuse power; not for way-above average financial gain; but to search diligently for solutions to crime, poverty, disease and rape of the environment. It is possible that some of today's politicians could re-invent themselves to serve the public first and foremost, but my forecast is that most will do their utmost to defend the status quo which gives them such comfortable lives.

Step forward, any politician prepared to vote for a reduction of 20% in all politicians' incomes and meantime, allocate such a proportion of your own finances to declared good causes – The Society for Action Against Crime perhaps. How many of you are willing to forego the range of goodies which have escalated in tandem with Party Politics.

My guesstimate is that for every current politician, there are more than a hundred other capable people who could far better fulfil what should be their role. Running a country is not rocket science and is much easier than running many a business. Businesses do not have the privilege of being able to dip sticky fingers into a pot of money which, not only belongs to others - but can be expanded upon demand. What makes politicians convince themselves that they are busy and hence, possibly useful, is that day to day, they are enmeshed in a maze of regulation and procedure which may indeed occupy much of their time. Unfortunately, this mainly irrelevant maze is of their own making and because they enjoy the cosiness of what essentially has become a very comfortable club, they never question either its aims, its values or its modus operandi. I am not, therefore, holding any high hopes that many of today's politicians will convert to becoming the better politicians of the future, willing to solve the problems which they themselves have either created or allowed to fester for decades.

Politicians already know they are held in low esteem by most of their public, they even discuss the matter from time to time, *but*, *but*, *but*, typical of the breed and typical of how they address most problems, that is all they do - talk.

So, we either continue with current spoof democracies in which mountebanks like Bush, Blair, Ahern and Chirac will always take power for their own purposes – or – we start the debate about how we can move towards a *true democracy* where the politicians work for the people and not just for themselves.

If you are interested, contact **truedemocracy@crimedown.org**. We propose some very innovative solutions.

To give you a flavour of one of many topics I wish to see brought into open debate, I have proposals to bring true democracy – as opposed to spoof democracy – much closer to the people. How much more comfortable most of us would be if our Governments included independent thinkers from the group below, any one of whom may have a mixture of views on any given topic. People, in fact, who would not blindly follow any Political Party's line, but who had some years of experience in their own fields. Experience which most legislators simply do not have, about how their laws affect everyday people.

It is these people who know far more than the great and the good, about how crime and other social issues impact upon their lives.

This is just one of a number of balls which we should start rolling. My years of research convince me that there is far more wisdom and common sense in the following groups than there is amongst today's politicians, most of whom have very limited experience in the real world of work or struggling to make ends meet.

Painters & decorators
Fire-fighters
Probation and prison officers
Police officers from Constables to Detective Inspectors
Hairdressers
Building workers
Those living on basic State pensions
Middle-rank amateur sportsmen and women
Small business entrepreneurs
Refuse collectors
Nurses and hospital porters
Bus, train, taxi and lorry drivers
Local supermarket personnel
Garage mechanics
Bar staffs and owners
Club security persons
Gas, electricity, water and telephone service personnel
Prostitutes
Carers
Shopkeepers
Fishermen – deep sea and recreational
Billposters
Postmen
and of course, others from everyday walks of life who may
wish to volunteer

There are numerous people from these groups with high moral standards who are every bit as capable as those with degrees in law or political science, but without their level of greed and lust for power.

I also have proposals to close the growing gap between rich and poor, sufficient to enable all of those at the bottom of the heap to live in dignity. Another issue which bears significantly on crime levels.

Party politicians will never convert high-crime countries to low-crime jurisdictions because they are now completely disconnected from their publics. Instead of promoting police officers based upon their records of catching criminals, they prefer Establishment figures prepared to do the Executives' bidding and support whatever dangerous or farcical measures are their flavours of the month.

In order to seem busy, successive American Presidents – not least today's Bible-thumping incumbent – have managed to add to the Holy Bible's Ten Commandments somewhat.

The children of Moses were subjected to only ten laws, of which Jesus believed only two to be important.

The poor children of George W. Bush, on the other hand, are bent double, with knees buckling and brains spinning, from the cancerous growth of laws, edicts, regulations, permits, certificates, licences etc.

In 1936, one of America's most villainous Presidents, Franklin D. Roosevelt, finally succumbed to public pressure and authorised the commencement of a *Federal Register of Regulations* which impacted upon the people. It comprised no less than 2,350 pages. Wow! You may well think …. but wait. Whilst the criminals were piling up serious crimes, America's Party politicians left them to it. *They* were comfortably indoors making even more unnecessary regulations to give them control of even the most trivial of human pursuits. Unfortunately, the vast majority of these were aimed not at serious villains but at the normally law-abiding sector of society.

Ignorance of the Law is no excuse, we are told by the political nabobs, but how can one not be ignorant?

I don't know about you, but I cannot take off more than two years from work to spend 8 hours a day, every day, simply to read through all of America's current mind-bending litter of law. Nor is there a man or woman alive who could understand all of the politi-babble contained therein. If you think you know of one, do please let me know and we can arrange an independent test.

To bring you "almost" up to date, the 2005 Federal Register now comprises not 2,350 pages, it contains *77,752 (seventy-seven thousand, seven hundred and fifty-two)* pages of regulatory detail. So if you neither slept, ate, drank or went to the bathroom – and it you never read a word – it would take you almost 3 days just to continuously turn the pages of this disgraceful Register of more than 10,000 (ten thousand) Regulations.

How did our Political Parties get such incredible control over you? Step by carefully-planned step, dear reader. Step by cunning step, so that you would never see how you were – and still are – being overwhelmed by the bureaucrats. Think Identity Cards. Think Health & Safety Regulations.

Churning out this nugatory effluence is just one of many reasons why our politicians are the weak link in the fight against crime. Their priorities are, quite simply, appalling, but of course, dreaming up new busybody laws is much easier than actually dealing with serious crime. How much more interesting it is to fly off to yet another contrived conference in a five-star hotel, at some exotic location, than it is to visit hospital accident and emergency departments to find out why patients are lying in pain on trolleys for many hours, or visiting prisons to find out why their governors are failing to prevent drugs getting into what are supposed to be our most secure and controlled establishments.

No further proof of Political Parties' misguided priorities and immorality is needed than their overt or clandestine use of other people's money in order to try to retain or gain power.

All Parties in Britain (just one example) seem to think they have a divine right to use taxpayers' funds for the express purpose of getting themselves elected and of course, this sneaky sleight of hand achieves, for the major Political Parties, precisely what is intended – the oppression of small Parties and of Independent candidates in order to retain perpetual power for the Bully Boy Parties.

Tony Blair and his cronies, in typically deceitful fashion, pretended to clean up the practice of financial support, but they structured the law in 2001 with such cunning that they left themselves a very convenient loophole which allowed them to continue to benefit from multi-million pounds of assistance without it being declared. Yet another dirty move which confirms my belief that *lawyers should not be permitted to draft any Country's laws* because they invariably do so with every intention of obfuscating and leaving room for varied interpretations. It is the nature of the beast.

Radical Solutions

I propose significant open debate designed to restore true democracy, by which I mean seriously diminishing the power of all of the major Political Parties and preventing any future Parties coming under the control of just one person or small clique. This will not be easy, but in the penultimate chapter, I show how freedom and democracy may be returned to the people of any Nation wanting it.

As of 2007, most spoof democracies are controlled by a tiny number of wealthy businessmen (male usually) and power-hungry political schemers (men <u>and</u> women).

Our aim should be to massively reduce the funds available to Political Parties and we do this by de-bunking the idea of the need for them.

John Prescott, the UK's buffoon Deputy Prime Minister on the 18th March 2006 said that if people wanted "an informed democracy, Political Parties must be provided with significant funds because campaigning is expensive". Since when did Party Political campaigning ever produce any form of democracy? As for "*informed*" Mr. Prescott? I think not. Ten months after the May 2005 UK General Election, neither you Mr. Deputy Prime Minister nor your Labour Party's Treasurer were "informed" about millions of pounds being loaned to its campaign funds by a few very wealthy businessmen, so it ill behoves you to lecture us about informed democracy.

So, let us do four major things :-

1. Stop – and I mean *stop* – any and all funding of any Political Party by the taxpayer. Taking your money and mine to advertise and promote a two/three Party system with which we may profoundly disagree is nothing but a dirty cartel practice. *It is theft by stealth and there is no justification whatsoever for using taxpayers' funds to enable Political Parties to sell their snake oil.*

2. Severely limit the amount of money which can be given or loaned to any Party or candidate, by anyone, including members of political parties. A maximum equal to one month's minimum wage rate would seem appropriate.

3. Make **all** hidden loans or gifts illegal with a mandatory 2 to 5-year prison sentence for any donor, intermediary, beneficiary or facilitator found guilty of such a crime.

4. Prohibit any business, Trade Union, profession or lobbying group etc. from making any block donations or loans to any Political Party. This would in no way interfere with the rights of any member of such groups to give as individuals up to the maximum suggested in clause 2, if they choose so to do. It will though put a stop to Trade Unions constantly bailing out the financially inept and profligate Labour Party, or wealthy lobbyists influencing any Party.

What will this achieve?

1. Stopping taxpayers' funds going to pay for Political Party campaigning would both end the theft and do something towards making Elections fair for every candidate.

    Taking Britain as an example, the Political Parties have conned the electorate by completely turning justice and fairness on their heads. I compare it with the Grand National, in which the horses with the greatest record of success are handicapped by having to carry extra weight in order to give the seemingly less powerful horses a fair chance. I accept that there is a valid argument not to do this and let each horse carry such weight as its owner and trainer chooses. ***However*** – what the main Political Parties have somehow managed to do by stealth, is handicap the small Parties, and even more seriously, destroy the chances of the individual candidates, by letting the best three horses (themselves) start half a mile ahead of all of the remainder. This defies logic, fairness, justice and freedom. The UK Liberal Party seems to have persuaded Sir Hayden Phillips that the public should give it yet another £1½ million to prevent the emergence of independent candidates.

    As at January 2007, the Political Parties have manoeuvred themselves into a position where they can each plunder their citizens' hard-earned taxes. If I told you the amounts they take, you would likely emigrate, as 10% of Brits have already one.

2. Severely limiting loans and donations will help return democracy where it belongs. To the people. Again I use Switzerland as a good example of a Country where Direct Democracy has resulted, because Elections there cannot be bought by any Political Party.

Tony Blair has amply demonstrated the dangers of having Elections decided by powerful, wealthy individuals having ego trip bun fights. Millions of pounds are spent by these Mr. Bigs funding what amounts to weeks and months of each Party slagging off the other and ensuring that their joint monopolising of the media further squeezes out Independent candidates and their opinions.

Taking many millions of pounds out of the Election processes of countries such as Britain, America, Ireland, Australia, France, Italy etc. can do nothing but good because one thing is for sure – these thefts, gifts and loans have not promoted democracy, they have seriously damaged it.

These countries never now get Governments chosen by the people. Instead, they get Governments chosen by that 20 or 30% of the population gullible enough to vote in accordance with the wishes of the mega-rich backers of the major Political Parties who are then permanently in hock to their fat-cat donors.

Currently, voters get almost no useful information from the massive advertising expenditures of the major Political Parties. Instead, they are bombarded with advertisements, half of which make very similar promises which are almost never honoured. The remaining millions are simply wasted by each Party simply sniping at their opponents.

I am on record as being critical of Political Party funding for many years and the issue reared its ugly head again in Britain mid-March 2006 when Tony Blair's sleight of hand on supposed "loans" to his Labour Party hit the fan. Between then and the publication of this book, I have no doubt that we shall see the major Political Parties focus all their energies on trying desperately to pretend that it is the most natural thing on God's earth for Political Parties to be entitled to be given huge amounts of money to spend on jousting with rhetoric. They will use all of their cosy media relationships to try to avoid the most useful question of all, which is – **Why should Political Parties be allowed to buy power by using either taxpayers' or rich people's money?**

3. Ending all exterior funding to Political Parties will instantly move true democracy up a few notches. Gone will be cash for Peerages, Knighthoods or other sinecures. Down, but not gone, will be the influence which a few wealthy people currently have on how Countries are run.

   The media, of course, have been far too cosy with big Political Parties and none seem to have run campaigns to put them on the spot with regards to their borrowings.

   I want to know "**How did/does any Political Party propose to repay the many millions of pounds of its debts?**" **From where could such repayment monies come?**

   Did Tony Blair and Michael Howard hope simply to rob tomorrow's Peters to repay yesterday's and today's Pauls? and –

   If Parliament, late in the day, outlaws both large gifts and loans – as it should – will any Party file for bankruptcy? or will their Party members and Members of Parliament particularly, dip into their own pockets to save them from the embarrassment of their insolvency?

4. Outlawing the block contributions which some Trade Unions, professions, media interests, lobbying groups or corporations make, will produce a number of benefits. It would eliminate the outrageous injustice wherein individual members of those groups currently see part of their fees or shareholdings used to help get a Political Party elected with whom they may profoundly disagree. Political Parties will have to recognise that their Election Manifestos cannot expect the automatic nod-through acceptance of these huge blocks and hence will have to be far more inclusive.

The elimination of block contributions will also remove the current perceived need for Party politicians to spend significant time and money (yours) courting those power groups whose payments can help their personal ambitions. Instead, they should be attending to the country's affairs, for which they are being paid.

Party politicians use a variety of techniques in order to manipulate their electorates and whilst this book is not the place for a comprehensive review of these, it is important that you have a better understanding of how Governments misuse your trust.

I will cover here just three methods which the control-freaks employ :-

Taking Sides - Step-by-Step - Manipulation of Statistics

- *Taking Sides.* People from a very early age have an inclination to take sides on a whole range of issues, some relatively harmless, others quite dangerous. Often we do this without logic and without having any conscious reason for our preferences. This is mainly because when our emotions are brought into play, the dorsolateral prefrontal cortexes of our brains, which handle reason, seem to be by-passed.

   Why, for example, do we support a particular sports team as opposed to another, often in the same city and with a not dissimilar record?

   Why do some prefer jazz to the exclusion of all other forms of music?

   Why did 70% of Americans – most of whom had no interest whatsoever in horseracing – become supporters of either War Admiral or Sea Biscuit when their head-to-head deciding race to determine "Best Horse" was imminent?

   Why did some people root for Steve Ovett and some for Seb Coe in their famous middle-distance races when they had no connection with either of them?

   Why do those, having had no personal contact with the police, divide so dramatically, with some seeing them as saviours whilst others believe them to be oppressive morons?

There are very few topics which will not cause the general public to divide and take sides and this book, incidentally, will be no exception. Some of you will see it as enlightening, innovative and a beacon of hope. Others will see it as disturbing and threatening.

I can live with both, helping the former to campaign against the latter.

Many people, having chosen a "side" will be hooked on it for life and it is this weakness which Political Parties have exploited to the full. By bombarding you with their rhetoric and promises, each major political grouping seeks to get you "on message" and close your ears to the ideas – hopefully for life - which even wiser and better-qualified independent candidates may have.

Fear is their weapon of choice.

In just the same way that many Inter-Milan supporters dislike A.C. Milan supporters – sometimes to the point of hatred and criminal violence – so it is with many of the hardcore supporters of Political Parties who seem oblivious to the criminality which hatred of the opposition has done to Italian soccer, which is to disgrace that lovely country.

Just listening to Blair, Bush, Chirac, De Villepin, Berlusconi, Howard, Cameron, Brown etc. confirms their excessive use of the fear weapon. They not only constantly warn you ***not to let the other side in***, they spend the major portion of their energies and financial resources on this incredibly negative activity.

Do not lose sight of the fact that Party Politicians' overwhelming priorities, at any given time, are winning the next Election and it is depressing that even the winners have this as their primary objective as soon as they gain or continue in Office. The next Election is always both the focus and limit of their horizon.

The Left-Wing Parties claim that if you do not vote for them, you will '***let in***' the Right-Wing Parties and of course vice versa. In fact, there is usually little or no difference between them. Neither is black or white – both are cynical grey – but exploiting this human frailty for coming down on one of only two sides has successfully prevented voters from considering alternatives for decades.

438

This wonderfully cosy system is fine for the leading members of major Political Parties but it has proved disastrous for almost everyone else. It has resulted in Governments comprised of Dictators, mountebanks, lawyers, buffoons and what Britain's once Home Secretary Charles Clarke described as "ne'er-do-wells". As far as these crafty politicians are concerned, exploiting this human weakness to take sides and then maximising this by the use of fear, is a win-win situation because the worst case scenario is that their Party ends up in opposition. Not bad eh?

Hopefully, reading this book will cause you to think about your own pre-conceived inclinations with a view to freeing yourself from this particularly debilitating form of brainwashing.

• *Step-By-Step* has been another time-honoured tactic by Party Politicians and bureaucrats, designed to increase their control over *you*. Only occasionally are the most serious aspects of any law made known to the public until it is too late. More usually, Draconian measures are only introduced in instalments.

For decades the true aims of the Federal Europhiles was kept hidden by the likes of Ted Heath and a highly-secretive group of co-conspirators and in fact, some had been planning for a *Federal* Europe since the 1920s. They knew absolutely that if they offered the convoluted European Union with its labyrinth of complex bureaucracies which is in situ in 2006, their publics would have shown them the door. So, typical of the sly breed, they chose instead to disguise their real objectives and move towards them very surreptitiously – step-by-step. This is well-documented should anyone find it difficult to believe.

Tony Blair, Charles Clarke, Jack Straw, Gordon Brown, David Blunkett, John Reid, Sir Ian Blair (Metropolitan Police Commissioner) etc. are all determined to have maximum control of every one of their citizens and there has been a *step-by-step* process in this direction for years and this – as did George Bush's schemes in America – started long before the 2001 terrorist attacks. 9/11 though, did give them the perfect excuse to ratchet up their attacks on individual freedom and privacy and boy, did they grab their chance.

People who have used the same bank for many years are now treated like terrorists and have to take documents **chosen by *The* Authorities** to their Bank Manager to prove who they are. Millions of completely innocent payments into and out of their banks must be reported by their once-friendly bank **to *The* Authorities**. This must be "in secret" and failure to comply can result in your bank facing horrendous fines or imprisonment. ***Just another step***, but one which not only costs both the banks and their customers huge amounts of money, but also damages life-long relationships by replacing trust with unjustified suspicion. It also puts banks, Accountants etc. in a very powerful position viz-a-viz their customers. Fall out with your bank, change your Accountant etc. and there is nothing to stop the spiteful from ensuring that the Authorities begin to delve into your affairs.

No matter that you are completely innocent of any crime, let alone terrorism, this could be a very uncomfortable and expensive experience for you. And please – do not tell me that there are not vindictive people around who would stoop to such malevolence for unworthy reasons of their own.

George Bush now believes his F.B.I./C.I.A./Customs/Revenue and many other Government departments should be able to bug or search your home without judicial authority and without either your prior or subsequent knowledge, despite this being unlawful under the Constitution of the U.S.A. ***Just another step***.

Britain has, for some years – again before 9/11 – had photo Driving Licences. ***Just another step***. All part of the grand plan for total control. Before they were introduced, there was far less crime.

Then along came Big Brother Blunkett, Jack Straw's successor as Britain's Home Secretary – Comrade Blunkett, the guy who has twice had to resign his post in the U.K. Cabinet due to loading the dice in his or his friends' favour. Identity Cards was his great love and he set in train a juicy prospect which Charles Clarke and John Reid have been oh so enthusiastic to run with. ***Just another step***.

Beginning to see the pattern?

To the gullible, each step may seem innocuous or little worse than the last and in their endeavours to handle their own credit card debt, rising heating bills, mortgage repayments and Council taxes – which are now worse than the Poll Tax could ever have been – many will have been too busy surviving to notice. Little different from the German people who were sleep-walked into Nazism in the 1930s and just what George Orwell so accurately forecast in the 1940s in his book *1984*.

Believe me, unless the people of all Countries kick all of the control-freaks out of Office, there are *far more serious steps to come*.

Biometric Passports for facial recognition are a *next step*. Apparently, Customs and Border Guards are suddenly going blind and are no longer able to match up your face to your photograph. Problem is, you will now have to travel to a designated centre to queue up to be processed and then pay a price for the privilege. Your cost for this travel, time and the final document cannot be less than several hundred pounds. What do Blunkett, Clarke, Reid and Gordon Brown propose should be done about those on basic State pensions or social security who cannot afford this?

An up-coming step which the UK Government admits, is that come 2008, British Citizens will be forced to submit themselves to "interview" to be finger-printed and quizzed about what schools they attended, where they have worked and at what addresses they have lived. None of their damned business. Again, another fee (tax) to be paid and because – unlike Tony Blair, Charles Clarke & co. – you cannot travel around in luxury at the taxpayers' expense, you will be lumbered with yet further costs and probably time off work to present yourself to The Authorities to be "interviewed". Perhaps, as Gordon Brown suggested, the police should be allowed to "interview" them, but hopefully not in custody for 90 days.

These are only the *steps* which the public knows about and how strange that so many of these involve Governments handing out massive I.T. contracts worth millions of pounds (your money) *to friends of senior politicians and Political Parties*.

Despite requests for information from the UK Home Office, I can get no information about how the Labour Party's headlong charge into Identity Cards is going to fit groups which cannot be pigeon-holed.

ID Cards, they claim, are to enable the authorities to trace everyone to their address, so what about :-

Gypsies and other travellers?

People who change their address frequently? Who pays for the up-date and what will be the penalties for failing to notify Big Brother of every address change?

The homeless, the druggies, the winos, the squatters etc. who have neither the awareness to get to a designated interview centre nor a birth certificate or other identification? Unless they steal some, they have no money to pay for an ID Card anyway. So, who is going to pay? And what use would an ID card be without a traceable address?

Or – are such groups going to be the really privileged class and be left out of the system completely, even though many of them are not exactly law-abiding?

Will the UK Labour Party make it illegal not to have a fixed address?

Hitler, of course, had an answer to the misfits.

Before too long, all Governments which succeed, without too much trouble, in making privacy and freedom a thing of the past, will get even bolder.

The British should not believe that their control-freak politicians will be satisfied with Radio Frequency Identification Chips which can only be read at a few centimetres distance. *Next Step* – your Government will tell you it is necessary to "read" the chip embedded in your enforced Identity Card at distance, so you will be passing hidden "readers" enabling your every movement to go into their mega computer. Where you have been, what you buy and where you buy it, your religion, what books you read, what travel arrangements you make, which hotels you use, what gifts you have sent to whom, which campaigning organisations or charities you support, what bank accounts you have and so on and so on. Governments right now are working with I.T. companies pursuing all of these capabilities, some of which are already developed and the rest and more are only just around the corner. Fortunately, not all of those working on these projects are prepared to remain silent about their dangers. We should all give our thanks and support to the whistle-blowers for whom freedom and conscience are an important priority.

442

If these bureaucratic controls do get past what should be public outrage, guess what the **next step** will be? Terrorists – your Governments will say – will stop carrying their R.F.I.D.-loaded plastic in order to avoid surveillance. They must be stopped. No problem, the Bush, Blair, Brown Big Brother Brigade will say. We will just have to "chip" the entire population, just as we did with the Driving Licences, Passports and ID Cards a few years ago, only this time you will have to trot along, by order of the Authorities, and get your R.F.I.D. chip **implanted into your body**. This is not science fiction. It is political fact. **Step-by-step-by-step**. That is the way Party politicians and bureaucrats work, whether it is constantly-rising tax rates, increased Government borrowings or Stasi-type identity controls.

Future steps. Unless many of us worldwide join together to prevent this enslavement, we will certainly be subjected to "even better" ID Cards, Passports and Driving Licences containing clever little R.F.I.D. chips.

These devious little buggers will be embedded, again at our cost, into all of our plastic – a bit like paying for our own hangman's rope really.

They will be able to track our every movement and contain more information about us than we know or can remember about ourselves.

If you have done nothing wrong, you have nothing to worry about, say The Authorities and the gullible. Absolutely untrue, I say.

Now, I don't know about you, but if I suffered from piles, had erection problems, had a colostomy bag, was having an affair with a Prime Minister's wife, had a liking for sheep, cross-dressing or was incontinent, I would not like every Jack and Jill official anywhere in the world logging-on to my personal private information and either having a good snigger at my expense or mistreating me in some way as a result.

Computer capacity is already enormous in 2006 but there is no doubt that in 2007/8, it will be possible for some Governments to have a file on every one of their citizens, available to any official with the appropriate handheld on his belt.

Next step, your Government will sign Treaties with other Governments giving them and their officials access to your file.

Now, you personally may think you have nothing to hide, but it is extremely doubtful that neither you nor any of your close relatives or friends will have nothing on your file which could not cause you serious problems with some countries' border or police personnel.

Your religion, sexual orientation, financial standing, political inclinations, relationships and personal habits are no-one's business but yours – unless you choose to make them public. However innocent of any wrongdoing an individual may be though, any of these factors coming up on some petty official's handheld computer can put any traveller in serious danger under certain circumstances.

Nor do I fancy having heavily-armed F.B.I. or S.O.C.A. teams crashing their way into my home in the middle of the night because, quite by coincidence, and unbeknown to me, I had been in the same place at the same time as a terrorist suspect.

I can tell you now, with R.F.I.D. chip surveillance, this will not be an uncommon occurrence. If you are lucky, you may get an apology. If you are unlucky, you could end up dead, as some already have. This is what happens when power-hungry Governments spend more resources poking their noses into the innocent affairs of their law-abiding citizens than they do catching and convicting the criminals.

Manipulation of Statistics

This is another common Government crime which, if committed in the private sector, quite rightly would see the perpetrators go to prison for fraud. Step by step, our Party politicians have de-sensitised us to the actual meaning and value of numbers – be they crime, debt, unemployment, inflation, pensions, hospital waiting lists, gross domestic product etc.

America first made the case for Government borrowings of up to a few million dollars. When there was no public reaction to this, they upped it to tens of millions. Still no protest, so why not borrow a hundred million dollars a year, being careful never to explain to the electors what a hundred million dollars represents. "Hey" said a succession of American Presidents "this is easy. We could borrow even more" – and so they did.

A hundred million dollars a year of debt became 200 million, became 300/400 million, half a billion dollars, with the debts of previous years still not paid off.

Note again the step-by-step stealth.

Only a tiny handful of U.S. politicians such as Congressman Ron Paul, tried to warn his colleagues of the dangers of America mortgaging its future by borrowing from countries around the world. Other weak countries copied America's borrowing solutions to plug the gaps created by their own greed, incompetence and power-trips but, even on a pro-rata basis, this paled into insignificance compared with Uncle Sam's lunacy.

Little wonder that a 2005 Gallup poll in 68 countries, commissioned by the British Broadcasting Corporation World Service, revealed that politicians were considered the group trusted least by the public. At 13%, they were at the bottom of the heap, with business leaders at 19% faring not much better. Journalists were trusted by twice as many people than politicians, who scored so abysmally – even before the publication of this book.

Two Bushes and a Clinton later, the original few millions of dollars of debt, which rose to half a billion dollars a year, has now ballooned into a National Debt of more than US$ 8 trillion, which is 8,000,000,000,000.00 dollars, just so America can stomp around the world trying to impose its own flawed version of democracy onto complete strangers whose cultures they have not even bothered to understand. With complete chutzpah, George W. Bush, President of by far the most indebted country the world has ever seen, blithely overlooks this disastrous financial situation and the fact that American citizens no longer have either democracy or freedom.

So – having de-sensitised the public to the meaning behind any numbers, American Presidents of both major Political Parties now feel free to tax, spend and borrow whatever they choose.

The U.S. Congress has now raised its National Debt limit for 2006 to 9 trillion dollars.

This 9 trillion, of course, is only the current debt. There are tens of trillions of dollars of Government debt waiting in the wings to pay for promises made on a whole range of future social goodies and wars. America cannot repay either its current or future debts because they greatly exceed its assets. In short, America is bankrupt and Bill Bonner and Addison Wiggin document this very lucidly in their book "*Empire of Debt*" (pub. John Wiley & Sons Inc.)

I will do what Clinton, Bush, Rumsfeld, Rice, Greenspan or Bernanke have determined not to do. I am going to give you some idea of what **nine trillion dollars** can represent. It is not easy. It takes only a second to say, but its implications are astronomic and the consequences for America's young people truly devastating, because this mountain of debt will be visited on them for generations.

- To spend that nine trillion, you would need to spend a million dollars a day, every day, for more than 24 thousand years.

- A new Wembley Sports Stadium could be built in every major city on earth, leaving over sufficient funds to eliminate malaria and carry out cataract operations on every person in need of them.

- 9,000,000,000,000 dollars would pay for desalination plants and deep water wells wherever they are needed and for continuous airdrops of food sufficient to save all of those close to starvation.

- Nine trillion dollars would have built fifty million schools, not that the world needs anything like that number, and fund the building of sufficient prisons to house every serious criminal.

- It would give $1,500 to every man, woman and child in the world.

- It could completely eliminate poverty worldwide.

- It would build barge-capable waterways in many countries sufficient to keep 75% of lorries off the road, as well as paying for massive updating of railways.

- Nine trillion dollars would have kept every river, lake and sea free of pollution and would have prevented global warming, had it not been thrown away on empire-building.

When the U.S. Congress next tries to slip yet a few more hundred billions onto its national debt, I recommend all Americans to start screaming, because it is not some ephemeral Government debt. It is owned by every man, woman and child and their future children and

446

grandchildren. The interest payments alone on nine trillion dollars are impossible to pay and the shortfalls on these dues is currently being added to the ever-growing outstanding principle.

Regrettably this outrageous borrowing by America has achieved almost nothing of value and instead of being spent on a combination of the above positive benefits, it has been frittered away. On What?

- On trying to bully the world via massive military expenditure which obviously it cannot finance from its own resources.

- On encouraging its citizens to borrow huge sums to buy houses, cars and other luxury goods at inflated prices which could not be afforded on their incomes.

- On numerous bureaucratic departments which achieve nothing, but which add hugely to the costs which they force individuals and businesses to bear.

- On interfering in the affairs of other nations, including some from whom America is borrowing huge sums of money.

- On supporting a seriously expensive, luxury living Government guarded by the most outrageously costly security machine the world has ever seen.

If America could afford such fripperies from their own resources and choose to waste money on them, fine, *but it is not their money* they are spending. They have borrowed it, and even their constant printing of ever more dollars cannot even begin to pay the interest. Only those who sell their dollars first, before its collapse, can hope to get back some of their money. For the rest – tough. America can never repay nine trillion dollars at anything approaching 2006 values. They may well, of course, take steps to trash their own currency in order to effect some reduction of their debt by repaying it with dollars of seriously-diminished worth. Don't take my world for it. It was Ben Bernanke, now Head of the Federal Reserve Bank who said that they have wonderful tools called printing presses and if necessary, he would crank these up and drop dollar bills from helicopters.

You should think about this and what nine trillion dollars of debt really means. It would be very unwise for anyone to continue holding U.S. dollars or dollar assets, thereby leaving themselves at risk to this criminal irresponsibility.

Manipulation of Statistics is absolutely commonplace and some Governments use their taxpayers' money to employ thousands of bureaucrats to dream up ways of presenting information in the most incomprehensible or even misleading form. Fortunately, there are some honest accountants in the private sector capable of seeing through many of these corruptions, some of which are nothing but straight fraud.

One of these guys, Walter John Williams (**www.shadowstats.com**) has analysed volumes of official statistics as they have evolved over decades and has proved how American Governments have managed to fool most of the world about their economy. Economic growth has been seriously overstated whilst inflation and unemployment have been systematically down-rated.

My previous remarks about Governments getting away with malpractices by using incremental step-by-step techniques are also reflected in Mr. Williams' findings about how the U.S. Government has manipulated G.D.P., employment and Consumer Price Index statistics for generations.

The C.P.I. figures, for example, were and are supposed to measure the rise or fall of a fixed basket of goods and services year-on-year ***but***, because so many social payments, pensions, contracts etc. use the C.P.I. as their indicator, this so scared the pants off the politicians and bureaucrats that they decided to start tweaking the figures. At first, this was by subtle substitutions of what was in the basket then, step-by-step, these subtle substitutions became blatant, until now (2007) the basket has very different contents indeed.

When some items were rising steeply in price, they were chucked out of the basket and substituted with something inferior and cheaper, so that like was no longer being measured with like.

A whole variety of other confusing and difficult-to-measure adjustments were introduced, including geometric weightings and chained substitutions, the outcome of which has been to massively reduce the amount which Governments, insurance companies etc. should have paid out to recipients due under C.P.I. up-weights.

But for this political sleight of hand, social security checks would now be 70% higher, because the true rate of inflation is not 3% but 7+%.

448

Switzerland now, according to the World Economic Forum, occupies the top spot as the world's most competitive economy with America slipping from first to sixth place.

The W. E. Forum is a respected Body financed by more than a thousand corporations and its findings are contributed to by eleven thousand corporate executives. It now ranks the U.S.A. at 69th for its overall economic environment because of its deficit spending, huge negative trade imbalance and doubts about the trustworthiness of the Bush administration.

In the U.S., unemployment is 8% - not the 5% proposed by Government, who cynically eliminate whole swathes of people from the register - people who, until Bill Clinton came up with a cunning wheeze, were quite rightly included in the statistics. Now, there are whole groups of people of working age, not disabled, whom the Government's statisticians have managed to worm off the unemployment register. Surprise, Surprise.

And so on and so on, with most western countries cooking the books in order to mislead and steal from their citizens.

Crime statistics are notoriously susceptible to manipulation and "interpretation", not least being those of the U.K. Government controlled *British Crime Survey*.

Only when it suits them, Blair, Blunkett, Clarke and Reid attempt to portray this joke organisation's findings as the authoritative measure of crime in the United Kingdom. It is, in fact, no such thing. It is both inaccurate and worthless, being based upon polling a tiny and wholly-unrepresentative sample of the population and its "conclusions" are of no value whatsoever to those of us calling for major reductions in crime.

The only use to which the British Crime Survey is put, is to help politicians downplay crime levels when the B.C.S. claims them to be lower than either police "recorded" crime or the public's experience and perception of it.

Scrap it – and spend the money on *fighting* crime.

David Blunkett – again – demonstrated how he and his co-power-chasers stopped at nothing to gain control of Britain. When asked why the Labour Party had cosied up – in the 1990s – to its arch enemy Rupert Murdoch, head of News International, Blunkett explained their U-turn thus :-

"A pact with the devil was a compromise well worth making in order to get elected" stated the creepy politician, who went on to abuse his power by demoralising, as Secretary of State for Education then the Home Office, both of those Ministries which, properly managed, could and should have been far more successful in the fight against crime.

That New Labour failed miserably to return Britain to being a low-crime country was confirmed on 29 January 2007 by their latest Home Secretary John Reid. When challenged in a BBC interview about the fiasco of grossly insufficient prison places, Mr. Reid attempted to defend the inadequacies of his Party's three previous Home Secretaries – Straw, Blunkett and Clarke, and of course, Tony Blair – by trotting out the usual mantra of supposed achievements, none of which ever stand up to close scrutiny. His main claim was that crime was down by 35% since 1997.

Well, I have news for Mr. Reid

- Statistics based upon the British Crime Survey are fallacious

- Putting that aside, a 35% reduction in crime in more than nine years is an admission of abysmal failure. It could and should have been 60 to 70%

- Much of even that poor lower crime level was due not to Government, but to more secure cars and to people seeing the necessity to barricade themselves into their homes

- His boasted extra 8,000 prison places "by 2012" are seriously too little and too late by 10 years. Mr. Reid's mantra of Home Office successes conveniently forgot to mention the 50 million crimes committed since Tony Blair's mob took Office, which remain unsolved, nor where he would put the perpetrators if only 1% of these criminals were caught and convicted

- Surprisingly, Home Secretary Reid also had to admit that despite our 15-year warnings about inadequate prison capacity, he has never had a meeting with the Prison Officers' Association.

I had hoped that John Reid would have acknowledged past failures in order to move ahead, but he blew his chance by reverting to type, by pretending that his predecessors were all fine, competent chaps.

Remember also – dishonest politicians do not beget honest populations. Only those who set good examples are likely to help reduce criminality. Most politicians now treat their citizens with disdain bordering on contempt.

The public, witnessing their empire-building and blatant plundering of their taxes, are not fooled. Some seek a measure of compensation by fiddling the Benefits System. Some decide crime is the route to gain a measure of redress. Others are playing a waiting game and meantime, venting their anger via the internet.

What many countries have today are **Sham Democracies** with genuine democracy having been hi-jacked by Political Party chicanery. Your once-every-few-years vote is worthless because in Government, all Parties pretty well ignore their electorate's wishes. You are, in effect, just taking part in a farcical process to decide which bunch of rogues is going to misgovern you.

Tony Blair and Gordon Brown in Britain, Jacques Chirac in France, George Bush in America, Bertie Ahern in Ireland, all promised to close the income gaps between the poor and the better off prior to each Election. Once in Office, they did no such thing – the richer got hugely richer and consequently, the have-nots in all of those countries have fallen further behind. Do the aforementioned western Leaders care? Absolutely not. They never even refer to it. Their priorities are to spend hundreds of billions of £s, $s, €s on ever more unnecessary unelected quangos stuffed to the gills with their overpaid friends, supporters and contacts.

America now has a staggering 397 Federal Agencies and most of these have branches in some or all of the 50 States. In total, this runs to thousands and on top of these are hundreds of quangos employing millions of parasites.

Britain is spending more than £100 billion a year on quangos alone, but on a per capita basis, no-one in the western world can top France for official spending. Try and swing a cat round in France and you are likely to knock a few bureaucrats or other spongers off their feet.

Who pays? I'll give you one guess.

Not surprisingly, the French disease is well-embedded in the EU and even Günter Verheugen, on behalf of the European Commission, admitted in November 2006 that form-filling was costing economies "around" €350 billion a year. He also acknowledged that companies are required to fill out compliance forms for EU laws which were scrapped long ago.

The more power which the complacency of citizens has allowed their politicians to grab, the more power they will seek and the greater will be the tax takes.

Any high crime country would be far better run if Government controlled a maximum of 20% of spending. It used to be far less in fact. In America, France, Britain and elsewhere, Governments now, either directly or indirectly, have managed to gain control of 45% to 65% of spending. In the U.S. in 1930 this figure was 12% - leaving the private sector with 88%.

More than 80% of people now think Governments have too much power and that politicians create more problems than they solve.

Political power and corruption seem almost like Siamese twins.

Sweden, for example, has its own unique form of corruption by the skilful rigging of Elections for years. The Social Democrats have guaranteed themselves huge advantages by spending $270 million of their taxpayers' funds on self propaganda. The SocDems also have an unhealthy relationship with a weird bunch called The Labour Movement which is kept wealthy by the monopoly State Lottery.

Added to this influence is LO, Sweden's biggest Trade Union which has about *4,000 employees.* Now, no Trade Union *needs* 4,000 employees to cater for only 2 million Members. Perhaps it has something to do with their having to be Members of the Social Democratic Party and being required to work full-time on campaigning to keep that single Party in power, if possible in perpetuity. To this end, the LO gave $10 million to the Social Democrats' campaign fund, which amount was as much as the campaign resources available to the other Political Parties combined. Think that is unfair?

Add in the 35,000 LO workers whose employers have to pay, in work time, to campaign for the Social Democratic Party and that adds another $50 million advantage and another kick in the teeth for genuine democracy.

See what I mean about true democracy being hi-jacked by *Party* politics? According to EU Observer, the Economist Intelligence Unit puts Sweden right at the top of world democracies, describing it as a near perfect democracy. Perhaps we should always suspect the research capabilities of any organisation with that misleading word "intelligence" in its title. All too often, it is just the opposite.

Notwithstanding these hugely rigged campaign advantages, the Swedish electorate has eventually wised-up and in their September 2006 General Election they inched the Social Democrats out of power. Considering the corrupt way in which the S.D.s have massaged unemployment figures, campaign funding and misused Government Departments in order to secure electoral advantage, this could mean that a substantial number of Swedes are beginning to realise how they have been conned over many years.

Ireland and America, on the other hand, are still amongst the countries where corrupt politicians and officials can usually avoid going to prison. Palms are greased, waters muddied, witnesses disappear or get promoted and suspects' memories selectively fail.

The European Union and the United Nations are also tainted by corruption, with the suits there hiving off huge amounts of money by a range of devious practices. Those working conscientiously for these organisations who discover the various malpractices, invariably experience major obstructions to having them independently investigated. Whistleblowers are likely to find their career prospects seriously damaged in these highly-secretive organisations. Some, including a former Chief Auditor at the U.N., kept quiet about frauds of which they had knowledge, until after their retirement.

In the European Commission, whistleblower Accountants who reported malpractices were usually fired or harassed into nervous breakdowns. Marta Andreason, Dorte Schmidt-Brown and Bob McCoy were amongst those persecuted and all Neil Kinnock - the Commissioner who was paid to root our corruption – could say on the subject was that what he described as creative finance was necessary to get the job done. What "the job" was, he failed to explain, but as the former Leader of the UK Labour Party, Mr. (now Lord, would you believe) Kinnock was an expert at evading explanations. The EU Court of Auditors incidentally, refused to sign off the European Commission's books for 11 years straight.

Top of the pile when it comes to greed and sleaze though, come those who slither and back-stab their way to power in France.

It has become traditional for French Leaders to pretend to be God. Louis XIV certainly set a disgraceful example during his reign, in which the popular Revolution was only a hiccough in the excesses of French elites, whether of Right or Left political persuasion.

De Gaulle and Mitterrand were amongst those surrounding themselves in luxury and frivolity at the expense of their taxpayers, but for sheer contempt of his electorate, Emperor Jacques Chirac takes the modern era prize for successfully plundering the State's coffers for personal aggrandisement. When flying, his plane has to ignore both the environmental and financial costs, by flying round in continuous circles before landing, in order to ensure a long sleep for his majesty.

His misuse of the Presidential jet is well-known, as is his penchant for lavish, over-the-top entertaining. When he was Mayor of Paris, he bought fine wines – for the City, with the City's money, of course. What was left was eventually sold in 2006 for a million euros, but whether the sale produced a profit or a loss is being kept secret.

King Chirac has also ensured that the Pot of Gold at his personal disposal keeps going ever higher. His annual budget is now €85 million.

He seems to make no connection between his own excesses and the increasing number of French citizens turning to crime. Luxuriating in the Élysée Palace with its courtesans and its numerous servants to indulge his every whim, he does not, of course, mix with the deprived ones who feel driven to torching more than a hundred vehicles in France every day. Perhaps Good Old Jacques rationalises this crime wave as being good business for Renault, Citroen and Michelin.

Chirac, of course, is only one man, but he is supported by the political process, so most of those involved are responsible to some degree - just another indication that when it comes to crime reduction initiatives, the politicians really are the weak links in the chain. They have had it within their power to tackle crime for decades, but because it involves treading on powerful toes, they have preferred to duck most of the important issues.

John Reid, Tony Blair's latest of four Home Secretaries, typifies the problems caused by politicians. On the 28th September 2006 he made the following inaccurate and/or dangerous statements:-

"Britain is facing serious terrorist threat for at least a generation and the chance to live without the fear of terrorism is the main Human Right." said Mr. Reid.

Well, I have been researching crime for far longer than John Reid and whilst it is true that many people live in fear of domestic crime, neither I nor The Society for Action Against Crime has come across anyone claiming to be living in fear of terrorism. One must therefore question the motives of anyone trying to link the two quite separate issues.

"I joined the Labour Party to work for a more equal society" claimed Mr. Reid.

Perhaps he will explain then, why under the Labour Party, the gap between the "have-littles" and the "have-loads" has expanded faster than at any time in history.

I would like John Reid to explain why, at a time when the UK Government is floundering on crime, the incomes of pensioners and those on minimum wage levels have fallen massively when compared with those of Labour Party Ministers and Prime Ministers. This has been happening for the entire 9 years of Tony Blair's stint as Prime Minister and is planned to get worse every year.

During the coming decade :-

Pensioners' incomes will rise from	£4,800	a year to	£6,450 a year
Minimum wage incomes will rise from	£ 10,000	a year to	£ 13,439 a year
Bog-standard MP's incomes will rise from	£ 62,085	a year to	£ 81,007 a year

Cabinet Ministers like John Reid
will see their mega incomes rise
from   £135,337   a year to   £181,881 a year

Tony Blair or his successor
will see his huge salary
rise from   £181,771   a year to   £249,660 a year

Many politicians train themselves in fake sincerity of course and either Home Secretary Reid is doing this when he pontificates that he joined the Labour Party to make a more equal society, or, he can understand neither the English language nor do basic arithmetic. The poor are suffering the high crime and the low incomes. The already rich are suffering less crime but enjoying massive income increases.

What is equal about that Mr. Reid?

Many of America's politicians are even more corrupt and incompetent than their European counterparts. Elections cannot be won without massive financial expenditure and dealing with crime is way down their list of priorities. There are big backhanders available to those who are buddy-buddy with the big agricultural and drug corporation lobbies. Big oil and those who supply the war machine can always get laws passed to their advantage. They can also call in favours for their Election financing to prevent laws being passed to protect the environment, where they would impact unfavourably on corporate profits. Put simply, there is far less easy money sloshing around to be picked up implementing anti-crime measures than there is in running unnecessary bureaucracies or pandering to big business.

Ireland has long suffered politicians of dubious probity, ranging from wild and incompetent misspending of taxpayers' money such as Justice Minister Michael McDowell to Taoiseach Teflon Bertie Ahern.

According to John Purcell, Ireland's Comptroller and Auditor-General, Michael McDowell had been responsible for the taxpayer being stung for almost €30 million for the purchase of Thornton Hall for a new prison when it could have been bought for €15 million. He and his predecessors should also be called to account for allowing the costs of keeping someone in gaol in Ireland to rise to €90,000 a year per prisoner by 2005. There is obviously something seriously wrong with Ireland's Justice Department's crime-fighting priorities.

A former Taoiseach (Prime Minister) was renowned for corruptly lining his own pockets via massive bribes or personal payments from business interests and today's Taoiseach Bertie Ahern now admits to having received the equivalent in Irish Punts of €60,000 in the early 1990s as loans from "friends" to help him out of his personal financial difficulties. The irony of getting himself into financial hot water whilst he was Ireland's Minister of Finance seems not to have occurred to either him or his Fianna Fail Party. Friends of Irish politicians have often been given quango appointments or contracts which they would not have got in the open market and such is the culture of favours and corruption in Ireland that crime gets minimal attention. So busy looking after their own financial interests, too many of the country's powerful politicians have neither the time, interest nor energy to tackle the avalanche of violent crime being suffered by many of their citizens.

In the unlikely event of this book finding any kind of distribution in China, I must acquaint readers there with the depressing news that the relaxations of recent years are under considerable threat. Your Communist politicians are already reverting to type and President Hu Jintao is attempting to cement his personal power base by rounding up and "disappearing" business executives and high-ranking officials. The Party is working overtime ensuring that the internet cannot become an independent and open communications medium, as it is trying to hide the huge amount of crime which has risen in tandem with China's excess of population and serious environmental damage.

Every nation must bear the responsibility of its own domestic crime level and it is up to its own citizens to secure reductions when crime gets out of hand. I am proposing, in this book, actions which can be taken in most countries to bring crime down significantly but China is a different cup of tea altogether.

The Communist Party still has an oppressive iron grip on every aspect of life – even in the apparently burgeoning market economy sector. Their Public Security Bureau is, in fact, a misnomer because the Communist hierarchy has little or no interest in the welfare of its public. Unless and until the Chinese people can rid themselves of their bureaucratic Communist masters I can offer no hope of ridding that sad country of its crime pandemic. That is bad enough, but far more serious is the ratcheting up of China's damage to the environment.

Unfortunately, not only is major damage being done within its own borders but China is now on course to oust America as the greatest destroyer of the global environment. The only possible optimism is that if and when most other countries wake up their politicians sufficiently to drive down crime from their current high levels, China will see the wisdom of following suit in its own best interests. It cannot enjoy the fruits of its limited capitalism whilst suppressing its people forever, because trade necessitates exchanges of people, ideas and information.

A growing number of Chinese are enjoying the benefits of global business already and having had a taste of what they perceive as being the Good Life, they will not easily be persuaded to give it up, however oppressive their politicians may be.

The choice then, is first to try to persuade our politicians to get serious about crime and this book is a Blueprint which can help them achieve a low crime goal.

Regrettably, too many countries' politicians have abysmal records on crime, so if they cannot be persuaded to get their act together, we need to replace them with politicians who will not be weak links in the fight against crime.

I explain in a later chapter how any concerned electorate can change from what has proved to be deeply-flawed **Big Government**, to a far more representative and more democratic version. What first has to be recognised is that neither Left nor Right Parties can resolve crime, terrorism, unfairness, poverty or environmental problems.

Left-winger Blair and Right-winger Bush may be on opposite sides of the Party political divide, but both have demonstrated an epic lack of wisdom. Their only skill has been manipulating themselves into power, then hanging on to it and to this end, both have big business, their military and intelligence arms and the media to mount a permanent propaganda blitz of lying to their electorates.

At least the Hungarian Government in 2006 had the good sense to admit that it had gained power by telling what it knew to be outrageous lies in order to win the last General Election.

Tony Blair and his side-kick, Attorney General Lord Goldsmith, on the other hand, demonstrated the depths to which politicians are prepared to sink by their failure to ensure that those involved in the bribery and corruption allegations surrounding a BAE/Saudi Arabia arms deal faced trial. Between them, they disgracefully pulled the plug on the prospect of the serious accusations being dealt with by the Courts, supposedly because this would be against the national interest. Tony Blair's Government had been got at by the Saudis threatening to stop helping in the war on terror. That amounts to conspiracy to pervert the course of justice, a serious crime with which those concerned should have, and should still be charged.

Even the Director of the Serious Fraud Office, Robert Wardle, wished the case inquiring into a £50 million slush fund operated by BAE Systems, allegedly used to bribe members of the Saudi royal family, to proceed. Its squashing, he agreed, amounted to giving in to blackmail.

Tony Blair never explained what kind of friendly nation could possibly threaten to stop supporting efforts to reduce terrorism, nor why he should feel the need to kow-tow to blackmailers.

Party politicians, dear reader – hard-wired never to admit even to failed policies; programmed never to give straight answers to even the simplest questions; and guaranteed to be the weak link in the fight against crime.

Further evidence of politicians' remoteness from the reality was provided by Tony Blair's and John Reid's statements on 16 February 2007 following a series of youth gun crimes within 2 weeks in South London – "They are not a metaphor for British Society", claimed Blair. Wrong – and how would he know?

I have repeatedly invited Tony Blair to come with me and tour some of Britain's city centre pubs, clubs and discos between 9 pm and 3 am when their drunken and drug-addicted customers are spilling out onto the streets. *Not once has he replied to my offer* which is a pity, because he would have learned that Britain now has a very ugly face.

Home Secretary John Reid pontificated that most Brits were an upright, law-abiding lot who just wanted a peaceful life and whilst there is some truth in that, it evades the issue of violent lawlessness completely.

In today's Britain, the only peaceful life ordinary citizens have is by restricting what they do and avoiding going to most of the places which were once fun venues for a night out but are now fraught with risk, where just looking at someone can get you accused of that ridiculous term "disrespect" and out will come the knives and increasingly, guns. Disrespect, in fact, is nothing more than an excuse for violent assault and it is a disgrace that Tony Blair and his Ministers seek to downplay the reality of 2007 Britain, which is that a substantial and growing minority of very nasty people have been allowed to develop without any meaningful challenge from Government. Pretending that eighty or so percent of decent folk counter-balances the lawless element is nothing but a dangerous deception, used by those who, for ten years, have shown themselves to be devoid of any understanding of criminality.

Tough on crime and tough on the causes of crime is easy to say. It is not, though, so easy to put into effect, as the British people are witnessing.

STOP PRESS squeezed in the day prior to Quicksands going to the printer, to cover Tony Blair's much-trumpeted *Summit on Gun Crime* on the 22nd February 2007. Regrettably, it turned out to be yet another damp squib, jointly conjured up by the Prime Minister and John Reid, his number four Home Secretary.

I was not at the Summit of course, but it was reported as being a three-point plan which included a supposed clarification that five-year mandatory prison sentences can now be passed on 17-year olds instead of 18-year olds found guilty of being in possession of an illegal firearm. This is tinkering of the most pathetic kind and will do little or nothing to stop gun crime.

There is to be a new National Police Unit to combat gun crime, but I have seen nothing explaining why this is different from the one announced in 2005/6 then inexplicably abandoned when the Serious Organised Crime Unit was set up.

Despite the fact that a working firearms tracking system is in place, Reid now promises another all-singing, all-dancing ballistics database by April 2008 – which is 13/14 months away.

On BBC Newsnight, Vernon Coaker, a Home Office Minister, was asked why a different firearms database is needed and why it is to take so long to bring into effect. He waffled. Properly compiled, such a database would be a useful facility for the police to have *but*, like the other panic measures announced, it is to do with solving – not preventing – gun crime. Nor should we forget that the British public was promised a Register of firearms by New Labour 10 years ago. There was, of course, the usual rhetoric about community partnership but this has been trotted out with boring regularity for 10 years.

No matter how many Summits or Home Secretaries Tony Blair has had, there will be no serious diminution in crime until the fundamental problems highlighted in this book are addressed.

Despite all his tinkering and clever spin, one inescapable fact remains, which is that gun crime in Britain *is up 50% since Tony Blair became its Prime Minister.*

CHAPTER 20

SUMMARY OF ANTI-CRIME PRIORITIES

In previous chapters I have covered most of the factors which contribute towards crime, but despite my extensive research and visits to numerous countries, it is not possible for anyone to offer a universal "must do" list of recommendations. In addition to face-to-face talks, and sourcing a vast amount of information available via the internet, I have read more than a hundred books and thousands of papers, articles and Reports in my search for solutions to high crime.

The following recommendations are therefore appropriate only for those countries suffering the problems of persistent, serious criminality and/or invasions of their liberties and freedoms by their own politicians and bureaucrats.

It is up to the citizens of each country to decide whether or not they suffer high crime and your opinion on this is every bit as valuable as is mine.

Countries seeking major reductions in crime will only secure maximum benefits by implementing *all* of the following corrections. Some countries, of course, will already have some of these measures in place whilst other low-crime countries such as Andorra need little of them because they never allowed serious crime to take root. Such small amount of crime as there is in the Principality is committed mainly by short-term visitors and very sensibly, the Andorrans have not set up an expensive bureaucracy to deal with them. They very simply, in most cases, take the offenders to either the French or Spanish border and kick them out.

Here then, are the anti-crime solutions without which the high-crime nations will remain high crime nations. I list them in the order of priority which I am confident will produce either the quickest reduction in crime – or – because they will take several years to reach maximum benefit, they should be started as a matter of urgency (Education, building prisons, environment protection etc.).

Although the following thirteen proposals are those to which priority should be given, in descending order of urgency, they are all important paths out of the crime quicksands. None should be delayed longer than is absolutely necessary because each will add weight and effectiveness to all of the other initiatives.

Here then are the first thirteen initiatives which all high-crime nations should bring into effect. These are in summary form only, so you will need to go back to the relevant chapters for fuller information.

Because politicians in some countries will resist some of my recommendations, the next chapter advises ordinary law-abiding citizens what they can do to persuade their elected representatives to stop dragging their feet on crime issues.

1. Put in place mandatory and compounding sentencing, based upon ten different crime categories.

2. Decriminalise all recreational drugs and significantly improve rehabilitation facilities.

3. Stop supporting or voting for large Political Parties and seek out more honest and independently-minded candidates.

4. Have adequate prison capacities, sufficient to confine the higher numbers of serious villains who will be caught and sentenced when other of my recommendations herein are in place.

5. Significantly increase police numbers, particularly uniformed Beat Officers on foot. Put simply, if there is high crime, there are too few quality police officers.

6. Establish "annual" targets to reduce all sectors of environmental damage and make good use of *genuine* earth-protection taxes.

7. Introduce a "Concern & Consequences" subject, with examinations, into all schools covering every aspect of crime and social responsibility.

8. Stop protecting juvenile criminals.

9. Change sentencing from Judges to juries in all trials for Category Five or Six and above crimes.

10. Resist all further attempts to diminish the personal freedoms and privacies of law-abiding citizens. Say 'absolutely not' to ID Cards or detention-without-charge for more than a few days.

11. Get serious, for the first time in history, about outlawing torture.

12. Close the gap between rich and poor and reign in the greedy Fat Cats.

13. Introduce major de-population measures.

1. ***Mandatory Sentence Categories.*** Without delay, all Governments should establish an open consultation procedure designed to put every crime into an appropriate one to ten category, with each category having a minimum to maximum range of sentences between which the Courts ***must choose and pass sentence upon the guilty***.

My chapter, New Sentencing Solutions, is a starting point and of course, I realise that there is the potential here for perpetual argument, but a start must be made and a strict timetable for progress must be brought into effect. Priority therefore, should be to allocate the most serious crimes to what initially seems to be the most appropriate category. Adjustments and the addition of the remainder of lesser crimes can follow. Consultation with the public is a must. They, after all, are the victims. They should be given full information via the media about the sentences appropriate to each Crime Category and then invited to nominate crimes which they believe should be allocated to particular Categories. I will happily contribute to debate about how such public consultation should be organised.

Mandatory Sentence Categories convey a clear warning to current and budding criminals and it is because at the moment, the villains are so confident that they will suffer only limited consequences (even if apprehended), that they choose to laugh at the law. In the short-term, my recommendations will necessitate more criminals, particularly violent ones, being sent to prison, but I have no doubt that this alone will reduce crime substantially. Many of today's offenders are career criminals because failed Governments have allowed them too much licence and too many chances. With mandatory sentencing though, career criminals will become a thing of the past and compounding sentences will ensure that they either decide to go straight or spend ever more of their lives incarcerated in gaol. Either way, the public will be enjoying maximum protection.

The early release of non-violent, non-dangerous prisoners should be put into effect very quickly in order to free-up many thousands of prison places for use by the really bad guys and dolls. Some should be released unconditionally, others with the remainder of their sentences suspended subject to not re-offending, or transferred to suitable Community Service programmes.

Compounding Sentences. In tandem with the aforementioned, ratcheting up custodial sentences is *the only way* to make serious inroads into serial offending. Repeatedly passing the same sentence for the same kind of offence (or letting them off with a caution) has proved to be a spectacular failure. It has cost the countries concerned billions of pounds/dollars/euros in unnecessary police and Court time and – much more seriously – it has been directly responsible for the murders, rapes and other sufferings of innocent victims whom the Governments and Courts failed to protect. We should all be very suspicious of anyone wishing to defend the status quo which, after generations of tinkering, has still left us with runaway crime and hordes of uncontrollable yobs.

Introduce mandatory sentences and reinforce them with ever higher compounding tariffs for subsequent offences and most criminals will soon get the message, for the first time, that crime really does not pay. Those too thick to read the writing on the wall will have only themselves to blame for spending much, possibly all of their lives in prison. It is their choice.

2. *De-criminalising Drugs.* Any country wanting the quickest fix to its problems with high crime need look no further than easily wiping out the evil drugs barons and dealers by killing their market. Decades of trying to do this by prohibition have failed completely and they always will fail.

Neither Governments, parents, social partnerships, focus groups, the judiciary, the police, anti-drugs armies, customs officials, aerial or maritime surveillance/ interception resources have – or ever will – stop a substantial percentage of most populations from experimenting with, enjoying, or suffering drugs. So – scrap these unbelievably expensive Bodies. Spend just a fraction of the trillions of dollars which will be saved, on creating a responsible, legal market for drugs and increasing – on a need basis – the number of rehabilitation facilities available to everyone wishing to kick their drugs habit. I do not pretend that this can be achieved by the wave of a wand, but it is certainly feasible and with 60 to 70% of crime being drugs related, it is by far the quickest route to major crime reduction.

Once de-criminalised, drugs ingredients could be grown in many countries, thereby keeping the price of the base products low enough to force out the dealers but high enough to give farmers – particularly those in third world countries – a better income than that forced upon them by the vicious and ruthless drugs barons and those politicians and war lords supporting them.

Suddenly, countries such as Afghanistan and Columbia would no longer be battlegrounds.

Want much less crime? Begin the process for de-criminalising drugs right now – 2007.

Do not wait to negotiate international treaties. That would simply be stalling and would take years, to the delight of the bureaucrats.

Any country could legalise drugs use starting in 2007 and release those who are in prison only for personal drugs use or possession of minor amounts. Dealers, traffickers and those who have committed crimes under the influence or drugs, or to fund their drugs habit, should absolutely *not* be released early from prison.

Starting in 2007, those countries which de-criminalise drugs can expect to see crime rates falling and before the end of

2008, crime could well be down by 30 to 40% from this single measure. An added benefit will be the huge financial savings and the freeing-up of police, Customs, Courts and military time to concentrate on other crimes such as violence, illegal immigration and environmental damage.

3. ***Stop supporting large Political Parties***. They have hi-jacked democracy and allowed crime to escalate for 40/50 years. Most countries have had the same two, occasionally three Parties in power for generations, so if their citizens are suffering high crime, it is the fault of those same Party Politicians in whom they mistakenly put their trust for far too long. Having read Chapter 19, I hope you will already understand that Big Government means high crime and that low crime levels only come from small Government, using maximum leverage.

The reaction of Political Parties to these proposals will be revealing. They will, of course, not be happy to see the support of their electorates slipping even further away from them if this particular recommendation is taken on board by many of my readers. Resistance by politicians to the other eleven of these main proposals may well hasten their demise, but their knee-jerk reactions are usually to oppose any initiatives which do not come from their own Party Leaders or from the powerful lobbying groups supporting them, sometimes corruptly. Time will tell.

Absolutely no Political Party should be allocated public/taxpayers/treasury money or taxes to promote or campaign for its own interests at any time, including Elections.

4. Without sufficient ***Prison Capacity*** no judicial system can function efficiently and to a large extent, the work of police services is sabotaged. Not having enough prison places restricts the Courts' ability to give custodial sentences, even where they are appropriate, and criminals are well-aware of this, realising that the chances of them escaping justice are pretty good.

The fact that most high-crime countries have had insufficient prison capacity for years is a disgrace. It has always been the fault of senior politicians who failed to see that keeping villains in prison is a lot cheaper and safer than having them roaming free, committing ever more crimes. Having spare capacity is never a problem, because empty cells incur little cost. Prison overcrowding, on the other hand, is hugely expensive, demoralising and ultimately dangerous. It creates huge logistical problems and forces the prison services to waste considerable time and financial resources trying to get a quart into a pint pot.

Every Prison Governor should spend two days every month doing one of the various jobs which his normal officers routinely do every working day. There can be no better way of understanding how any prison works than being in really close contact with the prisoners, staff at all levels, the visitors and the various outside contractors who help keep the buildings physically fit for purpose. College courses are fine as far as they go, but they are no substitute for the hands-on type of experience which I recommend should be introduced in all institutions of confinement. Governors should never be allowed to become remote from the harsh realities of the institutions which they serve.

5. More *Police Officers* are needed in every high-crime country, particularly those with huge backlogs of unsolved crimes because, by definition, that means that there are huge numbers of dangerous men and women on the loose, carrying on with their nefarious activities.

I have long advocated what a Carmarthen University Study of Violent Young Offenders confirmed in November 2006, which is that many of them actually like bullying, beating people up and even stabbing innocent victims. The robbery part of their mugging is often just incidental and many of these yobs admit to having committed as many as 50 crimes before being caught – just for the fun, they say.

The UK Home Office's four Home Secretaries in ten years have simply not got it. It needs – urgently – more prisons and at least 20,000 more police officers.

Friendly, well-visible, on-foot, uniformed officers are a necessary investment and any high-crime nation should start planning right now to increase their numbers by 25/30%. Probably around a third of these could come from restructuring – moving officers out of their stations and cars and onto the beat to mix with the public. The remainder will have to be newly-recruited and trained and because this takes time, the Governments in question must move quickly. As with Prison Governors, even the most senior police officer, from gold-braided Commissioner downwards, should participate positively in the tasks expected of their most junior officers.

6. Major *Environmental Damage* has already been done and some may never be corrected unless self-ignited catastrophes wipe out 90% of our population. We can though, stop adding to the damage and start reversing some of it, but every further day of delay will make recovery more difficult, more costly and less likely.

At least a half-century late, we absolutely must, starting in 2007, confront all aspects of environmental damage and to do this, *annual targets must be set and met*. Any politicians proposing 5, 10 or 40 years reduction targets – without immediate annual targets to check progress –are quite clearly not fit to be managing world affairs. They are simply attempting to postpone facing reality as they have been doing for decades. These verbose procrastinators must either get to grips or get out because disaster awaits us all if they do not. Anyone pretending that the initiatives necessary to rescue our planet from disaster can be painless is either seriously delusional or a dangerous villain. Annual targets are a must. They are urgent and they have to be tough.

Population excess is the cause of almost all environmental damage and it must be significantly reduced if disaster is to be avoided.

7. *Education*, claim Blair, Brown, Chirac, Ahern, Bush etc. has never been better. Exam passes by the billion and we must have more of the same. How wrong they are, and how come they never ask themselves – Why, with all these ever-increasing numbers of people with "qualifications",

we end up with such high crime levels? Well, I believe these guys have an extremely narrow and blinkered version of education. They measure it in University Degrees, in the number of people with memories good enough to regurgitate learned facts or processes, but they turn a blind eye to the number of warped people being churned out by our schools. Nor are all of these misfits academic failures, some being amongst those who have piled up lots of exam passes but still cannot see the dangers in regularly getting out of their skulls on booze and drugs; getting into knife fights; rapes; sexually-transmitted diseases; 100% mortgages etc. How "educated" is that?

It is time we measured the competence of schools by the quality of well-rounded citizens they turn out and to do this, we must stop piling ever more exam pressures on students and concentrate more on building character, honesty and generosity of spirit. I see the introduction of a Concern & Consequences examination subject into all schools as the only possible way to revert to education in the true meaning of the world. Go to **www.crimedown.org** if you wish to order The Society for Action Against Crime's Report on the subject of Education and Crime.

8. ***Stop Protecting Juvenile Criminals*** because they are tomorrow's big-time and serial criminals. Most serious and persistent law-breakers do not start in their 20s, 30s or older – they begin by being out-of-control, anti-social kids. It is at that tender age therefore, that they must be stopped in their tracks and those who try to protect them from the consequences of their crimes are doing neither the young offenders nor society any favours.

Crime is only rampant in those countries which have failed to teach their children that if they do bad things, they will be seriously punished. The problem usually, is that in recent decades the do-gooders have held sway and over-protected kids who all too often are far more villainous than they believe. Result? High crime levels as these juveniles are given carte blanche to develop their criminal tendencies under the protection of laws which mistakenly ignore what they are incubating.

9. ***Changing Sentencing Decisions*** is one of my more innovative and probably controversial proposals, but I believe Judges have too frequently dispensed faulty justice. All too often, juries have seen their guilty verdicts trashed by Judges giving ridiculously lenient sentences, but no-one seems to have asked if there may be a better alternative - there is. I wish to see Judges advise juries on matters of law; conduct trials in a fair and orderly manner; keep them reasonably short - but then leave both the verdict and the sentence to the jury, as outlined in my earlier chapter. Such a change, I am confident, would go a long way to ridding us of some very bizarre and inconsistent sentences passed by Judges, some of whom clearly see themselves as some kind of superior human beings. Analyses of sentences shows them to be mistaken.

The judgement of the average of a number of ordinary-citizen jurors, including that of the trial Judge, will in my view result in far more criminals receiving sentences appropriate to their crimes.

10. Without ***Freedom and Privacy*** for all law-abiding citizens, the State will eventually have a serious, probably irreversible stranglehold on us all. Control is the nature of the political/bureaucratic beast and we allow it to progress at our peril. Identity Cards are highly dangerous destroyers of freedom because they are not what they seem.

ID Cards are not - as they are portrayed - just a way of proving who you are, nor will they stop terrorism. The truth is that they are another step in the compilation of computer-based systems designed to have every possible aspect of your life available to a growing worldwide bureaucracy. Once you are hooked, you are hooked for life and that is when you get reeled in. Initially they are sold as being innocuous, but Big Brother would claim that, wouldn't he?

Governments hope that the naïve, the gullible and the complacent will help them get their anti-freedom measures onto the Statute Books. If they succeed, we can kiss goodbye to whatever is left of our liberty and every one of us will then be able to be pulled out of the Government's computer for whatever next pretext they dream up. Control should be of the criminals, not of the law-abiding citizens.

11. **Torture** is a dysfunction of humanity which has been around for centuries and it is to our shame that by 2007, there has not been a single major initiative to outlaw it. Lots of chat of course, from time-to-time, but nothing structured to bring the practice of torture out into the open with specific ideas for its demise. Torture is a foul, cowardly practice, whether carried out by Government Intelligence/military/ police personnel or a group of yobs kicking or stabbing some innocent victim. My research into torture and crime has, at times, brought me close to despair at the cruelty of what is a substantial minority of mankind and the temptation for me to move to a more civilised, low-crime country has never been far away in recent years.

My antidote to listening to and reading about the people who have suffered the most appalling abuse at the hands of their fellow men is, though, to try to do something about it. This book is part of my call to arms and as featured in my earlier chapter on torture, I have dreamed up a unique initiative designed to publicise and drive down torture. The first details of this will be announced within a few months of the publication of "*Quicksands of Crime*" and if you wish to support our efforts or would like more information shortly after launch-date, please email **torture@crimedown.org** and I will put you on my torture initiative mailing list.

12. *Reduce the gap between the rich and poor.* Until this is achieved, minimum crime levels will never be reached.

Right now – early in 2007 – this unfairness gap is not only immorally high, it is growing ever wider year-on-year. Regrettably, like power, greed seems to have no limits, so appealing to the consciences of those at the top of the pile is unlikely to produce a sufficient response to solve the problems. My next chapter offers a few alternative courses of action to reign in the Fat Cats to the benefit of the have-nots.

13. ***Unsustainable population***, in fact, merits first – not thirteenth – place in my list of initial crimedown measures, but it is undoubtedly the most difficult to address. It is highly unlikely that the world's population will drop substantially within the next five to ten years because big business is too powerful and Party politicians are too dim or uncaring to see what over-population is doing to our world. However, we have to start somewhere and the best I can hope for is that debate is opened and that we begin to challenge the ridiculous established notion that growth is either good or necessary. It is neither, for reasons already given, so let us start talking about how we can set about the thorny problem of reducing our world's population as quickly and by as much as possible.

Fail, and we will have either a very bleak future or perhaps none at all.

These then are the initiatives which, after my years of searching, are the ones which all high-crime countries must take if they wish to pull themselves out of the quicksands of crime.

CHAPTER 21

WHAT <u>YOU</u> CAN DO TO HELP
MAJOR CRIME REDUCTION

Whether individually or in groups you can, if you so choose, be instrumental in bringing crime down hugely, particularly if you live in a country where criminality has become entrenched.

You can start by taking notes from this book, of the ideas and proposals with which you are in agreement. Make yourself a list and then prioritise those items which *you* would most urgently like to see dealt with.

I have covered the subject of crime as comprehensively as is possible, but it is not for me to make decisions for my readers. Hopefully though, you will see the wisdom of doing something and focusing upon those crime-related aspects in "Quicksands" about which you feel most strongly. Having read this far, you will by now realise that the scope of subjects which feed through into crime is far wider than is usually discussed.

Some of you will have contacts in your own sphere who you can encourage to help you with your priorities. Some will have money which could help the campaigning which The Society for Action Against Crime will begin, following the publication of this book. **www.crimedown.org** shows how easy it is to contribute.

Others will have few contacts and little spare money but no matter, you can see shortly that this is no barrier to participation in work to reduce criminality.

Even some of those in categories of which I have been compelled to be critical, will wish to help. Many police officers are extremely unhappy with being the ones hand-cuffed by form-filling, political correctness and a seriously dysfunctional judicial system.

Not all bureaucrats are devoid of concern for their fellow citizens.

Not all academics are unaware that the education system is turning out far too many youngsters devoid of respect or compassion for anyone.

Very few prison officers are the sadistic morons which some criminals and do-gooders would have us believe. They are only too aware though, that the system in some countries is broke and needs fixing.

There may even be a few politicians honest enough to acknowledge to themselves that decades of Party Politics in many countries have failed to produce harmonious low-crime societies. How many will be willing to do anything about it though remains to be seen.

Politicians, of course, are the only ones already in a position to bring crime down most dramatically and quickly because for now, they control the purse strings and only they can bring in the necessary new laws. Their reactions to this book will demonstrate the extent of their willingness to re-think their attitudes to crime, but my forecast is that most of them will resist change and stick with complacency, hoping that their electors will let them off the hook.

I would love them to disprove my expectations by quickly getting to grips with crime, in which case I would give them every possible help. However, believing the prospect of our politicians accepting reality to be highly unlikely, we must develop strategies and tactics to overcome their anticipated obstruction. In this, I would welcome being proved wrong.

Here then, are some of the things *you* can do when you have decided upon your own anti-crime priorities.

- If you are able, form groups of like-minded friends, encouraging them to read this book with a view to lobbying as many politicians as possible. Use letters, emails, internet blogs and make personal visits to those politicians who make themselves available via surgeries to their constituents. Declaring support for the work herein and for The Society for Action Against Crime will add to the pressure which can be built up on those in power and the greater the numbers, the sooner we shall see changes.

- Contact Government Ministers by letter, outlining your concerns and asking them how and when they propose to take remedial action. Rarely do such letters elicit a satisfactory reply. Usually, the best you can expect is either a total fob-off standard letter from your Prime Minister's or President's office or a somewhat longer bit of meaningless rhetoric from a civil servant, which is nothing but the regurgitation of your Government's misleading spin.

I know. I have had hundreds of them over the years.

Do not worry if initially you seem to be hitting your head against a brick wall. The results will come as the campaign snowballs and politicians find themselves under a deluge of millions of communications, all demanding action on a whole range of anti-crime measures featured in the various chapters of this book. Decide your own priorities from my numbered one-to-thirteen actions list in the previous chapter and ask your political representatives how he or she will help bring them to fruition.

- Write to universities and Student Unions asking them to study and comment upon this book and inviting them to propose their own initiatives for reducing crime.

In co-operation with The Society for Action Against Crime, we will begin the publication of an on-line monthly newsletter – *The Crimedown Blueprint* – once we identify sufficient support for our proposals. This will list many names and communications details to whom we believe specified types of approaches could usefully be addressed. Its intention will be to bring the subject to the boil and keep it under constant review.

- Contact a range of media sources expressing your concerns about crime and your disapproval of politicians' failures to take what you know to be necessary corrective action.

Ask the BBC and other radio and TV operators if there is a blackout on commenting upon my anti-crime work. Ask why neither they nor any politician has said a single word about either my research or that of The Society for Action Against Crime (S.A.A.C.) in more than 15 years.

- Ask politicians what they *personally* have achieved in respect of reducing crime. Ask them in what areas they are currently working to reduce criminality. Ask them if they support my Crime Category Sentencing Proposals and if not, how *they* propose to end Judges' see-saw sentencing and persuade others that a career in crime is no longer going to be a soft option.

- Use your vote and at all times keep making it quite clear to incumbents that unless they match your aspirations by proposing suitable anti-crime measures, they will not get your support at any up-coming Election.

- When any Election is in the pipeline, use the prior weeks and months to contact all of the candidates. Tell them about this book. Ask them what they know about the work of the S.A.A.C. Ask them embarrassing questions and tell them if you consider their replies to be evasive waffle.

Make it clear to them that you are disillusioned with the way in which major Political Parties have abused the concept of Party Manifestos and that you are quite willing to cast your vote for whichever candidate seems most likely to take suitable new initiatives to make serious inroads into crime.

Leave no doubt that you will vote for an anti-crime independent candidate if necessary and **will not vote at all** if you can find no candidate sufficiently concerned about crime. When sufficient people say this and follow it through, this will be the first step in loosening the stranglehold which Political Parties have managed to gain over us all, step by step over many generations.

It is your individual vote, or its withholding, which can help restore privacy, freedom, decent standards and lower crime and ultimately, something closer to true democracy – not the Party political ping pong version.

What I will strive to do, following the publication of this book, is mount a major campaign, the size and effectiveness of which will depend upon the interest and support forthcoming. Clearly, I do not know many of my readers, nor they me, but I will do everything I can to bring together the energies of those who recognise that crime can be reduced hugely, but not without significant initiatives in many inter-related areas.

- Those wishing to choose aspects of unfairness which impact upon crime have a range of ways to bring about change.

Find out more about what the Board Directors' remunerations of the company for which you may be contemplating working. Ask how many times greater it is than that of the average and lowest-paid employee. If you come up against a brick wall of secrecy, or if you judge the executive salaries to be unjustified, you may prefer to work for a company driven not by the excessive greed of a handful of Directors to the impoverishment of its workforce.

I must repeat here that I am absolutely not against wealth.

Without dynamic entrepreneurs, we would all be poorer and if no-one could afford Ferrari cars, luxury yachts, 25-room mansions, outstanding works of art etc. the world would not only lose the millions of jobs involved in their making, it would be far more dreary. Like the corruption of power though, wealth becomes greed and the greed of some people without a shred of social conscience, knows no bounds. The depressing thing is, that some of the greed-freaks are not even the best people for the jobs they have secured, often by devious means.

Millions of shareholders are being criminally ripped-off by Board Directors and the financial services industry who, like Political Parties with democracy, have managed to turn things on their heads. Far too many public company executives have long since forgotten that the company which employs them is owned by the shareholders and is not their personal fiefdom which they can plunder at will. We are talking fraud and theft here.

Time for shareholders to hit back.

Study company Accounts and go to meetings.

Ask what each Director actually does, if he is claiming to be worth 5 times, 7 times, 10 or 50+ times that of the company's lowest-paid employee. Many of you would be as good or better at doing the C.E.O.'s job. Offer to do it at a 50% reduction in remuneration and advise institutional investors if you feel qualified to do this.

Ask what cash investment the Directors have made in the company. If it is low or non-existent, sell your shares. Why should *you* invest in any business in which its Directors have no confidence?

Ask for a copy of each Director's Contract/terms of employment and sell your shares if the Company Secretary refuses to give you the information.

Register official complaints with the Company Secretary if you consider Contracts to be too loaded in favour of the Directors.

Ask why the Directors feel entitled to such excessive rewards when their dividends to shareholders are either so parsimonious or non-existent.

Sell all of your shares in any public company where you consider the Board to be paying itself too much and go to the police if you suspect fraud.

- As a consumer, you can boycott products from companies who pay their Directors over-generously. You can often read about them in the press. Write to them and tell them why you are withdrawing your custom and advising your friends to shun the products or services of any company over-paying its Executives.

- We can all work peacefully to hasten the demise of the American Empire, that country being responsible for so many of the world's evils. Fat Cat salaries; school massacres; prohibitions; happy-slapping; generation separation; hard-porn films; sickeningly-violent video games; kids filming under-age sex; money and status being king; avalanches of frivolous law suits; corruption of the political system; rape of the environment; mega taxation; destruction of the Gold Standard and the serious erosion of citizens' freedoms and liberties are just some of the negatives which have either been born in the U.S. or refined there to abnormality. That, of course, would not be quite so bad if they kept their bad practices to themselves, but regrettably they use their undoubted marketing skills to spread them around the world. Even worse, they back this up by having their military based in more than a hundred countries around the globe and they use false pretexts to start wars, often against former friends.

Fortunately for the rest of the world, America has a very tender and very exposed Achilles heel. *They are trying to bully us with money which we, mainly foreigners, have lent to them.*

It is logical, therefore, for all cultures to turn away from the criminality which America has been exporting for generations and a good starting point is to *stop funding them*. This is very easy to do and the U.S. is in such a financial quagmire of its own making that it can do nothing to stop its creditors from withdrawing their support. Shrewd people will sell any U.S. dollar assets they may have, converting them to gold, silver (best options), euros, Swiss francs, Canadian/Australian dollars, Japanese yen, Chinese yuan/renminbi etc. In short, put an end to the crazy situation wherein the world's largest debtor also enjoys the undeserved privilege of being the world's reserve currency.

This is not individual financial advice I am broadcasting because in today's supposedly regulated world, I cannot do this, nor would I wish so to do. My advice is simply an indication of how the bankrupt American Empire can be forced to face reality and stop exporting so many practices which so plainly result in significantly higher global crime.

Dump those dollars now before the U.S. Treasury printing presses go into overdrive and churn out dollars like confetti. You don't have to take my word for America's plight. Even David Walker, the Head of the Government Accountability Office admitted, on Bloomberg television, that "The U.S.A. has been diagnosed with fiscal cancer". It is also sensible not to accept 50 or 100 dollar bills because the North Koreans have circulated millions of near-perfect forgeries which are also, of course, further decreasing the value of every other U.S. dollar already in existence.

- Contact prison Governors, asking them about their resources and what they routinely do to keep their regimes free of drugs. Even in countries where drugs are legalised, their prisons should be drug-free. Where appropriate, send on any responses you receive to your political representatives and the media, adding such comments of your own as you feel, to help move on the debate about any crime-related matters.

- Ask local schools what crimes have been conducted in the past three years by their pupils, either inside or outside their territorial boundaries and if they conduct weekly bullying research via questionnaires with all pupils. Take serious issue with any school which does not respond satisfactorily to your enquiries.

Involve local and national media, telling them that you are helping the Quicksands of Crime campaign.

- Be more pro-active on environmental issues by persuading your Government to introduce stringent laws to cut down on the polluters. Do not fall for the ridiculous Carbon Trading scam being proposed by some, to protect those with vested interests in continuing to foul our planet. Insist that *your* Government takes maximum measures to protect your environment and don't accept the delaying tactics of those claiming it to be a waste of time because, they say, America/India/China will carry on polluting. Every nation should do what is right and necessary, regardless of those dragging their feet. It will prove a very wise move to those who bite the bullet and tragedy for those who ignore environmental protections.

- **You** as an individual also have a voice in waking up the big polluting nations. Simply stop buying their products or services and stop visiting them. Buying only from the low-polluting countries may be a little more costly in the short-term, but if enough of us do this, America, India and China will soon get the message. They may be big but they cannot force you and me to buy their goods which are only cheaper because they are produced without concern for the environmental damage caused.

Remember, you are not alone. Many millions of others have been the victims of crime already and you may well be the next unfortunate.

As more and more individuals make crime-related approaches to a wide range of officials, the subject will reach critical importance and no-one will be able to offer themselves for election to Political Office without the threat of failure unless they have a clear programme addressing the issues raised in *Quicksands of Crime*.

The foregoing are just some of the measures we can all take to both reduce crime and to make our own country a cleaner, fairer, more civilised one in which we can be proud to live.

We should not despair. We are not as helpless as some would have us believe, so if you live in what you consider to be a high crime country or area, take heart and if some of my research conclusions and proposals strike a chord with you, do please make a start by doing something about it.

CHAPTER 22

CAN WE/WILL WE, WIN?

I have no doubt that any nation suffering high crime *can* substantially win the battles against those causing harm and distress to the peace-loving and law-abiding sectors of society. Implementing most of the recommendations in this book will achieve this in the shortest time and whilst I welcome contrary views which I always consider carefully, I must remain focused on what needs to be done. Neither I nor The Society for Action Against Crime are prepared to get side-tracked by endless academic argument, or Government spin doctors.

Having spent more than 15 years researching crime, discussing it with thousands of people, including prisoners, police personnel, lawyers, jurors, politicians, victims etc., I have not the slightest doubt that in high-crime countries, the problems can be brought down to below 20% of 2006 levels. This means *very significant drops in crime*, starting this year, 2007. Time scale – less than 5 years to have it down by at least 75% from current levels.

At the time of writing, I have no way of knowing how much interest "Quicksands" will arouse, but I am determined to continue my endeavours on the assumption that it will resonate with sufficient people to make serious crime reduction an attainable goal, so yes, absolutely we *can* very significantly win the battle against both the criminals and those of our political representatives too indolent, complacent, pompous or involved to start taking crime seriously.

The second part of my question – "*Will* we win?" - is more difficult because it is not yet possible to assess the level of 'active' support which is available out there in the big wide world. Many of my close associates are in substantial agreement with what I and the anti-crime Society are working towards, but right now, I simply do not know how much support we have from the millions of people with whom we have yet to make contact. Assuming that you have read this book, this potentially makes you one of these millions who can turn "Yes, we can win" into "Yes, we will win", but I must not be presumptuous. I am grateful to Bill Bonner of The Daily Reckoning for reminding me of Albert Einstein's cautionary words – "Two things are infinite: the universe and human stupidity; and I'm not sure about the universe"

If I have aroused your hope and interest, do please contact me with your views, offers of help, ideas, suggested contacts, experiences, whatever at **action@crimedown.org**. You may see merit also in recommending to others that "if you only read one more book – make sure it is Quicksands of Crime". You can also keep in touch with **www.crimedown.org** which gives just a flavour of what The Society for Action Against Crime is all about.

The publication of this book *can* be a watershed in the fight against crime. If it stirs sufficient interest, I plan to pull together the energies and resources of all of you who express a wish to help. This could include a regular Crimedown newsletter, open meetings, seminars and an on-going campaign to raise awareness of the issues surrounding crime. A range of activities, targeted to educating and persuading those who control the levers of power, will also be necessary. The success of our campaigning will be in direct proportion to the level of support we get from you, the general public and, having spent an unwise proportion of my own limited financial resources for well over a decade, I now have to reconsider my position.

Knowing that high crime can be significantly reduced, I have been passionate about doing something about it and regrettably, doing this on a shoestring has put a serious strain on some personal relationships. I have decided therefore, to concentrate my anti-crime endeavours from now on to helping only those countries where sufficient people express a willingness to help my campaigning. Having invested so much myself, in both time and money, it makes no sense to continue so doing in those places where too few people care sufficiently to back my work. In those countries where there is interest and support, I will be happy to continue devoting almost all of my time campaigning against crime, but I have promised my family that if no such prospect exists, I will call it a day and leave this book and The Society for Action Against Crime as stand-alone facilities for concerned folk to use as best they can.

Having little faith in most Governments, I have already identified, on behalf of friends and relatives, several peaceful venues in selected countries which have the best chance of surviving runaway crime, civil breakdown and serious environmental damage. The timing of my relocating there and spending my time fishing, canoeing, dancing and improving my harmonica-playing will depend upon whether or not there is support sufficient for me to campaign effectively against the vested interests who will resist, tooth and nail, the uncomfortable measures needed to make serious inroads into high crime levels.

So, to return to the question "***Will*** we win?" the answer is yes, but only in those countries where there are sufficient concerned people to step up to the plate. What is needed in each high crime country is:-

- Campaign funds which can come from caring wealthy benefactors and from multiple smaller donors concerned about crime

- Volunteers with a range of skills. A talented webmaster who, initially at least, may not be paid

- Fund-raisers, leaflet distributors, team organisers

- Free or low-cost campaign headquarters, computer and other office equipment

- Free or low-cost printing and advertising space

- Pro-bono legal, accountancy and public relations services

- Volunteer office personnel

- Local distributors to promote/sell Quicksands of Crime. The more widely it is read, the greater will be the pressure applied to those whose obstruction needs to be overcome

- Publishers/printers with whom I could work to create country-specific versions of Quicksands, translated into other languages as appropriate

I am initially self-publishing, but would not be averse to discussing business arrangements which freed me to concentrate more on the anti-crime aspects of my campaigning, provided that this could not lead to the suppression or curtailment of "Quicksands". With most of the above in place, I am confident that between us, we can achieve major reductions in crime, particularly in those countries suffering it the most.

Decision-time for you now, dear reader. You can:-

- Do nothing and stick Quicksands onto your bookshelf; bin it; or pass it on to someone who may have a greater interest in crime levels

- Implement some of the anti-crime measures contained herein. Do this and I wish you well and will always welcome any feedback, by email preferably, to **pancho@crimedown.org**

- Decide to join forces with like-minded friends to lobby locally for changes you would like to see, using Quicksands as your Crimedown Blueprint

- Contribute either financially or by voluntary effort to the wider campaigning which will follow publication of this book. This will include my revolutionary anti-torture initiative which I am going to launch regardless. Support, of course, will make the results from this both quicker and more effective.

The Society for Action Against Crime can be contacted by mail at:-

8 Darley Avenue, Carlton, Nottingham NG4 3PA, England

18 Phillips Avenue, Royston, Hertfordshire SG8 5ES, England

I can be contacted by mail at:-

Mountain View, Poulacapple East, Callan, Co. Kilkenny, Ireland

Email: pancho@crimedown.org

Together, we can achieve what has evaded all the tinkerers for decades. We can overcome all of the vested and established interests.

Together, we can put the criminals, instead of ourselves, on the defensive and see crime come tumbling down for the first time any of us can remember.

Together, we can significantly reduce the chances of either ourselves, our loved ones or our neighbours becoming victims of crime.

486

So let us start getting together, before the criminal fraternity becomes irreversibly out of control.

Remember Chapter 1 – "Life Can Be Wonderful With Minimum Crime".

I hope I have given *you* hope.

Peter Winstanley-Brown

Notes

Notes

Notes

Notes